LISA L. HANNETT hails from Ottawa, Canada but now lives in Adelaide, South Australia—city of churches, bizarre murders and pie floaters. Her short stories have been published in *Clarkesworld Magazine, Fantasy Magazine, Weird Tales, ChiZine, Shimmer, Steampunk II: Steampunk Reloaded, The Year's Best Australian Fantasy and Horror,* and *Imaginarium 2012: Best Canadian Speculative Fiction,* among other places. She has won three Aurealis Awards, including Best Collection for her first book, *Bluegrass Symphony* (Ticonderoga), which has also been nominated for a World Fantasy Award. Lisa has a PhD in medieval Icelandic literature and is a graduate of Clarion South. You can find her online at lisahannett.com and on Twitter @LisaLHannett.

ANGELA SLATTER is a Brisbane writer of dark fantasy and horror. In 2011 *The Girl with No Hands and Other Tales* (Ticonderoga) won the Aurealis Award for Best Collection and *Sourdough and Other Stories* (Tartarus) was shortlisted for the World Fantasy Award for Best Collection. "The February Dragon" (co-authored with Lisa L. Hannett) won the Aurealis for Best Fantasy Short Story. Her work has featured in both US and Australian *Best Of* collections, as well as *Fantasy Magazine, Lady Churchill's Rosebud Wristlet, Shimmer, Dreaming Again* and *Steampunk II: Steampunk Reloaded*. In 2012 "The Coffin-Maker's Daughter" (from the Stephen Jones edited *A Book of Horrors*) won the British Fantasy Award for Best Short Story. She has a PhD in Creative Writing and blogs at www.angelaslatter.com.

# *Midnight and Moonshine*

Also by

LISA L. HANNETT
*Bluegrass Symphony*

ANGELA SLATTER
*Sourdough and Other Stories*
*The Girl With No Hands and Other Tales*

# Midnight and Moonshine

Lisa L. Hannett and Angela Slatter

Ticonderoga publications

Huginn oc Muninn     fliúga hverian dag
iormungrund yfir;
óome ec of Hugin,     at hann aptr né komið
þó siámc meirr um Munin.


*Huginn and Muninn fly every day over the mighty earth;*
*I am afraid for Huginn, that he may not come back, but yet I*
*fear more for Muninn.*

*Grímnismál* (Sayings of Grímnir)

*Midnight and Moonshine* by Lisa L. Hannett and Angela Slatter

Published by Ticonderoga Publications

Copyright © 2012 Lisa L. Hannett and Angela Slatter

*All rights reserved. Without limiting the rights under copyright reserved above, no part of this publication may be reproduced, stored in or introduced into a retrieval system, or transmitted in any form or by any means (electronic, mechanical, recording or otherwise) without the express prior written permission of the copyright holder concerned.*

"Prohibition Blues" copyright © 2012 Lisa L. Hannett and Angela Slatter. First published in *Damnation and Dames*, Liz Grzyb and Amanda Pillar eds, Ticonderoga 2012.

All other stories appear here for the first time.

Introduction copyright © 2012 Kim Wilkins

Afterword copyright © 2012 Lisa L. Hannett and Angela Slatter

Cover artwork by Kathleen Jennings

Designed and edited by Russell B. Farr
Typeset in Sabon and Chopin Script

A Cataloging-in-Publications entry for this title is available from The National Library of Australia.

ISBN 978-1-921857-29-4 (hardcover)
978-1-921857-30-0 (trade paperback)
978-1-921857-31-7 (ebook)

Ticonderoga Publications
PO Box 29 Greenwood
Western Australia 6924

www.ticonderogapublications.com

10 9 8 7 6 5 4 3 2 1

Angela and Lisa would like to thank

*Thanks to Russell and Liz at Ticonderoga for their support and for facilitating* Midnight and Moonshine, *to Dr Kim Wilkins for her sparkling introduction, and to the wonderfully talented Kathleen Jennings for the cover illustration.*

Angela would like to thank

*Thank you and love always to my family: parents, Peter and Betty; sister, Michelle and nephew, Matthew; and my partner, David. And thank you as ever to my dear Brain, Lisa L. Hannett, without whom this book would have been only half done.*

Lisa would like to thank

*Huge thanks to my families for your love and enthusiasm. In Canada: Faye and David Gilliland, and my sisters, Kelly, Terri, Rachel, Sara and Amy. In Australia: Catherine Crout-Habel, and lovely Kirrily, Bruce, Jay, Cullen, Sylvia, Edan, Mia, and Jonah. I'm deeply grateful to Sara King for being such a dear friend and also the best patron in the world. Eternal thanks to Angela Slatter, beloved Brain, for being the most divine writing partner and making this project such a joy to work on. And to my wonderful fiancé Chad, a hundred thousand thanks for your unflagging love, encouragement and support.*

# Contents

Introduction, by Kim Wilkins ......... 13

Seeds ......... 17
Burning Seaweed for Salt ......... 29
The Morning is Wiser than the Evening ......... 45
The Third Who Went With Us ......... 77
To That Man, My Bitter Counsel ......... 93
Kveldúlfr ......... 121
The Red Wedding ......... 141
Midnight ......... 161
Of the Demon and the Drum ......... 189
Warp and Weft ......... 215
Bella Beaufort Goes to War ......... 239
Prohibition Blues ......... 255
Seven Sleepers ......... 283

Afterword ......... 313
Glossary ......... 317

# Introduction

## Kim Wilkins

Medieval Scandinavian history and culture still have the power to captivate contemporary audiences. Tales of the Aesir (who are somehow both supernaturally mighty and mortally vulnerable) and tales of the Aesir's worshippers keep circulating across media: in children's television, comic books, movies, videogames, and of course in literature. In fact, the Viking gods are so heavily associated with Viking history that the line between historical fact and cultural fantasy have become blurred: Odin seems almost as real as Svein Forkbeard; the sack of Lindisfarne is recounted in the same apocalytpic language as that used for Ragnarok.

This collection takes a minor character from Old Norse myth—Odin's raven Munin or memory, here reimagined as Mymnir—and spins a series of interlinked tales that span hundreds of years and spill across the sea and the American continent. Mymnir and her descendants love and feud through generations, their Fae blood always keeping them connected to their origins. Whether they are in the icy north in the ninth century, or the deep south in the twenty-first, they are strong, passionate, crafty, tenacious, often dangerous, sometimes ruthlessly practical. They are Vikings of a kind.

The writing, of course, is superb. I can't say I'm surprised: here are two of this country's most talented authors, with numerous honours in their wake both here and overseas. But the writing is not predictably superb, it doesn't have that too-clever gloss on it that can make a reader's attention slip right off. The word choice, the syntax, the attention paid to its medieval Scandinavian origins, results in the prose feeling strange, weighty, grim, shimmering like oil on dark sea:

> "In her hands, the bulbs break willingly. Thickened night spills from the glass, coalesces in a dense fog around her feet.... Pleating and weaving in the murk, Ingrid creates a voluminous cloak. She pulls it up over her shoulders and head, and becomes an absence, a shifting gap in the landscape. None can see her, but her presence is felt as a shiver of doubt..."

This is what Jimmy Page would have called "power, mystery, and the hammer of the gods", all the more an appropriate description because of the Viking DNA that this collection expresses. Like Mymnir's offspring, no matter how far from the source these ideas have wandered, they still have in their blood and bones traces of the rich literary history from which they draw.

Enjoy these magnificently rich tales. It is a collection to be reckoned with.

KIM WILKINS
BRISBANE, SEPTEMBER 2012

# *Seeds*

*It passed with mortals none the wiser.*

*The daylight hours darkened and there were storms; many silver-shod hooves were heard ringing against the vault of the sky. Thunder and lightning ruled, for a time, and humans lifted nervous eyes to the unseasonal display, clouds coloured gold one moment, red and blue the next. They watched as balls of fire fell and burst before they hit the ground.*

*Above the earth, Bifrost was sundered. Óðinn lay dead and Fenrir raged in the halls, devouring godly corpses and shitting them out only to begin the process anew the following day. Hel wandered, wondering what she might do next, then began to forget who she was. Frost giants, released from hatred and need, melted away. Fire giants burnt low and collapsed into stone embers. Cowards fled. The great serpent relaxed its coils and simply went back to sleep.*

*Miðgarðr remained otherwise untouched.*

*Ragnarok was an apocalypse for the gods alone.*

Gudrun Ælfwinsdóttir, Fragment from The Forgotten Sagas

"Little man," sneers Bjarni Herjólfsson as the passenger emerges from the ship's hold. "Little man, what is under that cover?"

He squints and leans over the hatch. In the darkness below, four thin blond men, all armed, huddle amid bales of homespun fabric, barrels of honey and bundled furs. Heavy air reeking of musk and damp wool issues from the hold, thick enough to choke. The pale swordsmen show no signs of discomfort. Expressionless, they surround a dome-shaped object, perhaps two feet in height and a foot in circumference. A cloth of oiled hide, its hem embroidered with silver thread in a pattern of vines twined around runes, is tucked tightly about the thing. The quartet sit facing outward, sharp ivory blades unsheathed across their folded knees. Poised and alert. Ready—but for what? Bjarni has no idea. The merchant is no slaver; he is not accustomed to ferrying live cargo, nor the odd ways of men stowed too long below decks.

The strangers have not shifted in days. At first, they would surface to relieve themselves over the strakes, or to stare up at the sky as though divining secret, cumulus messages. But after the sun rose thrice on their journey, as the ragged coastline diminished at their backs, the men were scarcely seen. When one did appear, the beardless foreigner, Snorri, left his post at the top of the stairs and took the other's place. The rest of the time, the runt trudged up and down the narrow steps, bringing food, hot drinks. Fussing as if they might be children liable to catch a chill. Though short, as he wended around cargo and men, he was forced to stoop to avoid crowning himself on the hold's low ceiling.

It is Snorri who speaks when required, who negotiated their fare and the conditions of their passage, who paid the three marks of silver Bjarni demanded. Snorri who'd hefted the group's packs onto the ship. Snorri who whispered as the hours of watching turned to days, forever chanting under his breath.

And it is Snorri who now faces Bjarni with a fierce kind of courage, the courage of a small man protecting a large secret.

"Answer!" Bjarni's voice rattles from deep in his chest. "So sly and sharp-witted. What mischief have you hidden in my ship's belly?"

Snorri stares at the captain, lips pursed. "Growl all you like, Bear. When I hired you, it was on the condition that no questions be asked. I'll thank you to stick to the terms of our agreement."

Bjarni laughs as Snorri turns and scurries back down to his charges, but he feels a chill when four blond heads simultaneously turn his way, their blue eyes flashing silver. A warning, he thinks, cursing himself for accepting the commission. It isn't greed that has guided the group's coins into Bjarni's purse. He's worked hard for the silver that funds his expeditions, and will travel far to get it. Constantinople, Rus, Frisia, Iona—his keel has tasted the salt of many seas, and his fair dealings have earned him the respect of kings.

No, it isn't greed that drives him westward, but lengthening nights and the cloak of frost settling firm on the shoulders of day. Winter depletes even the frugal man's storehouse; soon the seas will be too rough for trade. One last trip to Northumbrian shores, he's calculated, and his household will eat well until summer. Bjarni casts an eye to his sailors, their broad backs and strong arms more fit for mowing hay than fussing with rigging. He shakes his head, lifts his gaze skyward. Tries to ignore the two empty benches where Guthrum and Sihtric should be.

There had been a squall like no other not long after they left harbour. Fair winds had turned foul, and the sea boiled as if Niflheimr was bubbling up from the underworld. At midday the sky had been black, and some of the men swore they saw women in the clouds, armed and helmed, riding horses with flaming eyes and smoking nostrils. Bjarni himself had seen no such thing, but he wasn't a believer and that often made him blind to what others took for granted.

When the waters had finally subsided, his two sister-sons were missing, washed overboard by the temper of the waves. This storm was not natural, the survivors whispered; Njorðr, their friend these many years, had turned his back on seafarers. Something, they'd said, had angered their god. Eyeing the hatch, many thought *or someone*.

*Seven nights, no more*, sly Snorri had promised, as he paid Bjarni three times what anyone else would have. Transport to the ship's furthest port and a place to stow their goods undisturbed. The conditions were simple, and easily kept. *Stigandi*'s sail was robust, her rudder true: the *knörr* was in her element in a stiff breeze and had once made the journey in five turns of the moon. But her captain had not counted on the men's curiosity, nor on the strange events that had plagued them since their departure. Last night, two more of his crew disappeared. And on this, their sixth morning at sea with at least four yet to go, the ship is becalmed.

It bobs aimlessly while a carpenter scrambles to repair the mast, snapped under the force of northerly winds. The gale ambushed them at dawn, dying down almost as quick as it had roared to life.

*It was Ran with her nets,* the youngest ones murmur. *Weeds dripped from her bloated arms as she rose from the deeps, whirling her knotted webs overhead. Spinning them like horseshoes at Stigandi's post, intent on drowning us all.*

Bjarni paces between the benches, silencing the men's gossip with his presence. Quiet but not chastened, they sit rigid with halberds kept close, iron swords lodged in the planks at their feet. "Swing your hammers, not your jaws," he barks, even as his palm warms the hilt of his dagger. "The sooner our lady's mended, the sooner we'll be away."

Even with all hands contributing, it is late afternoon by the time the mast is erected, the stays, spreaders and fittings reattached. A square shadow stretches across the deck as ropes squeal through pulleys, hoisting the cloth once more.

"We're in your debt," Bjarni says, clapping Erlend the carpenter's back. Once the sail is aloft, the captain takes charge of the rudder himself. He works the broad oar, manoeuvring the vessel so as to face the setting sun. But no matter how he steers, the ship's bow points not at the orange horizon, but at a world turned to ash.

"Steady on, lads," he says, voice thin. Timbers creak and ripples lap against the hull, the sounds muffled. "Keep your heads. We've seen fog far worse than this."

Above them hollow rumbles roll, reverberate, setting iron amulets around the men's necks thrumming. Steel blades clank their thirst for blood. The thick mist swirls, condenses. Great chunks of sky splash into the ocean, darken, grow fins. Twice the length of a warrior, the creatures surface and dive. *Whales,* Bjarni thinks, and in the same instant sees faces, scales, rotting clothes. Teeth like white knives. Taloned fingers that grapple at clinker boards. *Not whales.*

The beasts circle the boat sleekly, hypnotically. The rhythm of their swimming draws the ship off course—Bjarni fights hard with the rudder, for naught. Damp air is expelled from blowholes, from gaping mouths, and pulls the sailors' attention down to the water. Away from the sky thickening. Thunderheads amassing, dispersing.

Exploding in a hail of black feathers.

———oo———

Bjarni is deafened by the sound of beating wings.

He cannot hear the men's swords singing as they are drawn from scabbards. Nor the slice of cold metal through flesh, the *thunk* of bodies being struck down. Nor beaks clashing against helms or puncturing windburnt skin. Nor hoarse shouts as wriggling figures haul themselves from the water onto *Stigandi*'s deck, adding grey slime to planks already treacherous with gore. Nor howls as sharp teeth sink into ankles, calves, thighs. The pounding of sailors against a hatch locked tight, Snorri and his charges safe and secure below. Bjarni's eyes register the scene unfolding before him. His hands, welded to the tiller, ache for the leather hilt of his blade. His feet seek purchase as the ship lists under the weight of battle. But in his ears, there is a grey whirring. The fluttering of hundreds, thousands, of birds.

A tornado of magpies, grackles and crows spins around the bondsmen. A spear tears through the whirlwind, disperses its ranks—which reassemble, numbers undiminished, almost before the shaft leaves the thrower's grip. As they spiral, so too does the fog. Or perhaps it's the ship that turns, swiftly, violently, and the world remains still around it. The vessel shudders, groans, the mast threatening to undo Erlend's hard work. Bjarni feels dizzy, and is soon heaving the contents of his stomach as he hasn't since he was a boy. Stars come out and tell him he's in the wrong place. Constellations he does not recognise guide him to realms unknown. A moment later it is day, the atmosphere tinted pink—another minute and the sun sizzles, extinguished beneath the waves. Still the men fight with edges too quickly dulled. Still the sea monsters feast on the fallen, and those about to fall. Still the flock flaps and eddies.

In the vortex overhead, the only point of calm in this unnatural storm, swoops a sleek black raven. The hardened sea captain stands, dumbstruck, as the beast descends. Now as large as a bull; now the size of a *dreki*, the span of its wings rivalling a dragonship's twenty-five oars. Round as Bjarni's wife, heavy with child, the dreadful bird darts between his smaller brethren, red eyes fixed on the ship's latticed hatch.

Bjarni does not see who threw the spear that pierces the dread raven's skull. Its cry turns his bowels to water; he finds himself ducking to avoid a swarm of beaks and claws that are no longer there. In an instant the skies clear, revealing the sun, allowing Bjarni to once again get his bearings.

*Impossible*, he thinks, as the raven plummets from the heavens, lands like doom at his feet.

---

The thing lies on the planks, its wings spread in the relaxation of death. Drops of blood spot its beak and the right eye hangs from its socket. One by one, men lower their weapons, catch their wind, and creep over to behold the creature they've felled.

Salty breezes play with the ship's rigging. Fresh spray douses the remaining men as the sail billows and grows taut. Bodies clunk against the hull; none look overboard to determine if the corpses are human or otherwise. For a time, all is quiet.

"Snorri Sæmundarsson!" yells Bjarni. Seeking out his steersman, at last he relinquishes his post. The captain's hands are stiff, curled around an invisible haft. He fumbles for a missing man's battle-axe, deeming his dagger not up to the task at hand. Spots dance before his eyes as he crosses the deck; the comfort of his disbelief in the supernatural now as dead as the abomination they'd slain. Bjarni rounds the carcass carefully as if it might turn draugr and spring back to life. "What have you brought upon us?"

The axe makes short work of the hatch, and Bjarni kicks the splintered wood away from the opening. From below there is only the gentle susurrus of waves and then a cry, poorly suppressed, clearly grief-stricken. It comes from the passengers. No. It comes from under the grey cover.

He lowers his eyes and meets Snorri's frightened, knowing gaze. The man's companions are all concentrating their attention on the dome and the wailing that comes from within it. Bjarni can hear them speaking in quiet tones, as if to soothe a wounded animal, but in no tongue he knows. The *sounds* are similar, they seem like ones he should recognise, but the words, the language escapes him, transformed somehow the instant it hits his ears.

Bjarni's long strides shrink the distance from stairs to sitters; before any of the quartet knows it, he has breached their circle and has a firm hold on their precious cargo. Anger fuels his movements. His footing is sure. He drags the thing upstairs and tears away the grey skin while Snorri and his companions are still fighting their way up the steps.

Beneath is a bird cage. Made of polished antler, carved and stained the hue of honey, each rail wound with silver wire. Inside, not clinging to a perch, but huddling at the bottom on a folded piece of gold cloth, is a bird.

A raven, in fact, twin to the dead one on the deck, only white, completely and utterly without pigmentation. A formidable creature that looks at Bjarni with liquid silver eyes and makes his heart clench. It opens its beak and a sound between a wail of grief and a howl of rage issues forth. Bjarni, acting on instinct, brings the axe down, driven solely by the gods-given need to destroy.

His tired arms betray him. The weapon smashes through the delicate antlers, shards flying. The silver wire becomes smoke once the spindles are broken, but the blade misses the raven altogether. As Bjarni draws back for a second blow, the bird flies at the breach in its prison, growing larger and larger as it passes through the wreckage, transmuting into something *other*.

Bjarni grunts and his grip on the axe is gone. The weapon falls with a loud crack, splitting to pieces on the deck like a dropped frost-cup.

The woman is so pale she hurts the eyes, shining with the same sheen as ancient ice. Her hair is long and silver-white, and her face ... For the briefest of instants, her face is thin and fine, translucent as the porcelain bowls Bjarni often obtains in the East. Blue highlights accentuate her high cheekbones and in place of eyebrows are long white feathers. Her irises swirl, now snow, now mercury. Then she settles. Her features firm, fill out, become almost human, but not quite, set apart by the perfection of her beauty. But it shifts, ever so slightly, vibrating from within, as if something prevents her from holding form too tightly. She wears a long-sleeved dress of arctic hues and a tunic that glistens like woven dew. Two oval box brooches adorn her chest, one on each side, just below her slender collarbone. Delicate chains link these hinged pieces to a third ornament, nestled between her breasts.

While the first two are the finest specimens Bjarni has seen, the latter is a dull lumpen thing that looks like a stone.

She is a head taller than Bjarni, than any other man on the ship, even her four fellows, whose human guises have been discarded. They stand lithe and elongated, facial feathers worn proudly as warriors' tattoos, silver hair moving with a will of its own, expressions haughty as outcast princes.

"Mymnir," mumbles Snorri helplessly. "My Lady."

She snarls at him and he cowers.

"You have failed, *vísla*."

"But, my Lady, my Queen . . . " He searches for words, eyes watering. "I gave my blood to protect your passage!"

And he had, too. In the early dawn before the ship set sail, he knelt beside the vessel and chanted to the hull. He grated his palm across barnacles encrusted there, smeared red into sea stains. Others saw him, thought it a fine idea, a good gift to the gods. Within a week, every man who set to sea sliced the fat pad of his hand and gave a little of himself to Njorðr.

"Wasn't enough, was it?" Her face fluctuates as she speaks, the brow feathers there and then gone again. She shoots him a last warning glare, then turns her gaze to the dead raven and makes her way towards it. The sailors fall back as she moves among them.

Bjarni watches, trying to rub away the pain in his sword arm; it feels like a frozen blade has pierced his flesh. He tries to speak but his mouth will not move. Like a sleepwalker, he follows the woman, stopping a few feet from where she crouches, her long hands reaching out to the heavy body. Her fingers glide across coal-black plumage, keeping contact on each stroke as long as she can, mewling all the while. Bjarni thinks he catches a name; it might be *Huginn*, but he cannot be sure, for the cold in his arm has crept upwards and is infecting his neck, face, ears. Everything sounds as if it comes across a great distance.

At last she rises, cradling the bird, its blood staining the blue of her dress. In a few steps she is at the rail. Without warning she heaves the carcass into the sea, where it bobs while the air leaves it, then sinks like unwanted treasure.

When she turns back her glare is dark as burnt wine.

"Put us ashore."

"There is no land," Bjarni manages, his tongue thick in his mouth.

"There." With an imperious gesture she points behind him and he turns, looks beyond her four companions and the snivelling vassal, and sees a beach and trees. Seagulls flying, surfing, nesting on rugged rocks and cliffs. The captain takes heed. He nods to his men, who readily tack the sail. A helpful breeze springs up as if commanded and sweeps them in like flotsam on the spray. This land could be filled with the richest of kings, Bjarni muses, but for once trade does not enter his mind.

"Anchor at the ready," he yells, scouring the coastline for a likely bay in which to moor, in which to offload his passengers.

---

Mymnir watches as the ship pulls away, leaving the six on the coast with only their packs. She had not demanded food or drink be left, but Bjarni hadn't questioned it. Too ill, she imagines. The *knörr* gets smaller and smaller and, when she judges hope might *just* have entered their hearts, she raises her arms and begins to sing.

The wave is strangely silent. It does not displace the liquid around it, as if it has been made separately from the ocean, a thing apart that hammers the vessel, overturns and smashes it, sending Bjarni and his men to join the black raven on the seabed.

Mymnir nods, satisfied. Away from the presence of iron weapons, from all that damned dampening metal, her powers grow stronger. She can feel the surge through her limbs, the settling of her form. She watches until the sea calms, until only memory can claim there once was a boat there, crewed by those with souls. She turns her back to the waters, skewering her guardians with a hard stare.

One of them, Harkon, bows and speaks, his voice coldly musical. "Forgive us, Lady, we did not expect a threat from the humans."

"No indeed. Too consumed with feeling sorry for yourselves. Too concerned with what has been burned and lost. You chose to come with me, all of you, so look forward or gods help me you will look upon nothing ever again."

"Yes, Lady," Eiðr says, and they all bow, even Snorri, although he is without Fae grace and his movements are comical and clumsy.

"Your brother, Lady. How did he find us?" Valdyr asks, brow creased.

"Perhaps Óðinn threw—" suggests Per, but is cut off.

"Óðinn is dead." She sets off along the shingle, toward an ascending the path, muttering. "*I will not die. I will not lie down and accept a fate not of my choosing.*"

Yet she knows that her twin must have followed her, left his post and tracked her down. And if he had, perhaps *others* might have too... No. Theirs is—was—a connection only one god shared, and that one-eyed bastard is a rotting corpse. No, her brother came because he's prone to fits of temper. Enraged and reckless, he attacked. Enraged and reckless he died, just so she would be forever yoked by his death, forever carrying it around her neck like a stone.

When they reach the top of the cliff, a flat expanse stretches out before them. In the far distance, a great thick forest bristles; closer, a river courses toward them over meadows and fields to career off the verge in a powerful, frothing arc. Wild grapes hang on vines, thick and lush, richly purple and fat. Mymnir nods.

"This will do. For now, this will have to do."

Snorri, forgotten Snorri, puffs behind them, making it to the plateau at last. Mymnir turns her eldritch gaze upon him and smiles. She waves him forward. He takes heart from that, and obeys.

One hand she lays on his shoulder and he beams, spine straightening him to new heights; with the other, she unclasps the left box brooch from her tunic and flips the intricate clasp that holds it closed. She releases it—and it floats to the ground, the open lid remaining upright. It settles on the luxuriant green grass and Mymnir squeezes, feeling Snorri's thin bones.

"You have been faithful, *vísla,* and for that I thank you."

"My Lady." Snorri lifts his head to stare into her eyes and does not see how the nail of her index finger lengthens and becomes white, hard as flint and sharp as hate. He barely feels it as it slices across his throat, as the blood pours over the tiny container at their feet.

Mymnir does not let him fall until he is dry. After a moment, she leans forward and whispers to the kingdom box, which shakes itself like a kitten waking after a nap then begins to hop about, struggling.

Once the first item springs from its depths—a fountain—others follow much more easily. In short order there are fine houses, more fountains, city squares, trees bearing strange fruit, horses and goats and shaggy cattle, byres and barns, a smithy, benches, paved streets and gardens and, finally, a palace, all glinting in the sun. The ground grumbles, then roars as stone rears from the earth. Jagged peaks push the construct up, so high its new rooftops seem to pierce the blue. Stone vines shoot from the soil, curl around the buildings, securing them to the ridge. Structures sprout granite roots, steeples and turrets are tethered to the mountainside by marble buttresses grown from sheer walls of rock. Mymnir crosses her arms, surveys her handiwork, whistling as it detaches from the continent, opening a league-wide channel between the two shores. Before the dust settles, an alabaster bridge stretches over the chasm, its railings topped with crystal orbs that catch the light, refracting rainbows up and down its length.

"Not quite Bifrost," she says, bending down to retrieve the box, which seems to gasp, exhausted.

"One last thing," she tells it and a sigh escapes the little thing. She flips it over and onto her unlined palm fall tiny seeds, silver and gold, perhaps a hundred. Mymnir exhales over them then flings them out before her.

Where each one lands a person unfurls. Maidens and lads, all Fae, all lovely and cold, and each one sinks before her into a deep bow. She nods once again.

"Home," she says. Her smile smug, regal. "For now, this is home."

# Burning Seaweed for Salt

That night, Guðmundr donned his black hood and crept across the meadow to Ingimundr's farmstead. While the household slept, Guðmundr carved plague runes into the fence posts, set the storehouse alight, then snuck back to his own holding to wait for Bergþora's return.

"What a dream I've just had," Bergþora said, waking in Ingimundr's bed-closet. "There was ash on the wind and all the beasts had manes of fire, both bad omens. I should not be surprised to find my husband has paid us a visit."

Ingimundr got dressed and ran outside. One by one his horses went mad, biting and kicking, tearing each other's hides with their teeth. By dawn, his fields were a sea of blood, his livestock dead or scattered. Any meat left on their bones was spoiled by the sorcerer's magic.

The next morning, Guðmundr heard beating hoofs on the ridge between his land and Ingimundr's. "That will be Bergþora," he thought, "and Gamli's dark son, begging for a place at my table. With no herds to support them, no bread, whey or cheese, they will starve unless they come crawling to me."

But the horse was riderless. It was Týrfaxi, Ingimundr's favourite steed, running wild-eyed and foaming. The creature leapt the fence and chased Guðmundr's stock around, ravaging them all before succumbing at last to the plague.

> "I have plenty of meat now for winter," Guðmundr said, clearing the seaweed from his smokehouse and burning it down to black-salt. Quickly, he flayed the carcasses and used the salt to preserve them. When he had finished the task he went inside, congratulating himself on his cleverness.
> That winter was the coldest this land has seen since Egill Gíslason helped Lóki steal the sun. Supplies ran low all over the district. Long before the weather broke, farmers were forced to slay their horses for meat—and when this source, too, was depleted, they survived by boiling and eating seaweed soup. For months Guðmundr waited for his wife and his neighbour to come, but they never arrived. All winter he sat alone in his house, nibbling on salted plague-meat, growing hungrier by the day. By spring he was shrivelled and black as a troll. From then on men called him Svartosattr, and refused to trade with him because, they said, his goods were rotten. Even seaweed soup was more nutritious than his cursed horsemeat. And they scoffed at him for behaving so rashly.
>
> From *Guðmundarþáttr Svartosatts (The Tale of Guðmundr Black-Salt)*

Aud shines.

Her skin, her hair, her face glow with not merely contentment, but active joy. She lies sleeping, naked on a tangle of sheets, the black of her tresses spreading across white pillows like a Valkyrie's rippling cape.

Ari brushes away the tendrils that curl at her forehead and temples. He lingers there a moment, lost in memory, then runs his hand down Aud's cheek, jaw, neck, shoulder, back, hip and then thigh. A light dampness coats his fingertips and he puts them to his mouth, tasting ambrosia.

Aud smiles and opens her eyes.

Happiness backlights them like cleverly placed lanterns.

Ari always comes here, straight from the other's bed, from cold flesh to warm sweet curves. Here in this storeroom, this solitary grotto etched out of the palace's foundations, Ari feels at home. Not because its pearlescent walls exude comfort, nor because its familiar clutter hides him from envious stares. A vast collection of tapestries muffles the space; its floor is stacked with camphor-lined boxes and layered with soft rugs. Even the enormous bed—which they'd foraged from the room's darkest corners, then hung with silk curtains and covered with fine linens—even *this* can't explain his gladness. He lies back, inhaling the spicy scent of the place, of Aud. He pulls her close, fulfilled. Here, together, they are safe.

"I must go," says Aud.

Through bleary eyes, Ari sees a mirage, as if tiny jewels float around her as she speaks. He admires the illusion even as he clamps on her wrist. They will wrestle, as they always do when the time for parting comes. Clinging to each other—now pulling, now pushing—they do their best to resist the outside world. To avoid the farce of courtly pandering, the fawning and feigning, the pretence of everyday life. For a few stolen minutes they are alone and honest. And yet, it's never enough.

Face red, petulant, Ari will let Aud go. He always does. He must. She smiles, a little sadly, a little wickedly. "The day will break soon, I can feel it. And Her Majesty will expect music with the dawning."

Born with moon tides and sun cycles in her blood, Aud knows what the time is, morning or night. The rising and setting of Earth's satellites is a singing in her veins.

"Stay," says Ari, tired as the argument he can't help but start.

She touches his face, runs her hand through his silver hair. Admires irises that are green one moment, argent-coal the next. "It's not worth it, my love, to arouse her suspicions. We would not survive."

Ari shakes his head, rolls over, a delinquent chafing at rules.

Aud persists. She climbs over her lover, sits by his knees and places her hand on his chest. "She *chose* you."

"What choice did I get?" Fury strangles the words. He throws the sheets back and swings his legs over the edge of the mattress. Slouching, elbows propped on his knees, he keeps his eyes averted and waits for Aud to leave. For the first time, he seems serious.

She watches him pick at his cuticles, intently not meeting scrutiny. His respiration is quiet, measured, but the air around him radiates tension. She leans over, kisses him, and he lets her go. It feels as if something has broken.

Perhaps today is not the day to share her news after all.

In the corner of the room is a shallow pool, heated by thermal springs. Aud is careful; she scrubs away all trace of their lovemaking.

Mymnir is a jealous mistress and Mymnir will know.

---

The white raven wakes to the sound of a harp caressed by Aud's clever fingers. *The girl has a rare talent*, Mymnir thinks, swooping from the nest she's built and rebuilt in the chamber's rafters for over two centuries, spun of myriad strands plucked from her past lovers' heads. She wings down through the bed's canopy and lands on the ermine coverlet. Layered sheers are drawn between the four carved corner posts, but Aud plays a light air that easily filters through the fine weave. Mymnir preens while she listens. The raven has never been much of a singer, though she has a sophisticated ear and her taste in music is exquisite. Not a day passes without song in the Fae Queen's household, nor without parvenu troubadours vying for position in her cortege.

*Upstarts.* She runs her beak along glossy feathers, then pulls until they grow into fingers, hands, arms. Flexing her claw-tipped toes, she relinquishes her avian form, sprouts feet, shins, thighs, hips, hair soft as down. Yawning, she transforms her features as easily as Aud's tune changes key. Mymnir slips into a silk robe, luxuriating as cool fabric slides against her bare skin. She nods appreciatively as Aud's wintry notes continue to trickle across the grand room. Unschooled bards and wandering minstrels could never compete with the Hrafn's Harpist, the fourth such to hold the title. The girl's pitch has been perfect since the day she was born; her first cries were madrigals, her first words heart-rending melodies. At her first childish strummings, her first clumsy pluckings, even the Æsir wept.

*The mother's influence*, every maestro agreed, knowing artistry ran strong in Helga's veins. *Aud clearly favours the Fae side of her lineage.* So at the age of five, the child had been removed from the servants' quarters, where all the *mixed* resided, and saved from a life of drudgery. She'd been privileged well above her station, granted the inheritance rights of a pureblood. Dedicated to a life of beauty.

A decade of training had refined Aud's talent. Two years as the Fae Queen's sole virtuoso had made it, and her, exceptional.

*You're welcome*, Mymnir thinks, as she does every morning, savouring each note in her private concert. She stretches and lengthens across the huge mattress, blankets still rumpled from Ari's last visit. Though he is certainly her favourite—her most *inventive* lover—like all the rest, he is banished from the bed as soon as their commerce is done. Ravens do not like to share anything, let alone their nests.

"Ivalo," says Mymnir and it is a command, not a question. There is no doubt in her tone that she will be answered.

"Yes, my Lady." Ivalo is short, stoop-shouldered and wizened. Like all half-breeds, she has unnaturally long life, but she cannot cheat the rigours of old age. She was given as a gift to Mymnir a century ago and has faithfully served her queen as a lady of the chamber, a lover for too short a time, and general factotum. Her heart has wavered only once; only once did another briefly take Mymnir's place.

As Mymnir sits on the edge of the bed, Ivalo scoops together the calf-length hair and deftly twists it into a plait, then curls it around until a fat bun rests at the nape of the Queen's neck. She leads the tall woman to her bath and does all that is needed to ensure Mymnir is washed, dried, perfumed and dressed to begin her day. The music plays on from Aud's hidden spot; a screened gallery running above the bedchamber, extending into the reception hall next door.

Ivalo secures a sapphire choker around the Queen's throat. Today it makes her eyes seem blue; tomorrow she might choose amethysts to give them a lilac sheen; emeralds the day after that so they are like limpid pools. When temper strikes, perhaps it will be rubies to mirror her mood. To warn those around her.

Mymnir crosses to the heavy velvet curtains that conceal an arched passageway between rooms. Ivalo hurries ahead and pulls aside the hangings so the Queen may pass through unhindered. She is early for the morning's business. There are no mercury-eyed courtiers here as yet, no supplicants begging for audience. The rill of Aud's harp crescendos, swelling like a waterfall after heavy rain. Its chorus surges up to the vaulted ceiling, washes across the stone floor and crashes around the chaise beside which Mymnir stands, smiling, bathed in the sound. Ivalo pours wine into a gold goblet and hands it to the Queen once she has seated herself comfortably.

Within seconds, a single knock resounds and double doors at the end of the hall swing open.

The Fae woman is fair and comely, though neither as tall nor as icily blonde as Mymnir. Her complexion has a bluish tinge, striking against the black of her kirtle, worn sleeveless despite the cold. Beaten bracelets of silver, gold and bronze clink on her wrists and upper arms as she treads a long thin carpet running from the entrance to the Queen's récamier. Mymnir raises an eyebrow at this intrusion. Ivalo stands vigil behind her, watchful as a hawk.

The woman carries a box, wooden and carved, the size of an infant. Gently she places it on the floor in front of the Queen, then offers the graceful drawn-out courtesy that Mymnir expects, hands fluttering behind her like wings. She rises, her face a mask. The harp's melody falters for an instant, no more than a beat, but it is enough to register on and twist Mymnir's lovely features.

Aud still misses her mother.

And Helga, it seems, still misses her daughter after twelve years.

*Emotional fools*, thinks the raven. *Grasping at ties that have long been dissolved.* Helga had carried Aud in her womb for a mere eighteen months—her human lover's seed burgeoning much more quickly than those of pure Fae stock. Aud's father, like so many of his short-lived brethren, was lured from the path, seduced by the mystery of the ones his people called *wanageeska*. In breeding, as in all things, humans insist on racing to the finish. Lovemaking, child-rearing, the span of their lives—all fervently pursued, all over so soon. Fae gestation is much longer, almost three years, and even then mothers barely get acquainted with their babies before they are born. Eighteen months for Helga and Aud, and a blink of years together after that . . . What bond could they have forged in such a brief time?

Mymnir, after all, practically raised the girl. *She* selected Aud as her personal accompanist. *She* has been, and will be, the subject of Aud's devotions for the length of her days. Nostalgic nonsense will not be tolerated.

"Your Majesty," says Helga, voice clear and low. She gestures with a hand that is both shorter and squarer than those of the Fae are wont to be—the digits stout and strong and scarred from her craft. Indeed, some whisper, though not too loudly, she carries a taint of Dwarfish blood. "Finished last night, for your pleasure."

"Then why do I see it only this morning?" demands Mymnir as Helga bends and unlocks the chest's lid. She meets the Queen's eye calmly.

"I did not think Your Majesty's sleep should be interrupted so late. Please excuse my presumption."

Mymnir knows Helga begs no forgiveness, but the Queen will not punish her sarcasm although she itches to do so. Helga Ögmundardóttir is respected among the Fae, popular and supported. The raven is cunning: she is a tyrant only so far and no more. Many rely on Helga for their adornments; Mymnir might face a rebellion if her court was deprived of its finest jeweller. Besides, though she is loathe to admit it, she herself wouldn't do without the artisan's inventions. And she is anxious to see the box's contents.

The lid rises slowly, oh so slowly, and Mymnir cranes forward to watch, hating that she must look like a greedy child.

On a bed of greenest velvet lies the necklace. A copy of the one Freyja sold her cunt for—the original improved upon, the gems somehow brighter, the metal seemingly more liquid, pulsing as if alive, the links in constant motion, catching the light. An enormous diamond mesmerises as the heartstone.

"Brisingamen," breathes Mymnir, then corrects herself, "My Brisingamen."

And although she had ordered it made, although she'd demanded it, she hadn't truly believed it possible. A fragment of the old world renewed, made *real*, in this one. She hadn't dared to hope . . . "Oh, Helga, how magnificent, how perfect. You may have one wish in return."

"I would speak with my daughter," says Helga without hesitation, and Mymnir knows herself trapped. Sensing the Queen's ire rising, Helga lifts the necklace and holds it out.

Mymnir strokes the sparkling, shivering gold, distracted. "What's this?"

The clasp is unfinished.

"It is not yet complete, Majesty." The jeweller flushes. "I wished to see how it hung on you, to get the required length for—*perfection*."

"Then I will consider your request when this is returned to me in a *perfect* state."

"Yes, Majesty." Helga bows stiffly. She moves to stand behind Mymnir and drapes the necklace around the other woman's throat. Making a show of measuring and adjusting, she clicks her tongue when the chain hangs too low; although truth be told her skill is so great, her eye so sharp, she could have done this simply by looking at the Queen. Mymnir knows this, as does Ivalo, who glares at Helga.

"By this evening," says the white raven.

"I look forward to speaking with Aud tonight, then." Helga folds the treasure back into its case, eschewing Mymnir's scrutiny as she rises and leaves the Queen to seethe and covet.

Helga thinks she feels her daughter's eyes follow her from the hall, but she cannot be sure. The music continues unabated.

---

Aud's fingers ache. She moves away from the harp and stretches, arching her back and rolling her shoulders and neck. Although she's exhausted, she cares for her instrument after working it so hard, much as a warrior does his steed. Before taking her leave, Aud relaxes the tuning pins and tends to the strings. She replaces any that need it, guaranteeing the delicate spun-gold wires will produce only the truest sounds. Pocketing the faulty ones, she drapes a cloth over the apparatus and silently promises to oil the soundboard later.

The sun has just dipped past its zenith. Outside the afternoon is warm, the lawns and flagstones dappled with inviting shade. Moments ago, the Queen called a recess from the morning's politics, then left to go and eat with her courtiers in the open air. Music does not travel well in the courtyards so Aud may rest until she is required to play as part of the evening's entertainment. Leaving the beloved thing in its place, she takes the narrow staircase down from her secluded balcony and steps out into the now empty reception hall.

Large hands grab her waist and strong arms whip around her, constricting. Her hair sweeps across her face, blinding, but she would recognise his scent anywhere: salt and sandalwood, and the fragrant oils Mymnir rubs into his skin.

"I'm so tired of sneaking," Ari says, nuzzling her neck. "So tired of hiding and being quiet and living life in the shadows, stealing what should be shared openly . . . Come away with me, Aud. Tonight. Please, let's leave this place. Leave *her*."

"But . . . My mother . . . "

Ari kisses Aud's eyelids, her lips. "Helga suffers more from your presence than your absence, my love."

Aud can't deny the truth in his words. *Mymnir is relentless whenever Mother is near* . . .

"And where would we go?" she asks, laughing, hoping to distract him by nibbling at his earlobe. *Where would we raise our child*, she wants to say, but hesitates. *Later. I'll tell him later.* She presses close—and through her pocket the worn harp strings jab her hip. Recoiling, she draws them out and plaits them together, then twines the braid like a torc around Ari's neck. "The woods in this land are wild."

"There are settlements beyond the palace," he says, admiring the makeshift necklace. "The skrælings and half-breeds haven't been idle in their exile. Humans can be quite resourceful when cut adrift—perhaps we could learn something from them?"

Aud stops trying to knot the strings' ends in place and instead pulls them tight, pushing Ari against the wall while pretending to garrotte him.

"Ah, but I have the advantage on that front," she says, wavering. "I am the best of both worlds . . . "

Ari shows her how much he agrees.

Pulling away, Aud grows serious. "She will hunt us, you know."

"Let her try."

Grinning, she rearranges the cord, ties it, and tucks it beneath his collar. Then she lets him kiss her fully, lets his hands roam where they will, wonders if—when—he'll detect the slight changes in her physique. They whisper and moan and see nothing beyond each other. They do not perceive Ivalo, who has come to get a shawl for the Queen, taking a shortcut through the hall. They do not hear her gasp, nor her subsequent weeping as she remembers days when Ari had held her just so. And they cannot know how she convinces herself that this jealousy, growing black and fertile within her, is on behalf of her wronged mistress. She does not admit there is a skerrick of mourning for her own loss and longing; that Ivalo, so often put aside, aches to hurt someone as she has so often been hurt.

By the time they break apart, Aud to go to her room to pack and Ari to sit at the Queen's table, Ivalo is gone, trailing news heavy with spite in her wake.

---

Mymnir's summons comes early and unexpectedly. Aud returns to the great hall as afternoon gropes for its cloak of twilight.

She senses something is amiss as soon as she steps inside, but does not associate it with herself. The room is packed with courtiers. Her mother stands in the deep rows of people, features pinched, fearful. Aud still does not understand. Head bowed, she tries to make her way towards her concealed stage, to play.

The crowd parts, not the way she wishes to go, but directly towards the Queen's dais. The chaise has been replaced by a throne of never-melting ice, but the chill issues from the sitter, not her seat.

Mymnir is deceptively relaxed. At her feet—*beneath* her feet—lies a body, shackles on wrists and ankles, long hair obscuring the face. Aud knows the body as well as she does her own, and the tiny child inside her seems to jump in response to her sudden fear. Her steps falter, but she forges ahead, hoping her shaking is not obvious. The fabric of her dress seems to shudder of its own accord. No-one could miss her terror.

With great effort, Aud holds her head high. Approaches the Queen.

"You are charged," declares Mymnir in a tone that makes the blood freeze, "with *theft*."

"We have done nothing but love each other." Aud's timid stutter makes Mymnir smile.

"You have taken my property. And after I raised you up—"

"You stole me from my mother!" The girl's voice hardens and Mymnir stops, shocked.

"*I* was your mother."

Aud shakes her head. "You were my *owner*. I have been nothing more than a favoured dog."

The barb lodges in Mymnir's craw and two spots of colour bloom in her cheeks. "And you would turn on me now," she says, "after I gave you a life, made you what you are . . . Very well, child." Mymnir lifts one hand, nothing more, and instantly Aud feels invisible whips lashing her. She yelps and stumbles forward, arms fluttering in a grotesque parody of the Queen's preferred courtesy. Her wrists are gripped by unseen forces and bent further and further back. Whimpering, Aud falls to her knees, twisting against the pain as her knuckles crack, almost at the point of breaking.

"Howl, *dog*—"

"Don't harm her," mumbles the man pinned under the Queen's slippers. Ari raises his head and Aud gasps. His eyes, his beautiful eyes . . . Blood has dried on his face and he seeks the room blindly, the orbs in his sockets gone, replaced by gold harp strings scrunched into balls. "Don't harm her."

Mymnir's anger has brought foam to the corners of her mouth. Ivalo leans forward to wipe it away. Releasing her magic, the Queen slaps at the stained, wrinkled hands, and the old woman subsides. She is both delighted and terrified by what she has done.

"I should have preserved your sight until you saw her burn. She will *shine*, my lover, I promise you."

Panting with relief, Aud cradles her quivering arms then gathers the strength to stand. She is unsteady on her feet, but defiant as she puts a protective hand to her belly. Mymnir notices the gesture and sneers.

Aud musters her courage. "For the sake of this child, be merciful. He is innocent in all this."

Mymnir's irises flash ruby. For a second Aud thinks the Queen may have relented, but then a wide smile spreads across her lovely face, teeth showing sharp and cruel.

"There is no greater mercy than giving him straight into the ancestors' care. Bypassing the heartbreaks of this lonely Earth, he'll be welcomed in the joyous halls beyond. You, however . . . There is only one end for your kind." Mymnir cocks an eyebrow and looks across the swaying mass of Fae, pleased to see one particularly stricken face.

"You may speak with your daughter, Helga, before she burns. Consider this a reward for your most excellent work, which I shall wear tonight when the little *thief* lights up the sky."

---

All these many years, they had obeyed the Queen.

Their family had benefitted from Aud's talent, from her *purchase*, arranged by Helga's father. But Helga had never been happy about the loss, no matter that the girl was *mixed*. Ögmundr had wanted this grandchild out of his sight; she was a constant reminder of his daughter's straying. It was not that he minded another half-breed in his line—it was honourable to provide servants for the realm—but he was humiliated by the affection his daughter bore the man who'd impregnated her. As studs and brood mares, humans were ideal; but they were temporary companions, too short-lived and naïve ever to be the Fae's equals. And when Helga softened with love for the child, when she refused to let the girl be reared as a lady's maid . . . Ögmundr could not bear the shame.

When he'd told her of the arrangement with the Queen, Helga had acquiesced. The contract was binding, permanent. There was nothing she could do. So she respected the transfer of ownership to Mymnir, but she had not been content. When she passed Aud in the palace's corridors she'd brush a hand over the girl's ebony locks—her touch so light that sometimes Aud wondered if she had really felt it. Helga had schooled the child not to run to her, to pretend her own mother did not exist, for she had been in the Queen's service for a lifetime. She knew the depths reserved for those who displeased the white raven.

"We have no time," Helga now says. The door of Aud's chamber is closed tightly behind them so the guards may not hear. "The bonfire—your funeral pyre—is even now being constructed."

Aud quakes and her mother's grip settles on her shoulders. "Listen to me carefully and do as I say." Helga hands her a dagger, black and silver metal with a blade that seems to drink in the coming night. "Use this when the time comes—do not be squeamish. And these are the words you must speak."

She whispers the spell, repeating it thrice until Aud's musician's ear has it firmly fixed.

"I'm sorry, so sorry," sobbed Aud, pressing her face to Helga's shoulder, until the woman feels hot tears coursing down her bare arm.

"No," she replies. "*I'm* sorry. I did not protect you and I should have." She reaches into the neck of her smock and pulls from her kirtle something that glimmers like moonbeams dancing over the sea. "Take this."

Aud gapes at the thing. Brisingamen is heart-heavy in her palm. She opens her mouth to speak, but the door begins to creak open, so she and Helga break apart. Aud slips the blade into one pocket of her skirt, and the necklace into another.

Ivalo stands framed in the doorway, a wicker washing basket propped on her hip. She looks between the two women, her expression sour and pleased.

"Time for you to go," she says to Helga.

Aud aches as her mother does not argue, but gives her a subtle warning glance. They nod, one to the other, and Helga turns her back. The guards close the door behind her.

Ivalo remains.

"I've something to show you." The old woman does not admit she was the author of Aud's predicament, but something in her satisfied manner reveals all. Ivalo lifts her chin and steps closer. She reaches into the basket and pulls out a ball.

No, not a ball. A head. With silver hair and melted gold in the cavities, shrunk down to a quarter of its size. Aud moans, attempts to touch Ari, but even in this Ivalo is spiteful. She yanks it away, tutting. "Soon it will be set in silver—the Queen will have your mother craft it into piece of jewellery. He will make a fine pendant, don't you think?"

Aud turns away and doubles over. Ivalo approaches, not from concern, but to better see her rival's pain. She drops the head back into the basket and then puts it on the floor, right in front of the girl's face. "Say farewell, lover," the old woman says, leaning close to rasp in Aud's ear. So eager is she to view Aud's grief, she does not notice the knife the girl holds along her thigh.

As soon as she can smell the old woman's sweat, Aud turns swiftly and, whispering the words her mother gave her, brings the blade up. It enters at Ivalo's pubis and splits the bone there before Aud slices skywards. Ivalo's cry is silent; the spell swells in her mouth and stoppers her throat. Her blood freezes, evaporates, spills out of the slit as radiant light. Her organs become steam, a fog that puffs from the body.

Aud hears high sharp chimes, a rushing of wind, and then she is holding Ivalo's skin draped over her arm, warm and pliable as a recently removed shirt. She allows herself no tears, no pause. She swallows down bitter bile and guilty regret.

She untangles the wrinkled membrane from its clothes, then strips off her own dress. Inside, the strange coat is sticky, slippery.

She steps into it as if pulling on hose, feet first, then carefully draws the old woman's leather up her legs, feeling her firm young belly swim in Ivalo's roomy pelvis. Next she works her arms in, then her hands, wiggling the skin-gloves until they fit, and finally flipping the head like a hood over her face. For a moment, there is nothing, then the skin quakes, convulses with an independent life, and tightens around her. As it adheres, pressing against her, she thinks she might suffocate. The two edges of the split meet, then close, sealing her in. The disguise settles, features falling back into place, folds and pouches all reasserting themselves. In the mirror, she is Ivalo—except for her eyes.

These alone are unmistakable.

She pulls Ivalo's clothing onto her stolen form, wincing at the smell, then slips Brisingamen and Ari's head into an oiled sack. This she hides in the wicker basket, under sheets she has torn from her bed. She wraps a shawl around the gash in her dress and a scarf tightly around her forehead, pulling it down until it touches the bridge of her nose. Fear tingles through her but she inhales deeply, calming her nerves and clearing her head. She can feel the sun dropping—soon it will be dusk, hours yet before the moon begins its climb. Before the many torches of Mymnir's palace are lit, before the bonfire is ready to receive her, she must make good her escape.

Heaving the basket onto her hip, she opens the door and limps between the guards, careful to keep her speed under control until she is beyond of their watchful sight. Truly, she need not worry—Ivalo's passage goes unremarked. The old woman rarely warrants anyone's attention.

---

On a small beach covered with smooth grey pebbles, Aud puts the basket down. She makes sure the bag containing Ari's head and the necklace is tied tight, then carefully loops its braided thongs around her neck. *This is not the departure you'd intended, my love . . . but tonight, at last, we leave here together.* She drops Ivalo's cloak and dress on the ground and takes one last look at her borrowed skin in the moonlight. From the cliffs above her she hears a commotion—her absence has finally been discovered.

*We will be safe*, she tells her son. *Safe when we cross these waters, when we enter the forests beyond, and lose ourselves in the mountain fastness. Safe when we are gone.*

Aud steps forward to meet the spray. The temperature of the water shocks her but she keeps moving, deeper and deeper until the sandy bottom drops off beneath her feet. The sack bobs against her spine as she dives into the darkness, a comforting weight. As she swims, the borrowed skin becomes softer and softer. It turns translucent, covering her in a foul-smelling goo, but soon enough the sea washes it away.

Licking the salt from her lips, Aud propels herself forward, arms and legs beating a three-quarter rhythm through the waves. The wind plays a tune only she can hear, encouraging, beckoning her on. Kicking against the brush of seaweed, she follows the ethereal song. Eyes set on the horizon, face shining beneath the stars, she draws ever closer to a new dawn.

# The Morning is Wiser than the Evening

"Go, hurry," said the children's nursemaid, who loved them as her own flesh and blood. They'd reached the riverbank not a moment too soon. Behind them, soldiers tramped up to the castle's grand gates, knocking, searching, shouting. High above waving torches and flashing swords, the crescent moon sailed peacefully toward the horizon.

"Seek the Bird of Truth," said the kindly old woman, heart breaking with the dawn. "She will set all to rights."

The twins were laid in a crystal casket and thrown into the water. Brave Rilla comforted her brother when the currents tossed their vessel hither and thither, when eels snapped at them through the glass, when the voyage seemed never-ending.

"But where will we find her?" Radigund asked for the thousandth time, a warble in his voice. Rilla kissed his cheek, dried his tears, but still had no answer to give.

Author unknown, *The Bird of Truth & the Teller of Lies*,
c.1380–1485, MS LK 748 I 4to

Magnus hears water splashing along a hidden brook and it makes him want to pee.

His horse is flea-bitten, sway-backed; its teeth are ground almost to the gums. One of its ears is, for the most part, absent, having lost a discussion with a black bear some time ago over drinking rights at a stream. The animal, needless to say, is quite stupid.

But it's the only beast Magnus has, and the largest part of his inheritance. One broken-down steed, one silver-grey pouch carrying a dried-up head that mutters to whoever will listen, and the last few shining links of a necklace comprise, sum and total, all the worldly goods his mother left him. She said the jewels were magnificent, once, that his grandmother had made them. Aud had sold off pieces as and when she could, bartering their way in life until disease took her. He didn't think she intended him to be alone, to fend for himself. Why, he'd lost their farm so quickly, so easily. It never would have happened if Aud had been there to watch over him.

Empty nets slap against his saddlebags—the snares in his pack haven't caught more than a scrawny hare all week. The *skræling* who'd traded Magnus the kit for his thickest blanket had sworn he'd earn a fortune in furs. *Sit yourself still for half a minute at sundown,* the swarthy man had promised, *and raccoons, minks, ermines—you name it—will throw themselves into your path.* But Magnus is convinced the trip-wires are too stiff, too slow. The bait is rank, repellent. The nets are woven too loosely—a buffalo could run through them. So he sets them when the mood strikes, eventide or otherwise, and tells himself that waiting and trapping are old men's games. A bit of hunger gives young hunters edge.

The demand of his bladder grows more insistent and he dismounts, unlacing his fly and letting forth a yellow cataract. The horse seems to sigh happily, relieved of Magnus' weight—he is not fat, no, but very tall and muscular. Relacing his trousers, Magnus decides his skins need filling as much as he needed emptying. He leads the nag away from the trail and pushes through the fir trees, towards the fluid rush.

Twigs and pine needles snag on his coat. Sap-coated limbs whip as he passes, threatening decapitation. Holding one arm up and his mare's head down for protection, he plunges through the dense forest. He is sticky, hot and sweaty by the time the woods relent, breaking abruptly into a large clearing. His mount, who Magnus often thinks of as Ekla, though he refuses to say the name aloud, isn't quite brainless enough to enjoy being flayed by primeval branches. As soon as they step onto the meadow, she snorts and tugs at the reins, trying to dislodge them from Magnus' clutches. Ekla stomps, points her long snout away from her master, and attempts a gallop. She nearly escapes, for Magnus is focused on the castle, an assemblage of granite and slate, half built into the scree-covered hill at the far side of the glade. At the last second, he yanks the lead hard, forcing the horse to stay by his side.

His feet move of their own volition, drawing him to the citadel. On the battlements are banners that flap in the breeze, pennants made not of silk and thread-of-gold, but rippling sheets of fire. Curving around the building is a moat; a semi-circle of fog that shrouds the foundations, lapping at the drawbridge and swirling up to the portcullis' threshold. Upon closer inspection Magnus sees it is more than just mist. Shards and slivers fly around in a glacial wind, lashing back and forth like a murmuration of crystal starlings, more effective a protection than some water-filled gully could ever be. Any man trying to ford *this* moat would be cut to shreds—and that's if, somehow, he managed to avoid the fosse-guardians.

Dozens of arctic foxes patrol the frost-ditch's depths, each larger than an ox. They leap and bound along the perimeter, herding the glimmering blades, unscathed. Their coats and teeth like diamond splinters, their movements deft smoke ribbons. Drawing closer and closer to the edge, Magnus almost loses himself watching the hypnotic fluctuations of white blight and glass, listening to its delicate chiming, its haunting moan. He feels dizzy, teeters, begins to plunge forward, hears the foxes' gleeful yelping, recognises his doom but cannot stop his own momentum.

A hand clamps around his upper arm, pulling him back and almost dislocating his shoulder as if the saviour does not know his own strength. Ekla whinnies and adds her muscle to the man's. Jerking the reins clean out of Magnus' grasp, she bolts, pitching him onto his arse as she tears off. He bites his tongue as his skull thunks against the hard ground. Spitting the rust-water taste of blood, he blinks at the sight of two feet planted a few inches away from his nose. Enormous things with steel—no! stone!—boots the size of a child's sled. He lifts his stare, taking in greaves, cuisses, haubergeon, gauntlets big as bucklers; the armour all hewn of flint and marble, articulated like fish scales. He sits up gingerly, careful not to teeter against the tree-trunk legs. On the man's chest is a device Magnus has not seen before: a white raven, *rousant*. It glints in the sunlight, undulating as though ruffling its wings. Long hair curls down to broad shoulders, ringlets of cloud and ash, now storm-charcoal, now a hint of ember, all framing a visage of hardened magma. And carved in it, features red and black and gold, irises that iridesce and flash and burn.

The fire giant reaches down to help him. Magnus grasps a thumb and a finger—his own grip cannot span the man's palm. He is lifted much as he was dropped, like a twig blown about by a force it cannot control. The giant settles him on his feet quite tenderly, brushing his clothes off as a father would a child after a fall. Checking for breaks, torn fabric. In spite of himself, Magnus laughs and so does the titan: a great sound, a good-humoured rumble from the depths of his belly.

"A lucky escape, my friend. I've lost four servants that way—the young ones keep forgetting not to look down." The giant moves over to the steed he rode in on and strokes its russet flank. The beast has eight legs and is almost thirty hands high by Magnus' reckoning. Its stirrups are just below the level of his nose.

"Thank you for your assistance." Magnus is not too proud to be grateful. His curiosity has often gotten him into trouble—it gladdens him that, this time, someone was there to prevent his fall. "I don't know how to repay you, but I owe you my life."

The giant laughs once more, his beautiful, terrible face lighting up with pleasure. "Keep me company for a while, accept my hospitality. That is all I ask. My wife is away and I am starved of good fellowship."

Magnus' asinine horse is grazing on the other side of the field. Contemplating the half-eaten hare in Ekla's saddlebag, his stomach complains. It has been too long since he's broken bread with anyone but the mare. *Let the stubborn thing roam where she will*, he thinks, and accepts the giant's offer with alacrity.

―⁂―

The carcass of an entire cow lies on Surtr's plate—a pewter tray, large as two shields laid end-to-end on the table. Magnus has acquitted himself well, but cannot compete with his host's appetite.

*The Morning is Wiser than the Evening*

The castle is not short of servants, yet the colossus does not speak to them except to give commands. Conversation with one's social inferiors is no conversation at all, he explains to Magnus.

"You, though, you have the look of a fine and noble fellow. Your phrases are as nicely turned as your legs—yes, your attire may be rough, but I'll wager you're well-suited for courtly life."

Surtr's mead cup is empty once more and it takes two men struggling with a cask to refill it. The giant sways in his seat, just a little, as he continues. "Perhaps you should go to the mountain, join the other fair folk, all those pretty ones bending the knee to Her Majesty, the White Queen. For all that you've fallen on hard times, a hale lad like you would most certainly capture the Hrafn's attention."

Magnus remembers how his mother's voice trembled when she spoke of the *fjallkona*, how she'd fervently warn him away from the palace. *You'll become no more than the raven's trinket*, Aud had said. *Not a person, not my charming boy; merely a bauble. And you'll be hers alone to play with . . .* His heart flounders, drowning in memory. How he'd try to distract his mother when her sombre moods struck, how he'd tell silly tales, how he'd sing—and how the music always made Aud wince. How she'd press her calloused fingers against his lips no matter the tune. Gently, firmly, silencing him. Now, Magnus scrubs a linen cloth across his mouth but he keeps his handsome, good-natured countenance blankly pleasant, not showing that the giant's words have caused any ructions in his soul.

Not that Surtr would notice. Absorbed in his cup, he slurs, "Majesty—*Her Majesty.* Pah!" He swallows deeply, grimacing at the taste, then snaps for wine before draining off the rest of his mead. "What has she done to earn such a title?"

"I've heard she has powerful magic," Magnus offers.

"Ah, so perhaps we should call her Magicsty instead?" Surtr chortles, but the laughter ebbs when his goblet remains dry a moment too long. As he looks around for a pageboy, his gaze catches on the pair of long axes hung crosswise on the wall behind him. His spine straightens with pride. Staggering to his feet, the giant hoists one of the weapons off its bracket. The handle is more than half his height, heavy steel banded with leather. The vicious double-moon blade is burnished by age and use, but its edge is honed to gleaming. He hefts its weight with ease, hands falling naturally to the grooves they've worn in the hilt. "Magic is but a tool, my friend. No more impressive than this *hatchet*, and no less—there is nothing inherently special about either. Power lies not in owning such tools, but in wielding them with honour. With nobility."

He widens his stance, braces himself, and swings the blade overhead. "From cradle to grave, it's our actions that define us. Not the shiny toys we are given, the inherited skills, nor the size and reach of our—" Surtr waggles his brows and gives a lurid grin, "—axes. It's what we do with them that matters."

Magnus laughs loudly as the giant splits the large barrel lately rolled into the room, lodging the steel head deep into the oak floor. Wine gushes, a cascade of red that puddles on the polished boards and soaks into silk carpets. Chuckling, he frees the weapon then slumps onto his seat, holding the dripping thing like a sceptre. One after another, he clunks his boots up onto the table and crosses them at the ankle.

"No matter what some little birds say, people aren't born into majesty. They earn it."

With that, the giant's countenance softens. He waves away the servants come to mop up the mess and, leaning his head against the chair's high back, watches the flames flickering in the hearth without really seeing them. A few minutes pass, until the silence stretches into tension. Magnus can see the huge man hasn't nodded off—his thick lashes continue to sweep up and down—but he isn't quite awake, either. Surtr has the same wistful look that Aud would get when the winters grew cold and the summers hot. When the moon was hidden by clouds, and when it shone too fiercely. When he smiled at her *just so*. When he dared tell her she was lovely.

Magnus clears his throat and wonders what songs might lift his host's spirits.

"Let us to bed, to bed, while there's still night left for slumber," Surtr says at last. "One can't meet adventure half-asleep."

"Adventure?" asks Magnus.

"Every day, my friend, is the first and last of its kind. This morning, we two were alone—you with none but a horse, me marking time until my wife's return—but tonight, how our lots have changed! Who knows what the morrow will bring? So to bed, to bed, and rest."

Surtr grunts as he heaves himself out of the chair. Ever courteous, Magnus stands along with his host, watching as he replaces the axe and makes his way toward the door.

"You've an air of luck about you," the giant says, pausing at Magnus' side. He is hot and reeks of drink. "Your future will be fire-bright, my friend. A knight in the making! A magistrate! Yes, you have a face people will trust." His voice trails off, muttering *trust, trust, yes, trust,* then booms, "And I trust you abide by the rules of hospitality? Yes? Splendid. Have I your word you will not offend against these laws? There are private rooms in this castle and they are so for good reason. You will not wander where curious feet should not tread?" Surtr gives Magnus' shoulder a sincere, bone-shuddering pat.

"The rules of your house are now my own, my lord." And he says it because he means it and because, no matter what, Magnus holds his honour dear.

"Good! Good." Surtr leans forward unsteadily, nearly knocking Magnus over as he shouts for a servant. "Jónsi! Jónsi, take my guest to his chamber. Good night, my friend—off to bed! A little *treat* awaits you."

Magnus opens his mouth to protest—the giant has been more than generous already—but Surtr cuts him off with a laugh and a wink. "You can thank me in the morning."

---

The room is lit only by a banked fire, but he can see how rich it is, with its canopied bed, thick furs covering the cold stone floors, the furniture highly polished and opulently sculpted. There is a wooden tub in one corner, steam rising from it. A bath! Now here is a treat.

He has stripped and lowered himself into the water before he notices the girl.

She has been waiting in the shadows between the bed and a single arched window. Quiet as a sylph, she moves to the fireplace and lights a taper, which she puts to the two golden candelabra at either end of the mantelpiece. A warm glow melts the darkness, surrounding the figure in a soft ochre nimbus. Her black hair falls to her knees, long as a peliçon. Each strand glistens with its own lustre as if it was spun from crushed stars. The girl turns and Magnus is convinced he will never again know sorrow.

He has had his fair share of pretty maids, *mixed*, full bloods, *skræling*, whoever has been willing—since Magnus, with his long silver hair and brave form, is like nectar to hummingbirds—but this one, this girl, this woman paralyses him. Her eyes, looming above sharp high cheekbones, are blue. The blue of the sky, of the sea, of the deepest midnight and the earliest dawn; they are all shades from azure to ultramarine and they meet his grey ones evenly, perfectly, as if designed for *this* moment, *this* gaze. He'll happily stay right here all night, chest-deep, muscles tense, clasping the tub's rim, if it means his mind will always be this focused, this blessedly clear. There is nothing else but her.

For a moment, strangely, he thinks she might bolt—but the feeling passes when she smiles. She smiles at him and through him and it's as if someone has crumpled his heart up into a ball like parchment and he tries his best to straighten it out, make it the right shape again, but he knows it's no use. He is hers, forever.

The bath is still steaming, a nightingale trilling, serenading the moon, the candles only just beginning to drip wax. Barely any time has passed and yet it feels like hours, days. Magnus is astounded love can happen so fast. He wonders if this is how it was for his mother and the man she refused to name. *Your father is gone*, she'd say whenever he asked. *Best not waste our time calling out to what's lost. Look forward, my son, ever forward.* But Magnus knows that she loved him, that unnamed man, knows not a day passed when she didn't wish him back. Through the wall between their sleeping rooms, he often heard her drenching his memory in tears. Was it like this, Aud's love? He doesn't know how it can feel like lightning, like burning, and he can still be alive.

"Soak much longer, my lord," the girl says with a grin, "and you'll shrivel away completely. And what use will you be to me then?"

As if in a dream, he holds out his dripping hand. She takes it, then hauls him up with uncanny strength, water sloshing everywhere. His fingers tingle when she releases her grip and her smile widens, as if she knows the effect she has. He steps out of the tub, fumbles for a towel. Her touch lingers on his wrist, forearm, bicep; it chases soapy droplets down his smooth chest. Flushing, Magnus' body responds to her explorations. He shakes with need, with desire—but he hesitates, afraid of frightening her, of chasing her away, of waking to discover that none of this is real.

She looks down, but not demurely. Not bashfully. Openly taking in the whole of him, slowly scrutinising every angle, every striation in his form. Head tilted. Moves so close, assessing, Magnus can smell the oil in her hair. A clean musk, like sun-baked leaves and freshly-turned loam. *She is no sylph, but a creature of flesh and bone.*

"Who are you?" he sputters, voice hoarse with want.

She lets the lapis robe slip from her naked shoulders.

Her name, she says, is Blue Dove.

---

For his good company, Surtr offers Magnus the second-best horse in his stables. A sleek Friesian with feathered fetlocks, eight hooves clip-clopping a powerful rhythm as a groom leads him out of his stall. "A noble steed, my lord," Magnus says, eyeing the animal warily. A stallion of this calibre must be ridden bareback. No stirrups, no spurs, only a hackamore so delicate it'd be hard-pressed to rein in a lamb. "I am humbled."

When his guest makes no move to mount up, Surtr realises his gaffe. Magnus' bearing and his personality make him seem even larger than he is—but not large enough for one of Sleipnir's progeny.

"Ámur is one of the most talented palfreys I've reared," the giant confides. "Best suited not for riding, but for herding and retrieving." He slaps the black's rump, sending him galloping across the dell. Soon enough the beast returns, flared nostrils the only sign of exertion, with Ekla following close behind. "Your own mare is much nimbler for hunting—let Ámur here round up the white-tails, let him drive them toward our arrows. Tonight, my friend, we sup on venison."

Magnus has never seen woods as abundant as those surrounding Surtr's castle, and has never before had such success catching game. The giant shows him how to properly set traps; how to make the most of his bait; how to fell two stags with one arrow; how to hone his sword so that it might hew a wild boar as precisely, as efficiently, as Surtr's axe separates bears from their heads. They feast the change of seasons, bidding farewell to the fruits and fish of summer and welcoming autumn with an endless harvest of pheasant, deer, rabbit, and succulent duck. Bushes burgeon with late berries, apples weigh heavily on the trees. Everywhere Magnus looks, there are signs of roundness, plenty, fecundity. Happiness.

Each evening, lying in bed, he rubs rosewater and sweet almond oil into the vivid red scar running between Blue Dove's breasts, and he echoes her sigh, thinking *This, yes, only this.*

Tonight, when her skin is slick with the perfumed liniment, she places her hand over his, presses until he stops. Beneath his fingertips he can feel the furrows of the weal, uneven, defiant and unexplained. So many nights he has thought *She will tell me now*, as he did this service. But she has not. The question sits like a pebble on his tongue, waiting to be spat out.

"Enough," she murmurs, and Magnus blushes to the tips of his ears. "Everything is changing. Soon you will leave me . . . "

There is a note of uncertainty in her voice, a wavering that worries him. He lifts himself up on one elbow, a crease darting up between his fair brows. "No, my heart, never. We will always be together."

Blue Dove winces slightly, but covers it by rolling onto her side and getting Magnus to tickle her back. He cannot see her face, but her bitter tone speaks for itself. "Together? You don't even let me keep the smallest thing here. Not even a comb." She laughs and it is a nasty sound, one he'd not thought to hear from her. It sours into nothingness before she continues. "The castle is so draughty, so vast. All the hallways and staircases that separate my room from this one—the rough stone and creaking timbers, the locks and catwalks and splintered beams—so much space to wander. And I am kept in a cupboard. Safe. *Protected.* Brought out only for your amusement."

Magnus says nothing and so Blue Dove rolls over, takes in his confused expression, and she can't help but smirk. His flush deepens, but she lessens the sting by kissing him gently.

"How do you think I spend my days, little calf? Cloistered in your chamber, while you and Surtr roam the countryside filling saddlebags with fresh meat and your lungs with fresh air? Should I pine by the window, just waiting for your return?"

She laughs again, but it comes out hollow.

In truth, Magnus hasn't given the matter much thought. Whenever he pictures Blue Dove, she looks just as she does now—reclined on the pillows, firelight burnishing her profile, sheets draped over the dip of her waist, the curve of her hip . . .

"You must think me such a fool," he says, throat tight with embarrassment. "I never—"

"Shhhhh," she replies, waving away his apologies. "You can make it up to me by fetching my things. Oh, don't think you're easily forgiven! It will be quite the scavenger hunt—I've been Surtr's guest for many a year, and I'm afraid my belongings are scattered across half the castle by now."

"I'll have you know, I was a treasure-hunter in a past life," Magnus says with a chuckle. Despite what Blue Dove says, he thinks he has indeed been let off lightly. Giddy with relief, he pushes himself to his knees and strikes an intrepid explorer's pose. "Point me in the right direction and the riches are yours."

"Little calf," she says lovingly, "you can't hope to retrieve it all tonight. But perhaps you could get just one thing?"

"Name it."

"It gets so hot with my hair hanging down. I can't bear its clinging—it feels like I'm being throttled. If only I could pin it up with my favourite comb . . . "

"Consider it procured, my lady," Magnus says, sketching an exaggerated bow. As he is dressing, Blue Dove gives him directions to the apartment in which she says she left the bauble. With his shirt half-tucked into his breeches, he hesitates. What if it's one of the places Surtr warned him was prohibited? The moment he asks her, he feels like an idiot. Worse, a coward. But she simply winks.

"I'm sure you'll find this one unlocked, oh daring adventurer. The pure of heart may always pass!" Stifling giggles, they mock the notion together and Magnus feels buoyed as surely as a gull on a thermal.

Servants have kept the way swept clean and well-lit. Fire blooms in scalloped alcoves at regular intervals down the corridors—not torches, Magnus observes, but live flames licking up from jets inset in each recess. As he treads quietly down the stairs, he loosens his collar. The walls exude such heat, he imagines veins of lava worming through the stone. Without incident, Magnus finds the room one floor down, on the other side of the stronghold. The journey took no more than a few minutes and the walk was an easy one. So easy, in fact, that for one uncharitable instant he thinks Blue Dove is lazy.

He shakes his head to rid it of such a thought—and to dislodge the chill that settles on him as he opens the door. It is unlocked, Blue Dove was right, but a creeping, shivering unease hangs like a curtain from its lintel, and as he enters the chamber Magnus shudders. Tiny flickerings graze his skin, as of ghostly wyrms tasting him, smelling him with their forked tongues, judging his worth.

A vanity dresser stands to the left, a rich polished walnut and maple burl creation with an oval mirror that, from this angle, seems to drink in the gloom, reflecting nothing. Decorative cages made of onyx and gold are clustered in the corners, dangling from exposed beams. The scent of moulting feathers is thick in the air but there isn't a peep from within; at this late hour, he reasons, all songbirds are asleep. Magnus determines to come back the next day to feed them, and to take a closer look at the artefacts Blue Dove has collected, to calculate how on earth he will transport them all to his chamber. Leather masks adorn the walls, brass-edged clothes chests skulk in the shadows, sarcophagi of various heights and widths are placed like stacking dolls beside a magnificent cupboard—ebony, perhaps, or burnt mahogany, engraved with stylised hearts. A round scarlet rug covers most of the floor— if he notices the spots where the hue is a deeper russet, then it does not trouble him more than half a second—and at its centre perches the bed. Raised on stilts to shoulder height, it is hard and narrow, clearly designed to accommodate one person alone. Its mattress appears lumpy beneath a starched, ill-fitting white sheet; stiff points drag on the carpet as if it was hastily thrown across the pallet. *No wonder Blue Dove is so fond of sleeping with me*, Magnus thinks, then instantly regrets the thought.

*It is love that draws her to me, not the comfort of my bed.*

Across the room, a pewter glint on a table between the dresser and bed draws his attention. *Oh, the lengths to which women will go for beauty*, he muses, examining the polished implements laid out in neat rows. Enormous tweezers, clippers of all sizes, singed sewing needles, scissors, and tongs—these last, he assumes, must be for curling hair. *Monstrous things*. He's glad Blue Dove seems to have abandoned the practice of torturing her locks into twists. Beside the impressive gleam of these tools, the comb appears dull, unremarkable, and while everything else is tidily in place, this one item has been tossed aside. Discarded. It isn't ivory or jade or tortoiseshell—the finest materials for such things, he recalls Aud telling him—and there is no sheen of nacre, no diamond, no sparkle. The tines are lifeless bone, the bridge a lacklustre slate. At its heart, snaggle-toothed prongs bite at blank spaces, any stones they once clutched torn from their settings.

*This ugly thing is her favourite?*

Blue Dove leaps up when Magnus returns, so delighted to see the comb that she claps like a child. She snatches it from him, then whirls around to see it better by the hearth light. Just as quickly she withers. Shoulders slumped, she wilts onto the bed, entranced by the awful trinket.

"My sapphires," she says, stroking the empty sockets, then clasping the adornment to her scarred chest. "They're gone."

Magnus frowns. "Who would pry a few paltry stones from a lady's hairpiece?"

Blue Dove swallows as though fighting back tears, but when she looks up all traces of misery are hidden. With the backs of her fingers, she pats the dew from her cheeks, then smiles.

"Ignore me, my love. I've grown forgetful. Surtr has the gems—which is not the only thing I've forgotten tonight. You have done me a great favour, little calf, and I have been remiss in not thanking you. Forgive me."

Any questions Magnus has—*what does the giant want with sapphires? when will he give them back?*—fly out of his head as Blue Dove draws him down beside her, and rewards him until he's exhausted.

---

"Are you well, my lord?"

Surtr grimaces and fidgets in his seat. His breakfast—great slabs of honeycomb, round loaves of sourdough, troughs of huckleberries and cherries, marbled pork belly and a full vat of *skyr*—lies untouched on the table before him. He thumps a fist against his sternum and screws his face up as if he's suffering heartburn. After gulping down a firkin of small beer, the giant releases a yeasty burp which does nothing to relieve the rancour in his expression.

"A bad night," he explains. "Truth be told, sleep eluded me for much of it. You'd think I'd have been exhausted, wouldn't you, after the chase that swine gave us yesterday!" For a moment, Surtr's features are less pinched and a glimmer of his jovial self resurfaces. Magnus grins as the big man claps him on the back; it was he who'd finally snared the bristled pig whose delicious meat now graces their plates, after Surtr had given up and gone in search of quail. "But even though my body ached for rest . . . Ah, my friend. Sadly, complaints of the muscle are as naught beside vexations of the mind. My bed was never more comfortable, yet I tossed and turned for hours, caught in the throes of anxiety—the source of which I cannot define. When at last I did manage to doze, demons took hold of my spirit and rode it into the dirt . . . Such nightmares, Magnus, as I haven't suffered since I first took up the axe, many a criminal's lifetime ago. Stupid as they seem in the glare of morning, still I can't dislodge their cold grip from my heart."

He falls silent long enough to extract a letter from his jerkin's breast pocket, and begins to read. Not for the first time, Magnus thinks, judging by the parchment's crinkled state.

"And now this appears," the giant continues. "My wife has been away for too long—and now this." Sparks ignite as Surtr scratches his chin, fingernails striking against his bristles. Absorbed in the missive, he absent-mindedly extinguishes the flames before they catch in the long coils of his hair. Reaching the end, he looks up and blinks as though surprised to find Magnus sitting there. With a self-deprecating snort, the giant regains his composure.

"Unless you are a complete knave, my young friend, when a beautiful woman beckons, you go."

"Of that there is no doubt," Magnus replies, recalling his midnight excursion and knowing he would do it all again if asked. He stabs another chunk of pork onto his dish, flips the knife and uses it to hack a bite-sized piece off. It's halfway to his mouth when Magnus loses his appetite.

"Even so, I will look back on these halcyon days of bachelorhood with great fondness," Surtr says, pushing away from the table, conceding defeat. "We've had quite the time these past few months, haven't we?"

The meat slips from Magnus' blade, lands with a wet smack on his plate. "Are they so soon come to an end, then?"

"I must attend to these matters at our holdings in the south, I'm afraid. My wife is a remarkable woman." Surtr puffs with pride. "She would not request my presence unless it were truly required."

Magnus' throat convulses and his mouth is so dry he can barely speak. What is he to do when his host leaves? There's a buzzing in his ears and he begins to choke. He has no house, no land. Just a one-eared horse, another he can't ride, and a bag of worthless heirlooms he hasn't even clapped eyes on since his arrival. Spots dance in his vision. The knife clatters from his numb fingers. He drops his shaking hands to his lap, conscious of the bulge he's developed at the beltline while keeping the giant's company. He's grown accustomed to the luxury of Surtr's chambers, the bounty in his hall. He had not thought it might end. What can he offer Blue Dove without these trappings, without these majestic ramparts around them? They'd find themselves living in a ditch before the end of the month, and would never find the means to crawl out of it. That's if Blue Dove condescends to go with him . . .

"These weeks have been like a dream," Magnus says miserably. "But I suppose it is time to wake."

"Oh," says Surtr, crestfallen. "I see. I've kept you too long—my wife tells me I have a habit of doing that. And all this time you've been so polite. Not a word to discomfit me. Not a complaint. I do hope you've been happy here."

Magnus assures him he's never been made more welcome, and his tone tells Surtr that all is not lost.

"And she—" The giant gestures in the direction of Magnus' room. "Is she, also—?"

Magnus saves his host the trouble of finishing. "She is radiant."

"Marvellous," Surtr booms, breaking into an enormous smile. Some of the tension he's been carrying in his shoulders eases, and his colour improves. "Then will you not remain as my guest? I'll only be away few days—certainly less than a week. And, true, things will change when my wife returns, but I know you'll adore her. Stay on, my friend. It will do this place good to have such a worthy yeoman here in my absence. And I shall be in your debt."

"Not at all," Magnus replies, feeling jittery and weak as the adrenaline rushes from his body. "I have yet to repay you for saving my life. This is the very least I can do."

---

Pleased as he is to remain, Magnus cannot relax. Palpitations overwhelm him as he watches Surtr feed the fosse-guardians before crossing the drawbridge, and he has to sit with his head between his knees to recover as the giant disappears into the forest. It isn't that he misses his host; he fears the reprieve Surtr has granted will be all too temporary. He feels as if a sword still hangs over his head. What if the man's affection for Magnus cools while he's away? What if his wife takes issue with having not only Blue Dove lodging with them, but now another stray?

Magnus clambers to his feet, thinking he hears a howl from the moat, a weeping, but assures himself it's just the wail of the rime-ridden wind harried by arctic foxes. His imagination is overworked, creating problems he does not actually have, engorging those he does, making them seem worse and worse.

His lover is napping when he enters their chamber. He watches her chest rise and fall, follows the lines of her form stretched on the chaise longue, the dip at the base of her neck, the arc of her belly. *Surtr said, once, that I am a lucky man ... And looking at her I believe him. But luck won't put food on the table—or indeed provide us with a table. And children,* he thinks, *what if there are children?*

"Out with it," Blue Dove says, arm draped over her face. "The whirring of your thoughts is disturbing my slumber. Unburden yourself, little calf, or else let me be."

Magnus intends to tell her about Surtr's departure, nothing more. But one word follows another like misshapen pearls on a string—they rattle out of him, each cruder and more honest than the previous, and the harder he tries to stop the faster they come, dropping from his lips, rolling across the floor to congregate at her fine-boned feet. By the time he's finished, there are no secrets left between them.

Blue Dove sits up, smooths her robe. Picks up Magnus' confessions and mulls them over, one by one. His non-existent status. His non-existent estate. His non-existent income. She stands and pads to the hearth. Lights a taper, much as she did the first night they met, and touches the flame to each wick on the mantle. One by one. Filling the chamber with a calming lambency.

"Surtr's sanctuary," she says, "lies in the furthest corner of the northernmost wing of this fortress. To reach it you must pass through an ancient hall of witchwood and amber. Some say it predates the castle by centuries, which may be true. Others that the first Fae Mymnir planted in this land travelled here, to this vale, and imbued every pillar and ceiling joint in the hall, every pointed window, every knot in the wretched timber with pieces of their souls. All a load of *skitr*, but Surtr believes it implicitly, and revels in walking its hallowed aisle to mark the beginning and end of his day." She rubs the scar on her chest nervously, unconsciously, worrying at the ridges. "Surtr is a creature of many habits, as one becomes when confined for long periods. In the evenings, after his stroll, he likes to tinker with precious stones and jewels, crafting and re-crafting them—including my sapphires."

She turns to Magnus then, but is backlit by the candles, so he can't decipher her expression. Her tone is sweeter, now, than all the kisses she has given him. "Those pretty blue shards will fetch an even prettier price at the Hrafn's court—her anaemic handmaidens will claw each other to shreds to add such colour to their finery. We'll leave as soon as you retrieve them, stopping first at the *fjallkona*'s isle to sell them, and then . . . " The index finger moves faster, harsher, across the cicatrice, her voice trembling with suppressed truths. "Then we will make a home."

Magnus is so happy, he doesn't know whether to laugh or to weep. So relieved, he ignores the sense that she is keeping something from him.

"Can we postpone our leave-taking for a few days," he asks. "Just a few days—no more than a week? It would be the highest insult to flee like a pair of thieves. After all Surtr has done for us . . . "

"Oh yes, my love," Blue Dove replies. "After all he has done, we'll wait and bid him a suitable farewell."

---

The whispers are insidious, pervasive.

*Coward.*
*Pauper.*
*Burden.*
*Leech.*

Little snippets buzz past his ears, butterfly phrases flutter across his mind, word-hornets ambush him as he walks toward Surtr's haven, stinging then withdrawing. They come at him from all directions, and none. He cannot see what spawns them or where they go once the damage is done. They become louder, more insistent and elaborate the further into the grand hallway he goes.

He throws back his shoulders and strides across the polished parquet like a courageous man, a man unafraid of death. *Fortune favours the brave*, he thinks. *The only way is forward.*

"You are weak," says Aud, adder-tongued.

"You are unwanted," says a man's voice, clipping his vowels exactly the way Magnus does. "You ruin everything."

"Father?" he asks, stopping short. The question is plucked like a dead leaf from his lips and hangs in the air, unanswered.

The passageway is dark, and grows ever darker. When he'd first approached, light had flooded from the doorway, as though the space beyond was illuminated by a hundred chandeliers. But as soon as he'd crossed the threshold, this brilliance dimmed. There were no lamps, no candles. Merely pockets of shine that receded with each step forward, smothered through thickening veils of dusk. Now, halfway to the doors looming at the far end of the hall, Magnus fumbles in umber twilight. Amber panels emit a sickly hue, barely enough to render the pillars that seem to keep pace beside him, to separate them from the shadows. His footfalls are muffled—the hard floor doesn't respond to the nervous shuffling and clunking of his heels. And though his breath rasps, though his heart pounds, though he wipes and wipes his hands against his rough homespun breeches, he makes no noise. Every sound is absorbed, except the whispers.

*Braggart.*
*Liar.*

"You are a fooooool," says Blue Dove.

Of all the voices in the growing murk, of all the words echoing from the high ceiling, of all the insults, this last cuts deepest.

Fists, teeth, muscles clench. He will not block his ears, he will not cry out, he will not give them the satisfaction. Onward, onward, one foot after the other, determined as an ox.

"Everything I gave up for you and look what you've become. Pathetic!"

He begins to feel he's walking along a precarious bridge, made of thin, crumbling marble, worn by years and elements. His path is so terribly high, strung over a precipice, stretched with no beginning and no end. An abyss lies beneath him. One wrong step is all it will take.

"You killed me. A murderer from the womb."

One wrong step to find a weakened seam in the stone.

"How can you protect me when you can barely keep your own body and soul together?"

He will trip, he will fall, he will be lost, and Blue Dove will be alone. He will never touch her again, never smell her, never wonder at the mystery of her.

"What can you possibly offer *me*?"

The words come as poisoned darts, paralysing. He can't turn for fear of losing direction in the gloom, can't progress, can't retreat. Teetering on the brink, he closes his eyes.

Exhales.

Focuses on the firmament behind his lids, dotted with blue and white stars. The voices rage, but he latches on to one throbbing light, one firefly of hope in the nothingness. One vibrant jewel, lapis lazuli, feathered with smoke and ice. It centres him, gives him strength.

Everything he has become in these past weeks, everything he might become, is due to her. But it's more than that, Magnus realises, opening his eyes. He is not here out of obligation. Not entirely.

*She needs me.*

It's not simply a matter of Blue Dove trusting him. Relying on him. Knowing he's there to please her. It can't just be a test of love. *She needs me*, he repeats, the thought fragile, wavering. He clings to it tentatively, carefully, trying not to strangle the valour it gives him to continue. The path seems endless, and brief. He's almost convinced himself, *she really needs me*, by the time he reaches the doors.

Golden-green witchwood, they are unvarnished but embellished with *bas-reliefs*, depicting a fable Magnus hasn't heard since he was a boy. A gnarled old tree trunk runs the full height where the doors meet; its abundant foliage fans up to the ceiling, spreads onto the frame, while the wood's deep grain camouflages two handles. Between the branches, a red squirrel pokes his head, ready to carry messages from the eagle sitting aloof high above all the way down to the dragon chewing on roots near the floor. A serpent slithers like a belt around the doors' waist, snapping at its own tail. The movement, Magnus sees, is more than a trick of low light. Leaves are stirred by his exhalations. A ravening wolf drools sap as he paces. Two ravens fly in opposite directions; one disappearing behind the clouds, the other a stark silhouette against a full moon. As Magnus twists the knobs and splits the scene down the middle, he suppresses the fear that one of the beasts might turn and take a piece out of him.

Within, the room is plain, freezing, and so sparsely furnished it feels abandoned. Glass spheres dangle from the rafters, dazzling with harsh flames that emit no warmth. Looking around, Magnus worries he has endured the whispering hall for nothing. *None could find rest here*, he thinks. *I've gone the wrong way*—but he calms himself and looks more carefully. The décor is minimal but telling. There is a gargantuan bed that could belong to no-one but Surtr. Above it hangs a handfasting cloth, its gay colours faded, obscured in places by what appear to be mud stains. Close to Magnus, a tall wardrobe stands ajar; inside he sees a few lovely gowns, simple and elegant, rich yet understated, a faint scent of honeysuckle and peppermint wafting from their fabric. There is a porcelain vase in the sole window's embrasure, and in it a single red tulip. *The wife's touch, no doubt.*

He turns his attention to a long workbench occupying the far wall, covered in a miscellany of lapidary tools: callipers and pliers, files and disc cutters, miniature hammers and mandrels. Small piles of stones, some cut with facets throwing tiny rainbows against the wall, others still crude ore. Magnus thinks it will be easy to find the sapphires, the blue chips his beloved so desires. He tries to remember where each gold wire, each pair of tweezers, each gem is set, so that he can leave everything as he found it after he's finished sifting. Reds and greens slip through his fingers; yellows, oranges and purples in varying intensities cross his palm. Chunks of mica, prisms of milk quartz, flakes of toffee beryl. Some the size and consistency of sand, others large, and cloudy as a storm-tossed sea. But not even the merest hint of cerulean, turquoise, or azure. Not the slightest bruise of blue.

He searches through the wardrobe, pinching the dresses' hems and seams to see if by some miracle the sapphires have been sewn in for safekeeping. He peers under the bed, finds dust. Trembling, he stops short of lifting the pillows, tossing the linens. It is useless. There is nothing for his dove here.

Barely controlling the desire to weep, Magnus turns away. He is not tempted to take any of Surtr's other jewels; he has the remains of Aud's once-marvellous necklace and he will never stoop to theft. Oblivious, now, to the wooden creatures frolicking across the chamber doors, he returns once more to the hall. He does not register the bulbs snuffing out behind him, nor does he hear the latch click shut as he leaves. Once more the light forsakes him and the voices slice, but they seem to have lost their enthusiasm, now simply off-handed, half-hearted.

*You are a disappointment,* they sneer. And Magnus agrees.

---

By the time he reaches his own chamber, Magnus has steadied his nerves enough to confront Blue Dove, an apology poised on his tongue. *We will find them,* he'll promise, and mean it. And she'll forgive him, won't she? She must forgive him. She must. Without a moment's pause, she'll devise a new plan—and he will enact it. All will be well. She'll forgive him and they will be fine. His love is clever; too clever to let this setback deter her. She will tell him what to do.

But as he goes to turn the handle, Magnus pauses, thrown. Surtr's haunted hall is far behind him, yet the murmurings seem to have tracked him back here . . . The relief he feels as he realises these voices are real is immediately replaced by disquiet. He presses his ear to the door. There is a man inside, and it isn't the giant. *This* voice, rustling like dry leaves, is so low he has to stifle his own breathing to hear.

"The boy may be thick as a ship's mast, but he's still my son. I won't have you ruining him."

"And what will you do, with your great arms and legs?" There are razors in Blue Dove's words, but she soon blunts them. "Rest easy, old one. I will watch over him. I will assure his future and make him prosperous. He'll be a man of influence, with a rich estate, weighty responsibilities. Many will come to him for aid—and he will provide it. And when he is settled, I'll bear him children so your line will live on. But I need him to help *me* first."

There is another pause. Finally, leaves grudgingly skitter, "All right. On your word: he will be safe?"

"In my care, no harm can befall him. Now, sleep and do not fear."

Magnus' hand quivers, rattling the catch. He has no choice but to enter; she can't think he's been skulking in the corridor, sneaking like a servant out to steal knowledge. Using more force than is strictly necessary, he throws the door open. It crashes against the chair upon which Blue Dove sits, and she leaps to her feet. Magnus doesn't want to be angry, but he is. She sent him on a fool's errand, had him risk his life—his sanity!—and here she is entertaining some old liar who claims to be his father!

"Do you have them?" She rushes to him, avid and greedy. He looks over her head at the chair she's vacated, then at the one mirroring it. Furs draped over the backs of both. The hideous comb on a low table between them. A book splayed on a cushion, half read. Ekla's saddlebag slumped on the floor where he'd left it. Nothing and no-one out of place.

*Where is he?* Magnus turns back to Blue Dove, who stares up at him feverishly. For the first time, he notices the sheen on her skin is a sweat not of passion, but of illness. Her colour is jaundiced as if she's suffering a swamp-borne disease; her hair hangs lank and dull. She seems to have lessened, to have begun dying, in the small time he has been gone. Worry tempers his ire, but not hers.

"They weren't there," he says, shame and concern pushing half-heard conversations and invisible men from his mind.

Her silence is desperate, disbelieving. "You must be mistaken. They must be there. How can you be so blind? Go back, go back for them."

"Forgive me, my love." He swallows hard to quell the wobble in his refusal. "I will not set foot in that place ever again, not even if my life depended on it."

"Mine does."

In that instant, she appears vulnerable, afraid. Frail and pleading for succour. All she has kept inside, all she has tightly suppressed, is untethered, revealed. And the sight of it undoes him.

"What else can I do?" Magnus makes for the water pitcher. She will not accept the goblet he offers. He takes her by the elbow, tries to steer her toward the bed, but she is anchored to her thoughts, immovable. Utterly helpless, he enfolds her in his arms. Rocks back and forth, a lullaby tempo, and hums a tune that was once Aud's favourite.

"I love you," he says between verses. "I love you."

"You will leave me here," she replies, flat as death.

"Never." He presses her head against his broad chest, holding it close, as if to convince her of his devotion through sheer strength of heartbeat alone. "We'll stay, together, until you are well. When you are, and only then, we'll leave. Together. Surtr will surely let me have my way in this. What is one less guest?"

Blue Dove wriggles free and rounds on him.

"You think he has *given* me to you? This is nothing more than a tease, a torment. Do you think yourself the first distraction Surtr has invited here to entertain me? To keep me from loneliness, he says. More like to keep me from harming the goods. Oh, Magnus. He will lend me out but he will never let me go!" She begins to pace the room, a caged creature thumping at her chest with one fist, muttering, *He has taken it, where has he taken it?*

She freezes as understanding dawns. Magnus, his jealousy and uncertainty forgotten, kneels before her. He is as sincere as he has ever been when he says, "My beloved, my heart. Whatever you want, I'll do. When the giant returns, I'll ask him to grant me a boon. Such a small gift, a few shards of stone; he will be my friend in this as in all things. Or, what? Tell me. There are many rooms in this castle—barred or open, I'll find a way in and scour every last one. Or I'll return to the hall and raze his sanctum. Anything. Anything. I cannot bear your suffering."

Blue Dove extends her free hand, inch by inch, as though Magnus is a wolf keen to bite. Instead, he kisses her palm. The gesture seems to open a valve inside her, releasing all the fight. She sinks to the floor and unleashes a flurry of words.

"Surtr—*this* Surtr—was born of embers. When the Hrafn came to this land, she had four guardians. Each of them smuggled a piece of their world, salvaged from destruction. Eiðr carried lore which he passed to his children, Valdyr a shaft of dreaded mistletoe, and Per bore a *hrímþursr*'s frozen skull. It was Harkon who brought cinders and coal from Múspellheimr, home of the fire giants. Some say they were chipped from the first Surtr's corpse, then stoked here to revive his spirit. Others believe Mymnir had Harkon infuse a golem with the Fire Lord's ashes, making a new one from the old to serve as her executioner. Either way, he took to his work with such fervour, she rewarded him with stewardship of the southlands. Recently, however, he's fallen into disfavour—this place is no prize, but an exile."

When Blue Dove speaks of Surtr, Magnus notices, her face darkens—indeed blood suffuses the skin in an all-consuming rage. Her voice lowers until it's barely more than a hiss.

"Surtr is but a spark struck from a greater creature—and like all copies he is *lesser*, somehow, than the original. Neither as strong nor as long-lived as his forebear, and all too aware of his mortality. But if he . . . if he takes part of another magic creature into himself, he can extend his life." Hot tears roll down her cheeks, splash cool on his skin.

For the first time, Magnus feels sure of Blue Dove's honesty. "These are not mere sapphires," he says.

She shakes her head, pulls back to draw the front of her robe wide. The scar between her breasts seems to throb with its own life. She scratches at it, agitated, checking for ruptures, as if it might open again independently, without the encouragement of Surtr's saws and hooks and pliers.

"I think he hopes it will regenerate," she says, "if he doesn't filch it all at once. So he rations himself, letting me survive another month, another year. Chipping off new pieces only when he burns through the previous ones."

"Burns?"

"In the furnace of his core. He swallows them, Magnus; he consumes them. My slow-melting years are fuel in his belly. And whatever fragments don't go down his gullet wind up on ornaments and blood-jewellery. Belt buckles. Armlets. Bronze collars. Combs. One shard after another, they shield and invigorate him, whether inside his body or adorning it. His time in this realm is prolonged, even as mine is abbreviated. Whole, I might be immortal. But like this . . . "

Any affection Magnus bore the giant dissolves, the memory of his company smothered in bitter soot. As passionate in hate as he is steadfast in love, Magnus hardens his resolve, reassured by the approval he sees in Blue Dove's eyes when he says, "Kill him."

"I would, my love," she says. "I've tried—but I am diminished. As long as Surtr lives, I am trapped. Wards bind me to this room, and to that other . . . " She stutters as small convulsions wrack her body. "I've fled, repeatedly, and each attempt is a greater failure than the last. By the time I reach the stairs my legs can barely support me; headaches overwhelm if I manage to make the first floor; and beyond the portcullis I suffer such vertigo it's near impossible to stand. Once, just once, I crawled to the forest before blacking out. And when I woke, I was back here, clean and in bed. My nose didn't stop bleeding for a week."

"Let me be your limbs, your sight, your sword. Wield me. Show me where to aim."

"Like any earthly being, Surtr can be injured by steel and arrow—but only injured. Only one enemy can destroy such a creature."

Magnus waits for her to go on.

"Just as Surtr began as embers," she says eventually, "so the thing in the moat was spawned from shavings of Argjöll's frozen skull. It was born of ice, and of ice it remains."

"Which makes it a frost giant?"

She shakes her head. "Partially—by now, what's left is mostly mind and soul, and even those are disarticulated, tormented. It's been confined for so long, hemmed in the ditch by those cursed foxes, it's been driven mad. And yet I suspect, even after all these years, the creature remembers freedom—and knows precisely who keeps it captive. Given half a chance it will tear Surtr limb from limb."

"And if he has your sapphires inside him . . . "

Blue Dove nods. "Exactly."

---

After some considerable searching, Magnus finds armour that fits him without too much adjustment. The servants, sensing something afoot, have shown no loyalty to their lord and have either run off to secret glens or disappeared in the kitchens and storerooms, waiting for the outcome to be known. Eyes survey the young master from some of the fortress's slit windows, their bearers recalling that kindness and politeness have never been beneath his dignity. They watch as he stands on the castle side of the drawbridge, agleam with polished mail, a two-handed sword ready in his grasp. He has eschewed a helm—which some think foolish, given Surtr's expertise as a headsman—and his hair catches the sunlight. He looks blessed.

Blue Dove stands tall by his side, nostrils flared, the muscles in her jaw working furiously. Lips the same shade as her name, curved in a rictus grin. Her battle is fought silently, internally, but she is determined. She *will* see the giant dead and no amount of pain will keep her away.

Magnus curses the moisture that slicks his palms. He is unaware of the servants' murmuring, can only hear the offended yipping of the restrained fosse-guardians. Trapped using the techniques Magnus learned at his host's knee, strung up by Blue Dove with the tiny spark of magic left to her, the arctic foxes are incensed, frothing at the indignity of capture. On the forest side of the moat, a sturdy makeshift ramp is angled into the trench. Magnus doubted the wisdom of lowering it already, but Blue Dove assured him. *The creature will not know itself until it senses the author of its agony.* He wipes his hands on his burnished cuisses, streaking sweat down his thighs. They'd received word this morning that Surtr would return within a matter of hours. So soon.

In the depths of the pit, the sleeping monstrosity stirs, but remains amorphous; a vacillating fog of hoarfrost and fumes. Its edges are diffuse and shambolic, almost lost entirely without the foxes to chase them to and fro. A few times it has nearly taken on the shape of a man, but at the last moment the form fails, fragmenting as if the effort of remembering is too much. Magnus feels sorry for the creature. It does not change his plans.

There is movement between the trees on the other side of the glade, and Surtr and the single squire he rode out with come into view. The giant spots Magnus and raises his hand in greeting, until he realises that his guest, his *protégé*, is not here to welcome him home. Even from this distance, Magnus can see the giant's scowl as he spurs his mount forward. The thunder of eight hoofs, all shod with Fae-forged ebony, resounds off the surrounding trees and the castle's curtain walls, and Magnus can feel the earth shuddering beneath his feet. His heart quakes, but he lifts his chin defiantly, tightening his grip on the sword.

Surtr is almost at the drawbridge when another beast streaks past him, sending the war-horse into a slide, then a rearing. Ekla, sleek and muscular after the weeks of good food and rest, canters down the ramp into the fosse.

"No, Ekla! No!" Magnus discovers his is not the only shout; Surtr has become equally fond of the stupid, stupid horse. Both men brace themselves for the mare's shrieks, her final frantic whinnies as the moat flenses her hide—

And the ice stops swirling.

Intrigued by the proximity of this curious animal and drawn by the pull of Surtr's presence, the maelstrom coalesces into a man three times the size of the fire giant. Solidly naked and transparent from crown to heel, Argjöll's joints grind together like fast-moving glaciers as he bends to pick up the horse. He cuddles Ekla like a kitten, chiselled chin dropped to his chest as he purrs and coos and pets her. Oddly subdued, the palfrey nestles into the crook of the giant's arm as he straightens and begins to scale the ramp. Magnus listens to the protesting wood and offers up prayers to any gods who will listen. *Please let this work.*

Surtr watches his phenomenal twin with horror. In this new world, this frangible place, he has had so little to fear, so little presents a threat to the likes of him. Now something elder strange is walking free and the foundations of his comfortable life are being compromised. But Surtr has not maintained his rule through cowardice. He kicks his mount's ribs and urges him forward.

The fire giant raises his burning battle-axe and swipes at the irresistible bull of his cold cousin. Diamond chips fly, shorn from his bicep, and Argjöll lets out a roar, more outrage than hurt. Turning away from his foe, he carefully puts Ekla down, ensuring her safety, while Surtr brings his steed around in a tight turn that strains the animal's forelegs. Blood-frenzied, the Lord of Fire cares nothing for the horse's distress, only that it continues to fight. Hooves pounding, he tilts again at the man-shaped mountain of rime, but misses. Wheels quickly back, reins and spurs biting deep, and comes at Argjöll side-on. Surtr lifts his weapon once more, deadly blades whistling as he bears down, but the blow does not connect.

The frost giant backhands Surtr, swatting him lazily, as one would a fly.

Magnus hears a most terrible cracking as the fire giant collides first with the mammoth knuckles, then with the ground. There is a scream from Surtr's horse as momentum snaps its front legs and it ploughs into the dirt, skidding to the moat and tipping over into the pit below. Wild at the sight of this tantalising feast, the ensnared foxes continue to caterwaul long after the stallion's cries have ceased.

Lying on the ridge, Surtr's moans are more awful still. He huffs like a bear clamped in the jaws of a trap, sad eyes turned skywards as he slowly bleeds out. Steam rises from his broken neck and magma oozes from his wounds, immediately calcifying into misshapen, charred growths as hot lava meets cool air. Magnus is transfixed as his friend writhes, wrecked, at the foot of his castle. As if wading through a thigh-high snowbank, Magnus trudges forward, his boots heavy and finding little purchase. Before he can reach Surtr, a lithe shape outstrips him and almost dances to the felled lord. Blue Dove, growing ever healthier and stronger as he weakens, kneels on the groaning giant's chest. Heedless of scalding, she digs into the ravaged flesh of his belly and tears it easily as parchment. Surtr shrieks and bawls as she plunges her reddened arm into the cavity, rummaging around inside him as if he is nothing more than a saddlebag that has swallowed her possessions. He thrashes beneath her, but she clamps her knees tight against his ribs and holds on. Pink spume bubbles from his lips and molten tears singe ruts into his temples. Overhead, the castle's glorious fire banners flap violently though the afternoon air is tranquil. The ramparts smoulder, billowing smoke as the flames die.

Blue Dove grunts with pain and withdraws her scorched hand from Surtr's carcass. Between her blistered fingers, rays of light so intense Magnus can see every vein illuminated from within, every graceful bone. He flinches from the glare.

Earthbound thunder peals as Argjöll finally turns his attention to them. The thing barrels in their direction, chasing a spooked

Ekla, or maybe coming to stomp Surtr's corpse to a pulp—Magnus isn't sure which. Hefting his sword and shield, he thinks, *Now* and tenses to run at the lumbering tower of man-ice.

A ball of white-heat whizzes past Magnus' ear. The sapphire, blazing from the forge of the Fire Lord's belly, strikes the frost giant square in the forehead. Argjöll stops dead, a look of utter surprise on his adamantine face as the gem burrows through his brainpan. Features are obliterated as his head caves in, the stone burning a channel down his neck, torso, pelvis, cleaving him in two. Both halves of his body collapse, shattering into a rapidly melting heap.

Lowering his arm, dropping his impotent weapon, Magnus can do nothing but gape.

Blue Dove briefly hugs him as she skips past. "I've had more than enough of giants for one lifetime," she says. Magnus watches as she points her toes and steps daintily into the rubble that once was Argjöll. Ribbons of skin dangling from her hands, she picks things up—knuckles, earlobes, teeth, testes—examining each chunk of ice then discarding it, until she gives a cry of triumph. She runs back to Magnus, cradling her treasure, and invites him to admire it, proud as a parent. The sapphire is much bigger than he'd expected. Not a thin shard at all, but a nugget the size of a pigeon's egg, its facets all jagged and sprouting rough edges. An aggregation of all the splinters shorn from Blue Dove's heart, now fused together. He catches a glimpse of blue, luminous as his lover's irises, before her fist closes over the gem.

Unabashed, she bares her chest and presses her hand against the livid scar. This time her hand passes through flesh, through bone; with a slurp, she is buried up to the wrist. Blue Dove exhales, a languid release of tension and hurt, and when she pulls free the palm is empty. She respires easily now, exuding serenity. As Magnus watches, the welt bleaches to white, a faint outline that echoes the curve of her cleavage. Burns and blisters fade from her arms. Her skin knits itself whole, perfect.

"Is that it?" he asks dully. "You're immortal again?"

Through her own exultation she hears his despair. Realises he thinks she will leave him, now that she is healed and free. She giggles, smooths the furrows from his forehead with an unblemished touch and says, "No."

He brushes her aside, not understanding.

"Surtr leached too much—the jewel's pulse is erratic, the damage irreparable. Oh, it yet courses with magic, but I won't live forever. Even so," she says, "I *will* live. And I owe it all to you, Magnus. My love, my *heart*. My life is yours: I will protect you, as you have me."

She touches him all over, just as when first she came to his bath. Goosebumps tingle from his scalp to his toes as his armour transforms, gleaming gold and indigo. Standing before her, Magnus feels hardier and healthier than he ever has before. She smiles, and he sees the future.

"I will make you great," she says.

And he believes her.

# The Third Who Went With Us

*They say Ymir was born of venom. Poisonous slag dripped from Élivágar rivers, shaping the first jötunn's colossal limbs, gouging canyons for his veins, filling these chasms with blood of gold and iron and silver ore. His bones were shafts of magnetite, black and sturdy and hale. From blood and bone Ymir's children sprang, the dvergar, stout and stony as the earth. Immediately these dwarves began to dig, deep, deep underground. Minerals and gems drew them down, blood calling to blood, bone calling to bone, an irresistible song. In caverns and mines, the dvergar lived in great packs; overwhelmed, physically, by a pull to return should they ever stray too far from their kin. Their metalwork was unparalleled—as were their tempers. Ymir's children inherited his poison along with his charm. Ever drawn together, ever repelled, the dwarves fought incessantly, even though such strife broke their hearts . . .*

Helga Ögmundardóttir, Fragment from *A Compendium of Dwarven Lore*

Birds dream, not of flight, but of endless oceans and silent caverns in the earth.

They are pragmatic creatures, sensible and shrewd. Knowledge is not a matter of space or size, but of depth: though tiny, these hollow-boned vessels carry infinite wisdom. Despite their reputations, winged ones are not simpletons. They know the most valuable treasures are buried, not left in plain sight. And so they long to plunge their rostra into the soil, to bathe in rich loam, to dig up what time has lost. Short beaks foil their plans, more often than not, but in their hearts most birds are archaeologists.

Later, when feasting on minnows or herring, they remember an age when their bodies were sinuous, flexible, covered by shell and scale. When they hunted in packs, clicking signals to each other across primeval forests. These memories make the birds ravenous; they pierce fish flesh, tear it to shreds, as though it were juicy red meat. Now most good things come from the sea, clever birds agree, swallowing, cooling their blood. And to its cold embrace all things will one day return. They feel this truth as a tugging in their feathered breasts. As an inexplicable desire to reach the liquid horizon. A yearning to dive into it, to swim, to sail.

While dreaming, their heads tilt, twitch, jerk. Their eyes are always open, rarely still. Some believe this means their attention is scattered. As though, following their dark irises, their thoughts are forever wandering, merely alighting on this or this or this or that. They seem mindless, ever hungry, ever cautious. But *seeming* is not being.

Flitting is not proof of confusion; it is a reflection of avian thoroughness. Birds will examine problems from all angles, quickly and with great imagination. Separated from their flocks, they will cock their heads, search the skies, investigate the treetops for evidence of their friends' passing. Loneliness makes those in exile jumpier than those who've remained with the clan; their stares grow sharper, their actions by turns aggressive and apathetic. Burdened with the weight of recollection, centuries of accumulated hopes and disappointments, certain ravens, for instance, will caw incessantly for their missing brethren. They will scour fields, woods, shorelines. Wings and mouths stretched wide, their calls stark black feathers against empty stretches of white sand. Crying out to the void. Listening for a reply that doesn't come. Waiting for someone to guide them home.

---

Ocean salt encrusts the white raven's nares, suffocating. She flies low, dips her beak into the water to clean it. Her wingtips skim the surface with each powerful stroke and the ruff of her breast clumps with sea spray, but she's reluctant to take to the heights. She hears the bones calling, calling her down. Their song resonates in her ribcage, the vibrations strongest when she's nearly submerged.

Behind her, the coastline recedes. Soon her palace—her bright refuge, the bower she made—is just a dark point on the horizon. For months she has ached to embark on this journey, ached down to the pit of her soul. But now she speeds over gentle waves, until around her is nothing but grey chopped with blue. Over land, she can travel hundreds of rastir in a day, yet here . . . Her muscles spasm, burning with exhaustion and a once-forgotten fear. This great *brine* is so deep, so wide. It sighs as she passes—it slurps. She imagines its wet tongues wrapped around her, swallowing her whole. Schools of fish wink in and out of the shadows below; one bold swimmer nips at her feet, mistaking her pale toes for worms. Wildly she spins, splashes, flaps heedlessly, aims for the clouds.

*My poor Huginn*, she thinks, in spite of all that passed between them, the rage and betrayal, the terrible, terrible loss. Her silver eyes gleam, perhaps with tears, as she propels herself away from danger. *What kind of grave is this for one such as thee?*

The higher she goes, the calmer she becomes. Cool breezes smooth her plumage and her nerves. Inhaling deeply, she smells the first hints of snow and smiles inwardly. Winter always reminds her of Gunnlöð, of how the frost giantess would tease her lover Óðinn by stealing his ravens right out from under his nose. How she'd feast the birds' health all season in Niflheimr, laughing as Óðinn fumbled to regain his winged children, his memories, the lost trace of his thoughts. How the grand woman would say Mymnir was her favourite, even with Huginn in earshot. The white raven's translucent feathers and gelid caw were perfect complements for Gunnlöð's arctic home, she'd said. And wouldn't it be best if they stayed together always? For a while, Mymnir and Gunnlöð hid from Óðinn in the giant's frozen halls, but in the end the raven always went back to the All-Father. From his mind she and her brother had sprung; to it they would ever return. Always, they could find him. Always, they'd be by his side.

Until . . .

*How simple it would be to forget*, she muses, feeling the lie like a hot poker in the belly. It was her burden, her lifeblood, to remember. She recalled every place her lord had been—in the old world. There, she could easily describe every one of Óðinn's favoured retreats, every crag of his weathered face. At times she would flee, teasing him as Gunnlöð did, but she would find him again whenever the mood struck. But here . . . Now . . .

She'd flown so far this time, so very, very far. She couldn't work out how to get back. Not on her own.

If only she'd bid him farewell before leaving. If only he knew it was his fault she'd gone.

She wings furiously on until her mountainous isle is once more within sight. *A silly plan*, she chides, shaking her head, leaving the ocean behind. *Surely Huginn is no longer the thinker he once was.* Surely all she feels are ghosts. Onward she travels, until sand turns to scrub, dune grasses stretch up into trees. Her heart clenches as gulls' shrieks fade away, pine-scented breezes replacing seaweed and salt. She drifts on currents of air, listless and weary for sorrow. The cry of her brother's bones grows shrill—then dwindles to a distant echo.

She knows what she must do and where she must go, for she has read the manuscripts often enough. Pored over them too many times, great vellum folios bound in calfskin, telling herself she is researching, embedding the knowledge, but deep down she knows it for procrastination.

Lóki's books.

Such a surprise to find, once her city sprang forth, that there was a library, fully stocked with the strangest volumes. She had not foreseen such treasures, although perhaps she should have— the trickster had always loved to hoard secrets, and the kingdom box she'd stolen had been his. And she, who had disdained Lóki's decrepit tomes for so long in the old world, she'd discovered that *here* they answered her need. In her mind, the call of the bones comes once again, a demand and a plea.

*I hear you, my dear.* Retracing her path, she flies until she can feel the beating, intense and loud once again. *I'm coming.*

---

The white raven is no water fowl.

Unlike her flat-billed cousins, she cannot bob on the ocean like a feathered boat. Hers is a realm of hunters, of brambles and berries and black tree trunks. She is a flash of light in dark woods, a phantom haunting wary travellers on the path, a soul-stealing vision tap-tapping at crofters' windows. In another guise, she is radiant, revered. Halls of live stone appear at her command, sumptuous chambers that rival any of Gunnlöð's. Courtiers erect ice palaces in her honour, shower her with jewels and fine scents, come as willing supplicants to her bed. Valets bring her baked salmon on silver platters, garnished with clustered pearls. A queen such as she does not fish for her own dinner.

Now, hovering over the spot where the pull of the bones is most fierce, where it reverberates with such force that her skull rattles and her ribs threaten to snap, she steels her nerves and points her sharp beak downward. The water is deep, so deep.

For what seems like the thousandth time, she attempts to reclaim her third form: in which she can be elusive at will, thin as smoke, a veil of memory clinging to her master's unruly black curls. In this shape she could simply seep through the waves, slipping gracefully around gaping jaws and spiked fins, sinking to the bottom without fear, without air. Closing her eyes, she concentrates. She imagines how things were before, when she was one third of a trio. A vital third, she reminds herself. A crucial third. When she sat on her lord's shoulder, looked into his good eye and, in her wisdom, advised him. And she *had* been wise, no matter what Huginn said, sitting smug and bloated with high thoughts on their master's right. The side of good, her brother had said, while she was relegated to the sinister. Shadows flicker across her mind, stinging, churning old hurts . . .

*No*, she thinks. *Focus.*

She waits for the frisson of transformation, to feel herself reduced, reshaped, turned to particles of spirit and water and air. A shudder rips through her body—but it's not right, not a sign of the metamorphosis she seeks. She is too heavy, too *full*.

It is so hard while they are apart.

Her wings stretch into arms as she sputters once more to the surface.

Feathers give way to skin; muscles elongate then seize with cold. Fingers, toes, nose replace claws and beak; the down on her body retreats to crooks and crevices. Splashing in circles, coughing up seawater, she tries to get her bearings while long strands of silver hair whip across her eyes. Sky: above. Ocean: below. All around, the lure of Huginn's song. She gasps in great lungfuls and struggles to slow the racing of her heart. *It is so dark down there...*

A spell chatters through her teeth, secret words shaped on lips limned blue. She falters, again and again, and wishes the cursed water didn't sap her energy so. With *terra firma* beneath her feet, she can raze forests with a glance, create mountains from pebbled beaches, or sculpt beautiful rambling cities from glaciers and lava—as she did, long ago, with the help of jötunn and dragons. Back then, by Óðinn's side, she'd play tricks on sailors—confuse them, bewilder them, make them believe they'd never before plotted a journey or mapped the stars. In fits of whimsy, she would help Njorðr and Atla stir up *bylgjur* to cleanse blood and gore from battle-wrecked shores. How she'd loved the refreshing crash of waves then; how it empowered her, made her roar.

The sundering, with its deluges, its storms, its interminable boat journeys, changed everything.

If she'd known, if only she'd known, perhaps she might not have started it.

*Steady*, she thinks, warmth flooding her limbs as weak Fae magic, the most she can muster out here, takes hold. Treading water, she gathers her power, concentrates it in her core. Her pulse regulates and she's immersed in calm. Lifting her arms up, tilting her face to the sun, she shakes away excess moisture, and dreams of flying. She is half transformed: her hair now a mantle of white feathers, her fingers and elbows barbed into plumes. But before she can beat a path into the sky, a clammy hand grabs her ankle, and *pulls*.

Bubbles swirl around her head, fluid pushes into her mouth and nose. Her screams are stifled in the black; her muffled shouts are taken up, mimicked, sent back by shrill marine voices. Their high-pitched laughter is deafening, vicious. No matter how hard she struggles, the chill grip on her leg can't be broken. Other hands join it. Sharp-taloned and brutish, they poke and pull and pinch all over. She wriggles and flails, but the instant she breaks free, tentacles slither around her waist and draw her back down. At last, suffocating, she relents.

*My dear Huginn*, she thinks, relaxing her wings and legs. *Will you catch me?*

But the *marbendlar* are not interested in drowning ravens, least of all one as valuable as she. They drag her to the surface, screeching, whispering.

"What will she give us?"

"Will she sate our hunger?"

"Can she?"

"A life saved is a debt owed."

"Indeed, indeed, indeed—"

"Indeed *not*," she says, imperious though bedraggled. "Unhand me."

Sliding free of several bothria, she extends her sodden wings and flaps, chanting silently until her human legs contract, shrivel, shrink into her abdomen. Yet she is weak, and the *marbendill* who first hooked her keeps firm his grip. Her scratching claws don't bother him in the least.

"Thrice, now, you've invaded our fields," he says, squeezing her tarsus relentlessly. His forearms are corded with muscle, his torso broad and bristling with coral. Slick with water, his navy skin shines in the sun, dappled with iridescent grey scales. A mane of anemones spills over his shoulders, thick and twisted dreadlocks. He continues quietly, his mouth hidden behind a tangle of foam. "Thrice you've disturbed our harvest and upset our cattle."

She studies the merman's companions. There *is* something bovine about a few of their long snouts . . .

"Do we plunder your clouds? Do we pillage your nests?" He shakes his head. "*Neh.* Generations have passed since our last trespass—and even then we had good reason. So what might yours be?"

The creature gives her no chance to respond. Leaning forward, he pulls her close and whispers, "I know you, little deserter. You may think me a poor farmer, stupidly tending deep-sea crops—but

I am older than the oceans you left behind. I witnessed the currents you made there, the rupture, the ruin. Countless ships would have wrecked on these shores, had I not guided them to safety—"

"Have you seen him?" She hates the traitorous hope in her voice, hates that her first thoughts, still, are of *him*.

"Ah," says the *marbendill*. "But of whom do you speak? The one whose corpse has rotted a great hole in my minnow garden? Or the third who once went everywhere with you?"

"Both," she replies, too quickly.

A juddering begins, fathoms within the man's chest. His face splits into a smile and a rank laugh issues from his maw. "Even yet you are selfish, little traitor." For a time, the *marbendill*'s mirth overwhelms him; he chuckles until his men's grumblings bring him back to himself.

"My bondsmen are hungry," he says, suddenly serious.

"I shan't make them much of a meal," she replies.

"*Neh*, stupid bird. Meat we have in plenty." The *marbendill* taps a pincer between her eyes. "It is for want of what's up here that my men are withering. As you are, I suppose, in your own way."

She digs her claws into his hand, cocks a beady eye at him, ruffles her feathers.

Again, the ancient creature laughs.

"Memories of the old world," he says. "You've stolen them in abundance, *neh*? How heavily they must weigh upon you . . . How *filling* they must be. Think how much quicker you might flee without the burden of all that knowledge."

The white raven freezes, but the merman carries on. "A trade then. Close your beak, *hrafn*, you're in no position to barter. The terms are mine alone to set."

She nods. And when he tells her how many years of her memory they want in exchange for her brother, which passages of her life she must relinquish, she agrees.

Most children are blessedly ignorant of how they came to be. Their first years of life are not something they know personally, but only experience second-hand, through the tales of others. She will not miss the image of her bloodless birth, the sight of Óðinn's head splitting in twain. Why should she? The *marbendlar* could sup until her skull was empty, and still she would know him as her lord. She will not miss the golden glow of the god's satisfaction as he looked down on the first of his offspring, imbued with his immortal memories, a child in nothing but age. She will not miss the gentle cast of his single eye, a bright fatherly eye, all those years before it hardened upon seeing her. No, she will miss none of it. Perhaps with fewer recollections, the guilt will not be so pressing.

Thoughtful Huginn will help to remind her, if she so desires.

Nothing is lost forever.

---

Now she flies with Huginn's bones strapped to her back, tied on with a seaweed rope, his wings a frail echo of her own. Each joint and empty shaft whistles in the wind; urgent speed underscored by her twin's haunting, ethereal music.

*Wake up, my dear,* she thinks, intently scanning the horizon. *You've slept long enough.*

Huginn's uncinated ribs flute a few low notes. She interprets this as a sign of her brother's rousing, and sings her approval.

South they travel, and still further south. One week passes, then two, the days growing ever hotter, the sea ever more vibrant until it shines a transparent, tropical blue. The raven stops only to rest on what spits of land interrupt her path, and to take fresh water where she can find it. Otherwise she presses on, eyes seeking a point beyond reckoning. She thanks the gods that Huginn is yet a skeleton. Beneath this sun he'd likely roast to death in his purple-black raiment—and strong though she is, even she couldn't carry his fully-fleshed weight in this heat.

*Fata morgana* shimmer in the distance, false archipelagos promising rest where there is none. But the raven is canny; she is not lured off course. The island she seeks will not waver or flicker with pathetic flashes of light. Her destination draws its power from the very bowels of the earth—it will make its presence known with a voice of flame and ash.

A blow takes her by surprise. She falters mid-flight, nosedives, her cargo fiercely rattling. It has been centuries since she last tumbled so awkwardly, a fledgling from Óðinn's shoulder. Now she harnesses the zephyrs buffeting her, pinpoints the horizon, and recovers. Regaining altitude, she casts about the clear sky for her attacker.

"Ah, a challenger!" There is a low snicker, and the raven is pressed back by a strong hot breeze. She hovers, blinking, and her eyes adjust as the air condenses above her. Droplets of golden liquid appear out of nowhere; collecting like dew, they begin to describe once-invisible limbs. Sunlight gathers and swells into knotted sinew, an enormous torso, thighs hefty as two ogres. A full mane of white-hot confetti spills over the gigantic man's shoulders and sparks from his face into a long beard. His eyes are wide-set, the irises luminous ochre, pupils tiny and perfectly black. Warmth radiates from his ever-changing skin, which flares and snuffs with its own auroras. He lazes on a cloud as if on a divan and wears wisps of it as a robe. Dwarfed by this entity, so like a fire giant but with none of its obvious weight, with no beholding to the pull of the earth, the raven widens the distance between them.

Beyond the creature, however, the island beckons.

"Fly away, little birdie with your little brain," he chortles.

She shakes her head. "I have come too far."

"And I say you must turn away," he insists, exhaling a sirocco. Behind him a glittering curtain of heat falls from an immeasurable height. The barrier stretches from left to right as far as the raven can see. "Posing riddles to your kind is simply not worth the effort. You shall not pass without answering correctly—*ergo*, you shall not pass."

"And I beg you to ask," she changes tack, and pleads. She recognises him for what he is: a bully with few opportunities to exercise his power. And she's noticed a rift in the wall he's so hastily constructed, a whirling blue aperture so small he hasn't detected it . . .

Her humiliation only makes him laugh harder.

"As you wish," he says, wiping tears from his cheeks. "Ignorance can be so very entertaining . . . All right. I'll go slowly, then, shall I? Pay attention."

She hangs her head, wings drooping. Dropping lower, she slowly glides closer. It takes all her self-control not to peck out his eyes.

"*Who are the two that run on ten feet? I'll give you a clue: they have three eyes, but only one tail . . .*"

Furious, her head whips up. *You think to stump* me *with* this? She sputters with anger—and the giant snorts, nestling further into his bed, so secure in his own authority, so unchallenged, he has already lost interest.

With a flick of her powerful wings, the bird feints, changes direction, comes up from beneath him and is behind him in a trice.

"Óðinn riding Sleipnir," she whispers, gouging her beak into his ear as she whistles past. Speeding towards the gateway, she hurtles through the gap before he realises where she's headed. Now it is her turn to laugh as the custodian roars in pain, in defeat.

"Pay attention," she says, cackling as she catches a final glimpse of the giant trying to squeeze his bulk through a too-small hole. "Or did you need me to go more slowly?"

---

Pristine beaches skirt the island, which is sharp at one end and broad at the other, curved like a mead horn. Three wing-beats see the raven across the sand, while the fourth plunges her into the shade of coconut and date palms. The incline from shore to centre is far from gentle; there is no room for meandering foothills on this small isle. The volcano's cone juts sheer and steep overhead, its slopes garbed in fronds of lush green. Its crown is charred, rocky lips smoking. And out of its mouth, spewing scarlet ire, phoenixes rise—orange, red, and gold—on coruscations of lava.

Soot coats the white raven until she is nearly as black as her brother once was, then sulphurous gusts wring her clean. In an instant she is parched: her Northern skin seems to shrivel, her wintry eyes dry into pebbles, all vital juices evaporate from her veins. Wheezing, she plummets to the charcoal-covered ground, not knowing or caring if Huginn's bones have survived the fall. Lying there, she can barely muster the energy to blink. She is too tired to do anything but watch the firebirds dance.

They dip into the magma, pull it up like taffy, shape it into whimsical structures of molten lace. Embers shower from their wingtips as they rise above the volcano's ridge to assess their work, all while sketching dainty loops through the sky. They soar, explode in puffs of ash, descending only to rise again. The raven tries to caw her appreciation, but her voice rasps into a cough. Frustrated, she attempts it again. Phoenixes are vain creatures—if she cannot pander to their egos, they will never help her.

The firebirds spot her almost immediately. She is so much fairer than they, so much prettier—and without the slightest lick of a flame! The largest one swoops; a Queen like the raven herself. Four nimble attendants follow soon after, flitting and fretting to arrange their mistress's train. Once primped, the grand phoenix shoos them away.

"No riddles," says the white Queen to the golden. She knows well that firebirds are cousin to dragons: befuddling strangers with puzzles and enigmas is a family trait. "I seek a boon and my need is dire. Please grant me a conversation spoken plainly."

"That's all?" The phoenix winks at her companions, then turns back to her visitor. "Your country must be verbose indeed, that you must travel such lengths for plain speech. But it is your boon, after all, and my pleasure to fulfil it. Perhaps this will do: "A thief shall stalk in the dark." You'll find none plainer!"

The glowing flock takes to the air, hysterics spouting from myriad beaks, and prepares its return to the volcano. The Queen bids the raven the traditional farewell of birds with a regal tilt of her head. "Fair winds, traveller."

Bones clatter as Mymnir sloughs her brother's frame and adopts a beggar's posture. Ignoring the phoenix's jest, she appeals to the creature's conceit. "My Lady," she begins, the honorific sticking in her dry throat. "I daren't engage in a battle of wills with one so clever as thee."

Preening, the firebird alights once more.

"Already you outshine me," the raven continues. "There's no need to make a spectacle of me as well—*that* I do well enough on my own."

"Undeniably." The golden Queen eyes her opponent's plumage, which flares white as truth, refusing to brown even so close to fire. "You most certainly do . . . See how my brethren gather on the ridge above? It's you, my plain-speaker, who has them in thrall. Plumes that blaze without spark! I've—*they've*—never before seen the like."

"They're yours, these plumes," says the raven. Then she gestures at Huginn. "But only if you grant my boon."

The phoenix's red eyes narrow, her crest and cowl bristle. "Do you know, child, what we paid for our hundred thousand births? What we lost to live and live and live again while all those around us die? It cannot be replaced with a few feathers, fetching though they may be."

Mymnir sighs, but the firebird continues. "Our *souls*, child. The very essence of our being. Exposed for all to see, to quench, to steal." She flaps her wings, swirling white, red, bronze tracers in front of the raven's face. "We burn not for merriment, not for pleasure, but merely to exist. Our spirit is on show, child. Forever. Inside is only emptiness."

"And again you prove most clever, my Lady. In trying to dissuade me, you've strengthened my resolve. Though you spoke of yourself, you've also described my brother as though you knew him intimately. If what you say is true, he'll be reborn as swiftly as any of your kin. My poor Huginn."

The phoenix startles at the name—for all birds are known to each other—but holds her tongue.

"Hollow now more than ever," the raven muses. "And before just as empty. Ha! There's a riddle for you." Her voice trails off. She hops over to the pile, caresses Huginn's beak with her own. "But that's just what you'd planned, wasn't it? A bit of riddling and some new trinkets to brighten your spirits? Well, you can have both, my Lady."

The phoenix scowls. "His spirit has travelled far . . . "

Mymnir fans her tail feathers, twelve lustrous spears for the Queen's taking. "Bring him back, please."

---

Though not plain, the phoenix Queen's words were spoken truly. Huginn, resurrected, now wears his soul on the outside—and it is as black as his gargantuan body.

"You killed me!" Death has ravaged the dark raven's voice. Words hiss from his throat, half-formed, moth-eaten exclamations. He pins Mymnir to the sand, lifts her, slams her back down. Without a rudder, flight is impossible. She is powerless to escape him.

"I brought you here," she protests. "I carried you. I gave you life!"

"Oh, did you now?" Huginn takes another swing, then claws his sister's scalp, her face, her back. "Well, I'm sure Óðinn will be interested to hear it. Shall we tell him, *ætt-morðingi*, how his delinquent daughter now claims the role of All-Father?"

Laughing, he pulls at Mymnir's wings, digs into the flesh around her shoulders, and begins to lift her into the sky. "Rage upon rage: first you take his world, now his status! *You gave me life*—ha! And well you should look frightened, kin-killer—just wait until you see his reaction!"

Mymnir goes limp in Huginn's clutches. She flushes, then shivers. Her extremities tingle, and her face goes numb.

"*Mín bróðir*," she whispers. "Oh, my sweet brother. You know where he is?"

"Of course," he replies casually. Lightly. "I can always find him, easy as thinking. Can't you?"

He glides to the level of the treetops and seems to wait for Mymnir's answer.

"Can't you?" he repeats, slowing his ascent.

Mymnir looks away, says nothing. She has never been able to tell her brother's truth from his lies. Is this a falsehood? Is this invention? Does he say this now to torment her with doubt and loss? Or is it worse: the truth?

Huginn caws his voice to shreds, his body shaking with delight. No longer blind with anger, he sees the desperation etched in Mymnir's features, the longing. It wasn't to save him that she expended such time and effort: when will he learn? Mymnir's greatest exertions are always self-serving.

Without a word, the black raven relaxes his grip, dropping his pale sister in the shallows. As she splashes and screams, he is wracked with such glee he is almost unable to fly. *Almost.*

---

The tide laps at Mymnir's feet as she patrols the fluid line where ocean meets shore.

In this part of the world, the days pass unremarked; neither growing longer nor shorter with the progression of months. She can't tell if it is weeks or years since Huginn left. Her tail feathers have all but regrown, though they are not yet strong enough to sustain the journey she faces. So she walks on soft sand to toughen her muscles, and on firm to harden her heart. Shifting between bird and human form, she hops to the left and right and creates three sets of prints, side by side on the strand. Two prong-footed, heavy as memory, light as thought, parentheses to the one with high arches and delicate toes.

Waves erase the right-hand prints first. *Good*, she thinks, setting her jaw. Turning to the middle set, she retraces her steps, deepens the imprints. But the water advances too quickly, waging relentless war on her efforts. What she needs, she realises, is reinforcement. She cannot preserve all her work alone.

The white raven sheds her human skin and focuses on bolstering the sinister side of the path. Her talons scoop great divots from the sand, and with every mile she feels stronger.

Her marks remain, deep and clear, long after the first two have dissolved.

# *To That Man, My Bitter Counsel*

*Keep doors always open when hosting a feast;*
*Guests freely in and out should roam.*
*Love becomes loathing if long one must sit*
*By the hearth in another man's home.*

'*Wary is the Wise Man*' *and other* lausavísur, compiled by
Tindr *hrafnaskáld*

Ingrid was once as pale and smooth as milk poured over marble. Her skin was translucent, thin and taut, with a fine sheen like mother-of-pearl. At the age of twelve she stood a foot taller than any of her female kin. By sixteen, if she'd been so inclined, she could easily have rested her elbows on the crowns of most men, including that of her first husband. When she entered Ármann's hall Ingrid kept her back straight, chin tilted slightly down. None could avoid catching her glance as she swept past to join him, their *séfinn*, at the head table perched on a dais.

Busy, siren-tongued Ármann, forever talking, forever *negotiating*, forever seeking. Engrossed in conversation with this envoy from Mymnir's estate or that emissary from the forest's red warriors, Ármann always kept a seat for Ingrid to his left. Guests and would-be courtiers could admire the lady of the house from this vantage, while she sat quietly listening. She, on the other hand, was afforded the best view of Ármann's back, his gesticulating arms, the shivering of his hair when his laughter, convincing proof of bonhomie and trustworthiness, roared forth.

Other Fae women, perfect beauties all, would peer up at her when they thought no-one was looking. They'd wish their already straight hair straighter, their feathered brows more plumed, their emerald eyes a lighter shade of gem, so they might each scintillate at court as Ingrid did. Half-human midwives with cracked red hands would smile as they delivered fair babes to these ladies. "White as Ingrid herself," they'd say proudly, as though they were somehow responsible for gifting the children with features of frost and snow. And for once, the Fae-wives allowed these low women their pride. For once they would return their smiles.

Half-blood nursemaids and pure Fae courtiers alike were speechless when Ingrid's own babies were born. Twin girls, more luck to her family name, and so bright you'd think the sun and moon were swaddled on their young mother's lap. So bright they brought a flush to the midwives' round cheeks. So bright they stilled Ármann's tongue, if only for a moment. So bright, they melted the newly-sparked jubilance from those other women's eyes, muddy green and heavily-lashed, all turned secretly in Ingrid's direction.

But not bright enough to dispel the long, dark shadow cast on her spotless reputation, the day the governess discovered the two empty cradles, not a week after they'd first been filled.

―――――∽∞∽―――――

Around the ephemeral crystal palace dusk bruises snow-covered fields, white-capped pines, a coastline jagged with ice.

Waves of night lap at the citadel's foundations where it hulks, half a mile back from the shore, a mere league away from the *fjallkona*'s island and its glorious bridge. The previous winter solstice festival, artisans had constructed the palace to resemble the *knörr* that carried their people to this land. A grand translucent ship, crafted of permafrost and firn; its wide rooftop festooned with icicle masts, each frozen trunk as round and tall as the great oaks the woodsmen had had cleared from the hillside. Seamstresses conjured up snowflake draperies then hung them as sails, which caught the wind and set the edifice to chiming.

# To That Man, My Bitter Counsel

This year, sculptors and architects joined forces to make last season's splendour seem like a sty. After weeks of planning and construction, Jötunheimr lived once more, recreated in all its glory—and then some. Where the original was an impregnable fortress, a slab of chiselled rock surrounded by an iceberg wall so high and slick none would dare scale it, this palace seems as light and fragile as mother-of-pearl. Flying buttresses sparkle like webs of carved sugar, supporting a behemoth of witch-glass and hoar. Its doors are filigreed things with frames meeting in delicate points overhead; the castle's aesthetic is not ruined by sharp portcullises, or ugly entrances tall enough to admit giants. There are no ramparts here, no crenellations. Brazenly facing the Fae Queen's forbidding stone island, impossibly thin steeples stretch from the tips of cloud-taffy towers, their finials dusted with stars.

Inside, on a third floor gallery above the cloistered central court, sunset refracts through a clear curved wall. Shards of rainbow light play across Ingrid's mottled face as she looks out, her eyes returning ever to the mountainous isle. She knows she is not the only one who has examined the *fjallkona* so intently over the past months. Halfway up the ridge, Mymnir's estate is fused with the living stone. From this distance it appears jagged and black. Harsh and cold, though Ingrid knows its avenues are illuminated by torchlight, its courtyards dotted with fine sculptures, its mead halls hung with thick tapestries and carpeted with silk. The hearths in its maze of chambers are always swept, always crackling with welcome fires; flames glinting off Mymnir's treasures are sure to raise a flush in the faces of her many guests, if not warm their blood. Though it's been years since she last walked the Fae Queen's halls, Ingrid can still feel the heat in those lofty rooms, the rugs' soft pile bending beneath her slippered feet. She closes her lids and for an instant still smells the musky scent of furs heaped on high mattresses. Mulling spices and wine left by servants. Fat tallow candles lit beside her bed.

Ingrid blinks and comes back to herself. There has been no warmth for her left in that mountain for many a long year. It is permanent and imposing, even in silhouette. She touches the glass and wonders how long it will take for her hand to melt a hole through. She's tempted to try, to weaken this ridiculous structure, to bring it tumbling down all around them. *In memory of giants,* she thinks, looking up to the glimmering joists in the ceiling, webs of hoarfrost. *Or so the architects claim.* Shivering, she steps back and tucks her hands under her arms. *But what use would creatures of flint and fire have for a palace made of ice?* Ingrid smiles, and imagines how Surtr would have guffawed at the sight of such delicate turrets, so many decorative clusters of moonstone.

*Fools, Skýja-Ingrid*, he would have said, his voice tinged with charcoal, as he surveyed the hubbub. *All those tiny Fae—flimsy little beings cowering so close to the ground. Not like you, my cloud-headed one.* Surtr would have ruffled the dense nimbus of Ingrid's now-black curls, as he often had when they were alone. Gently, oh so gently. Then he'd brush a knuckle along her purple jawline. Pride would split his face into a smile, which he'd quickly hide lest anyone here catch him looking anything less than fierce. He'd adopt a scowl at the unfolding scene, the mask of Surtr the Mighty slipped back in place. But from deep in his belly laughter would simmer, an earthquake of sound, as he watched the Fae hordes set up camp.

*Fools*, he would have repeated, echoing his wife's thoughts. *Building a city out of cloth and tree-bone.*

But Surtr is not here.

The many Húsringar have been gathering since late autumn. A fleet of pavilions, brilliant indigo- and garnet-dyed peaks, spills across a sea of winter white. Hundreds of timber and velvet structures dot the landscape, boasting fringed gables and leadlight windows, tapestries hung for insulation, fireplaces and heated floorboards to keep stewards from freezing to death while they tend to their noble suzerains. From far and wide caravans continue to crest the twilit horizon before colonising the coastline; their numbers swell as the solstice draws nigh. Makeshift stables are kept well away from the crystal palace, close to the tents: eight-legged thoroughbreds mean twice as many bucking silver horseshoes, and enough snorting and whinnying to keep servants cleaning steam from the outer walls all season.

Ingrid relaxes as shades of violet and gentian soften the view. She pulls her lace shawl tight, pretending it affords the same comfort as a giant palm engulfing her shoulders.

"Have you seen Mistress Klippel?" she asks a passing lackey. The dark-haired boy takes several steps before drawing to a halt, but at last he stops. *They're improving*, she thinks. *Magnus must have had a word with the Maester.* The boy's fidgeting sets his collection of *nátt-lamps* swinging, their swirling black bulbs clustered on a pole carried over his shoulder. He schools his expression, clears his throat. Barely flinches as he speaks.

"No, Mistress," he says, careful not to stare at the navy pattern on her left cheek. Stretched from temple to lip, the stain's edges have blurred over the years; it no longer so distinctly resembles the splayed print of a hand.

"No doubt she'll be in the promenade, tucked in an alcove somewhere with her hands up Liljana's skirts. Fetch her to me."

The boy gapes, but doesn't move.

"Drop the act, *snáði*. We both know there are no secrets between servants. Liljana is insatiable; Klippel earns her keep well. Now earn yours by bringing her here. Don't make me wait."

The boy looks down, as though the opalescent floors might reveal more than the smudged silhouettes of people beneath. Changing tack, he hoists the clutch of *nátt-lamps*. "I've got to hang these before eventide, else Maester will skin me alive."

*Any excuse to avoid taking orders from the jarl's Mistress*, Ingrid thinks.

She smiles, her magenta lips curling artfully to accentuate the bronze sheen of her skin, mirroring the deep purple crescents shading her large eyes. "I'll take one right here, thank you." She holds her arm straight out, palm down, and waits for the lamplighter to come to her. Reluctantly, he takes a dangling bulb from the bunch. The boy's soft shoes scuff across the hallway as he drags his feet into the gallery. Gingerly, he slides the thing onto Ingrid's forearm without touching the fuchsia stripes encircling her slim wrist.

The lamp's contents whirl like nightmares, grey madness spiralled with gloom. Regular chandeliers with garish tongues of yellow light are fine for regular houses: not so for the crystal palace. The heat of flames would wreak havoc on frozen windows, support beams, floors; the glare alone would be blinding once the full complement of candles was lit. With this in mind, the Queen's engineers made *nátt-lamps*: hurricane lanterns that absorb darkness rather than emit light, rendering transparent rooms in twilight until dawn. Their genesis belongs to Eiðr, he who was the last of Mymnir's four guardians. Old and a little mad, he dreams up insanities while those with more organised, practical minds set about making them real.

Ingrid holds the beacon aloft and imagines it leaching the black from her hair, leaving it long and straight and white. It doesn't, of course: she sees this clearly as disgust flashes across the young servant's face. *Not so well trained after all*, she muses, leaning forward to afford the boy a closer look at her colourful features. "My last husband gave me these curls," she whispers. "The day his flaming sword nearly severed my neck."

Ingrid laughs as the boy stumbles in his haste to retreat. "Lighten your load, *snáði*—leave another lamp here for Klippel. The sooner you've disposed of them, the sooner you can send her to me."

⁂

"They say Mymnir is gone."

Klippel sneers and pulls a long blonde hair out of her canapé. She tosses the morsel back onto a waiter's tray, and plucks another before he passes. Her pale pink lips, glossed to a shine, attract flecks of pepper as she nibbles a skewer of spiced hare. Ingrid passes her a handkerchief. She'd had to seek her friend out herself, after all; obviously the Maester's exhortations were not especially firm.

"They say many things," she replies. "But a wise man knows that truth thrives in silence."

"'Tis well we aren't men then, isn't it?" Klippel wipes her mouth, takes a swig of wine from a chilled goblet. "Aren't you curious?"

*About many things*, Ingrid thinks. Such as how someone like Magnus can rise to such prominence in so brief a time. A few decades, no more than a blink in the long lives of the Fae, and Ingrid's latest *séfinn* had graduated from courtier to courted. "What I want to know," she lowers her voice, forcing Klippel to lean so far forward the layers of her gown snag on the toothpick in her hand, "is what Liljana's husband intends to wear to the masquerade."

Klippel smirks at Ingrid's not-so-subtle change of topic. "He hasn't decided yet, apparently. But Liljana says he's narrowed it down to two choices: the Horned Man, or the Great Narwhal." The courtesan laughs, and signals the waiter to refill her glass. "Either way, it's absurd."

"Allow the man his overcompensations," Ingrid chuckles, "you've already taken his wife."

"Yes, well." Klippel watches the other hetaerae milling in the antechamber. Clusters of Fae companions—only full blooded were accorded the title 'Companion'; half-breeds were still 'hora'—the men as lovely as the women, all draped in shades of ivory and adorned with silver and quartz, loiter outside the palace's great hall while their *séfinnur* dine. Waiters flit from group to group, serving light victuals and drinking in gossip. All too soon the nobles will finish their evening meal. The service bells will peal out, beckoning these white butterflies in to feast on the scraps. The same routine every night.

"I've convinced Liljana to take whichever costume Arhus rejects." Klippel grins. "Whether it's whale or stag, when I ride into the hall on my lady's broad back, everyone will know who has the horn in their relationship."

The pair erupts in giggles, but Ingrid's laughter subsides well before her friend's. "So you'll be attending, then."

"Naturally," says Klippel. "Aren't you?"

Overhead, a chandelier of glass bells jingles with the sound of a thousand knives and forks being set upon emptied plates. At the far side of the room, two intricately spun doors swing open. Ingrid links arms with Klippel, and together they wait for the young, eager ones to swarm into the dining hall before them. "Darling," she begins, quietly admiring the fledglings' flawless pearl skin, their milkweed tresses. She squeezes Klippel's arm tightly, then clears the lump from her throat. "I've worn a costume for years. What need have I for a masque?"

---

Magnus comes quickly when he's excited.

"Mymnir is dead," he says, digging his fingers into Ingrid's hips, thrusting himself deeper and deeper into her as the pressure builds in his groin. "Or she's fled this world, though I don't see how that's possible." He reaches around Ingrid's front to grab her breast, leaning forward to quickly nuzzle the back of her neck. He licks the maroon lines circling her throat, as if a noose has been pulled tight and left its twisted echo, then straightens up. "We'd all have left this forsaken land centuries ago, if there was a way."

Ingrid shifts position to ease the ache in her knees and palms, amused that he speaks of himself as if he were pure Fae; she alone knows of his skræling ancestry. Still, he has enough Fae blood to keep him hale and hearty. His age does not show so much on him, although he must be approaching sixty by her calculations. She listens and fidgets as he goes on. She doesn't mind Magnus's ceaseless prattle during sex; it covers up her silence. But although her *séfinn* has spared no expense in furnishing his Mistress's tent, the wood flooring only has so much give.

"She must be dead." Magnus's voice goes up an octave. "It's been over a year." Grunting, now. "There's been talk of an Assembly. And an election . . . "

The words catch. He goes rigid, shudders, moans.

Ingrid drops to her elbows, wrists and knees throbbing. Black spots bloom there, swiftly stippling her forearms and calves. Soon the skin has turned leopard up to her biceps. She feels rosettes itching down to her ankles. The colour flares—deep purple lustre in the black—and Ingrid wonders if this time Magnus's mark will be permanent. She hides her arms beneath big throw-pillows on the floor. No use him seeing the ragged circles until—unless—they remain.

Quiet now, Magnus stays inside her, gently tracing his finger along Ingrid's mazarine spine as he softens. He works his way down, running his nails over the green striations stretching across her lower back. "Ármann?" he asks, plucking the tiger stripes like harp strings, gently pinching. Ingrid nods wordlessly, memories of her first husband's distrust still strong enough to choke.

*Where are the children, wife?* Not *my Queen.* Not *my love.* Wife.

*Stolen,* Ingrid had said. *Stolen!* she'd cried, trying to run, trying to escape Ármann's desperate hands, clawing green across her alabaster back as she scrambled.

*Where are they?* he'd whimpered, clinging, scraping. As though he might find them beneath her waistband, retreated back to her womb.

*Stolen,* she'd promised, even as he stepped away. Leaving her to the guards.

*Their* patches were mildew, bile, lichen orange. Magnus doesn't care to discuss the places those men had been.

He withdraws, and flips Ingrid over. Her stomach is a warm shade of gold, her breasts and inner thighs smeared with soot, her collarbone decorated with giant thumbprints each the same shape and hue as aubergines.

"And all this?" He kneads Ingrid's dark thighs, caressing the starbursts on her pelvis, tickles her ribs and nipples. His touch is just like any other: white as Ingrid's blood flees his fingertips, invisible as colour rushes back in. "How many others have painted you thus? Three? Seven? Twelve?"

"Magnus." Ingrid clicks her tongue.

"How many?"

She smiles. *Just one, you fool.*

"Did you know," she said, "Fire Giants make quite impressive executioners?"

"Don't change the subject, Ingrid. How many?"

Her smile broadens. She reaches up and brushes fine strands of damp hair away from Magnus's brow, the leopard in her arms all but faded. Stroking his temples, she says, "What did we agree?"

"I can't—"

Ingrid presses a finger to his lips. "No jealousy, my *séfinn*."

"Don't call me that," Magnus growls. "You are not my thrall. I do not command you."

"Let the name fit," she said. "I once was so fair—even more than you—Ármann's courtiers simply called me Hvíta. Nothing more, just *White*. I've since been called Skýja-Ingrid after the thundercloud on my head, the black storm in my eyes." She shrugs, and draws him down for a kiss. "Either way, I am still myself. And you *are* my lord." *Though never my master.* "But that is *not* the reason I stay."

*Not at all.*

Magnus pulls away. Without meeting Ingrid's eye, he refastens his dove breeches and straightens his tunic. "You refuse to answer?"

"Oh, it's honesty you're after? All right." Ingrid sits up and pretends to look for her dress; knowing it is simply that she has not given the answer he *wanted*. "Give me a moment and we'll go together to have a word with Osa."

"Don't try to threaten me," Magnus says, gathering his cloak and casting about for his ceremonial solstice-sword. It has fallen beneath the unused bed.

"Tell me, is what they say true? That the second wife is twice as jealous as the first?"

Magnus makes a sound like a bear with his patience tried. "Our affair is far from secret."

"True," Ingrid says, lying back, not shivering despite the chill air. "But does she want every last detail? Will that make her happy?"

Magnus stops, and lets the tent flap drop. He keeps his back to her, but doesn't leave.

"As I was saying." Ingrid reaches up to her bed, grabs the arctic fox blanket, a lush collection of pelts cured and stitched carefully together, with a lining of interwoven silk ribbons, and pulls it around her as she stands. She approaches him slowly, knowing Magnus gets skittish as a caribou when she mentions his first wife, and is just as likely to buck. Tenderly, she wraps her arms and the fur around him, and rests her chin on his shoulder. *He is tall*, she thinks, pressing her cold nose against his flushed cheek. *But not so tall as my Surtr.* "Fire Giants make extraordinary executioners."

"So you've said. And you know this how, exactly?"

"Listen." Ingrid slaps Magnus lightly, waking the ghost of a smile on his lips. "If Mymnir is truly gone—*if*—then what better way for you to assert your claim than by being the one to kill her, once and for all?"

Magnus spins to face Ingrid, his expression half grin, half confusion. "You're teasing me now."

Ingrid shakes her head. "We'll enlist the mummers. They'll fashion two costumes, the likes of which have never been seen. A Fire Giant with a flaming sword for you: on stilts you will tower over everyone, swinging your weapon above their simpering heads, howling for blood. For your wife, a gown and diadem fit for the Fae Queen herself—Osa will accompany you in the guise of Mymnir. And before the moon reaches its zenith, you will do the mummers proud, and enact the beheading of Mymnir for all to see. What better way to declare your candidacy for overlordship of the Fae? We cannot continue without a guiding hand, Magnus." Her tone shifts so subtly from frivolous to urgent that he does not notice the artistry in the inflection. "People need to be led, the Fae no less than the mortals that wash our feet. They need to be told what to do. Only you are fit for such command."

In reply, Magnus squeezes Ingrid, picks her up. As he spins her around, the points of the fox fur lift like long heavy wings.

*What better way to confirm their suspicions? That you are a love-blind fool?*

Hugging him in return, she laughs until she's empty.

---

The palace's central court, turned ballroom for the celebration, swirls with solstice colour. Its etched glass ceiling diffuses sunset, casting the revellers into a peach-hued gloaming. For this one night, the Fae doff their customary silvers and frosts, and drape themselves in springtime. Rose petal organza spills from slim waists as clusters of ladies skim from one side of the grand space to the other. Their elaborate coiffures twist skywards: plaited oaks dripping moss; hair nests resounding with enchanted wrens; ice antlers sprouting from beds of curls, nestled among currants and berries. Poppy collars skim the gentlemen's chins and tulip cuffs tickle their wrists as they sip sweet wines and flirt with their Mistresses. In turn, their wives catch paramours' eyes, smile, and pretend not to.

Near the banquet table is a huntress whose red armour ripples as she moves, its blood-arrows overlapping into one sharp-pointed skin. An ivory stag nuzzles her bow hand; her partner transformed for the evening. Ingrid searches for Klippel—finds her dressed as a sailor, harpoon in hand, carried pig-a-back by Liljana, finned and shiny in orca black. Beneath the *nátt-lamp* chandelier, owl-hooded counsellors alternately mumble and chuckle. So closely huddled, their feathered cloaks mesh; the costume now one giant bird with twelve heads. Around the room's cloistered perimeter, foxes and vultures and wolves gather in the shadows, scheming as they sample canapés. Courtesans weave through the crowd, filling glasses and smothering arguments. They alone remain clothed in white.

The dance floor is so full, Ingrid can't see the chequered tiles, but no-one has started dancing. Alone, she watches from the architects' catwalk, high up in the rafters. Down *there*, everyone is waiting.

As is she.

Mymnir's jarls, appointed to oversee parts of the kingdom beyond her holdings in the East, enter one at a time. Signy first, chieftain of the West, her garment made of beaten gold and fashioned into a chariot upon which she stands. Her locks are woven lengths of flax, two long ropes extending twelve metres from her head to join up with the bit in her husband's mouth. Örvar pulls his wife across the room—polite applause turns to catcalls when she lashes his centaur rump with a silk whip. Next comes Alvis, guardian in the North. Ingrid isn't quite sure what his outfit represents. He is nude, but painted red from head to foot, and laced with capillaries of white and blue. Pressed buttock-to-buttock with Kaspar, his husband, also naked but dyed marble blue. The pair walks together, muscular arms and legs moving as one, faces morose, glares sweeping slowly from side to side. *Hot and cold?* Ingrid wonders as the crowd parts to let the conjoined men through. *Ocean and desert?* She shakes her head. Either way, the message is confusing—not the best approach, if Alvis hopes to win support at the Assembly.

Noise swells as courtier and Fae alike wait for Magnus's entrance. Ingrid leans forward as far as she can without falling off, craning to see the hall's double doors more clearly. *Where is he?*

A waiter drops his tray, glass shattering on the frozen floor.

Ingrid's hands slip on the guardrail. Her breath catches as Mymnir strides into the room.

As one, the Fae genuflect and murmur blessings for their *fjallkona*. Music plays on, but even it seems cowed by the Hrafn's presence. A hush falls, swift and deep. Now Ingrid hears Mymnir's heels echo with each step; the susurrus of her straight silver-white hair brushing against the floor; the feathers fluttering on eyebrows and temples as she progresses down the silent aisle. Ingrid watches, spellbound, as the Queen looks down on her subjects. Skin like crushed opal. Irises like cut diamonds. Without a smudge of violet at her throat or even a wisp of thundercloud curls. She is imperious with confidence and beauty.

Ingrid's knees buckle. Tears glisten down her cheeks.

Osa is perfect.

"You think to escape me?" Magnus's voice booms, startling the crowd. Nervous laughter titters as the Fae realise the ruse—they get to their feet just as the Southern jarl barrels into the room. "None can cheat the executioner's sword!"

*I know one way . . .* Ingrid thinks with a sad smile. She wipes her face with a delicate handkerchief. *Oh, lover. You couldn't sound more foolish if I'd put the words into your mouth.* Titters develop into full-bellied guffaws as long-forgotten rumours of Ingrid's eleventh-hour marriage to Surtr instantly spring to the gossips' minds. Whispers that the Southern jarl nightly takes a giant's blood-wife to his bed. Magnus, however, makes no such connection; or perhaps ignores it. Determined to catch the fake Mymnir, he lumbers across the ballroom, swinging a flaming longsword. Barbarian leathers hold his suit of fur in place; its shaggy legs sewn six feet long to camouflage the stilts strapped to his feet. Signy and Alvis raise their glasses as he shuffles past, acknowledging their defeat in the costume stakes, though not in the election, which must surely be declared soon if the *true* Mymnir remains lost. Courtiers cheer him on, while the Fae make moves to get back to their conversations.

"I'll have your head, *fjallkona*!" Magnus bellows, ambling after Osa.

And then comes crashing down.

Ingrid leaps up, claps her hands over her mouth, too stunned at her good fortune to laugh. It all happens so quickly: either he's wielded the sword with too much enthusiasm, or his stilts have skidded on the sheer floor tiles . . . Either way, he's lost his footing. He's tumbling into the crowd, tearing delicate fabrics, setting hair sculptures alight. Glassware smashes as those closest to the mayhem scurry out of the way. Shouts and cries follow in his wake—and in a clatter of steel and wood, he's on the ground.

*That's it.* Ingrid stifles a whoop. *Magnus is revealed for a love-fool* and *an oaf. He's done for!*

Without missing a beat, Magnus dislodges his feet from the stirrups, launches himself into a graceful back-flip, and scoops up the smouldering sword. He makes short work of the distance between him and his wife: dashing to her left, he extends the blade to his right.

Osa freezes as it whistles to a stop just shy of her neck.

"No matter the obstacle," Magnus says, lowering the sword, "I always see my tasks through to the end."

The audience doesn't applaud at this declaration, but there are certainly more grins than frowns among their number. Magnus steals a kiss from his faux Mymnir, doffs an invisible cap at the crowd, then goes to collect the remnants of his costume.

*He's impressed them.*

High in the rafters, clinging to the catwalk railing until her knuckles whiten, Ingrid's heart plummets, smashes on the tiles far below. She watches as it's trodden to dust beneath delicate Fae feet.

---

The crystal palace still stands. The ice, sensing Mymnir's absence, refuses to melt. From seaside to far-distant plains, winter digs into the earth and grips tight, relentlessly cold, relentlessly present. And while the weather holds, the gathered hordes of Fae also remain, bickering and bustling, as though jostling for position might keep them warm.

Time trudges onwards.

Almost another year in which Magnus has been making a name for himself as a wise and respected man, good-humoured yet firm, brave yet even-tempered. At first there is subtle politicking among the Húsringar, favours sought and promised; gradually, though, the Fae have become restless, the jockeying more aggressive. Before it became obvious that the season's equinox would not pass, the convocation had agreed to wait until spring before making a move towards the Queen's isle. So it had been decided, and so it came to pass. Now, none may leave the encampment lest they think to ensconce themself in Mymnir's place, usurping the Hrafn's throne without the agreement of all. And as the unchanging weeks turn to unchanging months, the crystal palace's halls begin to echo with whispers. Plots. Plans.

Through it all, Magnus remains stable, dignified, surefooted. The jarl's self-confidence goes a long way to convincing those around him that he should be entrusted with much more than the lands to the South. That Mymnir's empty seat should be filled by him.

Still, the ice remains, and the only sign of spring is Ingrid's growing belly.

There had been no other child since the two who disappeared. Their going had left Ingrid stained with scorn, vulnerable to the discolouration of mortality. She tries not to think of the lost ones while she rubs her swollen stomach. The pregnancy has made all her patterns, all her bruises and plum-coloured markings more intense, more vibrant. She suffers no sickness. Ingrid dresses in the brightest hues, the richest fabrics—an entire wardrobe has been designed just for her, lightening Magnus's purse considerably. He does not care: he will refuse her nothing.

Osa has given him no children.

He had a son off his first wife, and raised him to be a chivalrous young man. But the son, near-grown, rejected the father—and Ingrid can only suspect why. *It was a matter of honour*, Magnus told her once, but wouldn't elaborate. And, truth be told, the second wife has the maternal instincts of a stone. But Osa knows a child would give her more than she already has: respect, a tangible hold on Magnus, a secure place among the coupled, assurance she'd never be demoted from wife to Companion.

*She may yet be*, Ingrid thinks, as the child nudges her ribs.

Ingrid's lush garments emphasise her new shape. The high waistline sits under her jutting breasts, which spill tantalisingly from the low-cut necklines, and highlights the ripeness of her belly. The underskirts are all woven in tints of summer, worn beneath split overskirts and long coats stitched from leaves darkening with a blush of autumn. She moves gracefully across great hall and snowy fields alike. No-one would think she has slowed down, merely that she has become languid, impossibly alluring with the promise of new life.

Magnus runs his hands over her even when they are in public, his pride, his glee palpable. For the moment, Ingrid does not bother to undermine him in her tidy, subtle way—he does this himself. Mooning over his mistress, waiting on the storm-cloud whore, letting all his peers see him led thus by his cock. The jarl is his own worst enemy.

Osa watches with hatred. Some days Ingrid can feel the other's stare burning into her—it reminds her of Surtr, how the giant could never quite smother the coals of his anger. She simply smiles, as she had so frequently when her husband's rages overtook him. *Fury and fire are in the jötunn's nature*, she thinks. *But as for the barren wife . . .* Calmly, steadily, she meets Osa's eyes, and lets her see a combination of pity and triumph.

When the baby comes, it is a boy, Fae in appearance but with Ingrid's black curls. A wine-coloured birthmark in the shape of a bear mars his little chest. Magnus displays it proudly to all who will look.

Pridbjørn is healthy, chubby, a happy infant who eats well, cries lustily and smiles when his father enters the tent.

"Such a fine boy!" Magnus likes to toss him into the air, not too high, and the baby huffs and gasps with delight. Ingrid's heart rises and falls with the child.

"Put him down, Magnus. He's too young to be thrown about like a sack of wheat. He'll be sick and then you'll look fine, all your silks and furs covered in vomit. How regal!" More and more, she has felt her own flames, revenge banked while the child grew within her, blaze up again. The desire to destroy burns hot.

"Nonsense! He's no milksop." But Magnus obeys and sits beside Ingrid, who lies on her bed, cocooned under piles of blankets against the long winter. She wants to pull the boy from his father's embrace and keep him beside her, enfolded in the soft nest of coverlets. Forever protected.

For the first week of her son's life, Ingrid had sat up all night, wide-eyed and vigilant, daring the fates to weave him out of her reach as they had her daughters. Swaddled and fed by nursemaids and nannies, the twins were almost untouched by her hand before they were stolen. And even as Ingrid was led to the executioner's block, she worried the girls would have no skin-memory of her, that they wouldn't think of themselves as loved. A legion of carers, a garrison full of Ármann's Húsringr guards, and the children had not been safe even then. *Gone after only six days* . . .

Time sneaks away behind Ingrid's back as she watches her new baby flourish. Now Pridbjørn is nearly five times the girls' age when they vanished, and Ingrid's lying-in is nearly over. All month, she has hidden herself in the bubble of her fine tent, the serenity broken only when Magnus comes by, either on his own or with gawking courtiers in tow, or when Klippel visits to gush over the plump boy. Osa appeared once, only once, when Magnus was busy with the Assembly. The second wife stood at the tent's entrance and glared at mother and child. Her footsteps utterly noiseless as she left.

Hungry, Pridbjørn reaches for Ingrid, and Magnus sits nearby as his son latches on to one full breast, the pattern of a peacock's feather decorating the sooty skin there. Droplets of milk slowly trace their way down, missed by a greedy mouth. Magnus smiles.

"Tomorrow," he says.

"Mmmm?" Ingrid's eyes are unfocused, dreamy. There is room only for her and her child here in this circle of care.

"Tomorrow," Magnus repeats, and his tone is filled with anticipation, desire, lust on the verge of being fulfilled. Wincing, she briefly wonders if she is to be treated to his attentions, but soon realises that this is something else. An excitement not even she can fuel. Suddenly, she is paying attention.

"What? Tomorrow what?"

"Tomorrow we will set out for the *fjallkona*."

"But . . . the agreement?"

"Yesterday, we reached another agreement. I shall take Mymnir's throne." His voice shakes. He seems to grow larger before her. This is all he has worked for, for so long. And all she has tried to prevent for even longer.

"But Mymnir's law. After each winter solstice the court can only return to the isle with her express permission." Ingrid knows she is clutching at straws. The child growls and struggles at the tit. She has stopped producing milk.

"There is no Mymnir, *uppáhald*. She's gone. And there's a throne for the taking."

---

Klippel cheerfully agrees to look after Pridbjørn, although it takes all of Ingrid's willpower to entrust the child to anyone. But she needs these hours—she needs this night. By tomorrow it will be too late.

"Take your time," the courtesan says with a wink. "Remind the old bear what warm beds are like. Guaranteed Osa has long forgotten how—and soon enough she, too, will be forgotten. Go on, now. We'll be fine, won't we, Bjørni? Go. *Go*. Show him what it means to have a queen by his side."

In the dim light of her *séfinn's* tent, Ingrid wakes Magnus with strong kisses. She straddles him and takes her pleasure angrily, which arouses him even more. By the time he is exhausted she too feels as if she could sleep for a week, but there are other imperatives.

"Wine, my lord?" She curses herself; the title slipped out.

"'My lord'? Are you being influenced by my new position, Ingrid?" Magnus laughs groggily, watching her leave the bed, naked, her skin swirling like disturbed darkness.

"You're not king yet, Magnus." She says it so softly he does not pick up on the undertone of hatred. He looks at her back as she pours wine from the etched quartz decanter into two frost-goblets. What he does not see is how she scrapes colour from her skin with a small sharp knife over one of the glasses, the hues becoming powder as they leave her. Dully luminescent purple, black and green, it hits the liquid's surface, floating and fizzing for precious seconds before finally being absorbed. Ingrid's rancour is rich, but she refrains from adding too much. Poison is too gentle, too easy an escape for this killer, this hypocrite. He deserves much, much worse.

She fusses, topping up the drinks and finally returning to him, bearing appropriate libation.

"To the soon-to-be-king," she says as they hoist the goblets, clinking their rims. As usual, Magnus swigs more deeply than she. He was ever a glutton.

Her skin cools as she watches him drowse. Her temper, however, does not. The drug will take hours from him; his slumber will last well beyond dawning and she will have all the time she needs.

"Do you think, ever, of those you have harmed?" She leans over and whispers, recoiling as she steps on something hard. A carved wooden box tumbles from Magnus's coat when she picks it up off the floor. *Another foolish gift.* The satin ribbon wrapped around it slides away easily and the hinges open without a sound. Cushioned on a bed of down, an elaborate comb—or is it a brooch?—fashioned from bone, onyx and sapphires twinkles up at Ingrid. Even in the darkened tent, the blue bird's facets gleam, glinting with inner light. *Where did he find this?* She startles when Magnus answers her earlier question.

"There are not so many, I think, who did not deserve it."

"And what of those who did not?"

He is silent for a while. "I have always lived to do justice, Ingrid. I freed Blu—my first wife—from a giant... You, too, I think. When one monster's downfall is the salvation of many it isn't a matter of *harm*. It's about doing what's right. Acting for the greater good."

Ingrid's rage rises at his arrogance, his self-belief, his delusional self-image—and his characterising her Surtr, her beloved rescuer, her tender executioner, as a 'monster'. Instead of stabbing Magnus with his own sharp trinket, she lifts his frost-goblet once more and tips the purple-red liquid into his mouth.

"Just a little more, my love," she insists. "It will help you sleep . . ."

---

The cordon around the Fae encampment has not been relaxed despite the concord of which Magnus spoke. The *nátt-lamps*, which Ingrid has hoarded as a dragon does gold, provide her solution.

In her hands, the bulbs break willingly. Thickened night spills from the glass, coalesces in a dense fog around her feet. A few whispered words, a few deft gestures and she crafts a shroud of darkness; the magic inherent in the little things is easily bent to any Fae will. Pleating and weaving the murk, Ingrid creates a voluminous cloak. She pulls it up over her shoulders and head, and becomes an absence, a shifting gap in the landscape. None can see her, but her presence is felt as a shiver of doubt, a bowel-clenching twist of uncertainty. As she passes errand boys running messages between the borders and the palace, hostlers tending to Sleipnir's progeny, and courtesans hurrying to perform for their *séfinnur*, Ingrid trails a chill that creeps up their spines, briefly turning their thoughts to the grave.

Hidden in this gloom, she slips between the sentries, her stout boots making no sound, and finds the path to the shoreline. Seven small boats are arrayed in the shallows, the sea too tumultuous to freeze around them. Wind whips the salty water against the crafts' clinkered hulls, clattering them one up against the other, a steady white noise that raises no alarm from the guards. Ingrid chooses the closest *faering* and soon weighs anchor. The vessel tosses wildly as she rows and spray blows across the stern, puddling beneath the benches. Wrapped tight in her disguise, Ingrid does not feel the chill; adrenaline courses through her veins, heating her to the core. The pull of the oars blisters her palms, but she does not pause. The isle comes closer and closer by the stroke.

Then there is a little beach, the keel scraping across its smooth pebbles. Ingrid stows the oars and drags the *faering* beyond the tideline. On this side of the channel, the air is still and heavy, muffling the mountain in an echoless pall. Shale clacks dully beneath her feet as she stumbles across the strand. Waterfalls flanking the steep road to Mymnir's kingdom cascade almost inaudibly down from the peaks. Gulls wheel overhead, their cries thin silver needles of sound glancing off the woollen sky. Ingrid's breath hangs in the atmosphere, cloying and damp, her lungs aching for a fresh breeze. Each inhalation is harder to take than the last. Spots begin to swim before her eyes, but she keeps her attention fixed on the city gates, and perseveres. If some clue to the raven's whereabouts is to be found, then Ingrid will only find it beyond those calcite doors. And if anyone can stop Magnus—if anyone can and will punish him for his presumption—it will be Mymnir.

Desperation propels her up the path.

The Queen's stronghold is hushed, all its magical torches snuffed. Snow drifts lazily across courtyards and along deserted streets, piling in sloped banks beneath dark windows and in corners. Buildings glisten under coats of frost. Slick roof tiles are jewelled with the stars' reflections and columns are sheathed in a thin diamond crust. Icicles spear down from eaves, blue, and sharp as witchwood. Ingrid sees, but does not register, the drip-drip-drip of melting water in the moonlight. Shuddering, she flits from shadow to shadow, approaching the palace as she would a tomb.

It looms on a rough promontory, walls of marble and jet and living stone perched at the apex of a statue-lined staircase. As Ingrid mounts the first step she begins to feel . . . exposed. Placing her feet carefully to avoid black ice, she seems to dance up the flight toward the entrance. Though the castle is clearly abandoned, the nape of her neck tingles; it takes all her self-control not to look back, to seek out the ghosts who are staring so intently with their dead eyes. Her pulse races as she passes beneath the portico, pushes open the great double doors and sees that her cloak is fading, becoming insubstantial.

*This shouldn't be happening . . . The* nátt-lamps' *power should last for hours yet.*

Frowning, she grasps at the dissipating magic, whispering words of binding. The sound returns to her redoubled, then trebled, the first echo she's heard on Mymnir's isle.

A voice—no, two distinct voices—not far away. One distracted, the other querulous. Ingrid waits to see if they'll grow any louder, if the speakers are moving any closer, if they'll appear around the corner and strike her down at first sight. A minute passes. Two.

Her shroud vanishes completely, but the conversation's volume remains unchanged.

Squaring her shoulders, Ingrid tightens her jaw and prepares to confront the pair. Uncovered, unnerved, alone.

---

She finds them in the labyrinthine library, huddled over immense stacks of books.

The oak table at which they sit is as narrow as a warship and twice as long—yet it is dwarfed by the sheer size of the room. Endless troops of wooden shelves form ranks across the marble floor, row after row marching into the gloom beyond the *nátt-lamps* dangling from ornate stands by the table. With so much valuable paper and vellum at hand, so much knowledge bound between flammable covers, it would be foolish to risk torches here—but streaks of soot staining fluted columns suggest that the library is no stranger to fire. Platforms run around its curved walls, facing more shelves jammed full with manuscripts, folios, scrolled parchments and maps. Floor upon floor of these walkways stretch for leagues overhead, connected by spiral staircases and hemmed in by a latticework of railings. Ingrid can't recall any evidence for such a tower from outside—yet although she cranes to see the ceiling, the only reward for her effort is a stiff neck. She looks down, taking in the mess of charcoal tablets and scribbled notes, the discarded quills and scrunched documents, the magnifying discs and astrolabes and crystal orbs ... And the Queen, fingers and sleeves smudged with ink, as beautiful and frightening as she was all those years ago, when Ingrid had been a welcome guest instead of a thief in the night.

Alone among the Fae, only Mymnir does not age, born as she was in the old world, a pure memory sprung from Óðinn's mind. She is still tall and silver-white, still flawless as silk, still lovely as a perfectly-honed blade.

Eiðr has no such advantage. He is yet blond, but his hair has thinned over the centuries, like gold hammered too many times, and there is a bald patch at the crown of his head. His grey robes are threadbare, wrinkled, and seemingly powdered with a layer of dust. Poring over illuminated manuscripts and fragments of runic engravings, he hunches as if the weight of this research is too much for his spine to bear. Propping his elbows on the table, the ancient liegeman rests his head in his hands, and stares bleakly at the tomes splayed like butterflies on Mymnir's board. When he speaks, his old man's voice seems to annoy the white raven.

"Believe me, my Queen, I have searched. I searched all the time you were gone and have searched ever since your return. I have been most thorough, my lady. And I've found nothing. It is not here." His tone is wounded; Ingrid suspects he has been sorely berated. She hadn't even noticed Eiðr's absence at the solstice . . . How long had he been here, alone?

"Where else would it be? Lóki's library has copies of everything ever written . . . *Everything.*" Mymnir is raging yet strangely mild, strangely distracted, as though this task occupies merely one part of her attention. "It must be here."

"I have served you all these years—"

"Hush, old fool. We have company."

They both turn and see Ingrid poised at the door, all trace of her shadow-cloak dissipated by proximity to Mymnir—no magic may survive that the Queen does not allow. Their two faces are expectant, less surprised than they might be, and quite polite. Ingrid finds herself at a loss.

"Your Majesty . . . "

Plumed brows rise expectantly.

"Who is that?" mutters Eiðr. "I haven't seen anyone in so long."

"The marked one."

"Eh?"

"The one who married her executioner to save her own life," snaps Mymnir.

"*Ætt-morðingi,*" Eiðr whispers, shaking his head. The Queen startles at the insult, but quickly regains her composure as the old man continues. "The one who murdered her dear little children?"

Eiðr begins to cough and cannot seem to stop. Ingrid doesn't know if it's because of her perceived sin or his desiccated lungs. Mymnir slaps him hard on the back and the blow seems to shock him into subsiding.

"I don't recall inviting you into my home, *snáði*," Mymnir says, eager to be going on with her work. "Explain this intrusion."

"The *séfinnur* plot against you, my Queen." Ingrid could add *They think you dead*, but does not. "They have elected Magnus *jötunsbani* king in your place. Tomorrow they will come here to claim your throne."

Mymnir stares at her for the longest time, then her mouth opens, widens until all Ingrid can see are white teeth and a red, red tongue. The Hrafn tilts her head and laughs, a rich, raucous sound that flies up to die in the library's far-distant rafters

"Let them come! Does a mother fear her naughty children?"

Ingrid gapes. "But . . . "

"Is she an idiot, do you think? Married to that giant, after all . . . " Eiðr asks, then lets loose a dusty fart. Mymnir ignores him.

"Go. Drift away little storm-cloud, there's nothing for you here. I thank you for your warning, but neither fear nor have time for their squabbles."

---

The iron brazier scalds Ingrid's palms as she tips embers on the ground outside Magnus's tent. Kneeling down, she blows on them gently until they flare orange and gold, like the first hints of dawn now gilding the landscape. The flames will be slow to catch, giving her time to collect her son. The chaos will allow them to slip safely away.

Fire. Yes, this is what Surtr would have done. Fire, always his answer, always her friend.

*Burn the traitor in his house, Skýja-Ingrid. Get him while he's comfortable. A wise man knows never to drop his guard.*

She moves swiftly towards Klippel's scarlet pavilion; it is dyed the most vibrant hue inside and out, so at first it's hard to distinguish the blood from the décor. The concubine is sprawled across her bed, a blossom of dark red growing across her dress. Her eyes are glazing, and her chest barely rising and falling.

With a wordless cry, Ingrid rushes to her friend and scoops her up in both arms. She holds her tight, shaking with anger and fear. She looks around the tent, desperately seeking Pridbjørn.

"Where?" she whispers. "Who?"

Klippel fights for air, then manages "Osa" in a crimson exhalation.

In dreadful certainty, Ingrid does not run to Osa's tent, but to Magnus's. His cursed wife would have taken the baby there, to show her husband how great a mother she could be. But no. *No.* Osa would not care to keep the bastard child. What good would that do her? Nothing, nothing. But a dead child? A missing one? Another of Ingrid's newborns disappeared into thin air?

There would be no marrying her executioner this time.

Heedless of obstacles and wild looks, Ingrid races back across the encampment. The world is a blur, a haze of tears and speed. If Pridbjørn is gone . . . Not even revenge would be enough to sustain her. She would not survive the loss. Smoke rises through holes burnt in the pavilion's silk panels. Tapestries and velvet draperies have ignited; wooden beams and support poles creak in the heat. All such perfect tinder for Ingrid's fire. Its sizzling is now like laughter in her ears, maliciously hissing admonishment. She rushes in, choking on fumes and fear.

Magnus's wife is placing Pridbjørn on the bed beside his still-sleeping sire. She straightens and faces Ingrid with a skewed smile. Red streaks her white gown. Her left arm is crooked, mangled; the right hangs limp behind her back. One glance is all Ingrid needs to see that here is one pushed too far.

Osa has not come to save her husband, but to let his son die with him.

The back wall of the tent is now a mass of orange and black. Noxious vapours fill their nostrils, making them dizzy. As Ingrid watches, a line of fire streaks overhead, splitting the ceiling and letting dawn peek through. Burning cinders drift down, threatening to ignite their hair, their clothing, their very skin. She is distracted for no more than a second—long enough that she very nearly dies under Osa's knife, still bright with Klippel's blood.

There is no telling whistle of steel through air, no grunt of exertion; Ingrid senses the other woman's lunge, and steps aside almost fast enough to avoid injury. Almost.

A seam of red opens up along her arm, from shoulder to elbow, where her sidestep gave Osa the chance to curve her blade around. In spite of the agony, Ingrid clasps her hands and before the crazed woman can collect herself for another attack, slams her doubled fists against the bridge of Osa's perfect nose. The *crunch* is loud even above the crackling of the flames. Magnus's wife falls slowly, staring up as Ingrid swoops.

The object in her hand catches the fire's bright light and flashes orange-blue sparks. The sturdy tines of the blue bird comb-brooch pierces Osa's throat, rake into the flesh. Ingrid yanks hard and turns it like a plough furrowing the soil. Osa gurgles her last.

Ingrid sweeps up her son, who is awake and bawling. She pauses, ever so briefly, to examine Magnus. He is still, frail and small in death. The smoke got to him before the flames—she both mourns him and is aggrieved that his passing was painless.

She stumbles from the burning tent.

Outside, clusters of Fae are gathering, staring at her and the raging bonfire. No-one tries to find water; they all know it's too late.

"Osa," Ingrid coughs when someone finally asks her what happened. "Osa killed Magnus and Klippel, and tried to kill my son!"

Somewhere in the crowd, Liljana wails. Her keening, raw and unrestrained, calls to Ingrid's pain, draws it out. Clinging to Pridbjørn, she falls to her knees and howls. *That* convinces them—a woman's weeping will sway the most powerful of doubters—that and the fact she is once again whiter than milk poured over marble. Whiter than a winter's dawn. Whiter, even, than Mymnir herself.

Even now, none dare touch her, none move to embrace or comfort the jarl's mistress. Ingrid's tears dry in the heat of the flames. Her composure returns on its own, unhindered but unhelped by the courtiers surrounding her. Getting to her feet, she moves away from the tent, pushing blindly through the throng. As she goes, she tells someone, she's unsure who, that if they return to the isle, they will find their Queen once more in residence. She does not mention the white raven's lack of interest in them. They will find out for themselves soon enough.

Pridbjørn, quietened with the prize of a full fat breast, dozes as Ingrid stands at a safe distance from the conflagration, jaw set, soot and blood now her only colouring. She does not face the fire, but rather watches the blaze's reflection dance across the crystal palace's slick facade. The frozen confection is melting. So close to the inferno, crenellations and turrets and vast picture windows have begun to drip and crack. The castle creaks and moans on its foundations, the structure's integrity already vulnerable; for days, unnoticed, spring zephyrs have warmed the coastline, heralding Mymnir's return.

Soon the fires will leap from pavilion to pavilion. Soon the Fae's longest solstice will end, their folly crashing around them, splashing into puddles that will seep into the thawing ground, erasing all trace of their presence. In the pandemonium that follows, fed by the fear that their Queen will discover their lack of faith, their petty squabbling, their contemplated treachery, Ingrid will plan her escape. She will attend to her arm and to her son's hurts. She will don a mourning gown, perform the mourning rituals, behave as is to be expected. And for a while, she will be scrutinised, maybe pitied, certainly disdained. She will ignore it all—their sneers and their condemnation alike. She is well-practised in feigning submission. But soon enough, when their glances begin to skim over her, when she blends into the sea of silver and white, no longer marked or remarkable, Ingrid will slip away. She will find the fir tree with signs of carefully disturbed earth at it base and dig up the satchel she buried there, filled with all the small valuable things she has collected. She will once more trace a path down to the boats and settle her son in the bottom of the strongest *faering*.

She will revel in being alone, free.

But for now, she will remain and contemplate her handiwork, smiling secretly.

# Kveldúlfr

*Oh, hark! Hear me sing for a pittance wage,*
*While I kneel to clean Her Majesty's stage;*
*Scrubbing away the one truth in this age:*
*We've a queen who eats seed and shits in a cage.*

Anonymous, *Servants' Quarters Doggerel*

Fálki knows something is lurking in the shadows.

He feels it watching as he creeps along the winding passage between the palace's great kitchens, with their ovens taller than a man and their tables fit for a giant, and the laundry, where the tubs of bubbling hot water are large enough to bathe in. Though he tells himself it's nothing, just a trick of the light, he has seen the glimmer of yellow orbs in the darkness between torches. He can't ignore the creature's stench, a gross undertone spoiling the warm aromas emanating from the cooks' fires. It laps Fálki's skin, damp and foetid, leaving him feeling unclean. And no matter how quietly he scurries from chore to chore, the sniffing, the snuffling stalks him. He knows it knows him by scent.

He tries not to imagine what the thing wants.

Fálki yearns to be brave, but he is not courageous and all the wishing in the world will not make him so. He start-stops along the servants' corridor, flitting from sconce to flickering sconce, lingering in the small pools of light long enough to calm his racing heart, then dashing through the black, praying his bladder won't betray him—again—before he makes it to the laundry. On his back is a bundle of linen, ready for boiling and steaming and pressing with heavy irons heated on huge stoves. He always carries his burdens in such a way that they might be used as a defence, a distraction, to buy him precious seconds. Fálki secretly hopes the extra bulk will convince others he is big. Threatening. Someone who can put up a good fight.

In truth, he is small and dark. With better nutrition he might become stocky as an adolescent and strong as a man, but in recent years Mymnir's generosity to the menials—those whose place is well below the stairs—has been strained. He gets enough only when he can steal it, but the under-cooks have gimlet eyes, and they are not kind. Especially not Hjötra.

This night, Fálki is tracked by two hunters, although he senses only one. Carefully placing each foot in front of the other, he chants to himself to be strong, be brave, be swift. But this night, it does not matter how gallant he is or how weak. As he creeps past the deepest black between two hefty columns, the murk moves, converges into teeth, nails, muscles—and lunges.

Taloned hands pluck him from the ground, coarse arms coil around him, constricting, suffocating. Then the creature bounds away with a satisfied humming that loosens the boy's bowels even as he passes out.

Perched in the rafters, the second observer catches only the briefest blur of motion. A shifting wrinkle in the gloom. Then a tumble of soiled linens, the torn bag of laundry deflated and abandoned. The boy's departure so swift he did not even get a chance to swing.

---

When Fálki wakes, he is bruised. His wrist stings and he finds it's bleeding from several marks that look like they were made by sharp teeth. He is lying on a pile of books—rather, pages ripped from books, dog-eared and rumpled and strewn in a rough circle around him. It's a strange sort of nest, the kind a fussy animal might make, but an animal nevertheless. The air is rank, pungent with musk. Fálki notes he has not been allowed on the dusty four-poster wedged between two bookshelves. In the middle of the chamber, there is a crude pine table, upon which sit slightly neater stacks of bound folios, rolls of parchment, quills stuck in inkwells, and a *nátt-lamp* feebly drawing blackness from the room. The lamp is *old*, the design of a sort that hasn't been used for many years. Fálki has seen etchings and woodcuts of the palace's early days, framed and displayed in the kitchens; of a time when bulbs such as this hung clustered from chandeliers, not scintillating but absorbing evening dark, complementing regular candles, which gleamed all the brighter in their opposites' company. Hjötra raps his knuckles each time she catches him mooning over the images, but that doesn't stop Fálki from looking. Once, just once, he'd love to be bathed in such a glow.

But this one weak lantern barely blots the deep grey pressing in from all sides. So close to the table, Fálki is rendered in charcoal and soot. He hears someone snuffling heavily, shuffling and scuffing just out of sight.

"I've been watching you." The voice, when it comes, it rough and raw, as if it's not been used in a long time; but the tone is playful, a little naughty.

"I know," says the boy and coughs. "My throat hurts."

"My grip was a little tight." Fálki senses that the speaker shrugs. "I haven't held anything so—carefully—for a long time. One forgets, where to place one's hands, how firmly to squeeze."

Fálki shivers. "What do you want? I'm nobody."

"On the contrary, my dear Fálki—see, I know your name, I have taken the trouble to learn it. Doesn't that tell you how important you are?" He falters, as if losing track of his purpose, then recapturing it. "Yes, very important. I'm afraid I need help and you are precisely what I am looking for."

"But I'm just a *kólbitr*."

"Coal-biter?"

"I clear ashes from the kitchen hearths, and from the fires beneath the laundry. Sometimes I carry things back and forth."

"My, what a specialised society that little bird has created! So clever, so ambitious a thief." The speaker laughs loudly, wildly; he experiments with modulation, as if trying to find what volume *should* do. "Now, Fálki, don't be alarmed."

The man who steps into the dim light isn't too frightening. He is taller, certainly, than the loftiest Fae. His skin has none of their translucence: his is an olive complexion. His hair is blacker than the filth Fálki scoops daily from the grates, as is his untidy goatee. His mouth is full and when he smiles, Fálki shivers. The teeth are long and white, but for the pink tint where Fálki's blood has left its mark. And the eyes, the large lupine eyes, are piercing, luminous amber.

"Not so fearsome?" asks the stranger. Fálki shakes his head and the man laughs. "A lie, but a brave one. We are helping each other already."

"But what can *I* do?" quavers Fálki, not feeling braver for this one's presence.

The large handsome head nods and the shoulders hunch forward as if to emphasise trust. He speaks with a low, conspiratorial fervour. "For weeks I've been planning a surprise for your Queen. Oh, I know what you're thinking: how do you surprise someone who already has everything? A whole kingdom, simpering courtiers, endless feasts, vassals to clean up after the revelry—not to mention little coal-biters like yourself. Well. You see this research? All the study?"

He gestures at the mess of papers crinkling beneath Fálki, then turns to the table. It does look like a lot of work.

"Oh, how Mymnir will jump to see me here after all these years, to see I've done all this for her! There is a book missing, though, a special book . . . Can you keep a secret?"

The boy gulps, but straightens up. He is no tattletale. Lovers' trysts, illegitimate births, premature deaths—he hears these and other mysteries whispered and grunted and moaned at night as he scours the chimney flues running from the cellars all the way up to the palace's top floors. Come morning, they are written in blood on the bed sheets Fálki carries to the laundry. And though he reads them well, he never says a word.

"There's a lad," says the man as Fálki, nodding, presses his lips firmly shut. "Inside this book is the perfect surprise for a queen—not the story, no. Something much, much dearer: a magic key."

Fálki's eyes widen.

"The most precious key in this great heap of rocks, and your queen has had it all along—without even knowing it! Can you imagine? So now it's up to us to get it from her. We'll polish it, make sure it still works, and then show her exactly what it does.

But for now, we must move quietly, unobtrusively. That's where you come in."

"You w-w-w-want me to steal from the Queen?" The boy thinks his heart might stop.

"Ah, how can you steal what she does not know she has? As for the book, you're merely borrowing it. We will return it when I have my—*the*—key." There is that smile again, reassuring, kind. "That's all right, isn't it?"

Fálki inclines his head slowly.

"Then we are friends and you shall help me. You can pass unseen in these halls, Fálki. No-one pays attention to you—I mean no offense, of course! It is a rare talent, to be invisible. Never underestimate its value, my young man."

"Why can't you look for it yourself?" asks Fálki, momentarily bold, then wishes to bite his own tongue off.

But the man guffaws. "What if she should catch me? I do not have your aptitude for passing unseen! Imagine me trying to sneak about? No, no. I am too clumsy, too cumbersome. The game will be ruined before it's begun."

Fálki recalls how the man has stalked him and thinks he does it well enough, but his sense of self-preservation wins out, and he simply nods once more.

"Begin your search immediately! The sooner we find the book, the sooner I shall present my gift to your Queen. The sooner she and I shall be reacquainted." The man helps him up, tenderly patting the wound on his wrist. The blood has become sluggish. "Go, now, and come back to me soonest."

The boy takes a few short steps, then hesitates. "There are so many, many books . . . How will I know I've found the right one?"

Chuckling, the man sidles up and leans in close. "Oh, you'll recognise it immediately." His breath clouds Fálki's vision, causing tears—but not because it is foul. The scent is suddenly heartbreaking: it's fresh summer air after a long dark winter; it's warm breezes across wide, open meadows after a lifetime spent cramped in a cool, damp cave; it's an endless moonlit night awash in silver after decades scorched in noontide sun. Fálki inhales and his lungs fill with distilled longing. He exhales and tastes the essence of promised joy.

"Follow your nose, boy. It won't lead you astray."

Blinking, Fálki asks, "But where am I?"

"Ah, yes. This is the eastern storeroom. No-one comes here anymore, although it is very comfortable. Out you go, boy—follow the furniture. When the beds end and become tables, and the tables become chairs, and the unused bookcases come up on your right, then turn left. It will take you a while, but you'll find yourself in a corridor that leads to the furnaces—no doubt you can find your way from there. Be quick about it and make sure no-one sees you."

The boy sets off uncertainly into the dark jungle of carved oak and mahogany and maple.

"Oh, and Fálki?"

He looks over his shoulder and sees the lamp manipulate the man's features in a way that makes him seem less than open, less than benign.

"Make *sure* no-one sees you."

---

When Hjötra considers Fálki she finds too much of herself in him. He reminds her of what she once was, what, in her heart, she still is: small and afraid and terribly unimportant. Once she was thin as he is, but with her hard-won position came the right to extra servings and the chance to steal as much food from the larder as she can stuff into her round cheeks. Now she waddles when she walks, constantly sweating from the effort of lugging her body around. Her dimpled knees ache when she stands and crack relentlessly until she sits, groaning and huffing as she lowers herself. Beneath a streaked layer of flour, she is always flushed. Her pulse is forever racing.

The other under-cooks and all the apprentices laugh when they think Hjötra cannot hear. Even so, she does not stop hoarding sweets, swilling thick cream, gnawing on fat slices of cheese. She licks every last glob of butter from her hands, then dips them back into the pot for more. Small loaves of white bread are flattened and squeezed into her apron pockets; she nibbles at them throughout the day, even after she is well and truly full. She looks at Fálki, acutely remembering what it was like to be him—alone, pathetic, hungry—and is compelled to eat some more.

Only her fingers are delicately plump; they nimbly roll pastries, knuckle dough with confidence, and can sugar any fruit without so much as bruising the skin. One day she will reign in the kitchens, head cook over all; she is a dab hand with spices and sauces. Mymnir, fussiest of eaters, can always be tempted by a dish seasoned with one of Hjötra's concoctions. And when the Queen is sated, promotions abound. The cooks tolerate Hjötra for this reason alone.

Tonight, when the boy creeps into the kitchen, she is first to spot him.

"Where have you been, little *kólbitr*? And look at you! Filthier than the hearthstones you've neglected all evening. Disgusting, lazy—ah! Get away!"

Wielding a hard wooden spoon, she raps him across the wrist as he tries to pilfer a scrap of smoked venison from a trencher on the table, and misses. Fálki sneers, a growl forming in the pit of his belly.

"I'm starving," he says, bolder than ever.

"No work, no food. And certainly none of our lady's meat!"

"But it's well past dinner—she's already had her fill . . . "

Salivating, the boy reaches out and hooks a juicy slice. *Yes, hooks*, Hjötra notices; his blackened nails dart across the board like spurs, like barbs. Then they're back to normal, cracked and small, with grime ingrained in each crease. Fálki wolfs down his catch and goes for another—but this time the under-cook is prepared.

"Enough," she says, spoon raising a red welt on his arm. "Go."

He scowls and gathers his shovel and broom.

"First the grease traps need emptying," she says, pinching him when he doesn't move fast enough for her liking. "Then the ashes."

Dropping his tools, the boy spins and glowers at her—and for a moment, it seems he glares *down* from an undue height. Hands clenched, he grits his teeth and fetches the slop bucket, the muscle in his jaw flexing and relaxing. Flexing and relaxing. Flexing.

*If he has the strength for such anger*, Hjötra thinks, *he is being fed too generously*. His rations, she decides, will be reduced by half.

---

*Neither of us is leaving here until you're done.*

The fat under-cook had plunked herself down on a high-backed chair between the fireplace and the door, and set to work shelling peas for the morrow's luncheon. The crisp sound of pods snapping, stems and tails plinking into one metal bowl, fruit plonking into another, had accompanied Fálki as he sloshed scum and fat and oil from traps beneath the spits. He'd carted the sludge to the dumbwaiter and lowered the lot down, bucket load by bucket load, to be rendered into tallow. Now he tamps the late-night embers with the back of his short iron shovel, his temper still as red as the coals. His stomach gurgles.

*How am I to find the book with her here?*
*Where do I even begin to look?*

The library is on the opposite side of the palace, much higher up the mountainside, well away from smithy and furnaces and glassblowers' fires. It would take most of the night to sneak there and days, if not weeks, to search through all the shelves . . . And no matter what the shadow-man says, Fálki has a hard time believing that none would notice his presence in the glittering corridors upstairs where only the fairest Fae dare tread.

He works his way from woodstove to bread oven, inglenook to grand hearth, his arms tired and covered in soot. It must be well beyond midnight, he thinks, body aching for the tiny cot awaiting him in the servants' quarters. Kneeling to scrub at the back of the kitchen's largest fireplace, Fálki feels a cool draught seeping down the chimney. Lifting his head, he catches a delicious scent on the breeze.

Longing. Moonlight. Wildflowers and . . . something much more tantalising.

Something warm and still and vulnerable . . .

He peers up the flue then over at Hjötra. The repetitive shunting of scoop and ash, the gentle whisking of broom across stones, has lulled her into a light doze. Patiently, the boy continues to sweep, bristles *shh-shhhh-shhhhhhh*ing a slow, clean rhythm, until his guard begins to snore. He waits a few moments longer, just to be sure she's really asleep, then downs tools. Quietly, he stands and cranes his neck, examining the chimney, assessing. The inner walls are blackened and a bit slippery, but the irregular stones jut out, offering plenty of finger- and toe-holds. The shaft is only slightly heated; at this late hour, most of the chambers' fires have been banked. Yellow light flickers three or four floors overhead, casting weird umbra and setting will-o-the-wisp sparks rising to the tiny rectangle of sky barely visible far, far above. No need to worry, though; those flames emanate from floors much higher than Fálki needs to climb. If he ascends just one level, he'll be free.

He licks his lips, runs his long tongue over serrated teeth.

Yes, that tang on the air is *freedom*.

---

The tabby isn't much to look at, but she smells divine.

Wedged in the flue, Fálki's legs start to shake—from the exertion of holding himself in position, but also excitement. Looking out from the throat of a first-floor fireplace, he can see the cat comfortably huddled on the hearthstones, sleeping soundly. His lips quiver and he's overwhelmed by an urge to bite down on her soft, round rump. Using his sleeve, he quickly brushes the cinders in front of him off to one side. Leaning further forward, he presses his stomach into the ledge until his ribs jam against the floor. Scrabbling for purchase with his nails, he digs his heels into the wall and hoists himself out of the chimney, tumbling into the room with a spill of clinkers and ash.

Two low armchairs sit unoccupied nearby. Between them a polished table is laden with goblets and decanters, waiting to be cleared. Heavy tapestries hang on all four walls, failing to trap warmth in the chilly space, and high arched doors bracket the chamber.

*A vestibule outside the grand refectory*, Fálki guesses, then all thoughts scatter as the cat wakes. She springs to her feet, bolts across the flagstones—and the boy's attention is riveted on the chase.

He skitters after her, primed, slavering for the hunt. They weave around rows of long tables in the feasting hall, ducking beneath some and clambering over others. Fálki's tongue lolls as he runs— he can practically taste the salt, the redness, the iron of fresh meat. Once, only once, his fingers brush the tip of the cat's tail and his energy soars. Panting, he follows her upstairs and down, along white marble corridors, sweeping galleries and colonnades, past chambermaids and guards and ethereal Fae gliding from one room to the next—and none of them pay him any attention. It's just as the prowling man had said! For an instant, the boy feels invisible. Invincible.

Hungry.

He wants to howl *I'm here! I'm alive!*

He wants to run for miles in the moonlight, wearing nothing but his skin.

But the cat is far cleverer than Fálki, and faster, smaller, more manoeuvrable. She bounds ahead, jinks to the left, then the right, leaving her pursuer utterly wrong-footed as she squeezes through a gap seemingly too narrow for her bulk. Fálki runs, face-first, into a wall, bounces back and thuds on his arse, shaking his head and tonguing at the thin trickle of blood coming from a cut on his lip.

When his addled brain clears, Fálki looks around. The cat has led him on such a chase that he doesn't know this corridor. He doesn't recognise a single stick of furniture, nor a painting, nor a nick in any of the stone walls. Fálki is utterly lost. He stands and, sighing, begins the long trudge to find a place where he belongs.

---

A single candle burns on a turned ivory table beside the empty bed. Fálki's footsteps echo across the chamber, telling him the space is far vaster than the low flame reveals. Gilded mirrors glint on the walls, and in their reflections Fálki discerns witch bottles on shelves, rich hangings, a grand harp without any strings. Jewels stud the bedposts between flimsy curtains, their facets twinkling like *græmlings'* eyes. He creeps further into the room, stepping from cold stone onto a great round rug, its pile so thick he feels like burrowing down into it and hibernating for months.

The book, however, compels him to keep moving.

He can smell it—the nip in the air, the promise of wide open spaces, the call of forests and valleys and waves crashing over his longship's prow—yes, yes, it's close. It's here, somewhere.

Though he's alone, Fálki is uneasy. He cocks his ears, hears animal-like scritching overhead. *Mice,* he thinks, *scurrying along the beams.* But he can't detect a hint of their feral odour, not even a whiff of spoor and decay. Just the book's beckoning perfume, another cloying scent like roses and spice and a damp tone that can only be sadness. *This is a lady's bower,* he realises as he approaches the light, sees the luxurious rabbit and fox furs strewn across the mattress and the fine dusting of down on their bristles. Pure white plumes float down out of the darkness, a gentle feathered snow.

Fálki peers upwards but the candle is too weak; he can't see much of anything past the canopy. Nerves grip him and he almost runs, runs like the rodents hiding in the ceiling, safe and small and inconsequential.

Oh, but that fragrance! He can't resist, he can't run. He won't. *I'll find the man's precious book ... and ask for a precious reward.*

A reward! Fálki hadn't considered payment until now, but the more he ponders the idea, the more he thinks it only fair. *No work, no food*, Hjötra was always telling him—justly, the man can't expect to get something for nothing. That's unreasonable. And, oh—what a good thought he's just had! He can hardly bear to contemplate it ...

The boy's bony chest swells and he thinks, at first, he'll be ill. He drops to his knees to catch his breath, clutching at his stomach and pressing his face against the coverlet's wonderfully soft fabric. Heart pounding, palms sweating, he feels a smile curve up his face and soon his cheeks are throbbing from the strength of it. His limbs are bloodless, they're made of wilted leaves, and the breeze of his quiet laughter threatens to blow them all away. Slumping onto the carpet, he rests his head on blades of silk and wool, the finest pillow he's ever known, and gives himself a minute to mull over his plan.

As he lies there, his vision adjusts to the gloom and he begins to make sense of the shapes beneath the lady's bed. Flat squares, tubes, rectangles. Papers, scrolls ... books. Dozens of them, scattered, caked in dust and fluff. His gaze alights on one unremarkable tome. No bigger than his two hands side-by-side, covered in worn black leather, bloated with fray-edged pages. It is small and plain—and it seems to sing to him. This one holds the man's key; he can smell it, he can taste it. Reaching out, he stretches until the muscles in his neck pull taut, fumbling at the piles until he comes up with the prize.

*This is hope*, he thinks. *This is hope.*

---

With the book carefully tucked into the front of his tunic, Fálki slips out the door. The palace's lavish corridors seem to welcome him now. Courtiers smile as he passes, their expressions inviting as they promenade the hallways, speaking to each other in fluting voices. The bracing scent of peppermint surrounding them seems designed for the boy's pleasure alone. He walks openly beneath a line of muted chandeliers and doesn't shy away from the torchlight when he passes decorative candelabras. Previously stern guards watch him make his way from room to room, nodding their approval.

*I will remain up here with you all soon enough*, Fálki thinks, grinning at everyone and everything. *And I will wear smart boots and a fine velvet coat, just like the valets.*

In exchange for the book, Fálki will ask his friend to take him on as a pageboy. From the mess in the storeroom it's clear the man doesn't yet have one . . . The boy has proven he can fetch books—he'll find all the volumes in the palace, if asked—and he can clean and lay fires and run errands. He will keep himself neat and tidy, he'll polish his new shoes, he'll tame his hair with a hat, he'll promise not to sleep in his new jacket. And he won't ask for much in return: a simple pallet and blanket, a hot meal once a day—even a cold one, he'd settle for cold—but most importantly, a life above ground. Days and nights spent outside the kitchens. Away from the fireplaces. Free of Hjötra.

As he trots through the ballroom toward the servants' passageway, he's so excited he can almost ignore the hollowness inside him, the acidic burning as his gut writhes with hunger. His ears perk at the sound of scrub-brushes rasping on the flecked marble tiles. Sniffing, he scrunches his nose; the half-breed women and children kneeling over soapy patches stink of unwashed bodies, skin and bones. His stomach turns. Mullioned windows run from floor to ceiling on Fálki's left, letting in great washes of silver-blue light. For a moment the cleaners look bloated and drowned, like the corpse Esther the laundress once found, floating face-down in her tub.

His excitement ebbs, then curdles as the moon comes into view; a sense of disquiet grows as his shadow stretches across the floor. It is elongated, alien, as all shadows are, but its reach is unsettling. It seems to be cast by a much taller person, a bulkier boy with bigger hands and unexpected tufts of hair. Fálki opens his mouth to gasp, but a gurgle escapes instead. He is overcome by a sudden and intense desire to sink his teeth into raw flesh, to tear and gnaw at it, to feed.

It will be safe now; Hjötra will have left her post, abashed that she nodded off while on duty. And his friend will not begrudge him a few minutes to fill his belly with stolen sweetmeats. Or perhaps the rest of that venison . . .

Leaving the bright upstairs world behind, Fálki ghosts through the scullery then tiptoes into the cavernous kitchen. Carefully crossing the cool flags, he wends around worktables and chopping blocks before ducking into one of the palace's larders. There are four, all large enough to be a noble's bed chamber, each with its own fire, table, shelving, and drying racks. Normally, this is Fálki's idea of bliss. Yet now that he's to be a lord's attendant—for his friend *must* be a lord, he's decided, otherwise he wouldn't have the gold for so many books, so much fine furniture—Fálki's bound to earn even better quarters. Again, he is tickled, but this pleasure is smothered by his ravenous appetite, and surprise.

The larder he's chosen is not empty.

Hjötra rounds on him.

"What are you doing here, little speck? Whelp? Come to steal again? When we're so good to you?" She still has a wooden spoon in her hand, which she whips back and forth just so the sound will frighten the boy.

But Fálki is strangely calm. He squares his shoulders, raises his chin and thinks, *This is what it feels like to be brave.*

---

When he wakes, Fálki is wet and sticky.

The sensation is unpleasant and the odour makes him feel ill. Conversely, his belly is full, as full as it's ever been, and for the first time in his life he is sated. He takes a moment to revel in that feeling, takes a moment of *elation*; but the smell is too much. The stickiness beneath him demands attention.

Shivering, he sits up. His muscles are stiff, pain lances his back, and a terrible ringing echoes in his ears. He knuckles the crust from his eyes, then freezes. For hours—all night? all day?—he has been nestled in a puddle of blood and entrails. Beside him is a torso, the ribcage visible through the torn flesh; he was curled around it in his sleep. Eight beautiful fingers are lined up next to him on the floor, their tips peeking out from under a spattered linen handkerchief. They look like little porcelain dolls lying there, white and smooth and lovely; like favourite toys he'd tucked into bed before nodding off. In one corner of the kitchen is a half-chewed leg; in the fireplace smoulders what appears to be an arm. The rich scent of roasting fills Fálki's nostrils and makes his mouth water. He swallows, blinks hard, looks up, trying to steel himself, caught between ecstasy and visceral nausea. On the spokes of an iron and antler chandelier suspended above the table hangs the other leg, its slipper pending precariously from the big toe. There is no sign of the other arm.

Slowly, Fálki rises. First to his hands and knees, stretching like a cat, then he stands and surveys the rest of the kitchen. Ah! There is the head, neatly placed in the centre of a great silver serving dish—an apple has been jammed between the under-cook's teeth. Next to the platter, on the table, surprisingly clean, is the book.

The boy's humanity gets the better of him and he vomits, long and hard. Someone will spend hours cleaning the mess, but Fálki knows it won't be him. He will be lucky to survive this day. He snatches up his prize and flees, heedless of the scritching and scratching ever following after him.

---

Covered in dark and drying red, Fálki stumbles into the man's sanctum, past the paper nest, to find his one and only friend balled in the middle of the four poster bed. His face is more densely bearded than before and his hands are shaggy and too pointed. In the dim light, his outline wavers: now expanding, an ogre's shape looming over the storeroom; now receding, a near-invisible shade, the mirage of a person on the mattress. As he sleeps, unaware of the boy's scrutiny, the creature's back legs twitch as if he chases rabbits in his dreams.

"What's happening to me?" wails Fálki and the slumberer sits bolt upright, instantly alert. "What have you done to me?"

"Oh, just a little nip." He smiles slyly. "You're welcome. Made you brave, didn't it? I take it *someone* won't be bothering you again."

Fálki senses the truth in the words but cannot get the smell of gore out of his nostrils. His heart sinks and he can't speak through the tears clogging his throat. Scrubbing at his cheeks and nose, he inches into the room. There will be no velvet coat, no upstairs, no sunshine for him. No such gifts from this man's scruffy hands, he realises.

The man's eyes go to the tome in the boy's trembling grip.

"You found it!" he shouts and bounces off the bed. "Oh, the waiting in the darkness, the endless waiting, watching her paw through all my books! She was at it forever! And you've soiled it—but that's all right, I'll forgive you because now, you wonderful boy, now I can leave this forsaken palace!"

But before he can get close enough to wrench the treasure from Fálki's crooked clutches a voice cuts through the musty air.

"Lóki, you look... different." Mymnir glides into view, trailing her own light with her. She is lovely, as ever, wearing a long satin robe that seems to drip around her curves. Unbound, her hair spills over her svelte shoulders and down to her calves. Her feet are bare—she treads silently—and apart from the delicate ribbon of a rose-coloured chain around her neck, the white raven goes unadorned.

The god watches her, his expression one of disappointment and disdain. Shaking his head, he pins on a smile, concentrates to lose his wolfish mien.

"Hello, thief!" He holds up a hand, displays the thickly raised flesh where a series of ridged scars have turned white. "Bitten by that fucking Fenrir, can you believe it? You try to rescue a fellow when the world starts crumbling—by the way, you outdid yourself there, little *hrafn*—and *this* is the thanks you get. Ah, offspring..."

Mymnir smirks. "And I gather this creature is yet another of them," she says smoothly, taking up position between god and wolf-boy. She views Fálki speculatively. *The perfect spy*, she thinks; she really would not have noticed him had she not been looking for him. "I almost didn't recognise you."

"You're one to talk, bird. Last time I saw you, you were winging through the stacks in my library, shitting on my scribes, blunting your talons on my oldest volumes. Always had a penchant for mindless destruction, haven't you? First my collection, then Ásgarðr..."

"Yet you survived."

"Of course I did. Of course. It will take a lot more than a meddlesome featherbrain to bring me down. I'll admit, though, that your tinkering has upset things somewhat... I forgot who I was for such a long time! Gradually, I came back to myself, but I simply cannot stop this shifting. Black-haired or red, man or woman, giant or billygoat—for years I'd fall asleep not knowing who I'd be once I woke. And you know me, love a good shift, but not when it's without my will. *Now*, however..."

Lóki grins and doubles in height. His tan deepens and the mess of sable ringlets blaze crimson, while his beard flashes red beneath an off-kilter nose. Muscular arms outstretched, he half-sketches a bow, towering over Mymnir. "It took ages to remember what I look like. And, if I let my mind wander, or idly think of something frivolous—poof! I'm a salmon. Very inconvenient."

"So that's how you got here? Swam upstream into this world?"

"No, no, no." Lóki clicks his tongue. "Unlike you, I learn from my mistakes... and Óðinn once made it clear that the fish shape is not my forté. But books! Books inside a library inside a kingdom box! Ah, that's something else entirely. You carried me here yourself, folded up, sleeping between pages. The folding is agony, you know—and so many paper cuts! But I suppose I owe you thanks, little thief. No point hiding myself away if I was simply left to burn with the rest of the Æsir." The god appears anything but grateful. "Enough chit-chat, child. What do you want?"

Mymnir bristles at the man's condescension. Her smile is venomous. "Boy—give me what you stole."

But Fálki is too caught up in his distress to respond. He looks from one to the other, tears cutting runnels through the reddish-brown smears on his cheeks.

"Uh-uh, no." All Lóki seems to do is turn, but then he is gone, flashing through the room like a phantasm, transforming just a little, just a tad, then he's beside the boy and plucking the book from Fálki's nerveless fingers. "I'll be taking that."

Mymnir's eyes narrow. Nothing else—a mere squint—and the temperature drops. A polar gale whips through the storeroom, fluttering scattered pages, long hair, rumpled sheets and tattered draperies. "You set wards, didn't you? Around the kingdom box?"

Reluctantly, Lóki nods. "How many souvenirs of Ásgarðr does one little bird need? Mistletoe spears, lore-guardians, and so many seeds—of course I set wards! But they went wrong. The magic got skewed on the journey from the old world, no doubt after someone—" he directs a pointed stare at Mymnir "—ran off with our memories. Instead of keeping others out, the ward-chains closed around *me*. I woke only when you started snooping—but I was no longer the tiny casket's master. Now, though . . . " His chuckle is deep, sonorous, and as savage as the Queen's expression. "Now I remember just enough."

Lóki balances the volume upright on his palms—it looks ridiculously small in his hands—and blows across the cut edges of the pages. The book falls open, willing as a whore. The god, still a touch lupine, grins. He runs the ivory points of his nails down the page, muttering, contorting his scarlet tongue around ancient phrases. As he speaks, glowing letters, accents, words rise off the page, floating and flickering like lantern bugs around him. Agog, Fálki watches. Mymnir's rasping breath inaudible under Lóki's triumphant spell. The Fae Queen is crouched, hands pressed against her ears as the stolen magic responds to its true master's voice; yet the thief can feel the wayward enchantments boring into her skin like fleas that threaten to undo her.

When it seems she can bear it no longer, Lóki's stream of words is spent, and he finishes with a shout: *lykill* and *ríki* and *svín-fylking*. The floating syllables shatter, burst, clot and finally transform. There are shapes, letters, yellow and orange like a smith's ingots, each swelling grunting, each becoming a spectral boar. The swine fall into line, forming a wedge-shaped phalanx.

Their ethereal trotters spark on the flagstones, the walls, the ceiling. They make one lap of the storeroom, snorting, sniffing, searching for the locks into which their tusks fit, before thundering out the door. The god whoops with glee.

"Watch," Lóki says, waving his hand, and matter becomes immaterial. Fálki can see through walls, he can see outside, see the animals coursing through the air, rushing beyond the building's confines, gouging their teeth into shimmering fortifications, shining chains, glimmering towers that have been there for centuries, hidden in the netherworld between the old and the new, only now visible around Mymnir's palace. One by one, the bonds are broken and those very same fortifications and chains and towers explode, disintegrating in a shower of gold dust. The boars progress from lock to lock with military precision, opening them before smashing each one as they would a foe.

Lóki's laughter takes on a shrill edge, a delight so powerful it borders on delirium.

He picks up a wilted Mymnir, slings his hands around her waist like an overly large belt, and they spin about as if they are at a masque, a courting couple. She is so wan, so drained from the wards' attack that she seems no threat, merely a rag doll in his arms. He does not watch *her*, instead keeps his attention on the swine-army as it forges his freedom, and so does not see Mymnir remove her necklace.

Had he paid attention, looked closer, he would have known by the marks in its metal, the strangely smooth links, that it is a dwarven ribbon-fetter. Strong enough to bind Fenrir. Forged by Helga Ögmundardóttir long, long ago. He feels the thing coiling up his bicep, determined as a snake. With a bellow, he throws it, and the Queen, across the room before the tether can take proper hold.

Mymnir hits the wall and is winded. If her bones were those of a bird, she might have been crushed, but as it is she is made of stronger mettle. She stands, squares her shoulders—she has not been manhandled in more than an aeon—and pride prevents her from gasping as she wants to.

"Do not think to pit your feeble magic against mine, little bird. You forget yourself: I am a god!"

"This world has more gods than you can imagine, Lóki." Mymnir laughs, but keeps a safe distance, thinking of all the wicked things the trickster has done in the name of amusing himself. Thinking, perhaps, of her aching back, the throbbing of her skull. Thinking, perhaps, that discretion is the better part of valour.

There is a new sound, a high chorus between a click and a squeal, issuing from many throats. All of the locks have been sundered, the boars' task complete. Lóki's roar splits the air; its force knocks Fálki, now forgotten, to the floor. The god, hair flaming behind him like a banner, strides towards the door.

"What will you do?" asks Mymnir, the words coming unbidden from her lips. This gives Lóki pause.

"I will . . . I will seek that which is lost."

And he is gone.

Fear trickles down Fálki's leg, soaks through his pants. *Not so brave now* . . . He whimpers as the Queen's feet appear near his face. Terror and the force of Lóki's betrayal have shaken his shape loose. Half-wolf, fangs gouge into his chin. Pointed ears twitch then lie flat against his head. Fálki shuts his lids, presses muzzle to knobbly knees and tries to shrink into oblivion. *It's a rare talent to be invisible*, his friend, the man, had said, but that talent has now abandoned him. Against his neck he feels the cold touch of metal, a metal that moves of its own volition. A metal beaten thin and fine and stronger than the earth and the stars and the sky combined. He feels it tighten.

The boy opens his eyes one last time to see Mymnir crouching, unladylike, in front of him, her face blank of everything but a curious appraisal. She holds the end of the dwarven fetter loosely in one hand, playing with it as she thinks.

"Some time in the darkness, I believe, will help you learn your place. Some long time in the *black*."

Fálki gives up, releases his humanity. Slavering and furious, he snarls and snaps at Mymnir. In his veins, he can feel the moon sliding towards the horizon, can feel its silvery strength coursing through him—but the Queen is stronger.

She wraps a second coil of the impenetrable cord over his head, snaps it back, and speaks low. "Behave, puppy."

She seeks out a bolt in the ceiling where once hung a chandelier. Smiling, she whispers to the end of the restraint and throws it upwards. The ribbon-chain flies and loops itself through the iron eyelet, then wraps and wraps and wraps around its own tail. The metal sizzles, burns red, and fuses with itself. Sturdy and permanent. Nodding, Mymnir drops a hand to the wolf-boy's crown, a tender caress as she passes, taking the antiquated *náttlamp* as she leaves.

Fálki's cold, cold howls echo after her.
*I'm here. I'm here.*
*Alone.*

# The Red Wedding

*Two days after Sturla died, Æsa went to sleep in the forest.*

*She had barely rested whilst nursing him, but for those brief moments snatched in between. Never long enough to truly rest. He had been ill for nigh on three weeks.*

*When he died, Æsa watched the last breath leave his body, watched it hover above the bed, a white mist with no real shape. It hung there momentarily then floated from the window. She followed, running down the stairs and out the kitchen door, into the herb garden, through the gate, almost falling because her eyes were glued to it, not the path, making its way across the lawn and into the woods.*

*Æsa pursued until it disappeared. She continued on, pushing through the afternoon long after she'd given up hope of finding that white wisp ever again. When night fell, she wove a cloak of grief to drape around her shoulders. When exhaustion finally took her, Æsa sat beneath an elm, curled into a crook in its roots, and closed her eyes.*

*The air was thick with fog when she woke, covered with moss. The ground had risen until she was chest-deep in earth. Her skin had changed, too. Cold to the touch and damp with condensation. Stone, Æsa was grey and hard, with glints of quartz catching what little light survived the haze.*

> *She struggled and fought, limbs grinding. At last she shrugged off the remnants of clinging dirt and stood. Stone, Æsa began to walk.*
>
> Fastríðr Grettisdóttir, *Æsa of the Stones*

The twins know Kanti's stories are wrong: there is no magic here.

All their lives, the old woman has sung to them. Tucking them into bed as children, she'd croon tales of crystal palaces, kingdoms on rocky islands and mysterious *chepi* queens, her low voice lulling them to sleep. While the girls' parents were busy overseeing the family's shareholdings, leaving bronze and fur offerings for the pale ones, or building them great castles of oak and yew, white-toothed Kanti would regale them with accounts of their birth.

"Oh, how your parents prayed for heirs," she'd say. "They'd wed when Sayen was barely fourteen, but she was well into her twenties by the time the two of you were found. Roland feared your mother was barren, but would never say so aloud. Not like the rest of them." Kanti always shook her head then, still disgusted after all these years. "Whisperings can do terrible things to a young lady's sanity, little *sáðsystr*. Such terrible, terrible things." Then she'd sing a tune about a woman whose wits were addled by ghostly voices—it was never a favourite. So they'd clap their tiny hands, and beg their old nanny to get back to *their* story.

"You, Aylen," she'd say, turning to a lithe little girl with platinum hair and periwinkle eyes, "got your looks and your name from the river. Clear and bright, just like the water that gave you life."

"I swum since the day I was born, didn't I?"

"Swam," corrected Kanti. "But yes, my dear. You certainly did. Sayen plucked you from the shallows that late winter morning— you kicked your legs something fierce, and gave her quite the chase. Your mother's kirtle was ruined, her legs frostbitten from the current. Oh, how she wanted you—there's no way she would let you go. To this day she swears she'd never seen such a quick child! And so blue!" Laughing, Kanti would lean back against the headboard, absentmindedly hiking up her long skirts to allow the cool evening air in to soothe her swollen ankles. "Even now, the sheen of that river is still on your skin, my girl. And chips of it are frozen in your gaze."

"And you, Addie," Kanti would say, as Adsila blinked irises every bit as blue as her sister's, "you poked your head up out of the scrub by the riverbank, fingers ruffling like flower petals in the breeze. A perfect little blossom you were—you didn't give Sayen any trouble. Plump and purple as a crocus, you reached your arms right up and waited to be plucked."

They aged much slower than other children, Kanti said, because perfection took time. The girls would giggle then, identical chirps, and nestle deeper into their blankets. Joints aching, their nanny would ease herself off the mattress, praying she'd be able to straighten once the children had planted winter-cold kisses on each of her wrinkled cheeks.

When they'd been naughty, Kanti's story changed.

If they snarled while she brushed their fine hair, or refused to practise the harp, or spoke in languages no-one else understood, or ran with the stableboys instead of stitching phoenix and escallop shell patterns onto their sable surcoats—sometimes it seemed if they did anything at all, Kanti's nostrils would flare and her left eyebrow would curve up into her linen scarf, rising like a hawk on a hot breeze—*then* her tales were sung in a minor key. The twins' arrival wasn't lovely and sweet. They weren't bobbing in the water like lilies, they didn't bloom like enchanted daffodils. No, they came from a witch's stronghold, Kanti would say. Dug from a dark nursery, from a cavern buried deep in forest loam. Stolen, she'd tell them, like two delicate eggs from a squawking bird's nest.

But Kanti had told them so many stories. They knew the rules as well as she did.

"If we were changelings," they'd counter, crawling into her lap, pulling crimson strands out from beneath her kerchief, "wouldn't we be shrivelled and black with roots for hair and mud in our mouths?" Kanti, with her creased face and strange locks untouched by frost, would slap away their smirks. Their infant skin remained white, she'd say, because of all the months they'd been swaddled in cobwebs. Spider poison flowed in their veins, not blood. Beetles rolled dung in their heads—there wasn't half a brain between them. It was the only explanation, when beautiful girls behaved so vilely.

Aylen and Adsila would wail and cry until their quartz skin flushed garnet, and they'd be sent to bed starved of music, the former forbidden to play and the latter to listen.

In the morning, when her temper had settled, Kanti would place a vial of pure spring water on Aylen's pillow, capped with a pure silver cork. Adsila would wake to find a peony blossom pinned in her hair, its petals embroidered with lace. It was all the apology Kanti gave, and all the twins ever needed.

Until they grew up.

---∞---

Aylen slips the most recent bottle into a pocket hidden in her long sleeve. Water, just as it's been these many years. She wishes it was something stronger. Deadlier.

"Hush now. Calmly, calmly, you'll lose your form," says Adsila, wiping tears from her sister's puffy eyes. Gently, she strokes Aylen's temples, brow, lashes; delicate white feathers sprout in response. Shaking hands betray her steady voice. "You'll make yourself sick."

"Fine," Aylen says, pulling away. "Perhaps then they'll call this performance off."

Looking in the mirror, one of the few furnishings left in the twins' chamber, Aylen straightens her tunic and smooths the surcoat over her narrow hips. Gone is the golden phoenix of her youth, gone the sable felt. White diamond and starburst shapes sewn on a ground of snowy fabric have replaced them, heralding her as bride to Húsringr Taregan. Her sleeves and hem are dagged into oak-leaf patterns to match her groom's tunic, and around her waist droops a belt of white gold inset with pearls. A floor-length cape of arctic fox fur is hooked onto her gown with silver clasps, soft and heavy against Aylen's back. Only the veil remains on the wooden chest, but she can't affix it properly without Kanti's help. Beside it lies Aylen's lute, all glowing caramel wood, silver frets and gut strings. She would not let it go on ahead; a gift, she was told, from the *fjallkona*'s court. Older than the forest, it is the last of its kind: an instrument hewn from the world tree. It—and her sister—will not leave her side. Kanti, however, is another matter.

"I begged her to come with us." Aylen rubs her eyes until the feathers disappear. "It was like talking to a stranger."

"She's just sad to bid us farewell," Adsila says, surveying her twin's glorious dress jealously. Her own is merely a slip, ivory linen laced along both sides with strands of freshwater pearls. Generous lengths of these cords snake around her; some wrap around her long neck sixteen times, once for each year of her life, others stretch down to coil around wrists and ankles. The stone floor numbs her bare feet. She flutters around, pearls clacking like coins in a purse, to distract her sister and keep herself warm. "Don't fret, dearest. She'll be there today."

"It's not that," Aylen whispers. "You didn't hear her. 'My work is almost done,' she said. Her voice was deep, like Father's after he's been in the mead. 'Your future is set. A bride until death.' She was quiet after that, no matter that I howled. She scoffed as I pleaded with her not to leave us."

Adsila joins her sister at the mirror. Frowning, she removes the peony from her hair and tosses it onto the bed. Aylen cocks an eyebrow.

"It doesn't match," Adsila says. "Besides, it would appear Taregan prefers diamonds." She spins Aylen around to get a better view of her embroidered surcoat. "Perhaps if I ask nicely," she makes a lewd gesture with her mouth, "he'll deign to give me some too?"

Aylen doesn't smile, despite her sister's nervous laughter. "You're enjoying this."

Adsila ignores, possibly for the first time ever, her sister's need. "What a bargain for Húsringr Taregan: a bride for heirs and a mistress for pleasure, sharing the same face. Be thankful, sister, that you have the dignity of marriage."

And Aylen, also for the first time, thinks that perhaps her twin is less than grateful to come with her. Less than grateful to be sold as another's whore, all so Aylen will not be alone. She opens her lips, but the moment is gone and Adsila is smiling again.

"The wedding is in an hour," Adsila says, suddenly serious. "Cast off your sorrows or cry your heart out. Whatever you wish. Our lord Taregan won't be the first man to wed a sobbing bride. Or the first whose concubine feigns pleasure."

"Perhaps we can return to the river? Find the *chepi* queen or the witch's nursery? Kanti said—"

Adsila places bloodless fingers across her sister's freezing lips. Swiftly, she replaces them with a kiss, then wraps her bare arms around Aylen's stiff shoulders.

"What will we do without her, Addie?"

"Survive."

In the terrace outside, garlands of ivy and bay leaves are draped from long tables and seat backs, lush greenery dotted with jessamine, oleander and meadow rue. Banners hang from rows of silver birch and poplar: half starbursts and diamonds, half golden phoenixes rising from the ash, creating a natural wall to enclose the U-shaped yard. Lanterns swing from low branches and are strung from ropes between the building's tall eaves—neither palace nor castle, for only the Fae may inhabit those, but a very fine mansion indeed. Thick candles are clustered on windowsills, tables, and tall candelabra fashioned of antler and bone. The sun has not quite dipped below the horizon, yet every wick is lit.

Waning rays filter through the trees, casting long umbra around guests and servants and groom. Taregan stands at the edge of the wood, his back to Húsringr Roland, wearing a crown of stars. His tunic gleams beneath a bulky cloak, burnished gold in the sun. Wide streaks of grey in his dark hair glint copper as he tilts his head, hearing Kanti's approach. The old woman draws close, her black robes startling against his white ones. They're so dark as she passes through shadow that, for a second, Aylen—watching from her window—loses sight of her altogether. But in a blink, Kanti reappears.

She reaches out, but refrains from touching Taregan's sleeve. Even from this distance, Aylen can see her nanny's arm shake, held in mid-air. Then it snaps to her side, and Kanti's back straightens. She nods as Taregan speaks, keeps nodding as he hands her a— what is it? Aylen leans closer to the glass. It is small, edged in lace. A handkerchief? A peony?

The old woman moves away from the groom, and Aylen is surprised by the expressions flitting across Kanti's unguarded face: need, want, fear. An instant later, the bride doubts what she's seen. There is a ripple, like a sheet being pulled across a secret, and Kanti is herself again. Knowing, determined, mischievous. She pauses once more, speaking to a small sallow youth carrying a wooden tray laden with mead cups. His head tilts slightly, the merest acknowledgement, and Kanti moves on. But the boy, as if sensing her scrutiny, lifts his chin and meets Aylen's gaze. He grins, audaciously, briefly. His teeth are sharp.

## The Red Wedding

"Let's try to get your veil on," Adsila says, startling her sister. Aylen quickly looks at the contraption she's supposed to wear, then turns back to the window. Kanti is gone, and so is the boy.

Taregan is alone. Guests mill about him, strolling the grounds and along dappled paths, shepherds and crofters gaping openly at Roland's wealth, neighbouring landholders slyly assessing the advocat's grand wooden manse. The twins' father has spared no expense today; all echelons have gathered to benefit from his hospitality, to witness the union of these two Húsringar. To be reminded of their superiority. To still the whispers about Roland's ageless girls.

*Where did she go*, Aylen wonders, before she spots Kanti stumbling through the crowd on the other side of the courtyard. She crashes into a young woman wearing teal, her sleeveless surcoat bearing a bird device woven into the fabric. A scowl already marred Galilahi's pretty face—indeed it has been there since this wedding was announced—and it grows deeper as she bends to help Kanti back to her feet. The twins' nanny clings to Galilahi, scrabbles up her trunk like a racoon. The girl tries to extract herself, not bothering to cover her look of distaste.

"The musicians have started. You need to finish dressing." Bursts of laughter erupt outside, not muffled enough through the wall to keep Aylen from blushing. And though Adsila is right—drummers have struck up a beat, bells are jingling, and pipes trilling to welcome the bride—she can't tear herself away from the old woman's spectacle.

Kanti brushes the dust from her fallen wedding day headscarf; black, but embroidered with jet, so it shines as if dark stars are embedded there. Her scarlet hair flows wild and loose. She raises her hand in apology, and presses something white and lacy into Galilahi's palm. With another bow, she slips out of sight.

"Come on!" Adsila turns Aylen around, just as Kanti strolls through the bedroom door, as neat and tidy as ever.

"Listen to your sister," she says, striding across the room. "She is, and will forever be, your most trusted advisor."

"Don't make me go out there," Aylen says. "I can't—I've too much to do still. Mother will need help with the baby. And there's the . . . " She flaps her arm lamely, gesturing at the nothingness in her chamber. The discolorations on the floor where treasured rugs used to lie, where the heavy oaken chests were stacked in corners for collection. All packed and sent by wagon to Taregan's estate days ago. Now there is just the empty wardrobe and plainly-made bed. "And poor Addie! We need to find her a cloak. She'll catch her death in that dress . . . "

Kanti slumps, makes herself small and unthreatening. She hobbles now, approaching Aylen as she would a frightened cat. Slowly, steadily, she grasps her charge by the shoulders and holds the girl at arm's length.

"This isn't about you, my dear, or your sister. There are more important things in this world than you two and more riding on this union than you can imagine." In Kanti's hand, a star sapphire brooch appears, pronged like a comb: a blue bird in profile, with wings outstretched. She jabs the teeth to Aylen's surcoat at the centre of its scooped neckline, securing the piece just below her collarbone. "Consider this an early morning gift from your groom."

Aylen catches Adsila's eye, *See what I mean?* written all over her expression. *Kanti makes no sense at all.* Kanti is old, they know— but old enough to begin losing her grip?

"Blue for sadness," the nanny says, her voice hoarse, masculine, as she pats the stones and leans back to admire her work. "Keep it locked in your breast. Let no more of it show on your face."

"But Taregan is *ancient*," Aylen attempts, listlessly.

"One can hope," Kanti says, taking the veil from Adsila. "One can certainly hope."

And with Adsila's delicate assistance, the elderly woman begins the timeworn process of obscuring the bride's dismay.

---

Galilahi can make things happen.

Her every word, thought or deed can be relied upon to have an effect, an echo, a *consequence*. She is used to having her own way in this colony of woodsmen and traders, settled well beyond the white Queen's ken or caring. Here, Galilahi has spent most of her twenty-five years manipulating those around her, subtly or otherwise, manoeuvring and positioning herself and others *just- so*. Here, Galilahi is Queen—or so her father tells her, just as her mother used to, perpetually smiling as he brokers his daughter's future. And her charms have not gone unnoticed. Since her twelfth naming day, she hasn't been short of suitors: Dagfinnr who has wandered farthest inland, who claims to own a thousand head of caribou and a majestic ice palace in the north; Janna *bláfótr*, whose soles are always black from running barefoot through the forests, who insists on wearing dresses of beaded leather though her family controls all trade in ermine, mink and beaver; even jarl Ármann once sent her a basket filled with dried pears and figs, sprinkled with a dusting of perfect diamonds. If he wasn't such a bitter rind of a man and hard as the stones he offered, Ármann might have won her hand. But while her father continued to negotiate, to field and decline offers, Galilahi blazed her own path to happiness behind closed doors, in a Húsringr her menfolk hadn't once considered.

It came as something of a shock to find, after all these months of trying, that she could not get Taregan to husband.

A dark boy—she heard the old woman call him Fóli? Færi? Fálki?—passes her before pausing to offer one of the richly wrought cups on his tray. She chooses one of silver with three turquoises set in its base. Galilahi drinks deeply, upending the goblet in record time. She dabs her lips with the lace handkerchief the old woman gave her. *Presumptuous hag—as if I'll shed any tears at this wedding . . .* The boy has waited, silent as a shadow, eyes averted but rarely still. His glance jumps around the quadrangle, alighting on one face, skipping to another. He squints as though taking stock of who is present, who's absent, calculating their worth, memorising.

*The little mixed-breed has probably never encountered such wealth*, Galilahi thinks, sneering at Húsringr Roland's garish display. *He'll probably boast of this day, the day he attended the great wedding of Roland's finest daughter. And the whoring of her sister.* This last makes Galilahi smile, knowing that someone else is suffering from this union.

She replaces the glass a little too heavily and helps herself to another, turning away to show the youth he should move on. In truth, she does not trust herself to stop drinking if he remains. Straightening, she starts up the aisle, casually, gradually. Let Taregan think it happenstance, a matter of taking whatever seat is available, when she sits in the front row. Absorbed in thought, she does not notice the way the servant sniffs the air where she has been, does not notice that her anger has an effect on him.

She sips her wine more slowly this time, feeling its pleasant burn. It does not make her relax, though, it does not dampen her ire. It does not make anything that has happened hurt less.

*I have no choice*, Taregan had said. *My legacy must come first.* She lay beside him, sticky and sweaty and happy, with that raw hum of anger quelled for a moment, completely incapable of understanding how she, Galilahi, came second in her lover's heart. All her plans freshly made and sweet in her head, instantly dashed. *But we promised. We promised each other.* She had begged him then—oh, how she'd begged—as she never had of anyone in her life. And she, clever Galilahi, strong Galilahi, unstoppable Galilahi, found that she could not move this man.

On the surface, Taregan was sad enough, regretful enough, but he would not budge. He would marry Aylen and take her twin to harlot; he would reap the rewards of marrying into Roland's clan, joining fortunes to increase the prestige of both houses. Reminding all and sundry that *these* families ranked behind the Fae alone.

Galilahi came from an impressive line, but clearly not impressive enough. Her golden skin and auburn mane had caught many an eye, but for a person of Taregan's standing, the lovely Galilahi was neither sufficiently lovely nor sufficiently pale. Daring Galilahi, stealing a temporary place in his bed, hoping it would soon become permanent. Foolish, foolish Galilahi, who had given everything away, who had risked it all, and lost.

She glares across the sea of guests, sees her father and brothers gathered in a group, laughing and talking, faces pinched with the knowledge that they could never compete with this splendour. Their spines are stiffer than usual, she thinks; their conversations more forced. At the moment they seem to merely chafe with want, slightly uncomfortable, no more. They help themselves to the delicacies spread on Roland's table, the rich liquors on his servants' trays, and neither gall nor hatred prevents them from eating. Dropping a hand to her belly, Galilahi plucks at her surcoat to ensure it isn't clinging, that the swelling there isn't yet noticeable. Soon enough that fine food will taste as ash in their mouths. Within weeks, maybe days, their jealous laughter will become sputtering, seething fury. Eyes reduced to slits, they will look at her with disappointment, with disgust, calculating how long it has been since her bloods stopped flowing, how much time they have to arrange a marriage before her shame is known to all.

No-one will buy a used wife.

For now, her father catches her eye and nods. She gives a wide, false smile and turns in her seat, looks towards the mansion.

Galilahi watches as Taregan takes up position at the front door, the groom's post, the *husband's*, to await his soon-to-be wife. She aches to turn away, but can't. Despite everything, she still finds him breathtaking. A growl claws at her throat, scratching and swirling, rising like vomit. Clenching teeth and hands, she swallows it down.

Through the crowd a pack of boys move deftly, clearing away the appetisers, topping up glasses, or carrying clean tablecloths from the kitchens in preparation for the banquet. Shoulders uniformly slouched, heads cocked and nostrils twitching, they lope from place to place, taking in a feast of sensations beyond human range. They all feel, these sharp-sensed youths, the shuddering vibration of Galilahi's frustration, the struggle within her as she barely stifles her anger. Such emotions, such power! They shiver with excitement. They lick their chops in anticipation.

---

Aylen dips her head to clear the lintel, then steps out of the bedroom she and Adsila have shared all their lives.

The corridor is dark, every candle brought outside for the evening. At the end of the grand hallway, the door stands open, as do they all in a house when a bride travels *out*. Weak yellow light follows the breeze in, but provides no comfort. It merely makes monsters out of familiar shapes. Trolls skulk near the entrance where once there were benches; impish jewels swing from the chandelier as Aylen's tall headdress brushes past; hags' fingers claw at her veil, high on the wall where, that morning, there were sconces. The sisters hold hands, fingers clenched until they lose feeling. Together, they make their way slowly towards their groom.

Taregan waits by the entrance, facing away. Even in silhouette, the silver in his hair is visible. Beneath layers of fine cloth, his build is lean, athletic. Much more robust than they'd expected for a man of his age.

His is a climber's form, Aylen thinks.

An equestrian's, muses Adsila.

A spearman's.

Aylen's step falters when she sees her parents waiting in the yard. Sayen sits heavily on a seat designed to accommodate two people. Her belly, finally round after a lifetime of disappointment, balloons under girded brocade. A sheen of sweat gilds her round face, despite the chill in the air. Shadows gather under the crescents of her eyes, lending her olive skin a sallow hue. At her side, Roland raises a glass, signalling the musicians to muffle their instruments. He glowers at the guests, who are moving into place, forming groups with their own families, until their laughter dies, and lively conversations dwindle to murmurs. The twins know he'd tell the trees to stop rustling, if only they'd listen. Until the vows are heard and acknowledged by all and sundry, silence will reign over his house.

She will miss Roland's baritone melding with Sayen's contralto, in perfect tune with her lute. Her mother's careful hands, which first showed Aylen how to cut and tighten strings, to keep the rose clean, to cradle the curved wooden belly against her own. And her father's beaming, so proud whenever Adsila composed a new duet for them to sing, the pieces increasingly challenging for Aylen to play, increasingly beautiful for all to hear. *Will Taregan frown upon my calluses? How will he feel about a wife who can pinpoint the key of every noise, every utterance, every sound? Does he even enjoy music?*

Adsila audibly exhales and nudges Aylen over the threshold.

Taregan's pace is stately, keeping the twins one step behind him. He maintains this distance as they proceed to the forest's outer limits. Whispers follow them as they wend through the crowd; from behind the gauze of her veil, Aylen sees mouths gaping and hands poised on the brink of applause.

*It's the antlers.* Eight-point whitetail, covered in tawny velvet, with branches spanning five feet above her head. Their stubbed ends dig into her scalp and the wires gouge mercilessly where Kanti twisted them around her skull. But the headdress sits firm. Aylen's translucent hair spills white down her back, the veil draping down just below her chin. With antlers balanced, she releases her sister's hand and follows Taregan. Carrying herself with unearthly grace as none of the women here could hope to achieve.

Even so, her stomach quakes.

Wavy locks of hair have worked loose of Taregan's queue; these he has tucked behind his ears. His left hand rests in the small of his back, posture straight but relaxed. Only his balled fist gives away any unease; the one sign of all the politicking and negotiating this day has required, of the deals struck and the offenses thereby caused. Aylen minds the narrow sword hung at his hip to ensure it doesn't get tangled in her skirts. They both face straight ahead, intently not looking at each other, nor at Adsila who flanks him on the right. The tension of walking slowly beside a complete stranger propels them all forward.

The groom's boots crunch on pine needles.

The bride's train whispers across gravel.

The third who walks with them treads without a sound.

Taregan repeatedly swallows and clears his throat. Quietly—a subdued communication that only Aylen can hear. It will be the first of many secret messages they'll share, she imagines, a coded language transmitted in loving gestures and soft sounds. She must believe this, else she'll fly back to her chamber and never emerge. She must trust in his kindness. She must see in his every act a promise of love. And it will become *love*; she must believe that. So Kanti has said in her kinder moments, and so her sister has sworn.

*He has been given Adsila for my sake.*

*It is for me that he will take her.* Only now does she quiver at the thought she has somehow made Adsila *less*.

*But she has never complained . . .*

The ceremony is short, the *prestr's* words clear and simple. As eldest, Aylen is wife. As second, Adsila is concubine. Together, they are Taregan's.

Together, their Húsringar will be matchless.

"Hear, hear," cries Roland, his speech drowned out by a boutade of pipe and tabors.

From the corner of her eye, Aylen sees the flush in her husband's cheek. A grin tickles the corners of her mouth. She imagines what he will look like when he smiles in return, when he takes her hand. When he does other things befitting a husband.

Aylen curtseys to make it easier for him to reach her veil. He fumbles with the fabric, so close now she can feel his heat. She arranges her countenance appropriately and, as the curtain lifts from her eyes, finally looks at her husband directly. Sees him up close for the very first time.

She looks to Adsila, whose skin is ashen, arms held stiff at her sides, then immediately back to Taregan. She can feel her smile contorting, drooping downwards. Her lips remain parted, but the muscles in her face have gone slack. Even so, her expression is nowhere near as grotesque as her husband's.

Deep red scars marble the right half of Taregan's visage, pulling one side of his mouth into a smile, Janus-like, while the other half frowns. But only for an instant—he schools his features, and tries not to register disappointment in her reaction.

His good eye remains steady, umber iris trained on his new wife, gauging the level and depth of her horror. The other, lost years ago, a smooth plane of skin; its lid sewn shut and criss-crossed with scar tissue, has been saved the pain of seeing Aylen struggle to keep her tears in.

He is grateful for such small mercies.

---

The first course has been served and the drinking well under way before Galilahi realises what the flash of blue at Aylen's throat is. During the interminable ceremony, she'd been trying to get a good look at it, but the bride fidgeted so appallingly that it was impossible to see more than her flapping arms, her blinding white dress. After the hand-fasting, well after the trio of vows were exchanged, Aylen was passed from well-wisher to well-wisher, crushed in besotted embraces, subject to all the kisses and pinches and gropings that are the newlywed's due. But now there she is, sitting at the high table, smug and gloating, having stolen too much, too much that is Galilahi's. Torches are added to a host of extra candles, all lit as the dusk deepens into night. Flames are drawn to the adornment Aylen wears, flickering and winking off its facets.

The comb. An heirloom gifted by her father to her mother and thence to her after her mother gave up the ghost. *Her* comb, worn as a brooch, with its blue bird sapphire; the hideous one she dons to please her father and her mother's shade. The thing that has become her sigil, her device.

Galilahi can't fathom how the harlot came to be wearing it, but she will have it back. It is hers, in all its shine, in all its ugliness. It is *hers*.

---

Aylen's breath catches when she sees Kanti approach. At last their nanny has changed her mind! A little sob of relief escapes Aylen's lips as she imagines how the old woman will make a fine toast, sing a travelling tune Adsila wrote for the occasion, and beg Taregan to allow her to accompany them; to care for his wives, her beloved charges, his darlings. And Taregan will give in—of course he will. He'll give anything to make up for the terror in his new wife's face when she saw his disfigurement. Anything to prove he isn't a monster.

But Kanti is humming a melody Aylen has never heard before; a simple canon, repeated over and over in the woman's phlegmatic chest.

"A favour, dear heart," she says, patting Aylen's hand before slipping her papery fingers up the bride's sleeve. Stepping back, Kanti nods her thanks. Deftly untwisting the vial's silver lid, she pours its clear liquid onto one large, square hand. Mist rises from her skin, a white wind that dies out as quickly as it began. Stopping a few *alen* from the marriage table, she holds out her hand, palm up, empty.

Behind her, the full moon, the wedding moon, is rising.

"That water's cold as the Hvergelmir, but you won't catch me shivering," Kanti says, directing her comments to Taregan. "These shifting bones of mine always hold true, even in the trickiest situations—but you know that already, don't you, old One-Eye?"

"Don't be rude," Adsila admonishes, but a sharp look from the nanny silences her.

Turning back to the maimed groom, Kanti keeps her arm steady as something sprouts from the dew coating her palm, or from the hand itself, or perhaps from thin air. At first it seems a seed, then it bloats to a bean. A worm. An adder. A baton. Now charcoal and platinum, it stretches to about two *alen* in length, but in girth it's no thicker than a cane. It squirms in the old woman's grip and continues to expand, surely as a cock kindly stroked. It grows until it is Kanti's height, and she seems to stretch in the inconstant light, half flickering gold, half limpid silver. A strange smile stalks her lips. Excitement ignites in her eyes.

Intently, she observes Taregan's every move, his every blink and fidget. Her voice, when it comes, is gruff. Virile and deep, it roughhouses with a single word, bullies it onto the groom's plate, serves it up as sacrifice: "Gungnir."

Óðinn's spear, the swaying one, always primed to strike any target. Óðinn's spear, which the god boldly wielded at the end of the world, its tip still encrusted with Fenrir's blood—for all the good stabbing that great beast did. The fen-dweller lives on through his sons, treachery and hate, Sköll and Hati. His furore survives in his trickster-sire's gambits.

"All is not lost," Kanti says, thrusting the weapon at Taregan. "Even here, Wise One, we have need of you."

Surely if the All-Father has forgotten himself then *this* will bring him back. This will bring him back and Kanti will not be so alone.

Taregan's single eye stares, uncomprehending. He looks to Aylen, to Adsila, then back at the old woman clinging to the lance so tightly her knuckles crack. "A princely gift," he says, fumbling for words. "I have never before seen its like."

Kanti feels something rend inside her—*the spear means nothing to him*—something that will be forever lost—*it is not him*—eternally broken. All the pieces she—he?—had shored up, all the *aspects* held in place since he—she?—had found his way out of the library, all those shards of the past, those splinters and remnants fly apart. All the fragments of himself, the memories he has cobbled together, all lost in a swirling vortex of disappointment, of loss, of despair.

Kanti sheds her disguise, the empty dugs of her woman-flesh swaying as she begins tearing away her skin. For a moment between she is male, she is Lóki, and then even the man-flesh is gone and he is all red fur and snapping jaws, she is the forgetful wolf, the image of his son and no less raging for being a copy.

Ever in tune with their maker's feelings, the servants immediately pick up on Lóki's distress. Led by Fálki, the young men burst from their shells, discarding their human coverings like unseasonal coats, donning bristling wild pelts and claws and hideous strength. Around the quadrangle the wolf-boys raise their snouts to the moon and howl. A plaintive sound and rapturous, heartbroken and full of hope. The long notes drain all trace of boyishness from the wolves, emptying them out, leaving them hollow and hungry.

As one, they turn lupine heads towards Úlfr-Lóki. Towards their master. And the moon, chased across the heavens by Fenrir's hateful child, the moon shows them the way.

---

Aylen, frozen.

She'd stumbled away from the table when Kanti began her transformation, tripping off the dais and falling into the scrambling crowd. The creature had leapt past her, lunging at Taregan; she, he, *it* snarled as it scrabbled over chairs and board, smashing dishes and tipping candles and torches in their decorative holders. Fire raced across wine-soaked linens and flames reflected in the russet wolf's eyes, Kanti's eyes, only harder, deadlier. Now Aylen can't move, not a single step. She can't turn to see where Adsila has gone, can't tell if her husband has escaped. Their screams, if there are any, are inaudible, indistinguishable in the din.

The bride stands, a girl carved of stone, unable to blink, as the massacre unfolds in front of her.

Then she is broadsided. A slap, with nails—not talons—leaves its mark on her face and she can feel warm blood welling from the gashes. Galilahi steps into her field of vision, her lovely face purple as an overripe plum.

"Thief! He wasn't enough for you?" One hand slaps again and the other fastens onto the comb, gripping tight. Aylen opens her mouth to protest—and a half-full ewer hits the side of Galilahi's head, ringing with a dull pewter echo. There's a high-pitched tearing, a strong tug at her neckline. Aylen pitches forward but manages to keep to her feet. Her bodice is ripped down to the waist, the jewelled bird gone. Its captor lies unconscious on the ground, a scrap of white fabric clenched in her fist.

"Come on!" shouts Adsila, tossing the makeshift weapon aside before tugging at her sister's hand, trying to pull her along, to make her take flight. "Our best chance is the woods—we'll find refuge in the river. We'll be safe near its waters, in its flowery beds, hidden until Mother and Father come to find us . . ."

"Oh, Addie, we can't go without them," wails Aylen, running frantically into the nightmare playing out in the courtyard, piercing the swirling smoke with her antlers. "Mother! Father! Mother!"

Adsila chases after her sister, crashing into her when she abruptly stops.

"My lute," Aylen says, her voice strained with panic. She squeals as a wolf-boy bowls her over, hurling himself onto the piper whose spirited music had accompanied the twins down the aisle. Scurrying away, she is soon back on her feet and yelling.

"It'll be destroyed! Fruit of the world tree—oh gods, you must get it!"

"*Now?*"

"Please, Addie, please! There's no time to argue—you fetch the lute, I'll find Mother and Father. We'll meet at the ford, where the river bends and the crocus blooms."

"And Taregan?" she asks, but Aylen is already gone, a wraith slipping between growling shadows.

Adsila sprints across the terrace, through the carnage, strangely untouched by the madness around her. Back inside the manse, blessedly free of the fire but not the mayhem. Glass shatters above and below; shards bite into her bare feet but she is numb to the pain, senseless with determination and terror. Barking and snarling resound through the halls, pouncing, moving from floor to floor. Feral laughter precedes screaming. Screaming and screaming and screaming . . . Lungs burning, gasping, she flies through the house, through passageways and rooms they were not meant to set foot in again, not for many months, not until Aylen—or indeed Adsila— had a womb rounding out nicely. Not until their place in Taregan's life was assured. Not until they were *anchored*.

Up the stairs, through all the open doors, doors that were supposed to let luck flow unbroken, and into their deserted bedchamber. On the chest lies the lute, luminous in the darkness. She sweeps it up and retraces her steps, so fast, so fleet she might be a deer, she might be a bird.

And out, out, out into the yard now awash with so much blood and so much gore she skids on the muck of it. In some part of her mind, she knows she is falling, knows the gravel should be scraping her, the skin peeling painfully from her knees—but she registers none of it.

Aylen is there, right there in front of her, right there, down at ground level.

And Aylen's white dress is all red.

Her veil is gone and clumps of scalp matt her hair. Antlers pierce her ribcage, her still-beating heart. Red pulses from her chest, froths down her cheek, oozes out of her nose. It spatters like rain—drip, drop onto Adsila's waxen face—as the beast snatches Aylen up. Drags her off to a bone-filled corner in one muscular, furred arm.

*Kanti? Oh, please do not let it be Kanti! Not this betrayal of all possible betrayals.*

Tightening her grip on the lute, Adsila begins to crawl. In her mind she is dashing after her sister, bounding over corpses, smashing left and right with the cursed instrument. In her mind she is singing a song she composed, one that will bring the dead back to life. In her mind, she is made of iron and Aylen is made of steel. Together, they cannot be harmed.

Boot heels crush her hands as she inches toward an overturned table. Claws score her calves, gouge craters in her thighs. A child's shriek deafens; his limp body flops into her path, its skull knocking against hers.

She feels none of it.

Not Taregan's arms as he scoops her up and holds her close. Not his long strides chewing furlongs, leagues, territories. Not the branches snagging in her hair, scratching her face, her eyes. Not the night's bitter wind, nor the morning sun's glare. She feels only a yawning hole in her chest, a chasm that widens the further he carries her, the further they travel from everyone she loved. Away from the red blur that had been her sister.

And as they go, she hears the birds singing with Aylen's sweet voice: Away and away and away . . .

# *Midnight*

*She came with a great army of wraiths and wolf-riders, wearing armour of moon-silver and stars. On that count, at least, all agree. Some say fury drove the Queen down from her mountain; others, madness. Still others won't hazard a guess. "Ancient history," one crone told me, her ruddy face shrivelled like a dried apple. The old woman was likely alive when these events took place—a century had passed between then and now, no more—but I refrained from observing as much in her company. (Note: she had before her a crude mortar and pestle, fashioned from basalt and bone. Pots of boiled marrow fat, lean strips of elk, and clay dishes of various fruits foraged from the woods. Choke cherries, blueberries, currants, &c. Ingredients for a restorative elixir, no doubt; perhaps a love potion. She certainly had the look of a witch about her; a New World Baba Yaga. Must tell M.)*

*From the east coast of this country, progressing westward, the Queen and her host travelled for seven days and seven nights. The campaign was undertaken in perpetual winter, several sources concur; more evidence of her Northern heritage. (Arguments to the contrary cannot be disregarded, however; the Queen has been known to voyage South without notice.) The population of the furthest settlements reduced by half after her visit; those nearest her own palace utterly decimated by the time she had been and gone. Thousands of hooves churned the soil to dust, caused rockslides and quakes, unearthed new wellsprings, changing the face of the landscape irrevocably. Yet all accounts are unanimous: she arrived silently, swiftly, a huntress stalking all the hearts that had forgotten or turned against her. No alarms, no warning. Vanishing as quickly as she came. Perhaps she*

An Example of 'Secretary Hand', mixed cursive script, *c.* mid-late 17thC.
Possibly a page from *Frontier Folklore: A Diary of Skræling Life* by "Ignace" (author unconfirmed)

Six months! Sophie-Élisabet scrunches the letter and throws it down. The cream-coloured paper is stained with half a world's worth of miles, dirt and fingerprints, but nowhere near enough words. Six months to hear from Madeleine, who could have swum back from the Americas in less time and tossed the four worthless lines at her in person. Six months. After all the letters composed on the ship, which the post boy had delivered in one precious slab so many, many weeks ago. A parcel of missives filled with inconsequential, everyday observations. *This was a mistake*, one of them read. *Conditions are ghastly, days and nights languishing in a floating coffin.* Another claimed, *I should never have left Paris.* Yet another: *Already I miss you too much, ma chère Erato.* They'd been wrapped in a red satin ribbon, sealed with ruby wax. Still smelling faintly of gardenia.

*Ma chère Erato.* Sophie's hand flutters to her diaphragm, the secret nickname ringing hollow. As if the meaning—*lovely, desired*—could somehow swell across the ocean, filling all the weeks, all the hours between now and when Madeleine first scribbled it down. As if those words could sustain them, those few lonely words, *Erato, lovely, desired*, as if they could stand on their own for six months, tied in ribbon and sealed in wax, without reinforcement, without repetition. As if they could replace the voice, the touch, the presence of she who wrote them. As if they could quell the ache.

It no longer surprises Sophie-Élisabet, how closely love resembles bitterness. How frequently yearning tastes of bile and gall. Her mouth floods with it, throat constricting, as she picks up the balled paper and smooths it against her stomach. How could Madeleine have sent this? After six months? This, only this, and no more?

*Shimmerings push back the gloom, the darkness under the mountain. They beckon with a carillon of voices, ringing with promised wonders.* Follow, *it seems they say,* follow. There is no place for you here.

Reason tells Sophie this final sentence refers to the voices. Just the voices.

Her heart says otherwise.

She tries not to think of what Madeleine has been doing all this time, what could have prevented her from writing something more meaningful. All the excuses she's invented—*her luggage was lost and with it her ink and pens; the mail carriage was waylaid by brigands, such a wild country; she's just getting settled, it's fine, everything is fine*—don't explain Madeleine's long silence. They don't explain away Sophie's doubts now that that silence has broken. With an effort, she bundles her worries and lodges them in the black pit of her bowels. She definitely doesn't think of the gentleman Madeleine mentioned in her final shipboard letter, hastily written and tucked in the bottom of the pack. Monsieur Ármann Alberi. A passing reference, no more.

*Monsieur Alberi tells me there is a rich tradition of fairy lore in the New Found Land of Virginia,* Madeleine had said, back when her letters still made sense, *particularly around certain uninhabitable isles off the coast. Hauntings, pixie mischief, suggestions of wendigo (this last seems unlikely, n'est-ce pas? too far South), the usual accounts of sinister folk lurking in the forest, superstitions warning against travelling under the light of a full moon, &c. I will explore further, ma chère; on that you have my oath. No collection of* Histoires ou Contes du Temps Passé *would be complete without such titbits—and I know you intend to be encyclopaedic. Perhaps Monsieur Ármann can be persuaded to lead an expedition . . .*

No, Sophie has decided, it was nothing remarkable. A casual observation about the man, tucked between ribald caricatures of other passengers and detailed criticisms of the food on board. That settled it, the glibness in Madeleine's tone. Sophie won't waste another second imagining the two of them traipsing across the wilderness, ostensibly doing research, sleeping under the stars, sleeping so close their heat mingles, sleeping *together*.

There are too many other things to consider at the moment, pressing things, like bagging the remaining clothes in her wardrobes and ensuring Jeanne lines their shelves with camphor, ignoring the lingering scent of gardenia as the maid packs her trunks, itemising all the notes she's taken, collating her manuscripts, deciding which chapters will come with her to the Americas and which relinquished to Barnabas for safe-keeping. Putting Madeleine's letters in her satchel, taking them out again.

Sighing, Sophie looks up at the gilded mirror hung next to the staircase sweeping a marble arc to the *hôtel particulier*'s second floor. If she was still here, Madeleine would laugh and call her vain, a raven attracted to the sparkle of her own reflection. And Sophie would scoff, lift her chin imperiously, a mischievous glint in her eye. Vanity, she'd argue, is largely scientific. A considered examination of the body's demise over time. Her tone is light when she jokes about ageing, but in truth, she is more concerned than she lets on. With every glance in the looking-glass, she gauges how her face traps each lost minute in a growing web of wrinkles, how its sepia skin brightens when smiling, darkens with frowns. With her tight curls pulled into a chignon and hidden under a cap, without the thick maquillage she's taken to wearing, and with a hint of exhaustion to offset the blue of her eyes, anyone would say she looks positively masculine. She is no longer as young as she once was, no, and too old to attract a noble husband—although, *Dieu merci*, her late father's wealth has saved her that worry. Secured her this house in the city, this blessed life of spinsterhood.

She looks up at the mirror, but sees nothing reflected. The glass is covered with a spotless white dustsheet, as is the hall stand, the ebony console, the pair of walnut chairs flanking the front door. All shrouded, all shapeless. Ghosts waiting for her to leave so that, in her absence, they might float gaily about. Unburdened by her presence. Free to roam. Fickle things, belongings, as fickle as lovers. After all the care she took in selecting them, in opening her home, finding the best places to set them down, to highlight their attributes, they've already forgotten her. They are not anticipating her return.

For days, however, Monsieur Barnabas has flitted like a bird around her, upset at the disturbance to their daily routine.

Standing in the doorway between the entrance and la grande salle, the steward clears his throat and once more offers to go with her ladyship.

"Mademoiselle needs a chaperone," he says, and Sophie wonders if it's exasperation she hears in his voice or merely defeat. He knows it's futile, trying to convince her to stay—she's made that clear—but he hasn't yet abandoned hope of her taking him along. Sliding the crumpled message into a pocket hidden in the abundant folds of her skirt, Sophie turns and clasps the old man's weathered hands. Hers a shade or two lighter than his, no more. A world of privilege marked in the difference.

"Go to Lyon, Henri. It has been far too long—surely your family is anxious to see you.

"Never fear," she teases as his brow furrows. "The house and all its dust will still be here come autumn, patiently awaiting our homecoming. Go, Monsieur. Go. You have earned this sabbatical." She stops short of kissing his cheek, but pats his hand tenderly, her expression warm as she shoos him away.

Mademoiselle doesn't need a chaperone, she thinks, watching the old man reluctantly mount the stairs to retrieve her luggage. Indeed, *Mademoiselle* will be left behind in Paris.

---

Dressed in the straight wool breeches favoured by seamen and a simple high-collared doublet, Sophie-Élisabet makes a terribly small man. The caraque offers little distraction for one as educated as he. No sailor, he, with his hands too delicate, his frame too fine for hauling hempen ropes as thick as a child's arm, or for clambering up rigging like the spider monkeys he once saw at the Sun King's Versailles menagerie. And Sophie-Élisabet has no head for heights, having spent most of his life stooped over low tables in his father's library, reading and annotating books. Merely looking up at the stature of the vessel's four masts, the pendulous swaying of a tiny crow's-nest on the main's pinnacle, is enough to make him dizzy. Remaining below decks is not much better for his *santé*. Humid darkness in the corridors beyond his cabin, the wafting reek of salt and bilge water and vomit, the erratic rocking of the hull, up and down and up and side to side and down around him, all conspire to turn Sophie's stomach.

Along with the other free men on board, Sophie-Élisabet has full liberty of the ship and he takes great advantage of it. With a knit cap pulled over his ears and a long cloak wrapped round him for warmth, Sophie spends the length of his journey outside on the raised platform at the stern of the big-bellied craft. For his passengers' convenience, the captain has had sturdy wooden chairs nailed to the decks; Sophie prefers the one sitting directly in the centre. Somehow the planks beneath his boots feel steadier here, more solid and tangible, less likely to tip. Crisp breezes clear his head as he looks through gaps in the decorative sterncastle. Deep blue waters stretch endlessly behind them, broken only by the vessel's sighing wake. It is a peaceful, contemplative view. Sophie latches onto it, hoping it will still the chatter in his mind and lend him the focus he needs to write.

*There is no place for you here . . .*

He doesn't compose any letters on this voyage—for to whom should he address them? *Mlle Madeleine Aveline, peut-être accompaniée par M. Alberi, près d'une Île Mystérieuse, Colonie de Virginie?* Or to Barnabas, *pauvre étoile,* who is by now too busy spoiling his plump nieces and nephews to worry about corresponding with the headstrong Mademoiselle? No. No. There is no point. Instead, Sophie spends time with his notes, his thoughts, his diary, though sea spray makes a puckered mess of them all.

———∞———

*. . . populations, often referred to as ~~scarlings~~?* (Corr.: skrælings), *cling to a range of mediaeval practices intended to defend the soul against beings referred to as "fades" (the term perhaps a malapropism of "shades"?) In local songs and genealogies, these creatures are commonly described as possessing "shimmer-milk" skin (notable, one presumes, because of a marked contrast to the skrælings' own sun-browned complexions?); they are incredibly long-lived, perhaps immortal; their tread so light and graceful they seem, universally, to be remembered more as spectres than as people. In fact, there is some confusion of tenses when "fades" are mentioned in oral accounts. Some storytellers use the past tense when describing these sprites, others the present; they are portrayed as beings who exist* in the now, *and also as phantoms who haunted*

their forebears. Thus, it remains unclear whether the rituals this society performs, and the various charms they employ, serve an apotropaic purpose for immediate cases of "soul vanishings" (present tense), or whether they are merely antediluvian tradition, maintained in homage to the ancestors: "those who fought the forest" (past tense).

A complete catalogue of these practices is a *desideratum*, not least because many need further explanation. Why do skrælings kill all species of *corvidae on* sight? Why do they light bonfires at the mouths of caves and burrows each night? Why do they string bells and beads in the gaps between ash trees and oak, setting the woods a-ringing around their encampments? Once believed to be selkies, due to their skill manoeuvring birch-bark vessels along streams and river-rapids, the skræling people now balk at sailing the ocean; refusing even to traverse the bay to collect gulls' eggs and seaweed from the stony island, not more than a league away. And what does any of this have to do with saving their souls from the "fades"?

---

23 mars 1682

Ma chère Erato,

This wild sea air, I've realised, is a tonic for the spirits.

Away from the city, away from the suffocating dark of its streets, away from the fields and marchés skirting les Jardins Tuileries, away from the Miracle Courts with their skin-girls and dupers and throat-slitters, away from the carriages and *les bals d'hiver*, away from your chaperones, your schedules, your places to be—

Away from all this, one can breathe. One can think.

Do you remember, ma chère, the day we first met? It was none of the times our circles spun together at court, when I'd curtsey to Mademoiselle Ignace and you, you would dip your delicate chin imperceptibly in response. But those weren't true meetings, they were merely peacocks' *menuets*—small steps, delicate poses, bird-brained rituals.

No, we met because of a fable.

It remains one of my favourites, in all its variations: a princess charged with murdering her sweet babes; the prince, distraught, banishing her from the realm (sometimes imprisoning her for twenty years, sometimes introducing her to the executioner); the children alive and well, living incognito; the children transformed into crows; the children drowned by a witch, their empty bodies afloat in the river. The grieving prince turning ogre, devouring every last soul in his kingdom. The happy prince remarrying, fathering new heirs. The deranged prince scouring the realm for a miracle, seeing his dead children everywhere and nowhere at all.

I had been in your service for, what, a week? Madame Laudine had passed so suddenly, and your father considered me a suitable companion for his *minou*. (He wasn't far wrong!) And delight of delights, his collection of *contes*—so many versions, so many translations, so many originals. Upon finding a new telling of the woeful prince, I turned to you.

And you were beautiful.

"C'est magnifique," I said. "Incomparable."

And you said, *Shhhhhhh, this is a library* . . .

I couldn't help but laugh!

For weeks now I've heard your *shhhhhhh* repeated in the waves, *shhhhhhh, shhhhhhh, shhhhhhhhhh,* and yearn for the lips that formed that fateful sound.

It is so peaceful today, Erato. So quiet.

You would love it.

*M.*

*Mardi, le 17 avril*
*à bord la* Cassiopée

*It cannot be the same man.*

*A brother, perhaps. An uncle? M didn't describe him—it was a passing comment, no more. Monsieur Alberi, she'd said. Monsieur Ármann. The slightest wisp of a mention. Nothing to suggest any lasting connection between them. Between that man and this.*

*And yet.*

*Such conversations I've had with this one, this other Alberi. He says I may call him Ármann, as is fitting between men, between friends. My travel papers refer to me merely as Ignace, and so, I said, should he. "A scholar's name," Ármann said, clapping me on the shoulder, as if that sealed it, my name, Ignace, "unknowing". Linking us. Our partnership built on a mutual desire for knowledge. I, for the world's stories, and he? What is it he pursues, I wonder? Deep down, what drives him? This gentleman—for such must he be, with skin untouched by the sun, hair so white and long he has no need for King Louis' fashionable periwigs (indeed, it would be a sin to cover his brilliant locks with so dull an imitation), and suits of velvet so fine one could almost believe they'd been spun by fairies—this Alberi is a hunter. And every once in a while, despite his easy smile and his refined bearing, there comes a desperate eagerness in his eyes, a flash of hope-tinged loss, that tells me he has not yet found what he seeks.*

*When he speaks, which he does at the slightest provocation, I am made to feel we've known each other for years. From the very first, Ármann has talked to me as a father to a son, sharing confidences, ideas, joys. He is decorous without artifice. Forthright without impropriety. Each day a torrent of words rushes between us, too many to record, too many, even, to remember. I often return to my quarters (that fearful cabin, the place where there is no sleep!) as the moon waxes large over the sea, content but befuddled. Overwhelmed with information, but unable to pinpoint exactly what it is we've discussed for so many hours. His passion for anthropology exceeds my own; of that there is no doubt. And it seems he's devoted a lifetime to studying the skrælings, their lore, their beliefs, their history. His approach is utterly immersive. Not merely reading stories, performing interviews, recording oral* legends, but blending into local ways of life, becoming familiar with the population—so familiar, in fact, it's as if he passes invisible through their world. The gift of a true anthropologist.

My dear M would have been charmed by his intellectual zeal. Perhaps she already has been. But, no. No. Perhaps this Alberi is that one's father? His son. It cannot be the same man.

Yet if it is . . .

Better to wait, to be certain. I daren't ask him of M's whereabouts only to discover that she is gone, fallen prey to some New World illness, a beautiful bauble impaled on a head-hunter's spear—or worse, that she is his. (Corr.: Ármann is acid-tongued when it comes to talk of love. Surely this Alberi could not have wooed one as romantic as my M?)

It's hard to explain. He is more open than any one I have met— and yet with each exchange he seems more remote, more alien, more obscure. Then, just as quickly, the clouds around him vanish. Beaming at me, he chatters on about Otherworlds and fairy hills. Rattle-bone weavers. Giants who weep cornflower tears. I get the impression he's been waiting some time to find a likeminded soul. Waiting to be a mentor, to pass on his knowledge, to lead.

He is a natural guide.

I wonder, did M follow him?

It cannot be the same man.

---

17 juin 1682

Mademoiselle Ignace,

Please excuse me for omitting such pleasantries as *I hope you are well* and *I trust your journey was an enjoyable one*. These sentiments drain the blood and leave a tired man feeling quite empty. No doubt, upon reading this, you will say I worry too much—was that not what drove you to leave no forwarding address? To avoid hampering your new, exciting life with dreary concerns from the old—at least until autumn, you said. Leave Paris to le Roi-Soleil, you said. At least until autumn. Forgive this intrusion, Mademoiselle, but I could not wait that long. (I look forward, whole-heartedly, to your mockery. I truly do.) Reports of Barbary pirates have reached us; of attacks on any ships that cross their path, from Constantinople all the way to Iceland. Cargo, passenger, slave; it makes no difference. All are boarded, ransacked and burnt. Including, we fear, *la Cassiopée*.

For luck, thirteen copies of this letter have been despatched. I pray one of them finds you and, yes, that it finds you well. Well, and whole and willing to write.

All of Lyon stands in vigil for your safe return.

Until that time, I remain,
Your most humble and very obedient servant,

Henri Barnabas
Lyon

---

Sophie-Élisabet only feels like herself at night, when she is free of costumes and expectations, free of deceit. It was so in Paris, as it is here. Days filled with interesting research, interminable nonetheless, as she waits to retire to her own rooms, to her own shack, the only places she can relinquish her various façades. There, that she cares only for men; here, that she is one.

At home in the library, Sophie would watch the candles shrink, millimetre by millimetre, a slow melt of hours, as she and Madeleine sat on opposite sides of her father's wide baroque table. Studying each other secretly, books open-mouthed on their laps. The lady of the house and her handmaiden, girded in stomachers and mantuas with high square necklines, held upright by stays and petticoats, both women as stiff and emotionless as their overskirts. Prim and proper. Paragons of gentility trapped within the confines of stifling day. But at night, only at night, stripped of these layers, Sophie was herself. Restless until Madeleine's soft tapping came at the chamber door. Relieved to hear their strumming. Aroused as they threaded through her curls, above and below. Slow explorations of touch and response, tender promises of togetherness. And later, naked, satiated, they would talk, outpourings of thoughts, dreams, plans, completing the transformation from day to night. After dark, Mademoiselle Ignace was silent. But Sophie-Élisabet had much to say.

Now, alone in her private shelter, one of Ármann's extra cabins, a storehouse for rotting antiques deep in a primitive grove, Sophie sheds her breeches and doublet for a few short hours, lets her chemise drape loose as perspiration trickles down her back and between her breasts. The humidity is relentless. Daily rainstorms provide no relief; they merely perpetuate the problem, and stir up swarms of mosquitos besides. To make things worse, bonfires blaze to life at twilight, no matter the temperature. Built facing tent flaps and hut entrances, at the foot of hollow trees, near ditches deeper and blacker than most. These people nurture superstitions about doorways—doorways and tunnels, windows and arches, corridors creeping like *hedera* through the ruins. Waystations between in and out. Whether the light is meant to warn folk away, or act as a beacon to attract, is unclear. Once the fires are lit and steadily seething, no-one goes anywhere near them.

*Probably concerned they'll evaporate in this ungodly heat, et à juste titre.* Sophie looks at her thinning arms, the protruding balls of her wrists. Slick with grease and sweat, sloughed of fat. She has shed far too much weight in the weeks since her departure. Seasickness followed by a diet of dried elk and smoked fish, neither of which she can keep down for long. She can't eat with a peach-pit of worry lodged in her throat. Her monthly bloods dried up, *Dieu merci*, and also the appetite that normally goes with them. Long treks through the wilderness, endless trudging from settlement to ramshackle settlement, seem to have stretched her garments. Her thighs, once plump and firm beneath Madeleine's caress, have wizened to sticks that scarcely graze the fabric of her breeches when she walks.

"Your friend is pining," one tale-teller confided, mid-interview. Nahuel's russet skin tinged blue with the coming dusk, tufts of pure white hair fluffing from his scalp, as if his head was a milkweed pod that had recently burst. He winked and Sophie's spirit roared. *Madeleine, he's seen Madeleine, and she misses me, oh she misses me . . .* But the sage was gazing over Sophie's head, at Monsieur Alberi. The friend, she realised, was herself.

Ármann had given no reply.

Nervous with wondering—*Where is she? Has he divined my secret? Where is she?*—the next morning, Sophie had sought out

Ármann. Her stomach a hard cluster of anxiety as she searched his face for signs of suspicion. Disappointment. Lust.

"They say Nahuel has gone to the stars," Alberi had said, crouched over a pot of succotash. He prodded the beans with a fork, watched them split. He hadn't once looked her way. "They'll farewell his spirit at sunset—you'll find there are no burials here. Perhaps that's worth noting?"

As Monsieur Ignace, Sophie has the freedom to question, to roam, to keep the company of other men. She'd attended the ceremony, she'd observed, she'd kept binding cloths tightly wound over her chest. But now, tonight, rid of her disguise, she can relax into herself, into her loneliness.

A single oil lamp sits before her, guttering, attracting moths. She crumbles dried lavender flowers into the flame, the sweet smoke helping to keep biting insects at bay. Sitting on a decrepit rug on the floor of her hut, Sophie-Élisabet transcribes the shorthand notes she took earlier today, panting a little in the heat. The wise-woman, Maiara, had regaled Sophie with myths drawn from the soil of this land. Tales of rampaging boars and enchanted drums, sapphire heart-stones, journeys of witches and gods. On second thought, she hadn't called them witches—Sophie flips through the pages, checking her entries. A-ha. *Fades*. Yes, like everyone else, the old woman had used that term. Soon after, the statement diminishes, deteriorates. What was lucid soon reads like the gibberish Madeleine sent, the four lines Sophie keeps folded, folded, so many times folded, in a locket, dangling next to her heart.

> **Maiara**: *Follow and follow and follow, whisper the voices.*
> **Ignace**: *Which voices, Madame? Mine? Yours?*
> **Maiara**: *Clay flutes and knuckle-bones, songs of the dead, echoes of those who've gone into the mountain before us. Gold and silver, starlight falls, glistening in the air. A comet gleaming before they all disappear. And they will . . .* [Subject covers her mouth. Stifling a sob. Corr.: Laughing. I give her time to control herself.]
> **Ignace**: *Go on.*
> **Maiara**: *Disappear. They will, they will, tomorrow, today. Ask the piper, the piper, oh shimmering wonder. There is no place for you here.*

Sophie-Élisabet puts down her pen, rubs the bridge of her nose with ink-stained fingers. What enchantment is this? One moment the stories, though fantastical, are perfectly logical. The next, the tellers' thoughts are scattered, maple keys spinning in the wind. It was the same with Madeleine... What inspires this rupture between mind and mouth? What spell befalls their tongues? What—

What was that?

Twigs snapping, a scuffle of feet over leaves. One set—no, two—sneaking past her shack, heading deeper into the woods.

She snuffs the lamp. Reaches for a penknife. Quickly dons her breeches and doublet.

---

The ruins writhe with rats. They squeak over fallen ramparts, little shadows darting along highwires that secure leather tarps to moss-covered stone. Tiny stars appear near decayed wooden floorboards, beneath platforms, on the rims of arched windows, next to barrels filled with crab-apples and acorns. They sparkle then wink out, flames blinked from the rodents' nocturnal eyes.

Falcons and hawks and owls in the treetops are the fattest Sophie has ever seen.

Quietly, he follows the sound of boots hastily making tracks through the tumble-down buildings. Avoiding open-roofed hallways where the feral beasts run thickest. Skulking across chambers and courtyards where the skrælings have erected their elaborate, ephemeral camp. A village of deer-hide pavilions in the grand hall. Hammocks bridging musicians' galleries and sculpted columns. Nests of silken tapestries and fur strewn in larders, fountains and drawing rooms. Rude lean-tos sheltering fireplaces, whole families sleeping in the hearths' maws. The stink of humanity barely camouflaged by summer pine and cedar, and by salty breezes creeping in from the sea, its shores visible through the coastal fringes of the forest.

Over it all, moonlight filters through black branches, black tiles, black rafters. Its silver offsets the golden flames, the ruby coals radiating below, and plunges the two figures in the distance into an unearthly lambency.

*Ármann.* Fluid white tresses, unmistakeable, as the silhouette on the left steps briefly into a clearing. Sophie's pulse races,

hiccups, nearly stops altogether. At the darkest edge of the glade, right where Ármann and his companion have melded back into the shadows, the air ripples between two mighty chestnuts. Suddenly their trunks are limned with spectral light, and then there are flashes—of what? of children? of women? no, no, of men?—and the bark is rimed with hoarfrost. A mint breeze slices through the mugginess, refreshing, fleeting. A dazzle of lightning, but no thunder, no impact, before the glare vanishes. Violet outlines trace its absence, glittering ghosts that are already waning.
*Fades.*
*Shimmerings.*
*Mon Dieu.*
Sophie tries to run after Ármann—*don't go*, he thinks, *not you too*—but a thick root strikes out in the dark. Teeth clash and knees jolt and palms scrape on pebbles, pine needles, dead leaves. The penknife sails, lands with a thud, lost in brambles. Air woofs from his lungs. A stone jabs his belly, and a hand presses him flat on the ground. A hot *hssssssst* in his ear.

"What a noise you make! Don't go chasing withywindles at midnight, fool child. Not here. No, especially not here. Come."

The hand pats his back, once, twice. Footsteps retreat as softly as they came.

Sophie springs up and strains his eyes for a sign of Ármann. He inhales the rich scent of loam and fungus and burning. But no mint. No gardenia.

"Come," the voice insists.

The man leads Sophie into a vestibule, through a ragged hole in one wall that gapes at the forest. It may have been a guardroom once, judging from the iron pegs nailed into what partitions remain, upon which swords and armour and helms could be hung. Granite benches huddle around a rectangular pit in the floor, the stones at its base smudged with centuries-old soot, littered with yellowed bones and much fresher carcasses. Rabbits, squirrels, foxes. The floor is carpeted with lichen that crunches underfoot. Weak flames lick up from bird skulls on the windowsills, little avian candles that barely push back the gloom. Spidersilk curtains flutter down from the ceiling beams. Gossamer strands that float, straggling toward the moonlight.

The stranger negotiates the space efficiently, easily, as if it was high noon. Without hesitation, he skirts around benches, rat-traps and pit. Crosses to the blackest side of the room, rummages through— something. A chest, perhaps. Sophie thinks he hears the creaking of hinges, a lid thunking on a hard surface. Then, *clink, clink,* flint sparks against steel. A torch flares, defeating one small corner of night. The man wedges it into a bracket above his head, turns and sits in an exquisite chair that would better suit Mademoiselle Ignace's home in Paris than this hovel in the middle of nowhere.

"Stay a while," he says, lifting his bare feet onto a threadbare ottoman. Sophie cringes. The man is *filthy,* of indeterminate age. It's been many long years since his shirt was white. Rent from the neck, where some few tenacious scraps of lace remain, to the waist, its cuffs are ragged, almost non-existent. His pants are stringed with muck, but Sophie can discern that, once, they were a fine thick fabric. He closes his eyes and scratches dirt and fleas from his matted black hair. At last, with a contented sigh, he continues. "I would offer you a seat, but I only have the one. And considering I just saved your life, well . . . "

"Where did they go?"

"That depends on which *they* you're talking about."

Sophie takes a step closer. He will not ask this boor about Madeleine. Disappointment after disappointment—no, the pain is too great. He will *not* ask. But, oh, how his heart lurches. The traitorous words come unbidden.

"Have you seen her? Another *française,* like me?" Sophie-Élisabet blurts out, forgetting he is no longer corseted and beribboned. "She's much prettier than I am, though. Yes, much. Tell me she's come this way. Tell me she's near."

The quiet between question and answer stretches so long Sophie fears the man has fallen asleep. Finally, he gets up, looks up. "*Française,*" he says to the heavens, then plucks the torch from its sconce. Holds it in front of him, affording his guest a clear view of his pock-marked face.

"My mother called me Beaufort," he says. "She was ever an optimist." He is neither beautiful nor strong. His muscles atrophied by some childhood disease, his cheeks staved in, his irises milky with cataracts. "The days of my seeings are long over, child. But I have a tale for your scratchings."

"Sit," he says, offering Sophie the chair. "Don't wish for parchment and quill, not yet. Memory is the best storyteller of all—she will regale you whenever you wish, so long as you pay her proper attention now. Just listen. Listen, and take heed."

---

*Midnight hanged himself when the blue raven stole his lover. A grand gesture, certainly, and certainly futile, as most grand gestures are. That's the thing about desperate last efforts—always too little, always too late. If only Midnight had shown half as much interest, half as much verve, when loyal Moonshine traded all her days for long nights. When she'd abandoned her sparks, fresh from the womb, to spend the velvet hours with him. If only he'd turned her head more frequently, wooed her, appreciated her, despite the repetition of years. If only his most winning smile hadn't been the one that smothered her light. If only he hadn't flashed it when Moonshine brushed her children away, when they fell like pure snow to the ground. If only he'd made her feel she was loved, and not just a lover.*

*If any of these onlys had been more than ifs, she might not have been so open to the theft.*

*Time stopped while he swung there on his pathetic gallows, for weeks, for months, who's to say? Refusing to budge, his corpse bloated blue-black, too heavy even for Dawn to lift on her broad shoulders. Midnight couldn't die, of course he couldn't, but he could make life miserable for everyone, if he so chose, as miserable as his own. And he so chose.*

*Selfish, yes, but what did you expect? This was a man who not only enabled clandestine trysts the world 'round, he also revelled in living them. He throve on drama, excitement, pivotal moments. He couldn't admit to having anything so ordinary as a wife. A steady, dedicated partner. Where was the romance in that? So to deny his attachment to Moonshine, he'd snub her publicly. Growing dark when she was brightest, gloating wide when she was dullest. Only making a fuss when she was no longer his to enjoy. Enter, the blue raven.*

*She wasn't malicious, not at first. She was lonely, I suppose, as only gods can be lonely. And with that glorious face, that lithesome body, Moonshine herself could almost pass as a god.*

*They were fitting companions; both set on shifting the burden of emptiness in the world, taking a little less for themselves, forcing a little more on others.*

"A lesson in give and take," the blue raven said, spearing a great cleft in the hillside, ushering Moonshine into the newly-formed cave.

As you'd expect, this land and its people withered under Midnight's reign. Crops failed, predators cleared the forests of prey, humans sickened and died. The blue raven wouldn't let the fades suffer—some say she *couldn't*. She herded them all, the children of moonlight, fair as their mother and brighter than dreams. "There is no place for you here," she said, urging those beautiful creatures to join their dam under the mountain. And they went, willing or unwilling, and consoled themselves with the prospect of reunion.

But Moonshine was unhappy. It had been so long since she'd given birth, she no longer recognised her offspring. They shone, as she did, but otherwise... She wasn't convinced they were hers. She couldn't see the resemblance. But, oh, how she missed the change in seasons, missed the wind and the rain, and, yes, most of all, she missed Midnight. Politely, she requested the Queen release her.

[The subject pauses; fumbles at his belt for a wineskin; drinks. Loses himself in reverie. I wait approx. five minutes.]

**Ignace:** "*What happened?*"

**Beaufort:** "*Why, the bird swallowed her. And from then on, she changed hue, glowed from beak to rectrices with Moonshine's trapped love. Like a fire blossom from the Far East, she shot into the sky, a streak of blinding white. Thinking his lover had returned at long last, Midnight lifted the siege, abandoned his noose, and pursued her. She taunts him still, relentlessly. Each night he gives the white raven chase, though he knows she's not Moonshine, though he knows he will never catch her.*

**Ignace:** "*I don't understand.*"

**Beaufort:** "*No, I suppose not.*" [Another pause.] "*Our kind seldom do.*"

*Vendredi, le 1 septembre*
*Colonie de Virginie (??); Quelque part*

The leaves are turning and there is a chill in the air. Ármann came back this morning—strange how, after that night, I am constantly surprised by his return—scouting, he says, for more settlements to include in my study. More settlements? More settlements. And yet I remain only in this one.

Many of the skrælings have vanished. A sickness plagues them, Ármann tells me, a sickness carried to this land on our ships. (Considering my own wasted form, I fear he is not far wrong. And I am sorry, so sorry.)

No letters from home, not a one. It seems even Barnabas has forgotten me. The Cassiopée has been and gone, but still I remain. I cannot go back without M. And yet. Twice I have buckled and begged Ármann to take me to the port; twice he has convinced me otherwise. "You have not yet achieved what you set out to accomplish." Single-minded in his goals, he thinks others should also be thus. But he is right. He is right. So we'll move no further up the coast, and no further inland. The island rears its head on the horizon. Jagged pilings jut from the channel between our forest camp and the floating mountain, a broken bridge that once spanned the distance from here to there, there to here. I have asked M. Alberi so many times about it and he always manages to avoid answering me. No, I lie. He said once, when pushed, "It is a broken thing," and no more. So strange when one considers how he loves to talk.

I spend, in spite of my initial repugnance, more and more time with Beaufort. Sometimes I find it hard to believe he is blind, so keenly does he navigate the ruins—the devil in me sometimes thinks to move his furniture, give him a test that can only be passed by the proof of physical hurt. But that is merely a spiteful urge when I am low.

I bring food and salves, culled from our provisions, for him. We eat and talk. I rub the unguents into the skin on his back where he cannot reach. I suspect it gives him no more pleasure than it does me, but I do it anyway and he submits to it. He has introduced me to the skræling weed, smoked by the likes of old Maiara and the other herb-women, to help them float, to have visions, to get closer to their dreams. But I . . . I woke wondering—believing—that Madeleine was no more than a figment of my imagination, a product of deprivation and desire.

And I dreamt . . . I dreamt that Beaufort and I . . . that we . . . But no. Mere fever-dreams.

Hallucinations.

Alberi comes and goes.

I speak to the few remaining skrælings, the old and the young, harvesting what stories and memories I may. I heard, today, another version of the prince deprived of his children. M would love it. My book grows fatter and fatter while my body grows thinner, leaner—hollow.

Alberi comes and goes.

---

**Jaci:** *He's a prince, you know. Mawmaw says so.*

**Ignace:** *Who is?*

**Jaci:** *But he never sleeps anymore, Mawmaw says, because secrets slip out when he's not guarding them. That's how she knows he's royal: night-talk. So he stays awake and travels and sneaks through the woods and then the tree-bells ring and ring.* [Subject is distracted by her woven-grass poupée. She chatters, as children do, without plot or planning.] *The prince goes into the shimmer whenever he wants, but he's the only one comes back.*

**Ignace:** *What is this "shimmer"? Where is it?* [Note: cross-reference the girl's comments with Beaufort's "withywindles". Connections?]

**Jaci** [singing to her doll]: *Shimmer, shimmer, under the mountain. Here, there, everywhere . . .*

[No other response is forthcoming; change tack.]

**Ignace:** *Why doesn't he stay—under the "mountain"?*

**Jaci:** *Because he hasn't found them yet.* [Subject looks exasperated, as if I am slow.] *Because they're still lost.*

**Ignace:** *And what did he lose? Must have been quite precious, to warrant the effort of all this searching. Perhaps something very small?*

**Jaci** [smiling, conspiratorial]: *Smaller than me, at first, but now probably much bigger.*

[Subject begins to unmake her toy, deliberately unplaiting its component parts. A thoughtful and efficient destruction. She waits for me to guess the answer to her riddle. I have led her far enough, though, and am far more patient than she. I will outwait her.]

**Jaci:** *Children, of course! His daughters.*

**Ignace:** *What happened to them? How does he know where to look?*

[Subject shrugs.]

**Ignace:** *Have you seen this prince, Jaci?*

**Jaci:** *He comes and goes. Don't take his hand.*

**Ignace:** *And if you do?*

**Jaci** [clearly bored]: *Shimmer, shimmer, under the mountain. Everyone goes eventually, Mawmaw says. But some he takes sooner rather than later.*

**Ignace:** *Why doesn't anyone stop him?*

[Subject snorts.] *Nobody lives forever.*

---

Beaufort is not in the garrison when Sophie-Élisabet goes to ask him about Ármann. Skull-candles are lit on the sill, a campfire crackling outside the door, but there is no other sign of the blind man. Beneath his breast bandages, Sophie's lungs constrict with sudden panic. Clouds gasp from his lips, cold as the late autumn wind. *Beaufort's gone*, he thinks. *Gone* gone. So many skrælings have disappeared these past months—no, they're dead, Sophie reminds himself, unconvinced. There have been no funerals. No mourning rites. Just a tightening of ranks, a clustering of families, a stoic disregard of the obvious.

Someone is stealing these people. Leading them astray.

Since transcribing it this afternoon, the little girl's story has repeated constantly through his mind. *He comes and goes*, she'd said. *Don't take his hand.*

Beaufort, he has observed, always takes whatever hand is offered.

*Please*, Sophie thinks, leaving the ruins in a rush. *Don't let the trusting fool be hurt—*

He stops as the last rays of sunset pierce through the foliage. Dusk. The time when Beaufort ranges through the undergrowth. Not far from the settlement, but just far enough. Laying traps to snag unwary meat for his dinner.

Sophie scratches at his scalp, so itchy under the cap, and heaves a sigh. Placated but not fully relieved. Not until he confirms that Beaufort is merely out hunting, not being hunted. It seems Jaci's 'prince' is indiscriminate in his victims, he thinks, heading for Ármann's hut. Men, women, children. Lovers. Now here, now vanished. Not dead. Led.

And Monsieur Alberi is a natural leader . . .

There is a field table in the anthropologist's shack, a collapsible chair, no bed. *He never sleeps anymore* . . . Drawings and etchings are pinned in straight rows along the log panels, manically neat. Portraits of the most beautiful faces Sophie-Élisabet has ever seen, people of all ages and, somehow, ageless. Birch baskets line the walls, arranged from largest to smallest. Deep round hampers are filled with winter hats and cloaks, folded and separated by colour; enough to clothe the settlement twice over. Gloves and handkerchiefs are stuffed into rectangular bins. The flattest containers, long wicker-rimmed trays, catch Sophie's eye and hold it. These are stacked with notes, journals, reports. Letters.

Between a decorative visiting card and a sheet of loose-leaf, a creamy page pokes out, the paper so individual, the hand so familiar, that his heart lurches. In his haste, he sends the piles skittering to the floor and must rifle, shaking, through the mess until, at last, he retrieves the right fragment. The ink is crisp and bold, just like she who employed it. There is no date, but Sophie believes—he *knows*—that if he unfurls the four lines in his locket, that page's top edge must certainly align with the bottom of this one.

*Ma chère Erato,*
*If only I were a painter, I might capture the beauty M. Alberi has shown me since our arrival. But my artistic skills are weak, I'm afraid, so writing must suffice, even though these black sentences are just so many twigs thrown on a white field—they cannot portray the variegations, the hues, the prismatic delights I've seen this past fortnight.*
*Ármann is, I think, a conjurer.*
*Mais j'anticipe! You should know, I've bored the poor man silly, regaling him with our plans. How you and I will be the first demoiselles to record a whole new realm of stories. "Ah, but*

*which realm? The visible, or the hidden? I can show you either."* He jests, incessantly, about this. And I laugh and laugh and tease him for thinking the snake in his trousers is like unto a world in itself—and for thinking I'd care to see it! I assure him, at great length, that I am most content with my Erato. And he, barbarian, seems unduly interested in our affairs. *"Two women? Together? How old are you?"* he says, positively leering, until I am forced to change the subject. But he is ancient and, I suppose, burdened by the backward thinking typical of his generation. I cannot fault him for finding us alluring. What's more, he has agreed to send this letter on my behalf, tomorrow, after he demonstrates his tricks and for that I am grateful.

And, yes, he *is* a conjurer—oh, if only you could see it! (How I wish you would come soon. You won't know yourself here! Trust me, ma chère. What a difference it makes, being free of civilisation.) Ármann summons portals, magic mirrors of spirit and light—spectacular legerdemain. They rock in the air like lullabies, enchanted shimmerings. Yes, that's the word. Shimmerings

Here the account ends, the page torn. Here Madeleine would have continued—had continued—*Shimmerings push back the gloom* . . . But why? Why did Ármann clip the note? Why why why only send a snippet? Sophie clenches his fist, hears the paper crunch, his knuckles crack.

The mystery of four lines, that's why.

It's more enticing, cut short. It's more certain to bring me here.

He wants us together.

Two women.

But Mademoiselle Ignace, Sophie reminds himself, was left behind in Paris.

He runs. Out of the hut, past the ruins, far beyond the reach of bonfires and torches. The moon hasn't yet risen. The stars, cowed by Sophie's anger, are hiding behind a steel wall of cloud. Running turns to stumbling, to falling and rising, pressing on, pressing on despite the uneven terrain, the slippery leaves, the knobbly roots. He trips, lands hard, and feels a small bone in his right hand break as it connects with quarried stone, an uplifted slab of pavement. Press on, press on. All energy, all strength poured into this one final, desperate trek through the forest. Toward the mountain.

Lead me, Sophie thinks. Lead me to her . . .

There! A flash between two chestnut trees; an oval sizzle of blue and white. There is no air in Sophie-Élisabet's lungs for shouting, only for pressing on, pressing on. Still he forces his legs to keep pumping, throwing him forward. There! He is briefly dazed by the flare as the shimmering veil bursts into life. Blinking hard, he continues to run, limping, not quite weeping, whimpering.

Bloodied and broken, he crashes through thickets and brush, tumbles to the grass at Ármann's feet. Occupied with helping two children step through the portal, the tall, aristocratic man pays Sophie's wheezing little attention.

"Ingrid will be so happy to see you," M. Alberi says to the girls, their long brown hair plaited in identical rows. Their expressions beatific, then openly delirious, as they cross into the snowy realm beyond the gate, and begin skipping toward a table laden with sugared fruits. Sophie pulls himself upright, hand throbbing.

"It's not them, Ármann. You must know it's not *them*. So why? Why bring them here?"

"If not these," M. Alberi replies, in the same instructional tone he used on the ship when discussing constellations or the lifespan of tsetse flies, "if not these, then perhaps the next will be, or the next. Collecting stragglers is slow, so many years!—I have not Mymnir's power, nor her army—but the result will repay the effort a hundredfold, a thousandfold, when we are reunited at last."

A woman's voice lilts through the opening, her cadences enticing, hypnotic. *Follow*, she seems to say, *follow. There is no place for you here.* Sophie thinks, for an instant, it is Madeleine.

"She is mine, not yours. You can't keep her, do you hear me? You. Can. Not. Give her back. Please. Give her back."

"Oh, no no no." Ármann clicks his tongue, waggles his index finger. "She loves you? All the better. Perhaps others love you *this* way too, as such a dashing man, perhaps my girls will follow you, young lover, perhaps they'll follow you home. Come, Ignace. Come. We must all be together, in one place, else I'll never find them. No, none shall go back. None will be left behind."

As Ármann steps over the threshold, Sophie looks into the Otherworld, looks *beyond*, and he can see, as if through a faintly warped glass, Madeleine on the other side. No conjuring, no illusion. It is her.

She doesn't speak, but she smiles, a slow dreamy smile, and helps the children to reach a bowl full of plums. Monsieur Alberi extends his hand, inviting, welcoming. Every instinct Sophie has urges him to run, to get away, but—there is Madeleine. Right there. Sophie draws closer, awash in gusts of *menthe* and gardenia, all nocturnal chirrupings and howlings around him drowned out by the loud *shhhhhhh, shhhhhhh, shhhhhhhing* emanating from the doorway, the portal, the magic mirror. It sounds like a waterfall, *shhhhhhh, shhhhhhh, shhhhhhh,* such a serene white noise, muffling all other sounds from Ármann's world. Behind Madeleine, there are emaciated, mercury-hued folk who stare back at Sophie lazily, as if he is a drab hen, stuck behind bars. They whisper to one another, *shhhhhhh, shhhhhhh, shhhhhhh,* so wan and colourless. Next to them, Madeleine is a parrot, red-headed and vibrant, a healthy flush on her lips. Sophie yanks off his cap, lets her corkscrew hair fly loose so her lover will recognise her. She tugs at her bindings, pinches roses into her cheeks, and yells, "I'm here! Ma chère, I'm here!"

*Shhhhhhh, shhhhhhh, shhhhhhh.*

The gap is closing, narrowing, the doorway is fading. Ármann withdraws slowly, purposefully, as if to say *Look at all you'll be missing.* She knows he'll be back—he comes and goes—but when? When? How many days, weeks, months, years? If she waits, she may never see Madeleine again. Desperation propels her, urgency lending her the strength to plunge through, to tear the veil with her teeth if need be.

"I'm coming," she whispers, preparing to dive.

And as she leans into the dying light, hands clamp on her shoulders, wrenching her back, away. Forcing her to stay.

"Do not leave me!" Beaufort is stronger than his skeletal form suggests. And he sees more than he lets on. Perhaps merely contours and shades; enough to let him find her, enough to protect her. She does not want protection.

Sophie-Élisabet struggles, flails, curses, bites, but cannot escape. The woods grow dark, then darker as the oval shrinks; as the fight leaves her and she sinks, listless, to the ground. Bleary-eyed, she takes in her last sight of the Otherworld, the living fairy tale.

At last, Madeleine meets her eye. She raises one hand in farewell.

She is happy, Sophie realises, squeezing Beaufort's rough arm, because it is there, because it is there and her lover is not.

Madeleine is happy, and she is beautiful, and she is gone.

*There is no place for you here.*

# Of the Demon and the Drum

*Whispered words bring ill luck: good tidings are ever spoken aloud.*
*A pair of ravens at the window marks a family's joy; a single bird tapping is a bad omen.*
*A harp without strings is like a body without soul; neither makes a welcome guest at the feast.*
*Never marry on the full moon.*
*Children born to dead fathers will lead charmed lives.*
*The doors of a wedding house must be kept open to allow the bride safe passage and prosperity.*
*Look to shore while sailing away, else to home you'll never return.*

Anonymous, *A Miscellany of Wishes, Good and Bad*

Water, almost as far as the eye can see.

"Maybe *Jé-rouge* what scared the cypress ladies off," say Miz Delphine Laveau, standing tall on the outside stairway ricketing down back of her house, wooden steps zigzagging from the attic all the way to the ground. Red-eyes been howling fierce for nigh on a week, skin-changing at dusk and bellowing til dawn, conversing in fits and snarls. Until this morning, they tracks churned between town and bayou, marking they territory with muddy prints, half man, half wolf. Now all signs of pacing and traipsing gone, washed away in the flood that rose up to the front doors overnight.

Young Claude say nothing. Pant legs dripping, he shift from foot to foot on the creaky landing, uneasy near Miz Delphine, uneasy looking out at a horizon free of all trees. There's a hitch in his movements, a crick and slow shuffle, but he try to pass it off as distress. Everything's lurid without cypress ladies' shade to darken bayou waters, to hold them in place. Sky and flood blend into one mass of brown-blue wet, broken only by sharp gables, houses proud as mountains, kings of the landscape. Low clouds press they fat bellies along rooftops, groping for trees and leaves, finding instead mud chimneys and daub. Between rolling arms, they trap the sun. Light glint off the street-murk, gold-heat smothering. Avenue streams slurp at the houses' half-timber siding, tongues lapping for a way into the cool, the dark, finally soaking through cracks in the boards.

"Can't you just imagine them," Delphine say, shaking her head. "All the old ones, gone trekking. Dozens of cypress ladies, all bent-backed and knobbly-armed. Lifting they knees and roots, kicking fish and gators with each step as they go, sludging they rachitic limbs up on out of here. What a sight, what a sight. Trailing they Spanish moss shawls and dresses and long long tresses, a green-veiled procession. Little ripples swirling behind, growing, swelling into waves. Great gushing waves. Waves that break loose once those bayou women leave they posts, overflowing the banks as they pass. What a sight to have missed."

Young Claude shrug, lower his tawny eyes. Reflections writhe up his deep brown cheeks as he lean over the railing, looking anywhere but at the ghost-woman beside him.

"Maybe they just gone strolling, no reason at all." Claude roll his shoulders, fidgeting the heavy hessian strap across his chest.

Delphine smile. "Maybe they want nothing but to piss off Lóki-Legba, that it?"

"Anyone know what set witchwood a-walking, that'd be you, Miz D."

She cock her head and laugh. "What you mean is *I'm* to go'on and find them."

Despite himself, Young Claude peer up at her, can't turn away. Mawmaw Brynja once tell him that all Laveaux serve the *Loa* with both hands; they whole family spin magics, light and dark, but Miz D most specially got a knack for the dark. Now, up close,

Young Claude see truth in his *mère*'s words. No leather pouches with baubles or spices or powdered juju are sewn into Delphine's sleeves, none worn on thongs at her neck and wrists; just that one thing, at her waist. Seem she doesn't need such tricks and trappings. With that spider web hair, those ivory fingernails, she the only charm-weaver with *gris-gris* sprouting straight from her pale pale skin.

"Everyone chip in for your trouble." Young Claude jiggle his pocket, heavy and clanking with the town's offering. Miz Delphine doesn't spot how he only use his left hand, though Claude i'nt a southpaw. "And all what goats ha'nt drown, and all what chickens, are yours for the picking. You'll want for nothing—please."

Again, Delphine laugh, loud and long. "I already want nothing but a dry sitting room, *p'tit*. Will a handful of *sous* get me that?"

Below, floating in a rowboat ten feet above street level, Louis hear that cackling and forget all about his brother, forget all about the promise he made Young Claude to wait for him. Paddles plunk, one-two, into the drink. Oarlocks swivel, squeal with each stroke as Louis strain to pull away.

"*Attends*," shout Young Claude. "*Attends!*"

He stop himself fleeing by gripping the railing hard. *Those Laveaux*, Mawmaw Brynja once explain, *are all so many mockingbirds. At first, they full of squawk and bluster and wind. But pay no mind to they taunting, son. Wait, wait and wait some more if you have to, and they puff will deflate.* Sweat run down his flushed face, salt stinging, but if he move to wipe it, he'll surely keep on moving and never look back. Shame rise in him, swift as the flood, at the thought of failing. *She's all bluster and wind, just bluster and wind* . . . Clenching his teeth, Young Claude await Miz Delphine's true answer, swaying with the effort of staying near her.

Delphine's fingertips spirit across his forehead, cold and slick as eels. "Hush, *p'tit*. I want no *sous* or goats or some sad, leaky boat. Tell me honest, once: you think *Jé-rouge* chase off our cypress queens?"

Not trusting his tongue, the boy give his head a quick shake.

"Hmph." The woman put on a sour expression, cross her arms, but Young Claude see her lips curl, her eyes shining while she look at him corner-wise. "What got our ladies riled so quick, then? They who ha'nt shifted long as I been alive."

*And how long that, I wonder?* Mawmaw Brynja say Delphine's great-gran, strange Galilahi, lived two hundred years—give or take—and may well have lasted two hundred more if the skin-changers ha'nt got to her at last. *Laveaux got more than their fair share of years,* she say. *They bayou-blood run deep and winding, stretching far beyond our ken.* Now Miz D stare at Young Claude with the same face she wore to stare at Mawmaw, back when she was Li'l Brynja. As young and as old as ever.

"Speak up or leave, boy. If I want gaping and dead-eye gawking, I'll go down the fish market and have my fill. Answer me something worthwhile, else swim after you skittish brother and be done with it."

"Might be," Young Claude say, who'd been mulling on it since the streets all turned swamp that morning, "our ladies been used as *coco macaque*."

"Well, there's a thought. Chase it up with another."

"Cypress women all made of wood, right? So, when you get to it, they really all giant bundles of sticks. And if these sticks been hexed, well, they owner can make them walk, can't he? They do his errands, his bidding, and wherever he send them to, they go. If he want, they kill his enemies. If he want."

Delphine sigh. "Child, you were doing so well. But now you go repeating yourself to no end. 'Might be they *coco macaque*,' you say—a fine start, I'll grant you. Then, using different words, longer phrases, you go'on conveying the same sense: 'They magic sticks what do his bidding if he want' is just another way to say 'Might be they *coco macaque*.' Wasted sayings. Offer me some *who*s and *why*s and *how*s, not just more *if*s."

Colour rise up Young Claude's neck. He pretend to shoo flies away from his curly head so's he can turn his back to the voudon, screw up his mouth and spit. "Way I see it, Miz D, *if*s always come before *why*s and *how*s. Question before answer, *n'est ce pas?*"

"I see," say Delphine. "You like working in a sequence, do you? Well then, tell me honest, second time: how many *bokors* you been looking at, A to B to C, before coming across Miz D's name on your list?"

"Can't say, *marraine* . . ."

"That your idea of honest, child?"

Young Claude clear his throat, but straighten up. That's twice now she call him that. No child, he. Turning eighteen before summer's end, he's a man what can face down a witch.

"All, Miz D. You we save for last." He try on a cheeky grin, though his belly twist and churn. "Last but not least."

Delphine trace the strong line of the boy's jaw, trawl her fingers down his neck and place her palm flat on his chest, damping a print on his cotton shirt. Shivering him with her touch. She draw so close, the shrink-head talisman she always wear looped on a long cornhusk rope around her waist, the one she whisper to when she think no-one's looking, jab into his hip. The boy smell the oil in her white dreads. The cool peppermint musk on her unique dress, a collection of handkerchiefs knotted and plaited around her old-young form, thin fabric covering the round bits of her, the full womanly bits, the firm. Young Claude's snake stir, raise its head. Miz D notice *that*. She lift one eyebrow, not laughing now. Considering.

Far in the distance, *Jé-rouge* pick up they hollering, one to another to another, wolves though it be broad daylight.

At last Delphine sough. "Tempting, *chèr*, so tempting. But, no. No, you calm that rabbit heart of yours. There's no time today for good grinding. Maybe I take you up on that later, once this business is said and done."

Delphine's skin is dank as a cellar even in this humidity, and is spiced with anise. Young Claude's head's a-spin with thoughts of what might be under that patch-rag dress. Feeling the hard press of her body, he think maybe Miz D i'nt so old after all.

A moment pass before Young Claude catch the courage to wriggle free. He cough, and they don't look at each other for a spell. They stare out across the near-blinding shine, squinting for moving shadows, studying for signs of long scaly snouts or amber-eyes winking on the surface. Beneath pilings and stoops, bullfrogs throat they pleasure at so much wet, all croaking "Knee-deep, knee-deep," while chickens stranded high on window sills and eaves cluck unhappy disagreement. Long-legged herons wade through wide intersections, careful-toe splashing around porches and makeshift rafts. Sleek heads appear then *plop* out of sight as confused nutria glide through the flood, they little nostrils huffing and rattails swishing them toward whatever embankment they can find. All the small creatures, from blowflies to gators, noise around, exploring, talking in they own way about the change. But the big ones, they with the words, leave all fussing and fixing to the two standing on Miz Delphine's landing.

They gazes drift with the slow currents over to other houses, then slide up muddy railings and crumble-plaster walls, settling where folk cling to high ground, waiting to hear what the voudon decide.

"Tell me honest, *last but not least*," Delphine say with a chuckle. "You want my help?"

"We all do, Miz D."

"None of this 'we all' tripe, Young Claude. It's you I see here come begging, last but not least, and not a soul else. So I ask again: *you* want my help?"

"Yes'm."

"Awright, then. You fetch me my drum, son, and we'll be off."

"Thought you might ask," Claude say, happy with himself. He swing the bag around and flip up its fabric flap, the motion making him gasp. For the first time, Miz Delphine heed the red streaking his unrolled sleeve, the dried spatter dabbing his right hand like some devil danced its fingerprints all over it.

"You should have shown me this first," she whisper, each word crisp and silver-white as her skin, all the bayou gone from her accent. Young Claude snatch away his limb. *Mockingbird Laveau*, he think, annoyed at his forgetting, even for an instant, that Miz D has a liar's tongue and a powerful way with glamours. Though she sound like she belong here, more often than not, and though it seem she know the right sayings and doings, truth is she's only an echo. A ghost hoping to be heard more than seen.

But the serious in her expression, the crackle of magic around her, remind Young Claude he in't the man to upset Delphine's illusions. So he stop, tense from skull to toes, and suffer the witch-woman's ministrations.

Gently, terribly gently, she reach and touch his fingers, lifting the sleeve to see three ragged gashes running the length of his forearm. Her frown deepen. Something's snuck in there, she can feel it. Something pulsing, something dark and shifting, something . . .

Without waiting for a response, the pale woman switch up her raggedy skirts and start down the steps, keeping on til she's wet up to her knees. She cup her hands round her mouth and shout with a volume that defy her small frame. "Louis! *Viens-t'en!*"

With no cypress ladies to block her call, Delphine's bellow sail clear across the water that once was her lawn. Through the great gap that yesterday was a sheltering copse, hiding her doings from prying town-spies. Down Rue Royal, over the market square, and up to Louis Arvidsson's red ears. Everyone round about hear that summoning, so there's no way for Louis to feign he didn't.

Slowly, slowly, the pirogue make its way once more to the charm-weaver's backwater.

---

"What use are you to me with your arm all mangled like that?"

Miz Delphine in't one to mince her words, so now Young Claude sit all rigid in the stern, affronted. Didn't he risk life and limb for that stupid drum, to impress her, maybe get a kind look? He stay quiet. Up forward, Louis's shoulders snicker up and down. Miz D lean in and swat at the back of the boy's head. "Don't you sass your brother when he act so brave."

Claude's heart swell. The woman's praise is balm for the spirit, just as her medicines soothe his wound. Cleaned and bandaged before they left, covered with some numbing herbal mix that mask the throbbing, the gouges don't bother him so much at the moment.

Delphine, cool beside him, continue, "When he act so brave and foolish."

"You wanted your drum," Young Claude say, even while he think *And you would know a thing or two about* acting *a part, wouldn't you?* She turn, meeting and holding his bewildered gaze. A hint of a smile play on her lips, but she keep it from full-blooming. Instead she nod once, approving that he said *wanted* not *needed*.

"And you stormed in and got it. You confronted the Baronesses."

Claude snort. "No, Miz D, I slipped in quiet as poison while Sjöfn and Gna and Hlin and all the rest were sleeping."

"Not all nine of 'em," she observe and he shake his head.

"No, I s'pose not. Don't know who got me—might be it was Var, might be it was Fulla, both are quick as catfish. Whoever did the chasing, I was too busy running and hanging onto your drum and thinking, *That Delphine Laveau gone kill me if I lose this.* And frankly, Miz D, I'm more scared of you than I am of the Baronesses."

Delphine's laugh burst out, clear and bubbling, a spring of elation finally released after being buried too long under frowns. It's contagious, melodic enough to enchant Claude into chortling, and Louis into pausing his strokes.

"Hustle now, Louis Arvidsson. We got further to go and not much time to get there," she say, poking at the boy's ribs with a thin finger. Claude's mirth redouble as a fearful squeak escape his brother. *Serve him right for running off.* As Young Claude gather his wits, the witcher hunch over and collect a bag from under the bench in front of them. The small boat rock a little as he shift to give her more elbow room—and to better see what she's doing.

Delphine turn the drum in her hands. Nodding slowly or clicking her tongue, she check every inch of it for damage. A giant, hollowed bone make up its body, yellowed and inscribed with sharp-edged scratchings Young Claude can't decipher. Its head, round as a wolf moon, i'nt covered with just any old hide. Thin, fine vellum, bright despite the oil Delphine worked into it before the Baronesses demanded it as tribute, stretch across the drum's mouth. The material pull down its sides into neat points, held in place with silver strings. Words ink all over it, cursive and black, written in a language of ghosts. Miz D trace the sentences with glance and touch, reading, reciting, verifying none of the meanings have changed.

She give the tympanum a tap, not too much, not so hard it shouts. Claude watch phrases rise like mist from its surface; not powerful ones, mind, just little scribbled whispers. Cradling the instrument in the crook of her arm, Miz D follow the letters' path with her sharp sight, and when they dissipate she tilt her head in satisfaction.

Around them, the bayou feel too empty. Its waters are smooth brown glass, dotted here and there with leaves, shaded by nothing taller than cattails. When they reach the river, it's wider than it should be, stripped of all the ladies, and the current make for hard rowing. Louis work the oars for an hour, then two, until the water level start to drop; the keel glides along a good few miles more before they leave the flood well and truly behind them. When scrub and brush begin to roughen the banks rising steep on either side, they see ruts where the cypress queens went, along with they twiggy handmaidens. Some of the smaller trees lie dead, fallen by the wayside in the witchwood exodus, not strong enough to complete they journey.

Focusing on the horizon, Delphine start to hum a sombre tune, susurrant and low. Louis's back is drenched with sweat, his thick arms pumping faster and faster, like he's trying to out-row the voudon's song. Birds and buzzers seem to lose they musics, the oarlocks spin silent like they been freshly oiled, and even the boat's prow parts the river without so much as a lick of sound. It's unnerving: Miz Delphine swaying, trance-like, her chant hushing all but one persistent noise.

"Miz D," Young Claude say. "Did you hear . . . "

Splashing behind them.

"I'nt nothing, child. Don't concern yourself," she say and as if to put a stop to any argument, Delphine strike up a slow cadence on her drum. The tune is lonesome, a northern gale, a wail across woods and snowy peaks. No bayou melody, this. This here's a song of the north.

But Young Claude can't deny it—something's tailing them. There's a creak through the undergrowth. A *kerplunk* of heavy wet landings. An exhale, definitely an exhale. The louder it get the more his stomach churn. He pick at his bandages then absentmindedly start to knead his injured arm. Knuckling it as he twist and turn on the bench, trying to see everything at once. Trying to rub away the ache slow-burning through the numb.

---

They stop where the water once more turn to swamp.

Louis steady the boat against the reeds, straining to keep it level as Delphine and Young Claude clamber out. Miz D doesn't bother hexing the boy not to go nowhere—she know his fear is too big for deft leavings. He's a-shaking and a-shivering, the whites of his eyes huge. Delphine run a hand over his head and give a blessing as she pass, hoping him safe for Claude's sake. She gather her skirts and her drum, then barefoots it up the slippery bank, limber as a goat.

Claude look hard at his brother, sure he'll be gone before they even get into the sparse cover to they left; bracken and shrubs wracked with gaping stump-holes, crushed saplings and rough furrows where the tree-walkers went. At last he shrug and turn away, follow Miz D up the path. He's as angry at the boy for being a coward as he is resentful that he himself cannot run too. As he watch the slim-hipped form pad in front of him, he hear oars dipping deep into water, his brother slipping away. He wonder if the boat feel heavier for Louis's shame.

"Come along, Young Claude. Best not to worry so on what's coming along behind. What's past is past—and those eyes of yours are stuck on the front of your head for a reason. We're all built to look forward, *p'tit*. Fear of the unknown make a person fleet, and only a halfwit won't mind the way he's flying. Besides, you didn't go looking backwards when you stole my drum, now did you?"

"No, Miz D. I did not. Not a once."

---

They find the first cypress queen about three hours later, trying to drag herself through the muck.

"She's in a bad way," Young Claude say, but Delphine doesn't need some fool boy to tell her that. Miz D can see the poor lady's situation clear as the humpback mountain curving his spine in the distance: hard and nasty and dark.

If it'd been yesterday, the tree's shaggy crown would've been scraping the blue eighty-odd feet up in the sky. But today her mossy hair gather nothing but mud, dried duckweed, pebbles, and dirt. The bark on her knees, elbows, and up her trunk is all chiselled raw and oozing sap; long strips of it peel away as she fight for leverage, as she flail her branches, desperate to haul her great bulk that much further. The walkers' thoroughfare stretch out before her, trudged down by so many marching roots, so many knotted legs. But the fallen tree is all crinkled with dry, all the jaunt drained from her twisted limbs. Hard to tell when it was, exactly, that she teetered—her crawl marks blend with the wider trample—hard to tell how long she struggled to keep up with her sisters. Yet it's easy enough to see how the other ladies had gone and done a Louis, leaving this poor soul behind to fend for herself.

"Oh," Delphine gasp, taking in the thickness of the creature's thighs, her waist's impressive girth, "this one's a grandmère, ancient as they come."

*Of the Demon and the Drum*

Young Claude bow his head respectfully, but he itch to keep going. He never did cope well with the ill and dying, no matter if they ailment was of the flesh, no matter if it was of leaves and wood. And with the beating-down sun on his skull, and the herb-plaster losing its effect, well, he'll be joining they ranks soon enough if he and Miz Delphine don't find themselves a patch of shade.

She, however, won't hear of leaving until the old bayou woman is let to rest.

"We don't have an axe," begin Young Claude, but Delphine shut his mouth with a sharp look. She click her tongue and suck air through her teeth.

"You stupid, boy? Talking of axes where a whole forest of magicked trees been a-walking? I'm sure they'll take kindly to that." Of a sudden, Miz Delphine's gone pink, and she spit a lava of fury Young Claude's way. "And remind me to come visit you when next you're sick a-bed—we can talk about how best to chop you up, maybe even pick out some bullets 'case you need putting down."

"Sorry, Miz D."

Another *tsk-tsk* is the witch-woman's only response. She focus on the cypress, edging closer, careful not to startle her. As she walk, she untie one handkerchief from her knotted dress. She lay the fabric across her drum and quick-tap a pulsing beat. It's over almost soon as it's begun, as though Delphine had a mind to keep the rhythm—and their presence—a secret. Crouching down beside the twitching tree's head, Miz D hold out a kerchief now glowing with soaked-up words.

"Your wishes are not mine to steal," Delphine say to the failing thing, relaxing into her regal accent. "So you must tell me if you wish to go on."

Bayou women speak in the language of rain on tranquil water and wind through fog-laden leaves. They sentences rustle. They voices rattle and creak. But even without knowing exactly what the fallen queen say, Delphine understand her meaning: the tree in't here of her own willing. Her many arms may thrash, her twigs may claw and claw to move forward, but she's being pulled by a force she'd rather resist. The witcher know this from the strain, the terror in those rolling green eyes. The lady want to be still. Silent and dreaming.

— 199 —

Miz D place the charmed handkerchief across the ridges and valleys of the old face, covering all but the mouth. Settling down into the dirt, the voudon rest her pure white cheek against the tree's coarse grey, drumming quietly as the queen's dying ruffles her dreadlocks.

"We might have been children together, you and I," Delphine whisper, smiling sadly. "It doesn't seem fair that I should survive you."

The venerable one breeze her last words. Maybe her agreement, maybe her curse, maybe her blessing. They all just so much soft air. Whatever they meaning, Miz Delphine Laveau catch the phrases in her cloth. Before tying it back onto her dress, she rub the kerchief over her drum, buffing the carved sides until the bone gleams and the fabric in her hand is worn clean. And as always, Delphine silently thank the deceased for her gift—*Your spirit's song will resonate throughout the ages, dear one, given voice by vibration and rhythm*—then she declare to the high heavens that her instrument never has had such a noble polish.

---

The trail climb higher and so do they. A while back, Miz D hiked up her skirt between her legs, tucked it into her belt; for miles Young Claude has watched her smooth calves, muscles flexing beneath her skin. It's almost enough to distract him from the dizzy in his head—almost. For a time, his mind spin nice fever-fancies of her and him, twisting together, writhing . . . but when the howling pain sear from his cuts, he can hardly see for hurting. He squeeze his lids shut then, short-winded, lips all but disappeared as he try to clench the agony from his body. And his hearing, well, it's been messing with him too. Mawmaw Brynja always say he has a real gift for true-listening, but if she were out here right about now, Claude's *mère* would swear the devil himself had lodged in her son's ears, and he was setting there to sing the child down to hell. More and more, he hear hisses and crackles and patterings behind them. He feel yellow with nausea whenever he turn—*something is coming up on us, damn it*—but each time he does, there is only flattened grass, trodden earth, thin copses of dead trees. Dandelion fluffs wandering over the ruin of it all like lost souls searching for they last hallelujah.

## Of the Demon and the Drum

Puffing, Delphine stop when she crest the rise. Claude sleeves the sweat off his brow and smooth the pinch in his features, then come up beside her. A meadow stretch about a hundred *alen* in front of them, its edge guarded by a circle of stone sentinels. The monolith hulks on the far side, grey rock rising so high they crane they necks to see its peak, with a dark split gashing its crag-belly like a wound.

"Cave?" ask Young Claude, shivering, the memory of the Baronesses' lair too fresh in his mind.

"Maybe," Delphine reply. "Seem to me, though, it's got the size for someone with leaves and full-spreading branches; plenty wide enough for our ladies' bustles to fit on in without too much trouble. Might be they saw a way through."

They start across the clearing, Claude nervous as a cat, staring at the henge. They're almost in the centre when an intonation come from the mouth of the trail, a chorus of many voices in one.

"Not so fast, witchlin'."

Miz D turn stiffly, as if her muscles were calcifying. Young Claude watch her first, then follow her eyes when he see the fleeting look on her face, something he never expected Miz Delphine to show. Fear.

There are only three Baronesses, and Delphine is thankful the others are playing shy today. Seems Sjöfn, Gna and Hlin have stepped out in all they black and purple finery: dresses with embroidered petticoats; pleated panniers curving round they bony hips in silk brocade; lace bursting from velvet-trimmed bodices; and frilled sleeves in a riot of gem colours. Bells of silver, gold and bronze jangle on they ankles, wrists and ears. Long chains of jet and sapphire, amethyst and emerald, citrine and turquoise drip from they wizened necks. All demanded or stolen. Dug up and stripped from the bodies of the dead. On the gorgeous fabrics, here a stain, there a tear. Woven into they fine hairstyles, fat curls piled into towering 'dos, there are cobwebs and bones. They faces, all saggy jaw lines and withered mouths, are now white, now black, now creamy brown, always shifting, never set.

"You have something that belong to us," come the trinity chantrel once more.

"Oh, Miz D. I'm so sorry." Young Claude fold in on himself, nursing his swollen arm, and start shaking.

"I'nt nothing to be sorry for, boy. This lot's been following for some time, got your scent when they claimed you. I just thought we might beat them here."

"*Claimed* me?"

She nod at his bandages. "They got they claws in. And anything they touch is good as taken."

"But—your drum."

"Sure, they want that too, but flesh is more fun than some old scuff-rag of a tambour, in't it?" She step past, smiling at him so fast he's not sure it was ever there. "Don't you fuss now."

Miz Delphine get a look on her like she's chewing steel as she greet the Baronesses, who've sidled up good and close. One of them—Hlin?—has a ribbon wrapped around her wrist, and held firm in her grip; a rosy-red thing that twist and float as if lifted by a breeze, though no such breeze is a-gusting. It stretch behind the Mystères, wriggling a ways back through the crush-tangle thicket, winding on down the way they came. Hlin give it a yank and a monstrous growl split the air. Now the scraggly bushes shake hard, and a thing what doesn't seem to know whether it's man or wolf burst through the remnants of the greenery. He's got a large muscular body, but is walking on all fours, pawing felled leaves with bare knuckles and toes. Wearing nothing but filthy tatters what don't leave much to the imagination, his tan skin is slick with grease and mud one minute and the next he's covered in matted fur, now black, now russet, now a mottled mix of both.

"Jé-Rouge," say Young Claude.

Mesmerised, Delphine can't quite focus on the animal, can't look elsewhere. "Hollering even by day . . . This one in't a regular—"

The beast lunge for Miz D. He move so quick, she ha'nt the time to blink, much less get out the way, and he go straight for that magnolia-soft throat of hers, jagged teeth gnashing—

The Baronesses seem set to let they pet feed—

"Delphine!" shout Young Claude—

Until Hlin tense, bend her knees, wrap both hands around the choke-string, and *pull*. The man-wolf jerk back, gobs of spit flying, trajectory cut short, and he fall. Oh how he fall! Knocking his skull on the ground, crumpling, writhing, snarling with disappointed hunger and rage.

"Now, now, Lóki-Legba," say the three. "That's no way to behave. No way to greet our friend."

"Friend?" ask Young Claude, eyebrow raised. "How d'you figure?" His forearm ache something fierce and the scratches burn like there's fire-ants gnawing, trying to get out—and these curse-throwers selling it as if they all genial?

"Don't you second-guess our fine Baronesses, *p'tit*. They telling us honest, just like I always ask you to."

Claude shoot Miz D a quizzical look, but she's already explaining: "You know what they say, don't you? 'Bout how the enemy of my enemy is my friend? Well, if this in't that kind of situation, I don't know what is. In't that right, ladies?"

"You fixing to cheat us, little hedgewitch? Trying to steal what's ours by right?"

"No, of course not." Delphine lower her lashes, all humble sincerity, and pat Young Claude reassuringly on the arm. "You'll get your due. I'm not here to dispute rightful claims—what you lay hands on is yours to keep, I know it. But I was hoping we might strike up a deal."

"You *are* trying to swindle—"

"Now just hear me out," Miz D snap. Then she inhale through gritted teeth, and smooth the ruffles in her temper before continuing. "You may have noticed a certain—now how should I describe it, Young Claude? A certain . . . "

"Expanded horizon?" he suggest, and Miz Delphine wink at him.

"Well put, child. To say it plain: there in't a tree from here to hell and back. The bayou ladies all gone a-walking and took they cousins along for the trip."

The Baronesses bristle. "We're neither blind nor stupid, little calf—and once upon a time, neither were you. But if you think we'd travel so far from our sisters, so far from the comforts of home, just to dig up this scrap of a man, well . . . "

*The comforts?* Young Claude think with a shudder. *If clammy caves stanking with the rot of blood and sacrifice is comfortable, what shape does miserable take?*

"People come to us, understand? They come begging for cures, begging us to have a word to Bondye on they behalf, begging that we bring back what's already good and lost. The worst fools come to light-finger what's ours." As one, the trio look at Young Claude. "And that's what the floods come and done. Washed out our fine rooms, every last one. Our treasures, our votives, our charms—all gone."

"You won't mind, then," say Miz Delphine, "if I borrow this here boy from you awhile longer. Oh, now, don't scrunch up your fine faces so—I'm not going to keep anything what's yours. The three of you should oughta come as well; we'll be needing all the strength we can get to rustle up those cypress queens and bring them on back where they belong."

The Baronesses slit they eyes, and give Miz D the hint of a sneer, trying to spy out the double in her tongue.

"Suit yourselves," Delphine say, fed up with negotiating. She push Young Claude toward the fissure, never mind what the Mystères say. "You think me a thief, well, so be it. I'll be taking your little treasure—pardon me, your *claim*—and y'all can curse me til I'm shrivelled as the head on my belt. *À toi de voir.* You want your share of him, you let me know."

As he step out of the glaring sun into the blessed cool of the rocky cleft, Young Claude hear Delphine call out, "Go'on set that old hound dog of yours on us while you're at it. Makes no mind to me."

She clap Claude on the back and mutter, "Plenty of sticks for him to chase where we're going."

---

The tunnel is cathedral-high and just as cavernous. The silken swish of the Baronesses' gowns and the jingle of bells on they ankles and wrists echo, magnified in the huge space—but not loud enough to overpower the whine and snuffle Lóki-Legba make as he drag along behind them. Nor loud enough to dispel the constant scritching-scratching, clicking-clacking, rustling down the corridor. Young Claude crunch over twigs and leaves the witchwood trees dropped, reassured with each treacherous step that they're heading the right way. The stone wall subtly curving up on his left is damp to the touch and nubbled here and there with moss, all grooved and bashed-up from the forest's passing. As much as he can, Young Claude keep to the edge of the path—as far from the Baronesses as possible without losing sight of Delphine. They shush-talking to each other in a language Claude doesn't understand; they words dart all around in the dark, now down at ear-level, now all the way up with the bats.

Miz D walk ahead of them, focused on the pointed arch of shining grey a ways off, what looks to be the exit of this ill-lit passage. But even though she's playing aloof, Claude can tell by the tilt of her head that she's listening. Maybe she understand what they saying, maybe not. Young Claude grunt. Probably this here's just one more of her language-tricks. Then again, might just be Miz Delphine Laveau know everything there is to know about the things what walk *between*. Claude concentrate on that same exit, on the splash of sky that promise they in't disappeared forever into the darkest of all holes in the world.

The creaking, crunching, crackling get noisier and noisier the further they go. By the time they reach the far end, the racket is overwhelming. Squinting, they emerge into a sunken valley cupped in the mountain's rounded palms. The sun is well and truly on the downslide to evening; rich black shadows drip from the peaks. Wildflowers and tall grasses blanket the slopes, soft ridges that undulate down to a lake so big the far shore is hazy, so wide they have to sweep they heads from side to side to take it all in. Might be, on a clear, calm day, its beauty would steal a person's breath; but as they step out, they all breathless on account of the ugliness.

Where the lake darkens from shallow grey to deep-water blue, the bayou ladies are climbing. Witchwood, saplings, twigs, leaves crawling up one another; entire forests squirming like insects; biting, sparking, snapping they branches; writhing, scrambling, clawing; grabbing themselves together, joining they limbs, twisting into position. Fashioning two giant legs, a torso, two arms, a great bearded head. A man, a god, shaped of living wood, his feet set deep in the soft muddy bottom, shins propped up by trees already drowned beneath the waters.

Nested in one enormous eye socket, sit a bloated black demon of a bird.

"What a view, what a view," say the raven, his declaration booming from a body big as Delphine's house, pretending he in't watching the small folk approach. But he sure can see them, his first courtiers. "Who wants a lifeless palace," he say, "when *this* audience hall befits a king!" All excited, he flap his wings, hop onto the tree-god's nose and caw, "*This! This! This!*" His red peepers twitch left, right, up, down, tracking his call's echo around the vale, trying to see all his claimed land at once. The fidget-bird jump from nose to shoulder. He preen his mangy feathers. Jump to cheek to ear. Shuffle his scrawny feet. Snip twigs and leaves with his beak. Jump to clavicle to chin to eye. Shout orders to everyone and no-one. So energetic, and yet so fat.

Delphine feel the pull of his will, realise she's been feeling the quease of it in her stomach all along. From her great-grandmère, she's heard tales of this one, stories of the long-ago, when he was a glorified pet, a hatchling of thought. Now Huginn look out of this twig-golem's eye, his master brought a-sprouting into shape, and this raven style himself a king. *All for this?*

*This! This! This!*

Miz D sense the Baronesses' annoyance and gesture as if gentling a spooked horse.

"Patience," she say, lips barely moving. "Be too anxious and you won't get your due."

With her left hand she urge the Mystères backward, and with her right Claude forward. She herself take careful steps toward the lake's edge and the great bird, *lèse-majesté*, huff and flap his terrible wings, taking to the air. In moments he *whoomph* down in front of her, the whirlwind of his landing almost knocking them both to the ground. Delphine keep her footing and drop into a low curtsy, holding the hem of her patchwork dress like it's some ladylike thing, frilled with satin and lace. Young Claude bow as if born to it.

"You bowed! You bowed to me!" trill the bird.

"My lord," Delphine say, using her fancy tones. "A king should never be first to show such courtesy."

"Of course not!" Huginn squawk then start to nip at fleas on his belly. "Such is the lot of baseborn and supplicants. But simply bending at the waist is not enough! Not enough! Kindly kneel before presenting your suit."

"But, sir," Young Claude say, cottoning on to Miz D's slant, "you can't be prostrating yourself while we do. In't right."

"Insolence," Huginn say, high-tailed and a-flutter. "I haven't so much as nodded at you yet."

"No disrespect, sir, but there's a distinct tilt," insist Claude.

"It's the trees," Delphine say.

"What do you mean?" Huginn jump up and down, an outburst that shake the earth.

"Our cypress ladies are the most impressive you'll find in these parts, but they are no match for you. See how your throne lists? Its fine visage will soon be in the mud—and that simply won't do."

"What throne?" ask Huginn. "I stand before you with feet buried deep in the soil of my lands, arms encompassing all that is mine. Am I not beautiful? The most royal of kings you have seen?"

"Awe-inspiring," say Young Claude.

"Most august and sovereign," agree Delphine, pointing to the leaning effigy. Huginn follow the direction of her finger, red irises jittering. "As such you need—*deserve*—support of equal bearing. A throne fit for the All-Father."

"All-Father?" the raven ask, pondering. He shake himself and arrow-shaped feathers float down. "Yes, I am him. I am Óðinn. Today, I am Óðinn, I am sure of it."

"I knew I was not mistaken! My lord, I have brought these—handmaidens—for you. Just say the word and I will have them ensure your throne is safe."

The raven prance and preen, nodding his acceptance.

"Sjöfn and Gna and Hlin!" Triple glares bore into Delphine, but she pay them no mind, so the women shuffle forward as bid. "Tend to this structure, make it fit for our king."

Mumbling and grumbling, the Baronesses levitate across the lake, they skirts not even skimming the surface. They encircle the wooden man, raise they arms and, all a-sudden, they bodies *grow*. Taller than gallows, taller than silos, the Mystères stretch and expand til they're grand enough to support a god-man. Reaching up to his shoulders, they push this way and that, trying to make the thing stable, anchoring they shadows on the lakebed. Delphine and Claude exchange worried glances; the groaning and rasping of witchwood is like the snap and crackle of a fire. The Baronesses hold on for dear life, but even so, it teeters. Lóki-Legba sit at they feet, watching, waiting, poised just above the lapping waves without a care.

"It keeps swaying! It will fall!" Huginn shriek and hop from foot to foot.

"Trust me, my lord," Delphine say and call out once again, the command resounding, amplified by water and valley. "Sjöfn and Gna and Hlin!"

So Hlin let Lóki-Legba's leash unroll, longer and longer, seemingly endless coils of it splashing into the depths. The instant the rope get slack, the wolf-man howl with delight as he think, just for a moment, he's bound for freedom. Elated, he run fast as his two-legs—now four-legs—will take him. But soon the howling turn violent. Try as he might to go straight and true, Lóki-Legba veer always in one direction. He run hard in circles, spiralling round the raven's grand perch, with the fetter snug round his gullet, the chain thin as thought, strong as a promise. Near and far other *Jé-Rouges* take up the baying, the shared refrain of anger and frustration competing with the witchwood's grating screeches.

Huginn whistle as Delphine, eyeing the twig man, say, "A king need a crown."

"Hmmm," say the bird. "No, no. Óðinn doesn't wear a crown. Never has."

"All the more reason to have one here. Magnificent and proud, lord of all you survey—you deserve a fine crown with precious gems. And music, yes, music for the coronation!"

Unsettled, unsure, Huginn flap his wings again, large as sails, sending foliage and dirt flying. Delphine doesn't give him a chance to think too long on what she suggested; immediately, she set to drumming. It's a fiery, patriotic beat, fit to stir the heart of any being. *Arise, arise*, sing the notes, *arise, quartz and mica and jasper*. The lake froth and roil; the raven watch with interest, then obvious glee. If he had hands, he would clap them. Stones and boulders emerge from the lake, some small as cantaloupes, many as big as a horse and cart. Streamers of water, strings of moss, algae and slime drip from them as they fly upwards, roughly faceted and gleaming in the late afternoon light.

"We'll fasten them on with ribbons of ebony and gold," Delphine say. "Up you go, Majesty, so we can fit it just right."

Huginn adjust his great fat belly and take off, soaring higher and higher until he is a speck, then spinning lazy circles back down to land once more in the tree-man's hollow socket. Even with the Baronesses' steadying hands, his bulk threaten to tip the wooden statue.

"Sjöfn and Gna and Hlin," Delphine say, and the Mystères balance themselves, fix they shadow-feet firm, while the drum's tempo changes. Complex ribbons of words, metallic licorice and lemon, lift from the drumhead; they ripple through the air, twist and surge like cursive dragons, up to the twig crown. They bind the stones in place, tighter than a lock, tighter than a chain, securing the coronet to the witchwood man's head. On and on, the streamers keep wrapping—then wrapping become hooking and hooking pulling. Pulling, pulling, pulling. All the while Huginn watch, cocking his head with concern as some strands begin to cover over the eye socket.

Claude, knowing a distraction is needed, wade into the shallows and genuflect. "Your Highness," he say, and the demon puffed with pride. As Huginn's beak dip towards his slimy feathered breast, Delphine mimic the gesture, nodding at Gna, at Hlin, at Sjöfn. She reel the song in, making it tight and small and short, just as the Baronesses release they hold on the branches. The Mystères shrink, turn themselves to mud and shell, slick down into the water, sludge through the roots and thrashing tree trunks, then ooze out onto shore, returning to their former human sizes.

Even as Delphine compliment the king on his accoutrement, there are tears on her cheeks. She let the drum drop and instead loop her hands around the song-cords. Hlin clutch the lead Lóki-Legba has looped round and round the writhing tree-legs and her sisters add their might. Together, they lean back and brace they feet as best they can, so they look like a tug-o-war team. Then ephemeral twine and fetter-rope all are given one mighty yank.

The behemoth topple, hitting the lake's surface with a great tearing splash. With a squawk, Huginn plummet without even a second to fly free. The head with its weighty crown, sink in the space of a hiccup, trapping its grotesque wearer in the deep.

Weeping, Miz D pick up her drum again. Young Claude recognise the tune: it's a dirge, an old lament Mawmaw Brynja sung at many a funeral. Delphine in't playing for the black demon, though; her sadness in't for none but the cypress ladies, the drowned queens she had to sacrifice. Young Claude take comfort in seeing there are survivors, grand ladies making their way to the shore, scrambling back towards the crag, the passageway, and home.

"Oh, clever, clever!"

The last beats of Delphine's song die away before the Mystères make their claim. They glances are admiring, even pretty, but that doesn't fool no-one. Playing lovely or harridan, they want what they're due. Delphine nudge Young Claude toward the great wolf, who, for the first time this evening, is sitting quiet as a househound. He know his job and he know the rules, what he may and may not take.

Delphine gather twigs and kindling; she make up a small fire while the Baronesses watch on.

"Our pet does not require his food cooked," they scoff as one.

"Time for that talk about bullets, Miz D?" ask Young Claude with a sick smile.

Delphine ignore them all and it's only when the fire is going good and proper, not smoking or choking on itself, but burning with a determined flame that she tell Claude to kneel before the beast.

He hesitate for a heartbeat, then two, letting his legs buckle only when the voudon take up her drum again. Soon as those knees strike ground, Lóki-Legba bring his jaws together around Young Claude's arm, just below the elbow, right where the first line of scratches start, and he take that forearm off lickety-split! Fast and neat and Claude almost doesn't know it's gone til Delphine rush up, hands a-blur. Drumming, drumming, she plant her foot on his chest and shove hard, pinning him flat on the ground. The heart of the fire seethe with her music, flaring hot and hotter. The tempo is frantic, the flames urgent. They devour branches and tinder with such speed, in a handful of seconds there's nothing left but raging embers. Losing no time, Miz D crouch and press Claude's bleeding stump into the coals, cauterising it, stopping the blood in its tracks. Saving his life and filling the air with the smell of roasting pork.

Delphine stand opposite the Baronesses, whose faces flash between colour and absence, between living and dead, between rage and amusement at the unexpected.

"Only what you claimed," she say, her fingertips now light as raindrops tap-tapping on the instrument. "Only bit you got your hands on was his forearm. You got your due to the letter."

"Oh, so clever!" Shrieks in triplicate, now rough, now smooth, now musical, now thunder. "'To the letter' she say!"

Young Claude try to concentrate through the pain. Things look sharper, like Delphine waiting there, head thrown back, chin lifted defiantly as she square up to the Baronesses. And the Baronesses as they raise they arms and point they digits at the witch-woman. And Lóki-Legba who, having settled himself on a broken pile of Huginn's tumbledown throne, is gnawing happily on Claude's very own meat.

"Seems her cold heart got all het up over this here boy." Tripartite laughter shrill in Claude's ears. "Seem he got her silvery blood a-boiling, the summer in that swagger of his made her love-bold, definitely made her stupid. 'Only what you claimed' she say, ignoring the first thing she owe us, forgetting the last. Might be her kind can only think straight when they've got the arctic shivers . . . "

"Might be," they agree with themselves, three times, "Might be."

From the tips of Gna's bony fingers, from Sjöfn's hooked nose, from Hlin's slightly parted lips pour a smoke, a frost that glint with ice. It billow toward Delphine and engulf her like a maelstrom, whipping through her, lashing any and all warmth from her core. For a minute there is no suffocating heat, no humidity; only marrow-chill convulsions, only gasping in the freezing air. Winter shoot down her arms and legs, race out through palms and soles. In her grip, the drum harden until it's brittle and mute. Its parchment head stiffen with verglas, shattering under her touch. With a loud crack, the bowl split in two and both halves fall, smashing to pieces on the ground. The earth rumble as long glacial lines project out from the shards, translucent streaks of blue-white skimming across the lake's shore, straight to the slowest bayou ladies, the weakest and smallest cypresses still struggling to get out of the valley to follow their stronger sisters back home.

Caught in the whirlwind, Delphine watch as the feeble trees creak to a standstill. Instantly, each sprig and bough rime with crystal. Knotted limbs lose they colour. Delicate branches appear sculpted from sparkling snow. Long grasses ripple in an unfelt wind, they green blades vibrant against the glistening, petrified white trunks.

Exhaling a final gust, the Baronesses turn as one to admire they work. Bit by bit sultry air return to the glade—but the forest, and

Delphine, remain frozen. She look down at what's left of her drum, then up at the Mystères, motionless for fear of what else might die if she budge even an inch.

"Don't be foolish, *chère*." Sjöfn glean Miz D's thoughts; flicking her wrist, she scatter the debris, leaving nothing of the instrument fit for repair. "What you felt coursing through you just now was pure Baroness—power of the Loa in't yours to keep. No need to fret; you're the same pathetic charm-weaver you ever was, minus one rhythm box. That toy was ours for breaking, the trees we helped ours for taking. Such was our due *to the letter*; we got no more than what we were owed."

"And I'm to simply accept your word," Delphine say, a tremble undermining her high tone. "That we aren't now connected, somehow, the four of us. That you won't channel your magic through me whenever the whim strikes. That I—" she swallow, noticeably not noticing Young Claude, "I won't freeze everything I touch?"

It make no difference whatsoever to the Baronesses if Miz D believe them or don't she. Far as they's concerned, Delphine's worries are hers alone to suffer: they owe her no explanations. Hlin reel in Lóki-Legba's lead, choking him tight close to her side. One grubby paw cling to her skirts, the other to a sucked-clean bone. Gna and Sjöfn lift they hems like debutants at a ball and, dragging that filthy Jé-Rouge behind them, the trio head up the mountain, leaving the voudon just as sneaky as they came.

Young Claude quiver to see them go. Not that he want them to stick around, mind. But he can still feel his lost limb, the one now swimming in Lóki-Legba's belly. He keep swiping at flies with a hand that in't there. He wonder how long that sensation will last, before he believe them truly gone. Jelly-kneed, he peer at Miz D, all folded in small, hugging herself in the deepening shade.

Delphine take in the lifeless trees, unshed tears like stars caught in her lashes. A modest copse, no more, but that was warning and reminder enough.

"The bayou in't a place for snow and ice, for this wrong season all of my making," she say, trying to rub some feeling back into her hands. "What if I carry the Baronesses' frigid wind with me forever?"

Gingerly, she squat beside the fire's dying embers. Reaching out, she sense no heat at all; flames tickle her skin like alpine showers, horribly refreshing. For a moment, just one moment, she's so alone that even her spirit seem to flee her. The world recede to nothingness, her vision shift to black. So far from a home she can't go back to, so numb from the impossible distance... Diamond drops plink from her tear ducts; one become five, five become ten. Grinding crystals with the heel of her palm, she try to stop crying. Afraid she'll weep herself dry, turn from flesh to stone.

Then Young Claude touch her with his good hand, thread his fingers through hers. They clasp is tremulous, shaking-scared, but tight.

"I do believe I've had enough heat to last me ten lifetimes," Claude say. "I wouldn't mind me a bit of winter."

"But, your family..."

"Never expected me to come back—why else d'you think Louis moved so fast? They mourned me soon as I went calling on the Baronesses, Miz D, and ha'nt treated me as nothing but a *zombi* since I got back."

Delphine hesitate. She know this is too much to ask of him. She know she can't ask it, she won't. But with the fire in that steady grip, the confidence fixed in those eyes, she also know she doesn't need to.

"North?" Young Claude suggest, conjuring images of long, dark nights and snow-capped ridges, a little cabin sheltered beneath birches and oaks. A nameless place far, far away. Somewhere to be cold, and thrive.

"North."

# Warp and Weft

My dear husband hopes to forget the past and live in the future, though he hasn't said it in so many words. Why else should we leave the refinements and luxuries of European society? Why else abandon Mother England, our Sovereign, our Home? Why else should we settle amongst savages and endless trees, Over There, in the wilds of the New World? Here, our proud nation's roots extend through the centuries: they are steadfast in the ages-old fossils cropping up on our shores; they sprout from mottes and tors in the form of roundhouses and baileys, true symbols of Honour, Chivalry, Perseverance and Might; they are embodied in the persons of Kings Ælfred and Richard, in our virginal Elizabeth, our Glorious Anne, may she rest in peace. Oh, Backwater of the North, where are your Raleighs? Your Shakespeares? Your Newtons? Where is your History? What is there for us that we cannot find, in greater abundance, here?

Opportunity, *says my lord husband, and his is the final word.*

And so, emigration. *A promise of bettering one's financial condition only by depriving oneself of all the pleasures of English life, all comfort but memory. Cold comfort, indeed.*

Excerpt from the Diary of Mrs. William (Grace) Chesshyre
Entry dated 18 May 1772

Susanna doesn't hear voices, *plural*.

There's only one, an old man's, whose dry-leaf tones infiltrate her small cabin on draughts of autumn wind. She once thought of him as Iago, and the name stuck, but it hasn't made his presence less disturbing. He is shy when her husband is near, as though Sten's pale skin, white eyebrows, and nimbus of tight titian-blond curls might dispel such shadow creatures. As though his green irises, translucent peridot discs, are bright enough to outshine anything Susanna might find unpleasant.

But sunlight features do her little good when their wearer is so frequently away.

*It's loneliness*, Susanna thinks, humming 'Greensleeves' to counter the chattering. When Kalle is there, his boy-noises are welcome distractions, but at the moment he's playing by the brook until she calls him in for dinner. And for the third time in as many weeks, Sten is out ranging in the forest, checking beaver snares and trapping raccoons, spending his nights trading furs with redskins and mountain men instead of sharing her bed. He rarely tells her before he leaves; doesn't ask her permission. In all the years she has known him, Susanna's husband has begged her approval only once. Iago reminds her of this daily.

*It's being alone in these woods.*

The clearing around her house is a tiny, stump-dotted island, an ineffective breakwater against the ridge's swell of trees. In one direction tenebrous rows of birch, alder and maple stretch down to the creek that curves along the property line; in the other, pine and aspen bristle up the slope to the snow cap. By day the canopy glows. Leaves of gold, red and amber catch the strong afternoon light, reflect it downward like devilish eyes. At night winking orbs descend to the forest floor as wendigoes and lynx take shelter under jumbled boughs, a landscape so unlike the manicured gardens at her mother's Surrey home it still leaves Susanna bewildered. She draws the curtains to catch the sun's dying rays and adds lyrics to her song, taking comfort in the solid sound of her voice.

*It's exhaustion*, she thinks, reaching the chorus. Nightmares kept Kalle awake again; her son wouldn't settle even when she left a lamp burning to prove there were no witches perched on his pillow. Repeating the second verse, Susanna sings with such passion she almost misses the strange sigh tickling her ear.

Almost.

*It's all in my mind*, she thinks.

But the whispers, always whispers, tell her things no sensible English woman could ever possibly know.

"Use chickweed, not tinder, to burn people in houses," Iago mutters. Then he whimpers as she stokes the stove and buries sweet potatoes and onions deep in its cast iron belly. Soon the smell of roasting vegetables wafts through the one-room house; she hears the smacking of lips. "Peel the victims' skins carefully, else the disguise will be worthless," he says, referring to people or potatoes or both—Susanna is rarely sure what he means. Her tune wavers as she takes a brand from the fire and uses it to light three candles on the table, one on the shelf hanging above her narrow bed, another set on the flat-topped chest the cold woman made when Sten was a boy.

She runs her hand over the wood's rough grain, the chisel marks and grooves as deep-set as its maker's wrinkles. Susanna sometimes wishes Delphine was still around, with her quaint herb lore and outlandish stories, her arthritic fingers drumming a metallic beat on Claude's cast-silver hand. Sten's father putting up with it stoically until the very end. Paying no mind to anything, really, except the rifle he kept for killing wolves. Claude lavished attention on the weapon—far more than he ever showed his son, that pasty, golden-headed child who looked—looks—so little like his father. Though Susanna knows the pair of them lived far beyond their years, she resents Sten's parents for having the audacity to die.

The whispers are much bolder, much more disruptive with them gone.

"You'll have to gut her if you're to escape," he says.

Imagined or not, the words are brittle things that crack as soon as they're spoken. Susanna's heels click loudly on Shenandoah timber as she crosses to the stove to fill copper warming pans with coals; she nestles one beneath the quilt on her son's short pallet and slips a second onto her mattress to leach the damp from its core.

She thinks back to the manor house in which she was raised, to servants who did this same, menial task at night, who made sure she didn't lift a finger, that her every need was met and her figure soft and white. She looks at her hands now, premature age spots dotting the backs, flesh beginning to shrivel. Too much time plunged in numbing water, scrubbing clothes on rocks, hefting the axe to replenish the firewood while Sten is away, her skin a mosaic of scars and rough calluses, nails torn to the quick. Blinking back tears she thought long gone, Susanna goes outside to get Kalle.

Winter nibbles at her nose as she picks her way across the sludge of their yard. No lawns here, no attractive flowerbeds. A rising tide of fear washes through her. England is lost; *this* is home. Perhaps, one day, she'll accept it. Gazing at the thin brown stream in the distance, she pulls her shawl tightly around her shoulders and wonders how long it will take for it to thicken with ice. Its waters are already sluggish, the shallows choked with fallen leaves. It requires all her strength to let her son spend time there; but she's well aware that prohibiting it will only give the creek allure, will only drive him there faster, when she's not looking. At least, this way, she always knows where he is.

Kalle plays with his favourite wooden horse on the banks, now and then throwing stones to ward off rusalki. *If only Sten would stop filling the boy's head with such tales*, she thinks, knowing he's just picking up where Delphine left off. Fae and selkies and God-knows-what else; enough to keep her son howling for hours the minute the candles are snuffed. Scaring him with superstitious rootwork, folk magic and the like, when there are real enough dangers in these woods.

"Kalle?" Even now, seven years after his christening, the name still grates whenever she says it aloud. She'd wanted to call him Henry—a king's name, that, and also her late father's—but Sten insisted on weighting the boy with *Karlemagnus*, a title more than twice the babe's size. Shortening it to 'Kalle' is still a mouthful she'd rather spit out, but at least it's palatable.

"Don't get wet," she calls. "You'll catch your death!" She imagines freezing ocean waves washing over her boy; sees him struggling for air; flailing for purchase as his ship is buffeted by winds, tossed well out of reach. The thought comes unbidden, uncontrollable. Bubbles of life oozing from his lips as he sinks into the green depths, a coral reef his only grave marker . . .

"Kalle!" *There's no need to panic the boy*, she thinks, smoothing her skirts as if that will help rid her of worry. *No need to give him new fears on top of old.* Ignoring the creek's babble, she closes her eyes and listens to the trees creaking. Leaves chattering. Captain

Gallop, Kalle's wooden toy, thudding onto dirt. Her son's high-pitched laughter every time the horse hits ground. For a few brief moments there is respite. Out here the only voices she hears come from avian throats, nesting calls of grackles and blue jays and crows. Steadied, she gives Kalle a smile and gently says, "Be careful."

---

Struck by a mood that suits invisibility, the three weavers do not break the silence. Unspooling skeins of transparent wool from hidden pockets in their cloaks, they watch Susanna slowly gather an armload of split logs from the dwindling pile stacked beneath a lean-to at the far end of the clearing. The breeze tugging at Susanna's long skirts, flapping her shawl like a ship's sail, doesn't bother the women in the least. Their irises shimmer with flecks of burgundy, sapphire, gold. Three opal sets that radiate with the effort of looking through time, focus, for now, on the present. Perched with their legs and threads dangling over the eaves of the cabin's shingled roof, the women watch, and bicker as only sisters can.

"A trick of yours?" Urðr squints at Skuld. "Raspy grave-dweller's curse to haunt our girl? Reincarnated spirit sent to remind her to give us our due?"

"Not mine," Skuld replies through rotted teeth, though it is true that Susanna has failed them for ten years. She hasn't once left gifts of creamed milk on the stoop, nor has she offered boiled bones from her cookpots for the trio to use as loom shuttles. Filaments run like spun glass through the weavers' taper-thin fingers. Reflective warp-fibres weighted with silver skulls sway as faces and likenesses not found in this country run up and down their sheer lengths. "No, my enchantments aren't so capricious."

Verðandi snorts and plucks a cardinal-red hair from her scalp, then knots it into the pattern growing before her. "The instance with Baldr and the mistletoe notwithstanding . . . "

Skuld scowls. "All I did was sew a few white berries in the cloth—you're the one who transformed them into a weapon." Reaching over, she uses her talons to snip a dozen intricately woven yarns off at their base. Between warp and weft, a great swathe of the image withers and dies, leaving a ragged gap in Verðandi's third of the fabric. Two thunderclouds shoot from the tips of singed strands; fat smoke walruses expand to the size of small mountains, and hang in the sky. The air crackles with ozone as the bulky clouds roll, casting the land immediately below into darkness. Lightning tusks clash as the beasts wrestle. With deafening barks, they grapple until one overpowers the other, flippers and teeth drawing gouts of rain.

Urðr clicks her tongue. "Now, now, children." Expression haughty, she smooths long white tufts away from her face, adjusts the pewter hourglass that fastens the cloak at her throat. The storm churns the yard into mud. "Behave."

Water slides over the women without leaving much trace of its passing. Droplets bead their protruding clavicles and prominent cheekbones like tiny pearls; the waxen flesh of their legs and feet, bare beneath the shadow-spun dresses they wear hitched up to the knee, remains dry. Verðandi leans toward the loom. Its warp-beam hangs unseen, centuries above their heads; the tapestry falls in a sheer curtain before them. Unlike earthly weaving, this ever-growing sheet falls skyward; eternal designs pushed up to the seat of the gods. Verðandi severs the clouds raging from her shorn fibrils. Pinching the frayed ends between her lips, she works them with her tongue until they sprout an equal number of new short tails, which ring like crystal bells as they wriggle. She tilts back and pulls, stretching them with her teeth.

"Our girl should watch her step," Urðr says, gesturing as Susanna drops the bundle of firewood, runs for Kalle. Her worsted slippers were designed for the high street, the sparkling comb in her locks better suited for stepping out to sip chocolate in civilised company, not for wild terrain such as this. But there are no high streets in this territory. No coffeehouses. Nothing remotely resembling civilisation, and still she *clings*.

Drenched, the woman's petticoats drag, collecting enough twigs, slop and debris to build a colony of birds' nests. The white lace of her neckerchief and apron now adhere like tissue to her hunter-green dress. She slides down the slope to the brook, collects Captain Gallop and drags Kalle from his imaginary playmates. Covered in muck, the boy digs in his heels as his mother alternately points at the cabin and pulls his arm.

"I do love a good mummer's farce," says Skuld as she embroiders autumn leaves onto her section of the arras with floss spun from her own golden hair.

Below, Susanna feigns defeat and takes two steps away from her son. His rigid posture relaxes as he prepares to return to the water's edge. The moment his back is turned, Susanna swoops. Grabbing the boy as local farmers would a greased piglet, she pins his limbs against her body, lifts him off the ground, then takes one measured footstep after another toward the house. The women know her legs are shaky beneath the sodden skirts, but her jaw is set. This strange mix of weakness and determination is why they forgive her omissions. Why they almost love her. Why they *wait*.

"Nicely played," says Verðandi.

"Why doesn't she wear a bonnet?" Urðr leans to her right, allowing Skuld to yank several white strands to use for depicting walrus-clouds, raindrops, and sodden lace. "Dirt takes the shine from raven-heads just as it does ivory . . . She must have to wash the grit from that mane at least twice a week."

"Dressed like that, our girl must take any excuse she can to preen . . . " Verðandi eyes the gash in the tapestry, sizes up the thickness of Susanna's plaited chignon, imagines the length required for such a magnificent twist.

"Such vanity should not be unrewarded," she says, with the ghost of a grin. "Why let her efforts go to waste? There's much darkness yet to be woven, my sisters. And it's been decades since we've seen such an abundance of fine black thread."

The other two, hearing the familiar longing, exchange a look that says *"Again?"*

Verðandi ignores them.

---

Susanna's brush has an ivory handle, the back inlaid with mother-of-pearl, but its bristles are thinning. A small oval mirror propped on the table against a pile of socks in need of darning, and held upright by a worn copy of *A Book of Common Prayer*, catches the candles' warm glow. In its spotted glass, she can see her son's slumbering form reflected. Tucked into her bed, his blond curls still glimmer with rain, his cheeks dewy and flushed. She hopes he rests well tonight.

"How to choose? How to choose?"

Susanna removes her comb and places it on the table, followed by a small haystack of foil pins. She unravels her braids, towels her storm-mussed tresses, then begins the process of redoing them. As she brushes her long hair, Mother's lessons resound. *Rouge and powder and a regal bearing are a lady's best companions.* But there are no cosmetics here, no companions but a sleeping boy and an incessant, ghostly prattle. Vigorously, she pulls the brush down until her biceps ache, each stroke a cacophony of boar bristles catching on tangles, a repetitive *shhhhhhh shhhhhhh shhhhhhhhing* she hopes will drown out Iago's gibbering.

"So beautiful, both of them: one a bright raven—oh, wicked, wicked and lovely—the other, an innocent, still new to this middle earth, hardly as long-lived as the first. To love both, not one . . . Why not? Why not? Two is better than one; yes, so much better . . . With much love to spend, how is a poor seed to choose? No choice. No choice at all."

For the first time, Susanna finds sense in the old man's ramblings. *He's talking about us.* Her hand stills. *Kalle and I: the young one and the raven.* Her back stiffens and she quickly looks around the room. Nothing is out of place. The whitewashed lumber walls, chinked with straw and horsehair, are no more askew than usual. The open cupboard boasts regular kitchen clutter: cutlery, plates, small packets of dried beans and flour. No footprints mar the soot-swept hearth; the woodstove crackles as it consumes dank logs. Kalle wheezes softly, in and out, the candle on the shelf above him casting his features in the calm patterns of oblivion. Sten's trunk is closed and locked as always, the key hanging next to his spare cloak on a hook by the entrance. Nothing but cobwebs and a shaded oil lamp hang from the rafters. No-one hides beneath the table at which Susanna sits. No hunchbacked men lurk in the corners.

*Only Sten calls me Raven*, she thinks, proceeding with her grooming, just to occupy her shaking hands. *And even he hasn't done so for years . . .*

She looks at the comb her husband gave her, long before they'd wed. Long before they'd fled.

---

"Hail, Raven-girl!"

Sten's bellow had echoed across the market square, resonant enough to shake white powder from wigs, to send awnings a-fluttering, and startle a flock of sparrows into flight.

Susanna remembers it perfectly: how she kept her eyes averted as her lover greeted her, decorum be damned, shouting without a trace of the colonies in his accent. *He'd done well to hide his ancestry*, she thinks now, convinced she wouldn't have been so keen to follow him if she'd known what backward province her fair trader called home.

Basket hooked over her arm, Susanna's heart raced as she strolled from stall to stall—the dressmaker's, the florist's, the twopenny baker's—occasionally leaning over her chaperone's shoulder to inspect a ream of brocade or a spool of delicate lace. Despite the season's chill, Susanna fluttered a fan to prevent Mrs Leeds from seeing the flush creeping up her neck. From the corner of her eye, she saw Sten wending through the bustling crowd. Though slicked back from his forehead and clubbed with a maroon ribbon, his strange hair gleamed in the rare Surrey sunshine. Amid a sea of tricornes, her lover went hatless; providing milliners with beaver felt did not mean Sten felt obliged to wear the product of his trade. Susanna caught herself smiling, then and now.

*Such rebellion*, she thinks, placing the brush on the table next to the comb. Using her fingernails, she traces a perfectly straight parting and splits the ebony fall into two sections, each spilling in waves to her waist. *What good does it do anyone?*

Business had been lively that brisk October morning. Cobbled walkways were invisible beneath a flurry of skirts and men's outmoded buckle-toed boots. Fashions moved slowly in Surrey, but gossip travelled quick as the plague. As Susanna waited for Mrs Leeds to haggle a lower price on two lengths of velvet ribbon, she heard rumours carried on winds from the south.

"It seems, lately, my husband's thoughts are consistently with the unfortunate Marie," said one woman, rearranging the apples in her cart, turning the fruits bruised-side down. Susanna couldn't hear the farmer's response, but the apple-seller barked out a laugh, a checkboard smile, black gaps where teeth should have been. Behind her, two milkmaids rested their pails in the shadow of the church's steeple; they, too, spoke of France's late queen, saying things, such horrible things—what mother would think to do such things? It made her gorge rise.

Dire thoughts fled the instant Sten appeared. He guided her to the farmer's wain with the deftest, barely-to-be-seen contact.

Feigning aloofness, she announced, "Mr Laveau," and quickly looked around. Yes, Mrs Leeds was still within sight: no-one could accuse her of impropriety. Clearing her throat, she picked up a piece of fruit, put it down, picked it up again. "Apple?"

He took her by the hand, pulled her aside. "We haven't time, Raven-girl."

Susanna tried not to giggle at her beau's impatience. She pried herself from his grasp and snapped her fan. Its emerald brocade fluttered like hummingbird wings. "We've all the time in the world . . ."

"Don't stain your tongue with such falsehoods," he said, barely audible above the clip-clop of horse-drawn calashes on the market's narrow passageways. Sten spoke to his feet, lips hardly moving as he opened the top three buttons on his coat. Should anyone look their way, they'd see nothing amiss: a young girl keeping the sun from her already olive skin; a stately gentleman searching his pockets for a handkerchief. "*Reinen* sails within the week, my love. And I shall go with her when she does."

Susanna made to turn away, but Sten's touch, soft as a snowflake on her wrist, stopped her. His hand travelled quickly from wrist to elbow to back, where it swiftly ran up her spine. She leaned into the embrace, nervous, excited.

"You must accept this," he said, pressing close. Too close.

"No," she said, spying Mrs Leeds counting out coins for the ribbon-maker, "we'll be caught. And Mother—"

Sten chuckled. His green gaze skimmed over the scarlet sashed gown, the high-necked frilled chemise, the foolish turban she wore—all to please her Mother. Mrs Edward Dalingridge, who'd lured many a suitor on her eldest daughter's behalf, with cunning words and an impressive dowry; who'd forced Susanna to pose, a picture of silent beauty for men of sufficient wealth to admire, in salons and dining rooms and balls; who'd hosted endless dinners, serving her daughter up on fine porcelain dishes that Susanna knew would never be hers, not with her clumsy hands . . . Yes, this same woman would blanch to see the expression on Sten's face. Not of a man who hungers for love, but of one who has already tasted it.

"You must accept this," he repeated, pressing a small handcrafted parcel into Susanna's palm. She could feel well-defined edges through the thin silk. "A token of my affection."

"Thank you," she began, but Sten had gone. Disappeared between the fishmonger's stall and the pen of sheep, perhaps, or down the laneway toward the apothecary's.

"No need to thank me, child," said Mrs Leeds, as she slipped the wrapped ribbons into Susanna's basket. The girl jumped; she hadn't heard her chaperone approach. "The coin what paid for these ribands came from your late father's coffers, not mine own."

"Of course, Mrs Leeds." Susanna quickly scanned the horizon, but her view was obstructed by carriages, coachmen, shoppers and many-coloured stalls. He was gone.

Later that night, in the safety of her chamber, she withdrew Sten's gift from her skirt pocket. Mrs Leeds had retired as soon as the latest suitor departed (a banker, dull as the notes he daily distributed), and before the scent of his cologne dissipated, Mother had dismissed Susanna with a disappointed click of her tongue. *Goodnight, goodnight,* she thought, so accustomed to her Mother's scowls that they only occasionally bothered her. She locked the door with a heavy key, crossed to her curtained bed, then placed the parcel on her pillow. Sitting cross-legged on the thick down coverlet, she untied the complicated knot slowly, savouring the mystery wrapped in pretty blue. Not for a moment did she believe this would be the last present Sten gave her.

*He won't leave,* she thought. *He mustn't.* A scrap of paper slid from the wrappings and lilted to the ground, revealing an unusual comb. The width of her palm, it was as heavy as a crystal goblet and just as well-made. Each of its long teeth was a tiny sharpened bone; joints fused to the decorative bridge, lengths fanned out like a bird's wing. Unlike the bones Susanna left on her plate at mealtimes, these were not flesh-stained grey but obsidian flecked with onyx. An absence of light masquerading as ornament in her hand. The piece's bridge was decorated with shards of sapphire and indigo, arranged into a flying bird shape. Not a bluebird, Susanna realised, despite its colouring. The olive branch in its beak, shaped of hardened lumps of ash, bespoke a dove.

*It's hideous,* she thought, reaching for the note Sten had enclosed.

*A strong charm for a strong spirit,* he wrote. *Protection passed from one generation of Laveau women to the next, for years* beyond counting. My Great-Greatmother would be honoured, should you agree to continue the tradition . . .

*That's it?* Susanna thought, tasting bile. After three weeks of sneaking, promising, compromising, loving: *I'm to please his Gran-dam?*

Bone tines scratched her fingers, drew blood as she went to throw the thing across the room. In the process, streaks of bright red smeared a tiny scroll wedged on the comb's underside. Lodged between the jewels' settings, it was small enough to be carried by pigeon.

*The first note was a ruse!* Smiling, Susanna sucked on her scratches. *A harmless letter, should Sten's gift fall into Mrs Leeds' or Mother's clutches.* She cursed her fumbling digits and frantically unrolled the blood-spattered message.

*Come with me*, it said. *Please.*

It was all the persuasion Susanna needed.

⁂

In her tresses the comb had shone like a mirage, a promise of beauty beyond rippling waters. Curved like the ship that would carry her to the New World, a new love, a new life. So much hope, spilled.

"Gods and seas, seas and gods." Iago sang a now-familiar refrain. "None can go back, none can return . . . Do you hear me, ladies? Sun, snow, and fire? You, with your half-knitted blankets. Ha! That got your attention, did it?" His chuckle was flimsy; leather snapping in the wind. "In the sky, over lakes, on the ground—the pathways, forever blocked. Believe what you will. Waves of chaos are yours, little Raven. Oceans of time and regret. Doomsday runs like a stream through your fingertips—always now, always then, always out of reach. Here is where you'll stay."

"*Enough.*" Plain pins gouge Susanna's scalp as she fastens her plaits in place. *He's gone.*

She rises and puts the mirror and brush away. Her stomach roils, just as it did all those years ago, on the deck of Sten's ship. Unrelenting rain had buffeted the galleon's sails as England became a ragged coastline in their wake, then a foggy smudge on the horizon, and then nothing at all. So many men swept overboard. So many lives lost. Overwhelmed by the wind's howling, the raging of the troubled sea, Susanna spent her days in the stifling, reeking hold.

The voyage is blurred in Susanna's memory; she glimpses it through portholes in her mind, tries to knuckle it away. "Give me peace," she says, quavering, though the old man's monologue has already subsided. "For once, damn you. Give me some peace."

With shaking hands, she pats her coiffure to ensure it is neat. She takes a deep, calming breath. Exhaling, she pats her eyes. Smooths invisible creases from her lace apron. Deciding to let Kalle sleep while he can, she sets the table for a solitary meal. Broth and bread, pottery and plate, warm milk and cheese. A well-used wooden spoon. Three candles, burned low. A scrap of faded blue silk dropped over her obsidian comb.

---

Verðandi's fingers throb as she weaves. A pair of lean horses and a shallow wagon appear, millimetre by millimetre, on the textile before her. If anyone asked, she'd honestly say she toils harder at this task than do her sisters—it's *her* choice of colour, *her* design, *her* vision, which set the tone for the tableau. She can't snooze the way Urðr is now, coiled on the foot of Susanna's bed. She can't stitch with only half her attention, like Skuld does every day, knowing if she goes slowly enough Verðandi will fill in the gaps herself. Unlike her siblings, who are happy to rework and reknot old sections without any plans for the future, Verðandi has responsibilities. She must make things happen. Only she knows where this story will end.

Which, she thinks, accounts for her scalded fingertips.

"Such an abundance of fine black thread," she'd said earlier as Susanna ran in from the storm. In one movement Verðandi had hooked her ankles beneath the cabin's eaves, held onto Skuld's forearm, and reached *down*—so far her arms and back stretched all out of proportion—and swiped a clump of their girl's hair. At least, that had been the plan.

Instead, her fingertips had made contact with jewel and bone. Recoiling, she'd nearly toppled to the earth as red welts erupted on her flesh. The points of her talons sizzled and smoked. Her body had snapped back to its original dimensions, and the prey entered the house unplucked.

"We go after her," Verðandi had said, all tolerance fled. "She's denied us long enough."

Skuld had shrugged noncommittally, then tied off a stitch. Urðr raised an eyebrow, but continued with her work. Verðandi grasped the shuttle, stilling its movement with her right hand. Around her, the world had gone quiet. Birds paused in mid-flight, the creek hushed its burbling, the woodland symphony of leaf and insect and beast fell silent. Clouds swirled to a halt. Below, hinges stopped mid-squeal. Kalle's curtailed laugh echoed in Verðandi's ears. Acting quickly, she'd stretched the length of her left arm across her sisters' chests and none-too-gently pushed them away from the loom.

"Ready?"

The trio reclined in unison. They sank through the roof, pulling reams of shimmering cloth down with them, and had fallen soft as dew to the floor inside. Silver skull-weights jangled from one side of the room to the other as the weavers adjusted their creation, drawing it over the ceiling rafters to dangle heavily down by their bare feet. Verðandi released the shuttle; it immediately resumed its scuttling journey, left to right to left. The world lurched back to life. Busy getting Kalle out of his wet jerkin, blotting his hair, putting a kettle on the stove and adjusting the warming pan in his bed, Susanna hummed and laughed with her son. Oblivious to the women's commotion.

When the child was asleep and Susanna preoccupied with her *toilette*, Verðandi abandoned the weaving and crept up to the table. She stood close enough to smell the rainwater on Susanna's skin, the musk of her underarms, the hint of mildew on the towel draped over her shoulders. For a moment, she was mesmerised by the way Susanna's locks drank in the candlelight, returning a vivid blue sheen.

Verðandi's talons hovered so close to Susanna's crown, they scarcely avoided getting clipped by the brush. She couldn't feel the same heat that had seared her earlier; no fire emanated from the woman's head. Even so, Verðandi resisted the temptation to grab handfuls of luxurious hair-thread. For now.

"I'm doing this for you," she said, calculating, planning, assessing. Her knuckles cracked with the effort of not-grabbing.

"Do you hear me, ladies? Sun, snow, and fire? You, with your half-knitted blankets."

Three sets of opal eyes looked up, searching.

"You've still got a troublesome tongue, old man," said Skuld.

"Ha! That got your attention, did it?"

"Still of this earth are you, Ari?" Urðr reached up and tugged at the tapestry. With Skuld's help she pulled, unrolled and folded six hundred years' of weaving, reading generation after generation of colourful lifelines and faded endings. "Ah," she said, tracing a ragged trajectory down metre after metre of the fabric. "Here you are." Every so often, a raven-shaped moonstone interrupted the pattern, extending some stories and abbreviating others. Ari's panels were heavily adorned with these pearlescent rooks: each time his strands wore thin, another corvine bead reinforced the design.

"I take it this is your doing," she said to Verðandi, who was notoriously fond of sparkle.

"Not mine." Her response was almost lost amid the sudden sound of flapping wings. "Remove them all—it makes no difference to me. Take him all the way back to Vinland for all I care."

Ari chuckled. "In the sky, over lakes, on the ground—the pathways, forever blocked."

Verðandi smirked. "Not for *her*. Mark my words: she'll find a way to take back what was lost."

"Believe what you will . . . "

"Stop humouring him," Skuld snapped. "Let's finish this and be gone."

"Agreed," said Verðandi, just as Ari sang, "Here is where you'll stay."

"Give me peace," cried Susanna. "For once, damn you. Give me some peace."

"Ease the tension on the girl's warp, dear sisters." Urðr snorted as she inspected Skuld's handiwork. "String her any tighter and she's going to snap."

Half-heartedly, Skuld loosened a stitch here and there. Verðandi strolled over to the arras and fiddled with one or two beads.

Outwardly calm, Susanna had tidied and set the table. Eaten a meagre dinner. Stared at a blue handkerchief, then finally swept it up and stuffed it into her skirt pocket.

Evening had fallen, cold and harsh. An overcast sky hid most of the stars; it was too dark to trek down to the creek for clean water. They'd watched as she stacked the dishes in a tidy pile to be washed in the morning. Her restlessness charged the air about them: she checked on her son; darned the heel of one sock then abandoned it; read half a page from her well-worn prayer book; stoked the fire only to bank it five minutes later. As the moon rose, she'd finally snuffed the candles, undressed, and retired.

Eyelids heavy as history, Urðr had followed her to bed soon after.

Leaving her younger sisters to weave without supervision.

———∘∘———

"I'll do it if you give me your cloak."

Verðandi schools her features as she considers Skuld's price. How many battles had she survived wearing it? How many hoof-carven fields had she crossed, each thick with corpses, dipping her garment in crimson pools until its hue was richer and darker than either of her sisters' mantles? For millennia she has added pockets to its lining to accommodate her fateful supplies. She knows precisely which pouch contains what; without looking she can retrieve any item she needs. But as she eyes the wisps that have worked loose from Susanna's plaits, her resolve weakens.

A great night scene is coming in her third of the composition, for which she desperately needs such an ungodly wool.

Verðandi fumbles with the clasp at her neckline, a miniature spyglass wrought from crystallised dreams, bedecked with garnets of hope. Even in the darkened room, it shines with the prismatic light of things yet to come. This is hers alone, no matter what deals she brokers with her older sister.

Skuld scoops up the cloak the instant it hits the floor. She tosses her own to Verðandi, who unhooks a golden brooch from the collar, fashioned from wheat and sunshine into the shape of Yggdrasil in full bloom.

"Give it here," says Skuld.

Passing the carelessly discarded amulet back, Verðandi latches onto her sister's wrist and draws her in close enough to bite. "Now sew."

"As you wish," Skuld replies, sneering. She pins the glowing tree to the woven image in front of her. The cabin's interior is captured in full detail: stove, cupboard, and table; calico curtains limned with wan light; Kalle sprawled on his own pallet now, arm wrapped around the toy horse; Susanna tossing and turning, not disturbing Urðr's rest in the least. Skuld's talons lengthen as she concentrates. Sharp, they grow, and sharper, until they are pointed for needlework, perforated with small holes for her thread. Tiptoeing around the room's perimeter, she drags their tips along baseboards and in corners, scraping up balls of dust and shredded spidersilk, careful to leave just enough on the floor for her purposes. Between her fingers, she spins this grey fluff into floss. One lap of the room done, she stands once more in front of her handiwork. And with Verðandi looking over her shoulder, she sews.

First one mouse, then two, on the floor by the table. A third on the windowsill, another on the bed's footboard. A fifth, cheeky and big-eared, crouches on Susanna's hip. Verðandi laughs as leftover dust and webs begin to whirl like tumbleweed across the cabin floor. She watches as they collect into small patches of fog—on the table, windowsill, bed panel and linens—held together by the weaver's determination and the deftness of her needle. Sweat glistens on Skuld's brow; she wipes it off between stitches, pressing the moisture into her embroidered mice.

"Will that do?" she asks, winded.

Verðandi nods. "For now. Let's see how they fare."

As if on cue, the rodents in the room squeak to life.

They scramble down walls and the table's turned legs. Down spindles, keeping away from Urðr. They scurry across patches of brown, taupe, blue and red, the blanket quilted in a variable star pattern. The closest one creeps up Susanna's ribs, upper arm, neck, cheek—then parks his rump on her temple and begins to chew at the nearest braid.

"How long will it take?" Verðandi asks, pacing over to the sleeping woman and back to the tapestry.

"Patience, child." Skuld caresses the stitched mice with her fingertip, latches them onto the loom shuttle, which carries them over to Verðandi's third. "I've done my part. It's up to you now to let them do theirs."

Verðandi combs the strings upward, pressing the mice into her design. After a few passes of the shuttle, she notices a blur in the image. A streak of yellow pine? Strips of leather . . . A bridle? Scowling, she leans forward for a closer look. "There's a flaw in the weave, Skuld—"

On the floor, three mice patter over Kalle's legs to join their brothers on Susanna's bed. The boy wakes screaming. He looks at the rodents, then at Verðandi and Skuld. "*Häxorna*, Mamma!"

Kalle jumps up. Kicking wildly, he squashes the mice on his pallet; small puffs of dust rise around his stockinged feet as he stomps. He shakes Susanna, slaps a fat mouse away from her. "Witches, Mamma! Witches!"

"What have you girls done?" Urðr wakes and launches herself away from the mattress, runs to the loom. Kalle catches the movement—he snatches up Captain Gallop, whips the wooden horse across the room after her. It sails harmlessly through the tapestry, past the women, and crashes into the far wall. The toy splinters with the force of his throw. In pieces, it clatters to a halt on top of Delphine's wooden chest.

"Ragnarok," says Ari. "Hooves across the vault of the sky!"

"Calm down, love." Susanna rolls over, not fully awake. "Hush now, it's only a dream."

Kalle's chest heaves. His eyes fill with tears as the little balls of his fists shake with fury. "Get out," he shouts, staring directly at Verðandi. "Cursed *häxorna*! Get out!"

"Shhhhh," says Susanna, peeling back the coverlets. "Climb in, darling. There are no witches here."

"It's time we take our leave, dear sisters." Urðr pulls the tapestry's right edge, gestures at Skuld to grab the middle. The blonde woman kneels and sweeps up an armful of weighted skulls before securing the work's ragged hem. Verðandi hesitates.

"We need her," she says. Still watching Kalle, she latches on to the weaving's left border. "The boy is a nuisance."

"Indeed," says Urðr.

"And?" asks Skuld.

As one, the women step backward. Slowly, slowly, so as not to fray the material on the cabin's rough-hewn rafters, its jagged shingles and arrow-peaked roof. They pull and step, pull and step, until they melt into the wall, dragging the cloth through with them. Outside, the trio retreats to the tree line, still well within sight of the cabin.

"He must be . . . unstitched." Verðandi looks for Urðr's approval, gets it. Turning to Skuld she says, "And I want my cloak back."

"Allow me," says Urðr, nudging Verðandi away from the front door. "You're completely tone-deaf. His timbre is deeper—that's the human taint for you—but even with that Southern twang, Sten still speaks with a Fae lilt."

With a quick tug, she checks the knotted, sticky cords drooping from the knob, trailing in three separate directions across the dirt. They hold firm. "Ready?"

Skuld nods, muscles tense. She lifts her arms, tightens her grip on the transparent ropes' ends. Verðandi loops cables twice around her waist, then prepares to sprint. "Try to keep up, old lady."

Urðr snorts. Lines weld to her ankles, keeping her long legs unencumbered for running, her arms free for grabbing. She clears her throat.

"*Lilla gullebit*," Urðr calls, projecting Sten's voice into the house. "Kalle, my little gold piece, I'm home!"

"Pappa!" comes the boy's muffled reply.

The scrape of one chair across floorboards, then another soon after. Dishes clank on the table. Leather soles slap, running. Wooden heels follow, tapping out a statelier pace. The knob turns.

To her sisters, Urðr mouths, "*Wait!*"

Out loud, with one hand raised in front of her lips to add distance to the sound: "I'm at the creek watering Kólfaxi. How I've missed you, *gullebit*!"

A boy-shaped whirlwind flies from the cabin. "We've missed you too, Pappa!"

"Now," cries Urðr.

The three leap into action. Skuld scales the home's outer walls. Moving so quickly her limbs are a blur, she clambers hand over foot, 'round and 'round, shrouding the rooftop and eaves with tightly-spun mesh. Verðandi circumnavigates the midsection, wrapping and rewrapping the building with her sturdy web until gauze covers windows, chimney, and door. Urðr, two beats slower off the mark, first nabs the boy then clamps a hand over his mouth. Carrying him like a baby, she speeds after her sisters. Running clockwise around the cabin's perimeter, she adds layer after layer of lucent fibres to the ones already barricading its only exit.

Wind ripples up and down the wrapped house. The casing billows and thrums like breakers crashing against cliffs. Kalle thrashes in Urðr's embrace as the weavers assess their work. His blond hair is glued to his temples. He tries to bite, fails. Urðr adjusts her grip on the child. "It's quite lovely, isn't it? You can almost hear the gulls."

Nodding, Verðandi gets a wistful look. She imagines Bifrost spanning upper worlds, the refreshing spray of giants splashing after white seals—until Kalle kicks, his small boot shattering her reverie. She fixes him with a calculating stare. "What's say we take our wriggling fish for a swim? The creek is a pathetic trickle compared with our Northern seas, but poor tools are better than none."

As they hurry toward the sodden banks, Urðr smiles to see Susanna's hazy silhouette appear. The mother's cries are indecipherable, her features a blur. She flaps her arms uselessly, a drowning woman trapped beneath ice.

---

Kalle shrieks—

A chorus of giggles, of cackles—

Blue jays and finches and blackbirds gossip, accuse—

Deep belly laugh; not Sten, it can't be Sten—

The old man repeats, "She's sharp! She's sharp! She'll slice her way out!"—

So many voices!

Susanna adds hers to the cacophony: "Kalle! Come back, Kalle!"

So many, many voices.

And a waterfall, loudest of all, gushing over windows. A rasping torrent of white cascading down. Deafening. Blocking the door.

Susanna falls to her knees, claws at her ears, jaw, cheeks, the comb in her hair. In her mind she's back in the ship's hold. Leaving home, entering a new world. Waves engulf creaking planks, bare feet thunder overhead, sails snap and wail against the storm. Sailors bark orders. The bosun whistles, all hands shout—another man overboard! Swallowed by the raging throat of the sea. Saltwater seeps through the deck, mermaids' tears falling on Susanna's fine dress. Huddled on the floor, she rocks from side to side. Side to side, her skirt chafing, soaked with salt, grinding the skin from her legs. She shivers and weeps, but does not cry out. Fear has rendered her mute. She is in the belly of the whale and will never escape.

*Mamma! Mamma!*

She opens her eyes. The way out is *right there*, but the water obscures her view, prevents her passage. Trees are blotches against a ground of liquid blue; fallen leaves ripple and gleam, embers on a flooded bed of brown. No matter how hard she looks, she can't see down the slope to the creek. Can't see her son.

"Kalle!" Still shaky, Susanna stands and reaches out to the barrier. Doesn't touch it.

"Kalle!" She calls again and again, but can't move forward. How could Sten do this? Bring her here, then leave her alone? Where is he? She inches closer to the threshold. The current is too powerful.

*I'll drown*, she thinks. *Where is he? We're all going to drown.*

"Rage," says the old man. "And vanity. Glamour. It's an illusion, I swear. A trick of the light. Not mine, no. *Hers.* Anger that cuts. Hack and slice and cut! The blade is honed, the neck is thin. One sweep of the arm: it all comes tumbling down!"

Susanna lashes out. Her hand rebounds against the obstruction, comes away dry. *It's not water.* She slaps it, still expecting to feel a splash against her face. Nothing. Pounding fervently with her fists, she rages just as Iago said she should. A primal growl strains against her clenched teeth as she punches and kicks. Again and again with such force the comb dislodges from her hair and crashes to the floor. Undaunted, she unleashes a whirlwind of elbows, knees, fists and feet. Fury strangles her. She fights until her chest is heaving, tears streaming down her cheeks. Unkempt, exhausted, bruised, she stares at the glistening portal and realises her efforts have achieved nothing.

Kalle's cries have grown weaker.

Iago is quiet.

She *must* get out.

Susanna reaches down, grabs the comb and throws it in a tantrum. She turns to the table, rummages among the breakfast dishes. Cups smash against plates, the pitcher topples, crusts of bread are shoved aside. Finally, the butter knife. Armed, she races back—and stops short.

Susanna loosens her grip. The blade clunks heavily at her feet.

A three-foot gash splits the barrier, the tines of Sten's gift sliced scalpel-clean. Lodged at the base of the cut, the comb's jewels twinkle in the early morning sunlight. Susanna has never found it more beautiful.

Renewed, she grabs the comb and shreds her way through the door. As she clambers outside, tatters cling to her like spidersilk, thick and heavy with dew. Everywhere, the stringy stuff sticks. To her hands and face. Across her eyes.

She blinks, and the world fills with monsters.

Salamander-faced goblins snuffle through the vegetable patch. Bat-winged girls with shrivelled grey hides dangle from the woodshed's eaves. In the birches' lowest boughs, fanged imps sprout like fleshy tumours from sparrows' wings. Up higher, squirrels are worn like scarves around the necks of maple dryads—sap and bark creatures whose twig-webbed brains interconnect, their thoughts intertwined, spanning the breadth of the mountainside. Fox-tailed nymphs the size of walnuts race through the undergrowth, their calls like grass bowing in the wind.

All these sights, Kalle's demons, vie for Susanna's attention—but she homes in on the three cloaked women wading in the stream. In their hands, icicle fishing rods trail lines of the same stuff that grips the cabin. Lines that flick back and forth, hooked on a struggling catch. A fish with blond hair and his father's astonishing eyes.

"Kalle!"

Susanna kicks her dainty green slippers aside, and runs. Stockinged feet fly across the yard, skid down the slope. Her shawl slips; she lets it go.

She keeps a firm grip on the comb, eyes locked on her son. Urgency lends her speed. In half a minute she's sinking in the bank's soft muck, fording through reeds and fallen branches in the shallows, seeking purchase on the slippery stone bed. No longer the sluggard it was yesterday, the current snatches her skirts, spins against her petticoats. Knee-deep, the chill water nips. Up to the waist, it bites. Susanna plunges on.

Kalle's head breaks the surface. He sputters, goes back under.

"What I wouldn't give to weave a vision so blue," Verðandi says wistfully as she looks at Kalle, submerged.

"Get away from him," Susanna shouts.

"One colour at a time," Skuld says, grinning. "First you *must* have black; now you yearn for blue. When did you become so greedy?"

*Warp and Weft*

"An artist with exacting standards is not *greedy*, dear sister. Masterpieces simply require the *best* raw materials."

"True," says Urðr. She flicks her wrist so the line dances. Again, Kalle rises, gasping.

"*Häxorna!*" The foreign word clunks from Susanna's lips, but its harshness suits the witches. She pushes at Urðr, who steps gracefully backwards. Stumbling past Skuld, Susanna meets Verðandi's stare. "Let him go!"

With all her might, she throws the comb at the weaver. The instant it flies, she dives. A hiss—"So that's what burnt"—then her ears fill with bubbling water. Carp-sized rusalki dart around Kalle's inert form. Susanna shoos them away, wraps her arms around the boy, drags him back to the surface, back to light and life.

As soon as she touches bottom and stands, Susanna's head jerks back. Verðandi grips a handful of her thick hair, and twists.

"One day you'll thank me for this," she says. With claws like shears, the witch cuts until Susanna's scalp goes numb. "Be free, little Raven."

———ο ο———

Urðr uses the skein of new thread sparingly. A hint to accentuate the bride's secret wedding to a young Sten. A series of jagged lines to represent storm-tossed waves: the ocean separating *there* from *here*, ancient history from the more recent past. To her right, Skuld weaves the brook, the cabin, shadows beneath Susanna's bed. A boy's broken horse. His tiny face, a perfect oval, bobbing momentarily above the waterline. She fills the forest with wondrous creatures, depicting the moment Susanna recognised that, even without her husband's presence, she'll never lack company. Twinkling green beads are sewn where brown used to be: Susanna's eyes now the same hue as her son's. Inside the cabin is where Skuld applies her share of the black, for blankets hastily folded and stuffed into packs, cupboards left bare, comb and mirror and outdated dresses burying a shrivelled head at the bottom of Sten's inherited chest.

Verðandi sings as she draws the shuttle to and fro, the image it shapes as dark as her song. Dust lifts behind a shallow wagon's spoked wheels. A path stretches through the oncoming woods, curves beyond the far-distant horizon—the actors in the cart may not see its end in their lifetime. A woman drives its small team of horses with a firm hand, son by her side, back straight. She wears a bonnet to cover her cropped hair. A cabin filled with memories of markets and coffeehouses, extravagant dresses and servants, stifling holds and exhilarating loves is sewn well off to the left. Scenery she's long outdistanced.

Her head is cocked as though listening.

Her eyes are turned to the future.

Satisfied, Verðandi ties off. For a moment, she lets the shuttle travel at its own pace.

# *Bella Beaufort Goes to War*

Volume Twelfth, 2nd Series, No. 312. July 19, 1873
QUERIES, cont'd:——
MAKING FATE & THE INFLUENCE OF NORNS IN THE NEW WORLD
*In pursing research for my book,* IN THE FASHION OF WOLVES, *I come, time and again, to the same pressing questions: Does the Norns' power stop when* certitude *does? When the idea that they decree* FATE *and tend to* YGGDRASIL *weakens, can such myths continue to exist? When faith in them ceases, to what thread might they cling? Without the lifeline of credulity are these* things *no more than the smoke of memory dispersed on the wind? Or are they weaving still, out of sight and mind, but not out of the world? Opinions and responses are most heartily desired.*

Valdís Brynjólfsdóttir
*South Carolina, United States of America*

"What do you see?"
Black things flap and snap on the wire fence running around the vacant land adjacent to the Laveau place. The sun is harsh, reflecting on the hard-packed dirt street, glaring off the two-storey house's peeling white paint; yet the old woman insists upon sitting

out on the verandah with the heat and light bouncing up at her, hitting the great diamond hanging like a monocle on a silver chain around her neck.

Sweat creeps down Bella's skin, soaking the armpits and back of her green gingham work dress, trickling from her temples, making her scalp itch worse than the lice she'd been afflicted with last summer. What she wouldn't give to scratch like a dog right about now, or to lift the thick russet hair off her crown like an unwanted hat. But she ignores the urge and concentrates on the widow's question. She squints, stares across overgrown cotton fields, and focuses on the shreds of—*what?*—writhing in the distance. While she gathers her thoughts, Eugenia, as usual, leaps in.

"Dead birds. Ravens. Big ones." This last was added in an uncertain tone, as though she realises she's wrong once again. The old lady's lip curls—she doesn't even bother to conceal it from her great-granddaughter nowadays—and then slides her eyes to Bella, who senses the expectation in that look, just as keenly as she feels Eugenia's resentment seething off her. Within the first few days of their apprenticeship, she'd overheard the other girl moaning to her *mémé*, saying it wasn't right, her teaching the two of them together. Her own rightful heir and Bella No-Blood. Bella Know-it-all. Bella Who-wasn't-even-family.

*Such a waste of effort, staring so hard at someone else's flaws,* the Widow Paris had said. *Take a close look at yourself, Eugenia Laveau, and tell me—what do you see?*

"It's skins," says Bella, who wasn't even family, as she smooths the white pin-tucks of her apron. "Skins taken so they can't fly anymore."

"They?" Eugenia sneers, white-blonde hair a striking contrast against her bronze skin. She props her elbows on the porch railing next to Bella, leans down to take another look from that vantage. Her sharp nose crinkling like there's a bad smell.

"They. Witches. Witches with their wings clipped, with their soul suits taken."

As if in answer, the feathered things wave in agreement, agitating like house-rugs left out for beating clean. The old woman nods brusquely, the closest she ever gets to showing approval. But Bella knows her mentor is pleased, though she covers a smile with her fan, a handsome thing of lace and mahogany. A gift, perhaps, from a grateful follower. The woman's fluttering hands are smooth, ageless. Unlike her face which, in recent months, has sagged dramatically, its rich brown becoming greyish. Against doctor's orders, the widow won't slow down. Knocking on eighty, and still she insists on sitting out in the heat, teaching them, trying to make sure they're receptacles of the knowledge only she can pass on. *Truth be told,* Bella thinks, *Miz Marie feels her time running away.*

"There you have it, child," the old woman says, peering over accordion folds at Eugenia, barely keeping the disappointment from her tone. "Focus. Pay attention. This isn't hairdressing school, no matter what folks been told. Make a mistake with *this* craft and you'll suffer much worse than burnt curls. You need to concentrate: be *certain* before you speak. Words are weapons, girl—you can't just fling them around, willy-nilly. Wield them carefully, accurately, else you'll unleash a world of hurt—on others, sure enough, but first and foremost, on yourself. Stop and *think*."

Eugenia's mouth tightens like she's fit to spit nails. A few seconds pass as she wrangles her temper. Splotches crawl up her neck, blooms of anger and shame. She straightens, pushes away from the bannister, away from Bella, and turns to stand with hands folded, white-knuckled, before the Widow Paris.

"Yes'm," she says through gritted teeth. "I'll bear that in mind."

"You do that. For now, go on in. Tidy up the brushes and arrange the curling rods by size—largest to smallest, handles out, on a tray near the fire—then scrub the combs and scissors. Miss What's-her-name from Olafsson House is coming 'round in an hour, and I haven't yet sussed if her appointment is for plaits or potions."

Eugenia, thus dismissed, bobs a curtsey, and flounces inside. Soon they hear utensils rattling into jars, iron tools clattering against tin, water splashing, the occasional grumble and mutter. When the screen door finally swings shut on its slow hinges, Bella looks over at the widow, whose rheumy brown eyes are fixed on her. Reduced to slits. Assessing.

She freezes like a hare, resists the desire to gulp. *Be certain before you speak . . .* The Widow Paris had been chastising Eugie, but Bella has a feeling the old herbwoman was talking double. Directing the dressing-down at her great-grandchild, but expecting them both to listen. Telling Bella that she's onto her. That she more than suspects, she *knows*.

That even though Bella's answer was right, it was obvious, to the widow at least, she had *guessed*.

She did it a lot, actually. Guessing. It wasn't laziness, not really. It's just, she can pick ideas out of the air. Sometimes. Most of the time. Very broad hints. And more often than not, they are precisely right. They are enough. Enough to ensure her instinct wins out over Eugenia's increasingly desperate shots in the dark.

Bella tries to distract the Widow Paris with a smile. It withers on her cheeks half-formed.

What if Eugenia finds out, that Bella guesses? Oh, rage, rage, such a rage. And lightning, no doubt. Whirlwinds. Hail. What Eugenia lacks in reading vibrations, ripples in water, tremors in the earth, the story of human expression, she more than makes up for with dark-limned magic. Spells of destruction, thunderous conjuration, explosions of fire and lava. These were her forté. *These* came to her easy as living.

*Eugie would make a powerful ally, if she wasn't such a pain in the backside.*

"Lemonade?" Bella asks, getting up from the white wicker chair. The old lady holds her gaze another instant, then shakes her head.

"That's enough for today. Better get home, young Isabella, before your uncle starts a-wondering what can possibly be taking so long."

As Bella collects her satchel and packs away the book in which she writes recipes, for hair tonics and potions alike, two men stroll down St Ann Street. Both pretend they don't know they're being watched, but they stand a little straighter, puff their chests a bit as they walk. One's a local parish boy, spends Sundays ushering people into church. The other's a regular jack-of-all trades—does everything from working the cotton gin to digging graves. The sight of him sets Bella's heart to pounding, as it no doubt does to most girls in town. Tall with blue eyes and bone china skin, a spill of Black Irish hair and a smile that makes the day brighter. Bella averts her eyes, but not soon enough.

"Careful, girl," says the old widow. "The worst thing in the world is getting what we desire. Help me inside before you go."

As she bends close to assist her teacher, their faces almost touching, Bella can smell the decay on the woman's sigh, the gust of death soughing up from inside. She squeezes the old lady's hand.

---

The trellis on the exterior wall is rickety, so Bella chooses the oak tree instead. Its branches are strong and thick and spread *everywhere*; one in convenient reach of her bedroom window, another trailing like a truncated staircase, with just a foot-long drop to the ground at the end. She's standing on the sill, ready to make the leap, when a single loud knock shudders the door behind her. Arms windmilling, she manages to hop back down and carefully arrange her face, a mix of umbrage and respect, before the knob slams into the wall. Only one person barges into her *chambre* so abruptly, trying to catch her out.

"Uncle Augustin."

"Evening, Bella. Have I disturbed you?" Her uncle's expression is hopeful, slightly lecherous. A distant cousin of her father's—not a *true* uncle, *not* a Beaufort—Augustin Fabron was willing to adopt poor, orphaned little Bella, after the accident. To take her in, not as a full family member, of course, but as a high level domestic in his plantation house. Daughter and servant and something else altogether. Something in between, not quite pure, existing in the social limbo dictated by her colouring. Hair red and irises green enough to say 'white', but skin a shade too dark, features a tad too Creole, to let her pass without question. Without the protection of papers and a wealthy not-uncle to vouch for her. To provide a room of her own. A safe enough space for now. She's got house duties and other . . . duties . . . Augustin hasn't commanded her to perform. At least, not yet. Not with Aunt Claudette around, and Uncle Augustin's tenure as lord of the manor secure only so long as she is—the property deeds being written in *her* name, after all, not his.

He blinks with eyes like a winter sky, close-set in a long cadaverous face framed with lank hair that greases down to his collar. They are of a height; Bella statuesque, Augustin spindly. It's been a few years since he's been able to look down at her, so he tilts his head slightly back whenever he speaks. Lines her up in his sight, and *peers*.

"Did you do your chores today?"

"Yes, Uncle," Bella says, hoping she remembered them all.

"Only, your Aunt said Evangeline couldn't find you when she wanted her hair done before dinner," he says smoothly. Bella doubts that Claudette's maid reported anything of the sort to him. "It's not that we mind you learning a trade—indeed we think it a sensible idea. After all, we won't be around to support you forever. But we are, however, here now. You must not forget your first duty."

"How could I," she says, thinking, *with you constantly reminding me*, "when you and Aunt Claudette have been so . . . kind."

"We wouldn't want to have to discontinue your apprenticeship, dear niece." Augustin's reply sounds as empty to Bella as hers must have to him. They both know he won't follow through. Claudette has been *delicate* as long as Bella has known her—as long, she suspects, as the woman has been wed. And Augustin is more than aware of what his ward has been learning at the Widow Paris's knee. He relies too heavily on the witch's remedies to keep his wife in reasonable health; when the old lady passes, he'll need Bella to continue administering Claudette's *treatments*.

*To keep her sedate*, she thinks. *Sedated*.

"No, Uncle. We wouldn't want that," she says, lowering her chin, feigning humility though it makes her pride squirm.

Mollified, Augustin gives unnecessary orders for the morning—her routine hasn't changed in seven years—and takes his leave. The door clicks shut behind him. She listens, for a minute, then two, waiting for him to move off the landing. The floorboards creak; he is still on the other side, listening for her too. She sits on her bed, wincing as the springs squeak loudly. Another moment passes and she blows out the lamp on her bedside table, knowing he has watched for the snuffing of the line of light under the door. At last, footsteps. Self-congratulatory and solid along the hallway. He thinks his point is made, that Bella remains under the thumb.

She doesn't move, even after she hears his tread on the stairs, wending their way down to the sitting room, where he will smoke cigars, drink whiskey and read those books he imports from France, the ones with the dirty pictures he thinks his wife knows nothing about. He'll be there for hours and now his *job* is done,

Uncle Augustin will not stir. To be safe, Bella waits an extra five minutes before setting off. More than enough time to do a cats-eye spell, to help her find her way under the slivered new moon.

The leap from sill to tree branch feels further, more exciting, more liberating than it actually is—a delusion she's happy to enjoy. Half a mile to the Widow Paris's, which Bella covers so quickly and quietly she seems to fly the distance. All the lights in the place are extinguished. A candle flickers to life, briefly, in the round porthole staring out from an attic gable. *Eugie's room.* It winks in and out of sight two or three times before being extinguished. *The fool never can settle, can she? Fidgeting even when she's alone.* Bella grabs a handful of wild sage from the roadside, some flax and a few black-eyed-susans and crushes them between her palms, scattering the bruised leaves and seeds on her toes, whispering ancient words to make her footfalls petal-soft.

The path between the house and the fairy hill beyond the wire fence is overrun with weeds and old cotton. Few dare tread across the Widow Paris's land in broad daylight, much less after dark, but Bella has no such fears. If pressed, she can identify the marks of everyone who's passed this way. The widow's stunted shuffle hasn't flattened the dirt here for years; but a set of Eugenia's prints, small and wide-spread and deep as a running deer's, head off to the bushes on her right. Wild blackberries grow there by the bucket-load, Bella remembers, and thinks she might follow the other girl's path next time. On her left, another series of tracks. Narrow and heavy-heeled, blurred with urgency. With excitement.

*These* Bella pursues.

Her boots make a *shhhhhhing* sound as she crosses to the field, barely raising a puff of dust. Mist winds through the shrubs, coalescing into sinuous smoke-women that slip around pecan trees along the field's borders. It seems they smile at her as she hurries to the fence and ducks under, careful not to catch her skirts. The witch-skins applaud her arrival. They shoo her toward the man leaning comfortably against the gentle slope of the fairy hill, as if he belongs there.

Tancred Carew sits with his long legs outstretched, crossed casually at the ankle. The hessian sack he always carries, with a flute he made and god-knows what else, is propped like a pillow behind his broad back. With her cats-eyes, Bella can see him perfectly—a bewitching sight that enthralls her. Cotton boles glowing white, little stars of the earth, surrounding his rumpled brown curls. Glints of moonlight winking in his blue eyes, glancing off his teeth as he chews his nails, beaming off them as he smiles.

"Evening, Miz Beaufort," he says, then wastes no more time talking. When they come up for air, Bella's lips are tingling. She bites them, savouring, and inhales the salty scent of Tancred's skin, sweaty underneath his open-collared shirt. He rests his chin on Bella's head and she can feel his Adam's apple bob against her temple as he talks.

"We should bury them," he says, gesturing at the black scraps caught on the fence. For a second, Bella hears a rustle of wings, loud as a dozen ravens taking flight at once. "It's not right, having them exposed like that."

Bella cranes her neck to look up at him. "We haven't any shovels."

"We've got hands, haven't we?"

She smirks. "Why, Mr. Carew. I can't possibly go fossicking in the earth wearing this, my Sunday best." She pulls away to give him a better view of her faded, ill-fitting gingham. "If I didn't know better, I'd say you had a mind to see me *digging* out of my petticoat."

"Wouldn't be the first time," Tancred grins.

Bella plays coy only so long, and no longer. Soon her dress, apron, smock and bloomers are tossed like offerings to the fairies. Tancred's buttons seem to melt beneath her fingers; the drawstring on his pants loosens of its own accord. Together they work up a sweat and when they're done, they lie on Bella's clothes like they're the finest bed in New Orleans. She traces patterns into his chest hair with her nails, resting her cheek on his lean bicep, and watches him soften. When he's recovered, Tancred looks down the slope to the rusty fence running along its base.

"We really should give them whatever peace the earth can offer."

"All right," says Bella, loving him for his passion, determination, caring. For keeping a noble thought in his head both before *and after* he's spent. Wearing nothing but their unders, they hoist the ragged skins off the wires. Two of them, a leathery jumble of feather and beaks, strands of long hair, boneless faces, and places that shouldn't have bones. Bella's stomach clenches—not with sick, with certainty. Her guess, as usual, had been right.

*Witch-skins.*

Collapsed, they are incredibly compact; the pair of them could easily fit inside Tancred's bag. Instead, he folds them in on themselves, ties each bundle off with its own hair, then passes it to Bella while he gets started on the digging. She stands there a moment, just watching. Admiring the way his muscles strain, the way dirt sticks to his chest, his ribs, his thighs. Almost unconsciously, she plucks at the witch-feathers, tearing at the desiccated flesh, at the matted tresses . . . And as she strikes cartilage, she feels a warmth in her belly, a heat of *knowing*. Ingredients potent as these can't go to waste.

Before she hands Tancred the neatly-tied parcels, she tucks a chunk of salvaged flesh up under her arm, unsure why she takes it, but determined to smuggle it home in the pocket of her apron.

---

A lamp, turned low, is burning in her room when Bella returns, stepping lightly over the sill. She doesn't really pay attention, happy as she is, reeking of Tancred's sweat, with tender parts tingling as if a charge has been sent through them. She puts her hands to the strings of her apron, the buttons at the back of her dress, doesn't notice the movement in the shadows, her cats-eye spell now thoroughly worn off. It's not until a bony hand closes around the hair at the nape of her neck, fingers gouging into the thick locks, that the magic of the night shatters and she realises she's not alone.

"Insolent little whore!" Spittle froths from Uncle Augustin's mouth, spatters her ear. Waves of malt fumes roll off him as he yells. He shakes her, bolstered by a rage that's simmered since she was a child; unheeded or outright defied by servants who check his orders with a mistress too frail to fulfil her marital duties, maids who lock their doors at night. Augustin fumbles with his trousers, trying to get them undone while keeping a grip on her. "I won't be ignored!"

He hooks a foot around her ankles, jerks hard. There's a jolt, hair ripping, as she tumbles free of his grasp—just for a second. Her head hits the floor. The blow is cushioned by the thick rug, but it's hard enough to make stars and suns pinwheel across her vision. Stunned, she scrambles for purchase, goes nowhere. It gives Augustin time to drop down beside her, shrug out of his suspenders. With one hand, he urgently shoves his pants down, while the other is busy loosening his narrow neck-tie, looping the noose over her head—as if he cannot decide which punishment will come first.

Bella tries to claw forward, but Augustin tightens the garrotte, pins her petticoat with his knees. Fabric tears. He yanks the ribbon tie, tighter, tighter. Bella tries to get words out, but the only sound she can produce is an animal whimper. Augustin's breath, hot, rank, slides across her cheek. Gagging, she tries to scream, tries to cry. And she flails, she flails, but his fingers jab, her skirts are lifted—

Her not-uncle, her un-uncle, grunts, then his grip relaxes enough to let her draw in great gusts of air. His hipbones dig into her rear, his ribs slam into her spine before he pushes himself upright again. Bella takes advantage, tries to shove him off, but he holds on. She realises there's been another noise, a new sound, unexpected. It's followed by a second, a loud, solid *thud*. Augustin slumps heavily onto her back; he tilts to the right, and drops, his arm draped across her calves. Bella kicks him aside, shimmies into a crouch. She blinks and blinks and finally looks up. Focuses on the shape looming over the fallen man.

Aunt Claudette, with shadows and lamplight dancing across her white nightgown, which is now spotted with a spray of wet red blossoms. In her shaking hand, a poker from the fireplace dangles between slackened fingers. The women stare at each without a word. Eventually, Bella heaves herself forward and checks for the pulse in Augustin's throat. It is slow, sluggish. She knows it won't be long before it stops, unless something is done.

She snatches her hand back, wipes it and wipes it on her torn skirt, turns to her Aunt for a cue.

Claudette is not as tall as Bella, nor as fit. She is *thin*, a bed-bound woman coddled to within an inch of her life. She stands there, swaying a little, her expression flicking between fear, hope, disbelief. Her glazed eyes meet Bella's and again her fingers tighten. She hefts the poker—as Bella gathers her wits and leaps up. She is at the casement in a few steps, out it in one bound and scampering down the tree like a squirrel.

As she hares into the woods, she can hear her name being called. In a small part of her mind—the same part that tells her a fluttering rag is a witch-skin, that interprets voices on the air—she *knows* it's not a cry of panic or condemnation; there is no tone of threat or accusation. In that same small part of her mind, she knows she should go back and help her not-aunt. *What if he wakes? She'll be alone . . .* But Bella is running, feet barely touching the ground. Running away from Augustin, from danger. Running to Tancred and safety. Without magic, her stride goes *thud, thud, thud* in time with her beating heart, and soon she is almost at the fairy hill—*he must still be there*—soon almost in Tancred's arms. On the path, she slows, tries to control her panting, the shaking and shuddering her body is committing without her say-so. Bella walks now, quickly, quietly and as she rounds the stand of trees that hid them both not even an hour ago, she sees Tancred's arms are otherwise engaged.

"Thanks for clearing those nasty old bird-skins."

"Couldn't have my best lady suffering the creeps, now could I?"

"I *am* your best, aren't I?"

Naked and gleaming, a girl with white, white hair and smooth bronze skin laughs, riding Bella's lover as if he's a steed, bouncing and writhing much as Bella was not so long—now, forever—ago.

---

The Widow Paris's front door is never locked—only the sorriest fool would enter there without permission—and Bella knows where all the fixings are, the ones she requires. In her pocket the pilfered piece of witch-skin weighs heavy; she pulls it out, lays it on the countertop.

She places the basalt mortar and pestle beside it, then begins. Collecting and adding ingredients, grinding and stirring them as she goes, making sure the mix is properly combined. There are scarlet rose petals, hyacinth oil, powdered mint leaves and rosemary, dried lavender, a tiny dash of the gold dust the Widow Paris is always so miserly with, a crush of indigo, a smear of marigold, two pansy petals and then half a spoon of the imported honey. She spits into the mess and whisks it about, hard and fast, then takes a knife, a small thing, fit for peeling fruit, and pulls it across her right palm. From the shallow cut drips fat jewels of blood to seal the deal—for all dark magic, all curses, all dreadful things dearly wished for, cost something personal. Bella needs no recipe for this potion; *this* alchemy comes from the deepest knowledge of heart and hurt.

Soon the paste is thick and dark and red, with a sheen that only hatred can give. So, they want each other, Tancred and Eugenia? They want to be together? Bella will give them what they want. She pours in a flacon of rainwater, takes the shreds of witch-skin and adds them to the admixture, bubbling of its own accord. The thin membranes float into the pestle and disintegrate as soon as they hit the liquid. Without hesitation, Bella whispers over it, feeling heat rise off the surface. "Here's my wish for you both: to love an ideal of each other without reason, to see an eidolon never a soul. Let your wings be clipped, let your love be a cage, let it trap you both forever." She murmurs their names across the brew so the spell will *know* them, so there can be no mistake, no misdirections. So the enchantment will hook its claws into the fabric of their lives and never let them go. *Happily ever after.*

When the spell leaves her Bella feels exhilarated and empty, as if a part of her soul has darkened in payment for this wicked wish, for this vengeance. The air seems thick and time still—until the front door creaks and Eugie's entrance echoes along the corridor. Hastily, Bella decants the potion into a small vial, stoppers it and slips it into her apron pocket. She runs a hand through her hair and waits to hear Eugie pass by the workroom. *So, what? I'm to sneak out?* Bella snorts. *Why should I creep around?* She opens the door and steps out into the hallway.

Halfway up the stairs, Eugenia spins around. "What are you doing here?"

But before Bella can answer, there is a crash and a thump upstairs, coming from the direction of the widow's room. Both girls race towards the sound.

---

"*Mémé!*" Eugenia's cry is heart-wrenching, or would be if Bella hadn't seen what she'd seen earlier. If her heart hadn't hardened.

The Widow Paris is half-on, half-off the bed, the linens caught up around her waist and legs, a knitted shawl 'round her shoulders despite the heat. While they watch, she slides fully to the floor with a thud. Her nightdress is open at the collar, the thin cotton clinging. Curls frizz out of her sleeping-bonnet, sticking to her ashen face, some tipped with droplets of cold sweat. High arched eyebrows, not much more than a few wisps on a shrivelled brow, frame lashless lids, closed on sunken eyes. Until she moans, Bella thinks she's already dead.

Death rattles the old woman's lungs as she blinks awake, her gaze unfocused, searching. "Mémé," Eugie wails, rushing to her great-grandmother's side, hugging her close.

"Get away, child. You're smothering me."

"But we've got to get you on up into bed—"

The Widow Paris waves the girl quiet. "Let me be. We all start low, Eugenia. Ashes to ashes, dust to dust, dirt to dirt—no matter what heights you reach in life, in the end it's all the same. Back to beginnings. I'm just saving y'all the trouble of hauling my old shell down off the bed. *No, I said.*" Eugenia's tugging her by the armpits, forcing her upright. She gets the woman into a seated position, then kneels, clings to her hand. The lady extricates her fingers, pushes the girl further away.

"Just let me be. Save your fussing for after I'm gone; I've no use for it." She coughs, long and sloppy, and Bella thinks, this time, the tide of her life must surely have ebbed for good.

"You in pain, Miz M?" she asks, mouse-quiet, coming close enough, but no closer.

"I'd expect more from you, Isabella Beaufort," the widow replies. "Sure you can *guess* what state I'm in." The widow blinks, and this time her eyes stay shut.

Her lips go slack and a puff of rancid meat air escapes them. Bella finds herself crouched beside Eugie, inhaling that stale gust. Finds her head resting on the old woman's scarecrow shoulder, ear pressed to her chest. Finds herself counting the seconds between heartbeats, tracing symbols across the desiccated breast, grasping at words, at spells to keep the faltering thing ticking.

"Take care of this house, Eugenia," the Widow Paris mumbles at last, eyes searching, unfixed. "I may crumble, but there's sure as Hell no reason it has to follow me into the earth."

"Don't say that, *mémé*. We'll get Doc Coffey down here, you'll be just fine, we'll—"

"Hush, now. Mind my house, child, that's all I ask. You do that for me?"

Eugie whimpers, tears coursing down her round cheeks, and nods.

"Good girl," the widow says, before turning to Bella. "Now, you." Marie folds her fingers around Bella's palm. She feels sharp angles, a cold glassy surface, a rough sphere with many facets.

"You," says the old woman, "*you* mind my business. You keep it going, my girl. You keep it going."

Bella opens her hand—there is the stone, the single biggest she will ever see. A white diamond the size of a child's heart.

"I will," Bella promises. "I am."

---

There is no moment of silence to honour the dead.

"She gave it to you! You! You're nobody! You're nothing. You're not even family." Eugenia's face boils crimson, and she's making a sound like a kettle left on the heat too long.

"Yet here we are, Eugie. Together with the one person who loved us both," says Bella smoothly. "Close as family."

Eugie weeps until she hiccups, hiccups until Bella thinks the girl might be sick in her own lap. She pours a glass of water from the bedside table and tips one, two, three drops from the vial into it—Eugie is too distracted to notice. The red liquid quickly disperses, tinting the clear fluid with only the slightest shade of pink. She hands it to Eugenia, who takes it without thanks, and gulps it down, down. All of it.

Bella smiles.

It will take. Oh, yes. It will sit inside her, stirring, gestating, ready to come to life the moment she sees Tancred. And when she does, the spell will uncurl, rise up and take hold. She'll be ruined in soulless love—there'll be nothing but obsession. The only tremors Eugenia will feel, the only excitement, the only fireworks, are the ones she casts with magic. It will be like eating, but never feeling full. She'll get nothing from Tancred, empty paragon of lies. And Tancred? Greedy, beautiful Tancred will take anything from Bella's hand, anything at all. He need only take this last thing. And he will.

While Eugenia sobs on the floor, Bella crosses to the window and looks out between the sheers. In the street below is the lady's maid Evangeline, gazing up at the house. Bella raises her hand, guessing, *knowing* she is safe. Aunt Claudette would not have sent Evangeline to *arrest* her; if that were the case, there would be constables roaming about by now. But there is nothing unusual on the road, in the fields. No-one but the servant.

Bella lets the curtains fall shut. Closing her eyes, she turns and perches on the sill. Runs her palms across her tattered apron, her twisted, torn skirt. *Eugie never even commented on it*, she muses, then blocks out all thoughts of the girl, all thoughts but the ones thrilling through the air. Quiet, she listens. Listens to the present, feels the truth of it in her belly. Her aunt's voice, not so feeble as it once was, explaining to Doc Coffey how Augustin has had a terrible accident, how he has fallen down the stairs. Listens to the doctor, who never liked the man, declare it's an open-and-shut case, no need to examine the wounds on his head. Listens to the night, replayed in her mind, and knows she will go back to that uncle-less house. She will tend to Claudette, who may not need her as much, in that uncle-less house, but Bella knows she'll want her there anyway. To keep an eye on her. To ensure her silence.

As she exhales, Bella senses the future, hears it through the other girl's wailing, hears the beat of what's to come, the pulse. Knowing Eugenia will ache for Tancred though he is hers, and Tancred will yearn for Eugenia, both fighting for more, neither getting enough, everyone getting what they deserve. And she, Bella Beaufort, will be there to see it all. To watch how the battle unfolds.

# Prohibition Blues

*One voice. A boy's, falsetto, angelic. High, more than high. Stratospheric. The child's instrument, effortlessly honed, unwavering, lifted. Singing.*

*He sustains a single note, just one perfect note, his mouth round and hollow as the cavern in which it resounds. It stretches, that note, while you listen, stretches until you feel sure he must break soon, he must stop, stretches as you feel breathless on his behalf, your own face reddening for oxygen, stretches until you squirm. And in that key of discomfort, that key of asphyxiation, you hear snow falling on crystal, you hear ships' timbers creaking, sailing frozen waters, you hear fjords and icebergs and glaciers, and you shiver, while you listen, you struggle for air, you wish that one icicle note suspended above you, falsetto, angelic, you'd wish it would shatter, become earthbound, you'd wish it would melt, you'd wish it would stop, that exquisite note, painfully pure, and you wonder, while you listen, while you wish, while you gasp, you wonder if you will ever again feel warmth.*

> 'On Achieving "Cold" in the Key of Fae Blood' in *Compositions for High C Voices: Or, Songs of the Displacement*
> Attributed to: Æringunnr Long-Gaze

Music drifts like smoke from beneath the closed door. Slow rhythms carry a baritone's chocolate voice out the house's open windows, drip it down the front porch and leave it pooling beneath Maeve's high-heeled Mary Janes. If this song had a colour, she thinks, it would be silver. Just like that dress she's been eyeing off in Trehaine's display: the slip's fringed hemline abbreviates at mid-thigh; over that, a sheer sheath beaded with oyster fruit; and, best of all, only available in sizes 2-5. As soon as they get paid, that dress is hers. It will show off her figure and blackberry hair to perfection. She shakes her head, focuses and yells.

"Tallulah! Get the hell out here or I'm going without you." For effect she bends down in front of Bella's dark green Model T and rolls the crank. The jazz cuts short as the jalopy sputters to life and she can hear her cousin's heels clattering down the wooden stairs inside. It will only be a moment before the front door is flung open and Tallulah appears, temper as hot as her bouncy red bob. Maeve grins. It's almost as easy pushing that girl's buttons as it is getting the yokels to open their wallets at the speakeasies night after night. A crimson tornado tears out the entryway to the ivy-covered, drunk-angled house they share. As Tallulah slams the front door shut and stalks toward her cousin, Maeve could swear steam is coming off her.

"Maeve Beaufort, you two bit chippy! Where are my—you are wearing my best shoes!"

"Oh, c'mon Tallulah. You know I can't find one of my strappy black ones and our outfits need to match. Don't take on. After tonight, we'll have plenty to throw around, more shoes than you can poke a stick at. Josephine Baker herself will turn green with envy."

Tallulah sighs. "But I haven't even worn those yet. You could've taken these ones."

"These fit better. Now hurry up and don't fuss. We can't afford to be late."

"Those Faerie types aren't keen on tardiness, cousin; you're quite right."

"Got everything?"

Tallulah holds up a battered brown suitcase with tarnished gold locks. She rattles it gently and slides one set of fine fingers along its edge. Glittering sparks shoot into the night and a delicate series of *clinks* ring out. "Hell, yes."

"Then let the good times roll."

―⁂―

The parties they frequent are always *two* parties, not just one. Oh, most folk who went along, all gussied up in their flapper finery, their gangster chic, were there for the canapés and the occasional bootlegged liquor. More often than not, the very people promoting the prohibition laws were the first ones to break them. Yet the majority of these wheelers and dealers, these hypocritical law-keepers, didn't generally know that the real action wasn't something *they* controlled; that in back halls, cellars, attics, and sometimes in hidden rooms that once sheltered those poor folk shuffling along the Underground Railroad, in those places the *other* parties are in full swing.

Few people realise that with the right lineage and a *bon mot* for the thugs manning the door, a girl can have a taste of the underworld and share in its riches. But as Tallulah and Maeve are only too aware, whether or not she survives to cash her cheque depends entirely on savvy and the quality of her performance.

The girls pull into a parking space on Clancy Robillard's front lawn. The antebellum mansion is lit up like a ship at sea, light rolling out into the night, chasing away the darkness as an unwelcome guest. They check their hair and make-up in pretty hand-held compacts and get out of the car, adjusting their matching red dresses, shimmying so all the glittering fringes fall *just so*. Maeve grabs the suitcase from the backseat and they walk up to the portico, arm in arm.

The two doormen are muscular, squat and very, very hairy. *Bitten*, thinks Tallulah, thankful the moon is nowhere near full. Bitten and making the best of it by working as bodyguards and security men—now that the newly-morally-correct police force won't employ them. She wonders what happens when that unfortunate time of the month rolls around; who locks them up and keeps them (and everyone else) safe while mistress moon holds her sway. She notches a smile to her lips, tight as a bowstring, so the men won't know what's on her mind.

Maeve does the same, tilting her head so the lustrous black of her locks falls across her high cheekbones. Tallulah plays peek-a-boo through her long fringe. Born flirts the both of them, their

Grandmamma used to say. *And who taught us?* the girls would ask and screech with laughter as she sent sparks shooting from her fingertips—not hot or hard enough to hurt, just to let them know she wouldn't be sassed. At least, not quite so much.

"Good evening, boys," purrs Maeve.

The shorter, squatter one looks them up and down. "Y'all the entertainment?"

Tallulah doesn't like his tone. Makes them sound like cheap hookers.

"We're the singers, *chèr*," Maeve drawls, playing out an accent she doesn't actually have. "Don't you be thinking otherwise."

The hairy one relaxes visibly and steps aside so they can go through. As Tallulah passes his companion, the man leans in and whispers, "Dry tonight. Feds are here."

She smiles and nods as if he's made a joke. Maeve's grip on her arm tells her she'd heard too. They need to be careful. If there's no booze here because of the long arm of the law, then chances are the other party, the under-party, might be known or suspected. They'll have to keep their wits about them. Neither girl plans on spending her youth in a federal penitentiary.

The chandelier-lit ballroom throngs with the rich, powerful and sober of Charleston. Maeve hides a smile—she's seen more than a few of the same faces at other *soirées*, leaning hard against walls, bow ties loose, dress straps slipping dangerously low as alcohol fumes fill the air. This evening they're all much more . . . temperate . . . why, butter wouldn't melt in their mouths. And—isn't that Lucille Vander-something-or-other? The last time Maeve encountered her at a shindig, that leading socialite and member of the Temperance League had been straddling Beauregard Fortescue in the back parlour of Libby Landorff's *pied-à-terre* in town. Maeve looks at her cousin and knows by her raised brows that Tallulah is remembering the same thing, or something very close to it.

They make their way through the crowd and find their host standing by the huge unlit fireplace, his elbow resting casually on the mantle, and surrounded by five or six other men, equally well-dressed and prosperous-looking. Mr Robillard tilts his head back when he speaks, perpetually looking down his nose at those around him. His voice holds all the zeal of a preacher and the shoddy conviction of a snake-handler. "Why even more invidious is its effect on our *own* people! I swear it won't be long before even Mickey Malone's own mother is set to join our campaign." A round of deep chuckles licks through the group. "Just imagine: young Mick, standing in his ma's parlour with a look of innocence so compelling she wouldn't have noticed the Tommy gun slung over his shoulder, the blood spattering his hands and suit. No matter how hard she looked, to her eyes his soul was so spotless it glowed! What a trick."

Chuckles develop into guffaws. "Soon as old Mrs Malone realised her son's squeaky clean image came out of a bottle of 'shine," Robillard continues, "that he hadn't earned his absolution like the rest of us but snorted it instead, word is she whacked him so hard he couldn't keep his bookies' numbers straight for a week." His laughter subsides. Wiping a tear from his eye, his face suddenly grows serious. "Filthy stuff, that 'shine. Even filthier that felons like him can still get their hands on it—and use it to fool their own mothers, no less! Mark my words, gentlemen. She'll come to us before moon dark."

All around, grunts and nods of assent. Robillard breaks off his speech when he spots the girls, and smiles fit to burst.

Tallulah thinks, not for the first time, that his teeth just aren't quite right. And he's running to fat—in a year he'll be giving a French bulldog competition in the jowls department.

"And here they are, the gorgeous Misses Beaufort, honouring us with their beauty and talent tonight. Gentlemen, we are spoilt."

"Why, Clancy, you are too kind." Maeve simpers. She knows Tallulah can't stand the man, but she gives her cousin credit for keeping a civil tongue, and not slapping Robillard as he looks her up and down like she's a piece of meat he might buy.

Their host stops his ogling long enough to make introductions to the men in his circle, which is all fine and dandy until he reaches someone they already know far too well.

"No introduction necessary, Clancy," says the tall blond man with a wide insincere smile and eyes as blue as his sapphire tie pin. "We're family."

"Why, Fayette, how charming to see you again." Tallulah's tone tells him clearly it is anything but. Here is the reason for the complete lack of booze. She'd wondered before if the Feds knew about the other party. If cousin Marc Fayette, the renegade of their family, the white sheep if you will, was at this gathering, if he was the face of the Feds, then hell yes, someone knew something was going down. Or had suspicions. And it means the girls must be extra careful.

"Tallulah, Maeve. Didn't expect to see you here. Still living in the old place?"

"Of course. No reason to leave the legacy behind, Fayette. *We* remember where we come from," Maeve replies. She pulls at Tallulah's arm. "You'll forgive us, we have a show to do. Do drop by sometime, if you can recall the way."

The girls can feel Fayette's glare long after they've found the room Robillard keeps aside for performers. As soon as the door shuts behind them, Maeve begins to swear.

"Shit. Shit, shit, shit."

"Can't you do better than that?"

"Double shit with a honey glaze."

Tallulah laughs in spite of herself. "Maeve, this is a bad idea. If Fayette's here, he's got an inkling. He'll be watching us."

"He'll stick to us like shit on a shoe, Tallulah. Dammit!" She wrings her hands like they're dish rags. "Maybe we shouldn't go through with it tonight?"

"Nuh-uh. We've got to stick to the plan. Feds or no, if we don't come through on this deal, they won't trust us again. It won't matter that we're the last of the Moonshining Beauforts or that our family have supplied for the last hundred years. None of that will amount to a hill of beans. The Fae don't forgive and they sure as hell don't forget."

"Shit," spits Maeve again and kicks at a fashionable side-table. One of its legs snaps and the whole structure wobbles. The expensive-looking vase on top teeters dangerously, but miraculously doesn't fall. "Shit."

"We go on stage. We do our thing, we muddle through." Tallulah grins. "Hell, we're smarter than Fayette, always were."

Maeve nods and returned the grin.

---

The band is on a raised dais, playing soft dignified tunes. The girls have worked with them many times before, so the musicians know what to do when Maeve and Tallulah appear.

There's a drum roll starting out like distant thunder and then building to an glass-vibrating crescendo; the trumpet player lets loose a wailing blow as the girls mount the stage all shimmering and shiny, then every member of the band produces an ear-splitting wolf-whistle. It has the desired effect, stopping the gathering in its tracks and bringing the attention of everyone in the enormous ballroom to the one place.

The Beaufort Girls have arrived and the tone of the evening, having no chance against their particular brand of charm, changes.

"Well, hello, good people of Charleston," Tallulah breathes, giving the room the glad eye.

Maeve makes a cupid's bow moue and sings out, "My, what a handsome group!"

With just the right amount of preliminary eyelash fluttering and pouting, they launch into a round of songs, belting out favourites like *Ain't Misbehaving*, *Love Me or Leave Me*, and *Lovesick Blues*. Previously sedate butter and egg men take their hands off their bankrolls, and applaud wildly after each number. To keep themselves amused, before each gig the girls arbitrarily select the audience members they'll lavish with particular attention. One night it's men without jackets, the next it's those with. Sometimes black hair would seal the deal, others it's ginger bucks who tickle their fancies. This little extra attentiveness has been known to ensure handsome gifts and cash donations from besotted admirers. So when Tallulah had declared this afternoon, "Ascots. The more outrageous the better," ascots it was.

Between sets, Maeve takes a swig of water, covers her microphone. "Striped and purple, stage left. Pinned with an emerald the size of my knuckle."

Tallulah glances at the balding gent with the designated tie. "Oh, my. Gotcha. That would pay to replace the roof at home," she states. Taking her mic from its stand, she catches the gentleman's eye and holds it. Sauntering to the front of the stage, the fringes of her dress swaying enticingly, she gives her tone a throaty edge, "Our next tune is real close to my heart." She tilts her head earnestly, trying not to laugh at the sweat beading Purple Ascot's forehead. "It's a gem, sung for a real gem of an audience."

Over her shoulder, Tallulah calls out, *"Embraceable You*, boys."

Purple Ascot can't contain himself: he bends his tongue back and whistles like he's slumming it at a barrel house.

"Easy tiger," Tallulah giggles. "We're only getting started."

The band carries the crowd through set after set of smoky blues and old-fashioned ragtime tunes; the girls by turns flutter their fingers and swing their hips in Maroon Striped, Eggyolk Yellow and Beige Herringbone Ascots' direction. In the middle of their third encore, Tallulah selects their final tie for the evening.

"White with a full moon clip, diamond in it like you would not believe," she whispers, while she and Maeve have their backs to the crowd, their arms and legs swinging in the frenzied dance that's making their town famous. "Caught a peek of it over near Fayette's circle of Feds."

Maeve spins on her heel and scans the room, already planning what she'll say before breaking the poor man's heart with her last chorus. Waiters holding trays of soda and lemon water negotiate the throng, taking no offense when people nip out to steal a swig from hidden flasks. The suit-clad Feds and uniformed local constabulary, secretly wishing they could join the train of revellers as they move in and out of the ballroom, work the crowd halfheartedly unless Fayette is nearby. Maeve spies her cousin and a couple of his deputies next to the Mayor and Charleston's Chief of Police. Standing between them, just hidden by the Chief's overly large form, is a stark white pantsuit. The type that's topped off perfectly with an equally white ascot tie.

"Thank y'all for coming," she says, the band playing and replaying the bridge until they get Maeve's cue to wrap it up. "You're in our hearts, each and every one of you—but this last number is reserved for the boys in blue over there."

Judging by the noise, this crowd is as expert at feigning love for its lawmen as the Beaufort girls. Maeve whoops, twirls her finger at the pianist, and she and Tallulah turn to their mics in unison. "*I love my man,*" they begin, putting their all into it—and both falter, just a little, when the white ascot's wearer comes fully into view.

The woman's platinum blonde hair is slicked back in a bun. Her dead brown eyes are ringed with black eyeliner, and though they are directed at the men in front of her as she nods in agreement to whatever they're saying, those orbs seemed to focus on twelve different places at once. Eugenia Laveau doesn't seem to notice them, although Tallulah doubts she could have avoided it. Eugenia Laveau: practising sorceress; local crime boss; descendant of New Orleans' witch queen, Marie. The woman who knows where the bodies are buried because she'd put them there. Possessor of a drunk, good-for-nothing husband who had disappeared some years ago, *not of his own volition*, the rumours say. Once Grandmamma Bella's sworn enemy and rival. The woman who'd worn a feline smile as she stood at the edge of Bella's funeral service.

Tallulah signals to the band to finish with a drum solo. Hearts pounding furiously, the girls blow kisses at their admirers, curtsey to their detractors, then beat a hasty retreat from the stage. Quickly, they duck into the performers' room to collect the battered brown case, before slipping along a deserted corridor until the music becomes nothing more than a burbling hum.

"That was too close," Maeve hisses, pushing open the door to the basement stairs. "We're lucky she didn't recognise us."

Tallulah's hot on her heels. "Don't count your chickens, doll." She senses it's only a matter of time before Eugenia catches wind of their presence. The rest will be dominoes: Beaufort girls mean moonshine; which means there'll be Fae prowling around the joint; which means deals are being struck beneath Laveau's nose.

Without her say-so.

On her turf.

Much to her displeasure.

The heavy wooden door swings shut behind them, muffling the demands of a crowed too fired up to remark on the girls' clumsy exit.

---

The tunnels beneath Clancy's house are filthy. Tallulah shies away from the spiders' webs mainly because they have spiders dangling in them. The shining steel door at the end of the tunnel is attended by two burly guards. Maeve judges they do a reasonable job of passing as human, but "Work on the aftershave, boys," she says as one of them pulls the enormous bolt on the barrier and the other pushes it open. "The peppermint's a dead giveaway."

"A rasher of bacon in your pocket will do the trick," Tallulah suggests with a wink. The men grunt before closing the door behind them. Fae aren't easy prey for the girls' charms.

The ante-chamber they step into is like a storm porch, a spot where you can tidy yourself up after being outside. Carefully placing the suitcase on the ground, Maeve checks her hair for spiders and webs. Tallulah rubs her arms as if imaginary arachnids dance on her skin. Each uses the other as a mirror, making sure they're clean and lovely and nothing less than they can possibly be. One thing they can't escape, though, is the smell of smoke in their hair. There are so many folk upstairs puffing out white clouds that the girls' locks reek—their lavender toilet water is no match for Charleston tobacco.

This is their first solo deal. The first time they've done anything since Grandmamma died in the accident. Since the main still she'd kept out in the swamps had somehow ruptured, frying Bella Beaufort and leaving a hole in the ground where gators and gars now swim quite happily. It had taken months to set up a new still, to get the recipe right, to make enough to fill the order they'd received—and when it came, it was not only an order for goods, it was an *order* as in there was no choice as to whether or not they supplied. They'd been the couriers before, delivering Bella's best to under-parties all through Charleston, but this time they are *it*.

A last barrier barricade stands before them. One final dash of bravado, deep and steadying, then Tallulah picks up the case and Maeve turns the handle on the door.

---

The light is almost blinding.

The room is the white of snow and almost as cold. The furniture, what little there is of it, is pale Nordic pine, silver metal, thickly blown glass strong as a diamond. Mirrors edged with linear etchings stretch from floor to ceiling along the near and far walls, making the space look infinite as the girls enter, positioned briefly to see their own reflections. For a few seconds, hundreds of Tallulahs and Maeves step across the marble floor, the bright red of their lipstick, the deep berry shades of their hair, and the sparkle of their dresses almost garish against the bleached backdrop. It's a relief to move beyond the frames. The air is redolent of peppermint and a haze of white fume, almost a mist, floats near the ceiling as if the people can command the clouds.

Tallulah believes they might be able to, if they wanted. If they ever troubled themselves to do anything so pointless, so frivolous. Maybe these ones would—these who sneak around on their own kind, doing things that might just get them exiled—if they weren't already outcast. Shoulders back, heads held high, the girls thread their way through the crowd. The group is select, maybe thirty of the Fae folk, mostly male. Real daisies, the lot of them. All tall and thin to the point of emaciation, not burdened by the weight having a soul lends human frames. A handful of them recline on elegant chaises, crystal wine flutes loosely clutched, while the rest stand in pairs or perch on painfully spare barstools. They seem as if they've all been cast from the same refined mould, inhabitants and barstools alike. Both are sculptural and appear liable to shatter at the slightest disturbance. Both, Tallulah knows, are stronger than they seem and can break your neck if pushed the wrong way.

Those who deign to notice the girls at all, regard the pair as if they are something *less*, a subspecies. Tallulah doesn't believe they have any right to be so high and mighty, not when they're buying what they were buying. Not when they're no better than those human addicts who hide themselves away to chase the dragon. No right to be so uppity when their own folk would hand down terrible judgment on them if it were to be discovered they're using what the Beaufort girls make; what's in the case they have with them. Tallulah feels the sweat from her palm slicking the handle.

"Miss Maeve?" A voice, feather-light, slides through the air and catches their attention. "And Miss Tallulah. Thank you for coming."

"You say that like we had a choice." Tallulah doesn't mince her words. Her cousin put a gentle hand on her shoulder.

"Mr Indridi?" Maeve inquires and receives a minimal nod in reply, unsure whether it's all her client thinks is needed or all he can be bothered to give. She decides she doesn't really care. Though most of the club's patrons are doing a fine job pretending the girls aren't there, Maeve senses they're being watched. From the corner of her eye, she can see heads turn to follow their progression in the mirrors. She's tempted to pivot and wink at them.

But this is business, not pleasure.

"You have the product?" Navan Indridi asks. He's dressed in a grey so anaemic it is nearly white. Slim-cut slacks accentuate the length of his legs; a silk shirt, buttoned up to a high collar and linked three times at the cuff, skims across his lean torso like water. The only suggestion of colour is the green of his narrow tie, precisely the cold hue of his eyes.

"Yes. We've got your 'shine, Mr Indridi." Tallulah notes, with no little satisfaction, that he cringes at the word. She bites down on a smile.

"Not here." Clasping his hands behind his back, he gestures with his head to a curtained door on the far side. "This way." He doesn't tell them twice, doesn't turn to see if they follow.

The click of their heels echoes as they walk across the main room, the sound as stark as the music they can hear softly playing. A very different music to that of the upstairs party. Single piano notes seem to drop from above; a double bass plucked at random, its tones mournful next to the icicle clarity of the piano. Occasionally, a violin ties the two together, its fine wail setting Maeve's teeth on edge. There's no band, no musicians to speak of, so she can't pinpoint where the sound comes from. Goosebumps pimple her bare arms as she hurries to keep up with the Fae.

"The curtain," he says, once they've all crossed the threshold into a private dining room. Tallulah looks at her cousin and lifts the case as if to say, "Hands full," then waits for Indridi to invite them to sit in any one of the sixteen high-backed chrome chairs flanking the long birch table. She's still waiting, even after Maeve loosens tasselled ropes around the hooks embedded in the doorframe, letting the heavy fabric fall shut.

"We mustn't excite the masses," Indridi declares, taking a seat. He crosses his legs, folds his hands on his knees. His face, perfectly illuminated beneath a cluster of triangular chandeliers, betrays no emotion. "If the vintage of these spirits proves less than what we've bargained for, it's best they don't get so much as a whiff of it. I'm not sure I could assure your safety in that instance." He removes his steel-framed glasses, examines the lenses for a speck of non-existent dust, then replaces them on the bridge of his pointed nose. "There's nothing worse than taking a hit of coffin varnish when what you need is something pure."

"You *faekes* sure have some nerve—"

Maeve cuts Tallulah off before her sharp tongue gets them firmly on Indridi's bad side. "Bella always used to tell us," she confides, silently daring her cousin to contradict her, "that your establishments are no average juice joints."

"Is that so." Indridi's tone is flat. "An insightful woman, your Greatmother."

Keeping her eyes locked on his, Maeve smiles a dimple into her cheek. "Pardon me, but it's *Grand*—"

Noticing the correction, and the faint flush rising up the Fae's neck, Tallulah slides the case onto the table top. She clicks the clasps, quickly opens it, deftly removes the false bottom, and displays the contents as she would a picture book to a child. "You couldn't be righter, doll," she says to Maeve. "Beaufort Moonshine is *grand*. Always has been, always will be. Have a belt, Mr Indridi. You won't be disappointed."

His schooled expression transforms when he catches sight of the twenty-four cut-glass bottles, each the length of a man's hand and three of his fingers wide, topped with silver filigree caps shaped like corks and nestling into custom-fit grooves. Though its violet sateen lining is worn and dull in places and the padding flattened from years of use, the box emits a glow so bright it makes the milk-white walls look beige in comparison. The girls relax, seeing the flint melt from Indridi's eyes. Now *this* is a look they recognise: they'd just seen it on half their audiences faces.

Their smiles widen. Whether it was sported by man, woman or Fae, red hot hunger is unmistakeable. Longing is longing no matter who wears it.

Tallulah plucks a phial at random, unstops it and waves it beneath the Fae's nose. She gives him barely long enough to catch the moonshine's complex aroma before whisking it away, covering its mouth with her thumb. When the tension eases in her client's shoulders, and his posture slackens ever so slightly, she knows the mixture is as potent as she and Maeve suspected. Even she can detect the lingering musk of humanity, taunting him. And she also knows, before he even opens his mouth, that he'll want another sample.

"Too short," he complains, jaw clenched to retain his veneer of calm. "I couldn't quite catch the afterglow. No deal if it mellows too quickly."

"Do we look like the type of girls to brew up a batch of mellow?" Maeve's laugh is the throaty one she's practised a thousand times on stage. "Give him another kick, Tallulah," she says, and is tempted to let her heels match her words, but realises that, just now, Indridi is in no state to appreciate the finer points of cabaret timing.

With a wink for Maeve, Tallulah holds the bottle out for three solid seconds. Indridi inhales deeply, drinking in the scent of starlight mixed with a dash of love, loss, hope—the essence of a human soul. The delight of such foreign emotions breaks his concentration. For the briefest instant, he forgets to maintain his guise: his glasses vanish and white feathers sprout where his eyebrows had been; cheekbones lengthen and gain an icy blue sheen; his irises, already pastel, lose all hint of colour and swirl with washes of iridescent white. The neat silver braid restraining his long hair unravels, his tresses lift, caught in a whirlwind no-one else can feel. Crystal dust flakes from his lashes when, almost immediately, he sneezes. With that, he regains his composure. The only evidence of the lapse is a slight reddening of his cheeks, which he masks by dabbing at his nose with a linen handkerchief.

"Right, then." Tallulah replaces the phial, closes the old brown suitcase. "Peppy enough for you?"

Maeve picks up her cousin's line of questioning. "And the soul's afterglow: tell me that's not pure as a babe on Sunday morning." She sidles over to Indridi, leans up against the table. For the first time that evening, it feels like the Fae is exuding warmth.

"It'll do," he concedes, a shade louder than a whisper. The corner of his mouth twitches with the beginnings of a smile.

"Dandy," Tallulah says, placing the case on the floor behind her. "Let's talk about the twenty large this lot'll cost you."

"Bandying numbers is so crass," Indridi begins.

"Then call me crass to your heart's content, Mr Indridi, but let's talk about money while you do it." Tallulah tosses her head carelessly then fixes the Fae with a stare that says she means business.

He opens his lips to begin negotiations.

Beyond the curtain, the stark Fae music abruptly stops. Chairs and barstools scrape on the marble floor, then these too fall silent. Around them, the girls notice, the dining room walls go from polished white to dingy brick. Mould and damp rot the baseboards, staining the ceiling in an instant. The chandeliers burst like bubbles and are replaced by a single bare bulb dangling from a tattered cord. Its feeble light leaves them mostly in the dark. Curtain, table and chairs vanish—mops, tin pails and spartan shelves appear in their place. Through the door, Tallulah can now see exposed water pipes dripping condensation. Where the Fae chaises had lounged, now boxes with faded labels are stacked in haphazard rows. Piles of dirty linens wait to be ferried into the laundry down the hall. Whispers rise and fall in the empty basement, then rustle into the room like dry leaves.

"We've got company, *séfinn*."

Tallulah's ears pop when the Fae's disembodied voice fades away. Maeve shivers. "What's going on?"

Footsteps moving quickly strike the floorboards over their heads. Indridi's eyes focus. Once more they grow sharp, serious. Cool with disappointment.

"Tut, tut," he says, looking beyond the broom closet, through the basement to the door opposite. Yellow light traces its outline as the sound of clomping boots reaches the anteroom. The door handle turns from horizontal to vertical. "Should've known you kittens would've had tails."

---

Tallulah and Maeve are far too pretty for jail.

"What happened to the guards?" Maeve asks as the door swing open, releasing a swarm of dark-suited Feds and blue-uniformed Charleston flatfoots into the basement, headed by their bastard of a cousin. The girls groan at the sight of Fayette and retreat further into the shadows. Pressing their backs against the cold wall, they peer into the adjoining room, scanning the place for another way out.

"Over there," Indridi mutters. No longer kitted out like a pair of ham-fisted bouncers, the Fae security men now wear impressive imitations of the Feds' double-breasted jackets. Like the real bulls, their black Oxfords shine beneath perfectly pleated trousers. There are so many law-enforcement officers crowded into the room, in the confusion no-one will question a couple of unfamiliar faces. Their batons swing menacingly as the interlopers survey the place, ensuring their Fae kinsmen can make a clean sneak.

"Do that voice thing y'all just did—tell them to steer the herd clear of us." When she looks back at Indridi, Maeve faces the spitting image of one of Charleston's finest. Dark, round-cheeked and sweaty, with a belly large enough to make a joke of the twin rows of brass buttons running down his front, the Fae takes Maeve by the elbow. His grip is firm, its heat cooling rapidly as the effects of the 'shine he'd snuffed wear off.

"The merchandise," he mumbles at Tallulah. Soon as she grasps the handle the case becomes a small brown evening bag, but she keeps her surprise in check. Indridi locks onto her upper arm, and raises his voice:

"Call off the search, boys. Look'ee, look'ee who I found sticking their mugs where they don't belong." Indridi shuffles the girls forward, their protestations at being manhandled adding a nice touch of realism to the act.

"Get your paws off me, Mr—" Tallulah's voice drops away as the crowd of coppers parts, leaving an avenue wide enough for Fayette and his smug grin to pass through.

"What have we got here, Lieutenant?" Fayette saunters over to the trio. He stands so close, they can smell the red onions he'd had with lunch. "This what you call keeping the Beaufort name alive, ladies?"

"Want me to get on the blower, sir?" Indridi catches Maeve's eye, holds it. "Give the boys down at the watchhouse time to *shine* the cage up for these canaries?"

Maeve understands the Fae's drift: *Make tracks before the bulls sniff out the 'shine.* She doesn't give her holier-than-thou cousin the opportunity to reply. "Don't bother playing so high and mighty with us, Fayette. Can't nab us for something you're guilty of yourself, unless you're hankering for a family reunion down at the Big House."

Fayette clears his throat. "Your mind's gone off the track, hasn't it?" He smirks. "Just like the old bat's did before she blew herself to kingdom come."

Tallulah ignores the gibe although she dearly wants to apply the toe of her shoe to Fayette's backside. For now, she picks up Maeve's thread, and improvises the way they used to for Mr Ziegfeld's show. "You're a known lurker at Clancy's séances, Marc—don't you try to deny it."

Fury turns Fayette's olive skin a shade lighter. Maeve pretends not to notice how his eyes harden when she continues: "Keeping such fun to yourself—well, it's downright selfish. So we asked ourselves, 'Why not go downstairs and get an eyeful of the hocus pocus?'"

"'We could catch up with our old pal Fayette in the process.'"

"'And keep our friends close, but our family closer'—isn't that just what we were thinking, Tallulah?"

"Sure was." She directs her next comment to the elephant ears hanging on their every word. "See, my dumb Dora of a cousin here's lost one of her snazziest shoes." Maeve shrugs, widens her eyes, and puckers her lips in the best Helen Kane impression this side of the Ashley river. The men chuckle despite their superior's frown. Tallulah leans as far forward as she can without breaking Indridi's hold, and whispers conspiratorially: "We were hoping a real live witch like the ones Clancy hires for his get-togethers might be able to track it down for us. Now, is that a crime?"

"In some places." A woman's voice echoes from the back. "Yes, it is."

The subterranean temperature, already chill, drops another few degrees as Eugenia Laveau enters. Hands in her pockets, she walks unhurriedly but with purpose. Her eyebrows lift when she spies the clutch Tallulah carries. They raise even further when she turn to the broom closet; her forehead creases to the roots of her hair as she investigates its dim interior. Stooping down, she runs her fingers along the floor where the Fae table used to stand. She sniffs the sparkling crystal dust on her fingertips. Licks it. Nodding, she plucks a single white feather from beneath the rim of an overturned bucket. Before straightening up, she tucks it in her pocket, head tilted back as though she's been struck by an elusive thought. As though she is on the brink of a sneeze.

Fayette's eyes follow Laveau's impressive frame. Tallulah can tell he isn't happy to have her there. "Hang whatever will stick on them," he says to Indridi. "Just get them out of here."

"Find anything of interest, officer?" Laveau's gaze is still averted, focusing on the floor and walls, but it's clear to whom she's addressing her question.

"Not to my knowledge," Indridi replies, his voice suitably gruff. He tightens his hold on the girls and begins to move towards the door. Laveau glides into his path, and the tension in the room ratchets up. Maeve starches up her nerves. She catches sight of

Fayette's expression. He looks an awful lot like Bella on her lightning temper days; he steps between Eugenia and her prey, just as she's pulling a hand from her pocket, raising it towards Indridi's chest.

Marc is brave, Tallulah will give him that. Or stupid. Or he just really doesn't want anyone pissing on his patch, especially not some spell-shooting, voodoo-doll pinning, crime boss. She can see Eugenia hesitate, like she really wants to hex him, but decides not to—like there are too many Feds here even for her. And she can bide her time. She will wait.

"Lieutenant, get the suspects out of here," orders Fayette. "And you, Miz Laveau, have no place here. Kindly remove yourself from *my* investigation."

Maeve catches a smile from Eugenia that makes her think of the Bitten Ones and she shivers. Indridi nods dutifully to Fayette, and then half-pushes, half-drags her and Tallulah out, through the storm room, along the corridor, then up the steps once more. As soon as the light at the top of the stairs shows, Maeve starts to breathe again.

*Maybe,* she dares hope, *just maybe we'll get away with this.*

---

"Little ladies! Y'all are back at last," hoots a fat industrialist with a penchant for plaid trousers. It seems he and quite a few others have taken the opportune disappearance of the sterner bluecoats to openly indulge. Over his shoulder Tallulah watches the Chief of Police taking a swig from a hip flask offered by Clancy Robillard's son, Trosclair. She laughs, and feels an overwhelming urge to kiss the boy.

"Now, when is the next set, my sweets?" continues their inebriated beau.

"Not now, darlin'," croons Maeve. "Show's over."

"Oh," he says and his face falls like a child denied candy. Then he brightens as if a very clever thought has occurred. "Party's not over until I say so!"

He swings towards Tallulah to sweep her up. "Oh, enough futzing around," she snaps. Her right hand barely moves. Only someone watching closely would see it, but a stream of thin blue-gold sparks flies from the tips of her fingers and hits him in the chest and shoulders. He jumps back and does a jig, slapping himself as if to put out a fire no-one but he can see or feel. It distracts him long enough for Indridi to bustle the girls past.

"Impressive, Miss Tallulah. Tell me, do you have any other tricks?"

Maeve answers, "Nope. That's pretty much the extent of our mixed blood heritage: cheap fireworks. Nothing like what Bella Beaufort had in her arsenal."

They're almost at the exit. No-one is paying them any attention now: the girls have consciously dimmed their showgirl sparkle, and Indridi's magic helps dampen their natural glamour. They slouch and imagine themselves small and nondescript as they head to one of the house's less employed back doors, so they make it to their goal unmolested. All three move out into the cool night air, sighing with relief.

"Lordy, lordy, something smells out here," drawls a low rough voice. Maeve whips around. Two stout, hirsute men step out of the darkness, moonlight accentuating the crags in their cheeks and around their yellow eyes. Bitten Ones, smaller and nastier than the two posted out front, noses crinkling at the smell of Fae blood and not, she suspects, in the employ of their host. It isn't full moon, they can't *shift*, but they're still mean and dangerous, with one hell of a bite. They move quickly despite their stunted legs; before Maeve blinks twice the men are closing in. Indridi pushes the girls aside, spits words: two silver chains streak from his mouth, shifting like snakes in the air, coiling around the torsos of Eugenia's men, who begin to snarl and scream. Tallulah gets a whiff of burning fur and flesh as the links tighten and take hold.

"You're right, gentlemen," she agrees, sniffing and daintily blocking her nose with the back of her hand. "What a stench!"

The Bitten Ones' howls of rage intensify and are taken up all around the house's perimeter. Shadows bob across Robillard's manicured lawns, stretching from the direction of the side and front yards as the other guards' lupine voices draw nearer and nearer.

"Don't just stand there," hisses Indridi. "Run!"

"Told you we should have turned right," grumbles Tallulah as one foot plunges into the quagmire of the bayou. "Oh, my second-best pair of shoes!"

"If you could concentrate on surviving instead of moaning about fashion, we'd all be better off, Miss Tallulah," shoot back Indridi. The Fae has dropped his copper's façade, and is doing his best to ignore both the cloying humidity and the mud stains seeping up the exquisite fabric of his trousers.

"All well and good for you, Mr Faeke, but these pumps are Herman Delmans—the closest I'll ever get to a pair of André Perugias at this rate!"

"Not to mention Ferragamos," Maeve mutters.

Tallulah exhales sharply, lowers her voice. "And they're my *only* other pair of shoes. Of course, someone as flush as you wouldn't be familiar with that problem."

As she speaks, she hears a splash and a whole lot of cursing. Maeve is struggling to get out of a knee-deep bog. When she frees herself, her left foot is unshod and the right is a high-heeled mess of mud and muck.

Tallulah sighs as she helps her cousin. "And now I have *no* shoes."

"Get us out of this and I will buy you all the damned shoes you want!"

Indridi, considers Maeve, is displaying rather more human emotions than one of his kind is wont to do. Of course, Tallulah can be a trial and would drive a saint to distraction—why not a Fae? She shrugs, proud of her cousin.

"Don't fuss so, Mr Indridi. We know this place like the backs of our hands." Idly she turns her left hand over and examines it with vague surprise. "Well, look at that. Of course, normally we're here in daylight. And it was a few years ago . . . " A small vertical wrinkle grows between Maeve's eyebrows as she concentrates.

Feeling the greedy mud eager to claim her right shoe, she lurches forward. Stumbling into Tallulah, Maeve surveys the shadowy landscape.

"I want to say this all looks familiar, but . . . "

Everything is so dark, so similar. Hundreds of trees loom like ghosts out of the bayou. Moonlight dapples through the leafy canopy overhead, its reflection lost in the fog curling across the water's surface. Stray beams strike the eyes of watchful gators trailing the trio idly. In places long reeds and cattails poke their heads out of the haze, marking the boundary between riverbank and solid ground. Bullfrogs hum and croak, the sound hemming the three in. If only they could find a point of reference, or one of Bella's markers. Maeve has heard of people gauging their position by looking at the stars—so she releases Tallulah's arm, cranes her neck and strains to locate the Big Dipper. She takes a few steps forward, seeking the brightest star in Orion's belt, and—

"Watch out!" Tallulah warns, waiting for the splash as Maeve topples off the path and disappears into the murk.

Instead, there is a squeal, a thump, and the sound of timber snapping.

"Shit," Maeve hisses as she rights herself, inspecting her dress for snags and her palms for splinters. "Those railings were much sturdier when we were kids . . . "

Tallulah snorts. "There are more graceful ways of making an entrance, you know."

Maeve puts on a serious face, but her relief at having found the causeway to Bella's second storehouse is irresistible. She smiles and retorts, "It's a new dance move, called the 'Told you we were going the right way' step. Nice, huh?"

Tallulah hefts the case and grins. "That's enough out of you."

Water laps the walkway's planks, which are soft and slick with algae from years of disuse. It zigzags across the bayou, its furthest pilings invisible more than ten metres out. The trio step carefully, clutching the handrails only when absolutely necessary. After five minutes their legs ache from walking so unnaturally—and by the time they reach the copse of trees sheltering Bella's shack, they're stiffer than a shot of cheap whisky.

Indridi sneers at the sight of the dilapidated cabin. Its foundations are propped on a network of stilts two feet above the waterline; its walls weathered and its red tin roof sags. "*This* is where you intend me to stay?"

"Take it or leave it," Tallulah offers, casually swinging the valise. "The Feds are bound to look for us at home, and they surely know where Bella's main warehouse was, given the explosion and all . . . And since you won't whisk us back to your place—"

"Not *won't*, Miss Tallulah. *Can't*. Not with all this water around . . . and you might find worse dangers there."

"Like I said, since Faerieland is apparently too good for the likes of us, this is what we're left with. You want the 'shine, Mr Indridi? Then you have to help see us through til morning, wait til the heat's a little less intense."

"I'm afraid that isn't going to happen any time soon, cousin."

Fayette eases himself off the sturdy bench Bella Beaufort kept on the shack's front porch. *Sore feet make a person stingy*, the old woman used to say. *The most profitable deals are the ones negotiated sitting down.* Maeve always thought that was just a line her Grandmamma spun to teach the girls about hospitality—anyone who dealt with Bella knew she judged the weight of a man's wallet by the clink his arse made on that bench. But now, looking at Indridi's ragged appearance and thinking of the money she and Tallulah still haven't seen, Maeve wonders if she shouldn't have listened closer to that piece of advice.

"Don't make things difficult," Fayette says. "We want the case. Leave now and I'll even forget you two were fraternising with twinkle-toes there—consider it a family favour."

"Bastard!" Tallulah storms up the steps as quickly as the slippery surface will allow. "How dare you come here!" She stops short on the landing, her momentum broken by the .38 in her cousin's hand, and the chorus of low growls coming from inside the shack. Keeping the gun steady, Fayette moves aside. The cabin door creaks open behind him.

"Get a wiggle on, ladies. That's our cue to make an exit," Indridi begins, his words trailing away as three of the Bitten Ones they'd eluded back at Robillard's step outside, followed by their sleek-haired boss, Eugenia Laveau.

Maeve and Tallulah's faces are twin masks of disgust and anger. "What the hell are you playing at, *cousin*? Since when did you become the witch's lapdog?"

"It's not that simple—"

"Bullshit!"

"Watch that tongue of yours, kitten." The sorceress's outfit is miraculously pristine, all things considered. Sharp and ice-white, just like her voice. "My boys here are only too fond of chasing after waggling meat. Besides, you're too hard on your cousin."

Maeve's pulse races; she sees Fayette's sapphire tie pin placed just below Laveau's, gleaming like a trophy on her ascot. Fayette has been compelled. "Dry up, hag."

Laveau shakes her head, removes her hands from her pockets. Blue fire crackles along her fingertips. "You Beaufort women are all the same. Stupid rubes, the lot of you. Taking things that don't belong, queering up things that were right." There's a hiccup in her voice, but her face remains a mask of disdain. "I should've known you'd be too thick to learn from the lesson I taught old Bella."

Tallulah retreats, overwhelmed by visions of the distillery in flames; the calm night screaming with moonshine explosions; Bella's charred skin, singed hair, lifeless eyes. And the diamond she always wore on a chain gone—they thought the bayou had swallowed it. But now that gem of Eugenia's is looking awfully familiar close-up, reset and remade . . . She stumbles on the bottom step, but keeps her balance. "It was you."

"Give the girl a hand, boys." Eugenia applauds while the men fill the air with catcalls. "She can add two plus two."

The muzzle of Fayette's gun droops as he looks sideways at the sorceress. "Just give her the case and we'll be through here." Squinting at the pure energy licking up Laveau's wrists, he growls, "Now." Maeve is gratified, just a little, to see him struggle against the witch's hex. He may be an arse, he may have fought with their grandmamma, but he was family.

"I'll pay you double to listen to him, Miss Tallulah." Indridi edges forward, keeping one eye on the pistol and the other on Eugenia. Feathers ruffle across his brow; his features stretch, harden. Maeve remembers the white feather Laveau had pocketed and wonders if the witch's magic will work on the Fae.

"What—this case?" Tallulah asks, throwing it to Maeve, just as one of the Bitten Ones taunts, "Too much a *faery* to fight like a man?"

"That's the kicker, isn't it?" Indridi watches Maeve open the battered suitcase and remove two bottles of 'shine. He licks his lips, and for a fleeting moment his face darkens. "I'm not a man."

In an instant, his plumage turns to white fur. His nose elongates in perfect imitation of the Bitten Ones' full-moon snouts and his mouth grows ragged with deadly teeth. His tailored suit stretches, turns to flesh and muscle, lending his slight frame a werewolf's weight. Then he smiles, and his eyes glow with the light of a thousand fireflies.

On the porch, Laveau stretches out her arm, launches a streak of lightning at the Fae.

Before the spell hits, Indridi disappears. Blue fire blasts a hole through the walkway where he'd been, sending Maeve flying. She scrambles on her hands and knees, slides across slimy boards, and gathers the scattered bottles of 'shine back into the case. Holding two in one hand, she pulls their stoppers, snaps her fingers until a shower of sparks cascades into each. "Thanks, Bella," she whispers, quickly replacing the caps, and shaking them until the glass grows too hot to hold.

"Tallulah," she cries. "Duck!"

In quick succession the phials of 'shine sail over Tallulah's head as she creeps up the stairs, crouching low to avoid the bullets Fayette is spraying in Maeve's direction. As his free will wars with Laveau's spell, the shots go wide—or his aim is particularly bad—at any rate none, as yet, meet their target. Tallulah lunges for his legs just as the first bottle of 'shine explodes against the shack wall behind him.

A deep concussion shakes the cabin. Rainbow embers flare, blindingly bright. The whole structure rocks on its stilts, tilts dangerously to the left. Fayette pitches forward, down the stairs, still shooting wildly. He collides with Tallulah, who bears the brunt of his weight on her back and shoulders. Instinctively, she straightens up and propels him away from her. The pistol falls from his grasp, skitters down the steps and lands at her feet.

Indridi, in werewolf shape, appears on the porch as the second bottle lands. It strikes the floorboards between the sorceress and the cluster of men to her left, the explosion knocking two of them over the right-hand railing. Maeve has never met a Bitten One who could swim: these were no exception. She watches the pair flail their arms as they try to keep afloat—then the waters around them begin to churn and the gators' patience is rewarded. The howls are drowned out by the incredible sound of the shack's roof caving in. Windows smash, spitting shards of glass. Indridi leaps out of harm's way, straight into the path of the third goon.

The Fae-in-wolf's-clothing and the wolf-in-man's-clothing wrestle, their strength evenly matched: Indridi bolstered by magic, his opponent hyped on adrenaline and hot blood. Oblivious to their struggle, Eugenia Laveau stares down at Maeve. Hands alive with elemental fire, the witch once more lifts her arms, takes aim, and unleashes a searing bolt of light at Bella's granddaughter.

The night splits with the snap of released electricity. Fayette shudders as though struggling to wake. His body sways, head drunkenly bobbing from side to side as he looks around him. Eyes focussing, he steps into the path of the blast. While Maeve cowers on the ground not ten feet in front of him, Fayette's torso takes the brunt of Laveau's casting. His camel-hair coat and stiff-collared shirt are instantly reduced to a pile of witch ash; the skin beneath first scalds, then bubbles, then blackens. The beam of light holds him upright even after his knees buckle and his body goes slack.

Tallulah snatches up Fayette's lost weapon, aims at the sorceress, squeezes her eyes shut and pulls the trigger. The bullet lodges in Eugenia's shoulder, red blossoming on the white fabric, throwing her aim wide just long enough to release Fayette. He slumps on the walkway and half slides into the water, one of the widely-spaced pilings the only barrier between him and complete submersion.

Still clutching the gun, now empty, Tallulah turns and runs towards Maeve. "Keep tossing those pineapples, girl!"

Maeve reaches for another bottle, sparks and shakes it, and throws it hard. Too low: it shatters on the steps, about a foot from where the witch stands. Though wood erupts in a shower of splinters, Eugenia smirks, keeps her feet—until the floor lurches beneath them. The platform supporting the shack rumbles, then squeals as it twists and shudders. Indridi, teeth clamped around the Bitten One's neck, shuffles awkwardly backwards and collides with Laveau. Maeve's shot might've missed her, but it had ruptured the last solid strut supporting Grandmamma's not-so-secret storehouse. The shack, groaning in defeat, completes its lean to the left, and collapses into the bayou, taking both Fae and witch with it.

Tallulah and Maeve crawl to Fayette. While they haul their cousin's waterlogged body from the mire, they don't speak; their attention is focused on scanning the water's black surface, waiting for Eugenia's alabaster head to emerge. Hoping as hard as they can for any grace the gators might bestow.

"Don't bother: she's gone." Indridi's bare skin gleams as he hoists himself onto the walkway beside them. "Perhaps not dead, but gone."

The Fae offers no further explanation. The girls don't press the issue, merely keep their eyes averted while the naked Fae shakes himself like a dog. Water flies from him like honeydew in the moonlight, then he shifts himself back into his stained clothing. They turn their attention to Fayette. He smells like something roasted too long, and he's glowing with residual magic.

"Aw, Marc. Shit," sighs Tallulah, trying to find a non-burnt spot on his head to rest her hand. But the thick blonde locks are singed beyond belief.

"Give me the case," Indridi says.

"Is that all you think about? Getting high?" Maeve yells, disgusted, a catch in her voice.

"I take it you want him to die then?"

"Well, no, but what the hell can you do about it?"

"Give him the damned case, Maeve!" shouts Tallulah. Indridi hadn't fallen victim to Laveau's hex; he's more than a man. Maeve flings open the lid and hands him one of the phials.

Indridi uncaps it with his teeth, holding Fayette's head on one hand, then pours most of the contents into the unconscious man's mouth. When there are a couple of swallows left, the Fae holds the bottle under his own nose and inhales, several deep huffs. His form loses any semblance of humanity. The girls are aware only of a sharp-featured face and an intense white plumage that seems to illuminate the night. Squinting, they watch as he leans over, places his lips on Fayette's, and exhales. He repeats the motion again and again until he wheezes with the effort. Wisps of lavender, yellow and green mist escape as Indridi finally breaks away, taking a ragged breath.

Fayette's blackened chest spasms. His shrivelled features convulse, then lengthen and grow calm as the charred flesh fills out. Deep blue feathers sprout around his jaw and wrists, and along the length of his spine. As they watch, he grows taller, just a few inches, but it seem to make him thinner, as if he's been stretched.

"Oh, my. Diluted blood plus 'shine," whistles Tallulah.

"And a modicum of magic," Indridi offers, quietly pleased.

"There is certainly more to you than meets the eye, Mr Indridi," admits Maeve.

Indridi inclines his head, "I might say the very same about you, Misses." They help Fayette to his feet. Stunned, he blinks wordlessly until Tallulah bursts out laughing. "Now, Marc, if we hadn't brewed that 'shine, where would you be?"

"The very least you can do is show your gratitude," adds Maeve, smiling.

"God, I'm *ruined*." Fayette's eyes are wild as he brushes at his facial feathers like handlebar moustaches. He scowls at the girls. "I won't help you keep breaking the law, you know. Even like this."

"And who asked you to? Hell, we'll be happy to have some of those feathers though." Maeve reaches out as if to souvenir one. Fayette slaps at her hands and Tallulah goes back to business, barely stifling her mirth.

"As for you, Mr Indridi. Consider that bottle a freebie, but the other ones will cost you. Plus interest."

"Interest?"

"Yeah: the kind that comes in red, black, and silver," Maeve sings.

"Ferragamo. Patent leather with heels as long as your index finger. One pair each in all three colours. Size seven," Tallulah fairly trills.

"We'll discuss particulars in the morning, shall we?"

"Let's finish it now—talking money is too *crass* to dwell on. Don't you agree, Mr Faeke?" Tallulah grins and winks at Maeve.

"I couldn't have said it better myself, cousin."

"Oh, and one more thing."

Exasperation wrinkles Indridi's face. "What?"

"Ask them to engrave our initials into the soles, will you? Let Maeve lose her own shoes for a change."

Maeve crosses her arms and huffs. "Fine idea. But make mine six-and-a-halfs. I've got a more delicate bone structure than Amazon Queen over there . . . "

"Oh, cousin, think twice before you fling insults," hoots Tallulah. She scrambles along a section of slowly sinking boardwalk and bends down quickly, then skips back to firmer ground. She holds up her prize. Eugenia Laveau's tie pin loves the moonlight surely as her wolfmen did. "Things are looking up."

# Seven Sleepers

A hoarder as well as a notorious thief, the raven will frequently hide what it steals, often leaving 'treasure' concealed for such a long time that the precise location of its cache is forgotten. The point, it seems, is not to use the object regularly, but merely to have it. To keep it well after the owner has given up all hope of recovery. So it was with the Æsir and Vanir's memories: stolen away and hidden for too long. Stolen away on the eve of the battle that most required their wits.

The fact remains, that since the day Mymnir left Ásgarðr, lore and remembrance, history and magic have been problematic things. Some say this is why she created her own people: Fae so newly born they would never know of her great sins.

> Fríða Ragnarsdóttir, *A Commentary on The Forgotten Sagas of Gudrun Ælfwinsdóttir*

She will say it began with small things.

Seeds, spilled from a brooch. So many tiny kernels smuggled onto a ship, nestled in a filigreed oval box. Hard, iridescent little things, germinated in a bed of blood and pebbles, propagated in this new world. She wonders if they still shine, that first generation, her children, her flowering Fae. Or are they now as dull as the jewellery that once carried them? The silver ornaments adorning her dress are tarnished almost beyond recognition, bruised purple and green; the chain linking these to the central pendant a mottled, rotten blue.

*Helga has been lax,* she thinks, *leaving this so long unpolished, leaving the clasp unfinished.*

But, no. No. That can't be right. Helga is a smudge, like the rest of them. A blur of dust ingrained in the simple weave of the Queen's tunic, brushed over her head along with the antique garment she donned this morning before descending into the cavern. Her cavern. Carved into the earth beneath the Southern live oak she planted herself, many centuries ago, and nurtured from acorn to majesty. Small things. Seeds, acorns, roots. While watering the seedling with melted ice, she trained the radicles not to dig straight down, forced the stems to weave walls underground, to fashion a cathedral chamber as deep and wide below as its trunk and branches would stretch above. A space more than large enough for seven biers, seven grottos in which ancient sleepers could comfortably rest.

Damp and warm, the undercroft floor is abundant with life-giving mud, the air thick with spores. It's a cave only she can access; withywindles guard the gnarled entrance at the tree's base. Dangling, at night, from twisted limbs and boughs, these glowing spectres frighten the locals, who believe the oak haunted by ghosts, by angels, of dead slaves. No-one dares follow the Queen into her retreat, her secret cocoon, her womb.

She rolls up filthy long sleeves, wipes begrimed hands on the ragged blue fabric of her skirt. Gone are the silks, the furs, the brocades it's been her pleasure to wear over the years. Gone are the cages and guards—or guardians?—what were their names? There were four, she thinks. Maybe more? No matter. She needs no retinue now, no sentinels, no servants, no companions but the ones she creates. The ones she revives. Dew drips from the ceiling, spatters like tears on her kirtle. It's a pretty, natural pattern; midnight starbursts across her sternum, moonflower blossoms. She smiles. A basic dress for a basic setting, and a fundamental task. Yes, today, she is going back to beginnings. Seeds, acorns, roots. Clay.

Her fingers skim across the right-hand brooch and follow the drooping chain that connects it to its twin on her left shoulder. In the middle, they pause, and close around the stone fastened there, dangling over the firm shelf of her breasts. It is not an attractive gem, a blob of hardened grey sludge, misshapen and pocked, but no less precious for its ugliness. Closing her eyes, she presses it against her chest. Feels her heart beating, strong, steady. Feels the life coursing through her. Flowing into it.

As she warms the lump of primal clay in her hands, softens it, makes it pliable, she casts her mind further back, back to the smallest beginning, the first and only beginning she knows. The earliest details are sketchy, worm-eaten. A birth, of a sort. A one-eyed man and his offspring. A raven of thought who grew much too big. A raven of memory who emerged so small, so small.

---

Finn wakes when lightning strikes the power pole outside her window. She opens her eyes in time to see sparks erupt, then rapidly die. The street is dark, the line of lamp posts extinguished, everything still in the terrible silence of *after*. Finn is thankful, though; the sudden fright pulled her from a nightmare, leaving nothing but echoes of birds screeching, glass smashing. All the curiosities she has allowed to bubble up from the lower floor—all the things she doesn't want to sell—look strange in the moonlight, their shadows threatening. The over-stuffed badger, his coat silvered by age; the Hebridean chessmen carved of walrus ivory, with gap-toothed crowns and berserkir biting their shields; the porcelain Mandarin doll in full regalia (a golden phoenix flying across his *yuanlingshan*); the shrunken heads hanging like a decrepit bouquet from the ceiling; the hatstand moulded like a tree with spreading branches. From downstairs, she can hear Reg mumbling to himself; he probably hasn't stopped since she dropped off. She looks to the clock on the bedside table but finds no insistent red numerals. Her wrist watch is beside it and the slim green hands point to luminous digits.

*Two a.m.*

She's dozed for an hour, no more. Sweat has soaked through her t-shirt, the sheets are sleep-tossed and damp. In her slumber she'd scuttled across the mattress and the place where Lucien usually lies is as much a mess as her side.

The floor is cool and gritty—housework has never been high on her priority list—and she feels the slight *crunch* as her feet touch down. She makes a mental note to vacuum soon, before Lucien writes his name in the dust again to underscore a point. If Lucien comes back. *When* Lucien comes back. She glances out the window once more, through the security bars, sees the coin of the moon unobscured by clouds. The opposite wall, where she has hung all the pretty mirrors, looks like a gallery of eyes, silvered by moonlight and mercury reflections.

She strips the mattress and tosses the linens in the approximate direction of the bathroom's clothes hamper. From a vast closet she pulls crisp fresh sheets and remakes the antique brass bed, then contemplates the smooth panes of the pale pink and fluffy pillows. Finn can't bring herself to lie down yet; her adrenaline is still pumping, and she feels too awake for this ungodly hour. She finds the pair of running shorts she discarded last night—not that they've ever been worn for running. Finn's metabolism is an unreliable thing, sometimes working too much, sometimes not at all, leading her to swing between teen-thin and Rubenesque in a matter of months. At the moment she is leaning towards the latter, but made peace with her curves ages ago. She twists her long red hair up and knots it, then grabs a clean shirt from the teetering ironing pile, knowing it will be clinging to her all too soon in the sultry air. She notices, as she heads down the creaking stairs, that despite the lightning, no rain has fallen to relieve the heat.

If she can't sleep, there are other things she can do, like the books, the dishes, maybe the vacuuming. Probably not the vacuuming.

The steps are polished wood, with a threadbare carpet running along the centre; flowers, hares and foxes flowing like woolly water. She slips into the box-filled back room, and looks through the curtain of purple beads hanging in the doorway to the shop proper, filled with all manner of what her Grandmamma Tallulah refers to as "crazy crap".

Pieces of furniture incorporating animals and plants: a gorilla armchair, a lion coffee table, a dresser shaped like a lotus that opens up when you want to do your hair. Display cases, set a little too close together, filled with jewellery, some fine and lovely, other pieces just plain, well, nasty. Earrings made of baby teeth, *memento mori* lockets holding dried hair of the long-dead, finger-bone reliquaries of uncertain provenance. Some gris-gris and voodoo dolls, so old they might disintegrate in a strong breeze, take up space on a corner unit that wouldn't be out of place in an ossuary. Next to it is a shelf of skulls, all with a patina of age, some decorated with pewter and gold, some with ink and lace. On the far wall a construct of antlers (eight-point whitetail, most of the tawny velvet rubbed away) and corroded metal threads; the branches span five feet and scrape at the roof. Tenacious scraps of decaying, once-white fabric droop from it, some of their edges rust-red. Bird cages of varying sizes litter the ceiling, creating an aerial minefield for those above average height; some are of wood, some of metal, one particularly fine specimen is made of amber spindles and copper wire. They are, for the most part, empty: one or two hold children's shoes; another, a red-painted wooden fire truck; another, a harmonica, its ivory parts yellowed with years. A clockwork bird flies, when wound, from cage to cage, only perching on top of, never entering, them.

Some nights Finn walks through the store, touching each piece that has washed up here, not turning on a light, but navigating by the soles of her feet and their intrinsic memory of this territory which is hers and hers alone. Yes, some nights she will stalk the front room, but not tonight. She moves toward the oversized cherrywood roll-top desk waiting in the nook where two walls meet.

She finds an antique hurricane lantern and matches on the floor behind the desk, where she left them last time the electricity failed. Finn gives it a gentle shake to ensure there's some fuel left and the thing gurgles a cheerful affirmative. When lit, the colours from the enamel paint decorating the glass throw a night-rainbow across the desk, and flicker up the wall to the grotesque.

Perched on a small shelf and tied to the mounting board behind it, almost as if it wears the board as a parachute, the creature owes much to the fake mermaids of old, half primate, half manatee. This thing has a shrivelled head, almost recognisable as a man's, sewn (badly) onto the body of a rather small Capuchin monkey. Only by looking closely can one notice that the lashless lids move up and down, the golden eyes side to side, in a sort of insane Charleston.

Finn sits, rolls the desk lid up and catches with practised hands the loose sales receipts that immediately spill out. She heaps them into a pile and opens the accounts book. The embroidered cushion on the chair is lumpy and she thinks again that she should replace it, then kneads it firmly, tolerantly, into the small of her back.

"Can't make money from junk," comes the voice from above. A voice of a thousand leaves tossed on tundra winds. A voice that repeats what it hears, makes up new nonsense, and does it all over again. Spruik, rinse, repeat. Finn doesn't remember a time when it hasn't talked. As a child this used to creep her out, but when she decided, at age five, to name him, he lost much of his creepiness. Rowan gets cranky with her about it, but as he was christened so the head has remained.

"Shut up, Reg," she mutters. He's parroting Great-Aunt Maeve—she knows this because Grandmamma Tallulah would have said, "Can't make money from shit".

Finn sorts the receipts, laying them out in date order across the desktop. She feels puffed with virtue, but that's as far as she gets before there's a great *crack* in the street once more. *Lightning striking twice?*

"Beware the feathers, beware the breath," rants Reg. "Beware the things in-between."

"Oh, shut *up*," she snaps and rises, hearing a scratching and metallic scrambling as of a key in the lock. She moves through the beaded curtain, enjoying, as always, the click-clack of plastic gems bobbing against each other. The shop is not glass-fronted, so Finn can't peek out. She steps towards the front entrance and reaches for the handle.

The door swings open in her face, and she lets out a yelp.

Looming before her, a silhouette. Tall and broad and, for a moment, completely unfamiliar. The click of a switch and Finn's vision fills with red sunbursts from the ruby-glass chandelier above, pulsing with restored power.

"Finn? What's up, babe? Finn? Are you sleepwalking?" The voice is lighter than one might expect from a man of his size, but in no way feminine.

"I don't sleepwalk," she lies, grumpy. Not because of his comment, but because he's back and she's relieved and she hadn't admitted to herself how afraid she was that he wouldn't return. She won't—can't—admit to him this fear, can't—won't—show him the hurt that's been worming its way through her for the past three days. The aching, insidious idea that his family would *win*.

She wraps her arms around his waist, buries her face in his neck. His stubble, black as the scruffy hair on his head, tickles her ear. He holds her close then tips her chin so she's looking into his brown eyes, his handsome, weathered face, with its kind, constantly amused grin.

"Did you miss me?" he asks.

"No," she says, and they laugh.

"You're the worst liar." He kisses her and says, vaguely reproachful, "I did text to say I was coming home."

She nods guiltily, knowing that her mobile is entombed in the arse-end of her too-large handbag. Buried there so she wouldn't be tempted to check it constantly. So it couldn't tell her anything good or bad.

"How did it go? With your family?" she asks even though she doesn't want to ruin the warmth of his homecoming, doesn't want to paint the toenails of the elephant in the room. His smile slips and he shakes his head. She pulls him back into a hug and runs her palms up and down his spine. She's grateful they're not kids, not teens; that being in their thirties gives them a tiny protective shell, a resistance to the demands of old families. *Whatever's gone before*, Lucien has said more than once, *is ancient history*. "Tomorrow. We'll talk tomorrow."

Outside, the storm finally breaks. More lightning, thunder and drops of rain large as tangerines and just as juicy as they hit the ground. Lucien kicks the door shut behind him and they head upstairs. Absorbed in her lover, Finn doesn't hear the sound of a dozen small feathered bodies hurtling into the wood of the shopfront.

---

They have laid here the greater part of a millennium, stretched on stone slabs beneath the grand oak, sleeping, not dreaming. One needs spirit for such night-travels, not just a body, not just form. Even gods can't dream without souls to send over the waves. Without memories to draw them back home again.

Crafting the seven facsimiles was easy enough. A hundred years, maybe two, was dedicated to each. Collecting bones and skins, finding and assembling all the Vanir and Æsir, the god-shaped detritus, that had followed her into this world. Time well spent,

Mymnir thinks, looking at the placid creatures slumbering before her. One by one, she has cobbled them together, piece by piece. The divine beings she once fled, she once ruined. So long ago.

How they roared as her beak pierced their skulls! How they raged when she pilfered their recollections! When she flew away, faster than Freyja's legs spreading, their memories held fast in her breast. The clamour still rings in her ears when she's alone, when she ruminates on what she's done. Now, though, all their bluster is gone. There is a hush in the cavern, broken only by the rhythmic *plink-plink* of condensation. Today the gods are but marble shells. Their chests rise and fall imperceptibly; a single breath is taken over the full span of a day, exhaled the next. Empty, but sustaining, motions. Enough to keep them from decaying, their bodies from crumbling, not enough to jolt them to life.

More is needed.

She strolls between the biers silently, admiring her handiwork. Touching a nose here, a cheek there, double-checking that all is in place. Pausing. Sweet Baldr, brightest, purest of them all. Mistletoe threaded through his jerkin, holding the fabric together. Mayweed strewn across his fair brow. Dear Baldr. He has always been kind to her, treating her like a true lady, never shouting or slapping her when she wouldn't do his bidding. If the Norns were right, he'll be reborn in the new world—in this world? Wait. Is he dead? Mymnir pauses, shakes her head, tries to remember. She touches his stiff flaxen hair. Sweet Baldr, brightest, purest of them all. Mistletoe threaded through his jerkin . . . Mayweed strewn across . . . Dear Baldr. Always kind. His return, more than the rest, will please her.

After so much kneading, the clay is warm putty in Mymnir's hands. She tears a dollop off, rolls it in her palms, then buries it deep in Baldr's chest. As she moves on, his shrunken flesh adopts a healthier hue. It plumps up like dough. The raven performs a similar process at each catafalque. "Dawn has broken," she whispers to Þórr, frowning; *something is not quite right*. Her face clears and she nibbles a hole in her fingertip, streaking his beard and hair red with her blood before plunging the worked alluvium where his heart should be. "Today bears your name—a good omen, if any was needed. Prepare your hammer and harness your goats; the heavens cry out for thunder."

Another clump is pressed between the dragon keels and cresting waves inscribed on Njorðr's ribs. "Fear not," she tells him as the clay begins its work, "salt breezes will refresh you soon enough." He has always hated mountains and dirt, and loathes the howling of wolves. *So ugly a noise,* he once told Mymnir, *after hearing the beautiful song of swans.* Njorðr's children are next. Freyr with his phallus erect even now, his goatee just as prominent, curving up from the chin. Around his muscular waist, *Skíðblaðnir*, best of all ships, is folded up like a handkerchief in a pouch, stored until it should be needed. "Soon," the raven promises, before turning to Freyja. A thick braid drapes over each sturdy shoulder and a cloak of falcon feathers is tied around her neck—an exact duplicate of the one Frigg wears beside her. But Freyja's long white throat remains bare. Mymnir embeds a piece of softened stone in the goddess' gullet, marking the place where Brisingamen's heartstone once sat. Frigg, on the other hand, clutching a distaff, wears several strands beneath her cloak, long, looping chains jewelled with thousands of crystallised drops. *A mother's tears, shed when Baldr died.* Mymnir brusquely pushes them aside, quickly implants Frigg's hollow chest cavity, watches it swell. *Yet you did not weep for me.*

Óðinn she saves for last. The hoary-faced All-Father, sharing the granite bed with his replacement spear. Light as mosquitos, her hands hover above his closed eyes. There are two perfectly shaped orbs, two black irises beneath those lids, two pupils through which he might see her. Her craftsmanship is impeccable. The lashes, the veins, the lovely pair of convex arcs bracketing the strong bridge of his nose. In all her life, she has never seen such an exquisite set of eyes. She stares at them both a long time. Beetles crawl through the rootwork overhead. Water drips and drips. At last she digs her thumb deep into the second socket, gouging and grinding with her nail until gore splashes up her wrist, a combination of mud and shell and stone. She pulps the eyeball, jabs and jabs until the cheekbone is ruined, the temple caving in. Then she stops. Exhales through flared nostrils. Leans over and kisses the damage. It takes hours to repair and he still looks ruined, but she doesn't mind; that's how he was in life. When it's bolstered once more, Mymnir seals the hole with every last bit of slurry.

Then, like a baker, she waits for it to prove.
She waits for them to rise.

———∾∽———

The rain, initially so reluctant to fall last night, has not stopped since. Finn and Lucien stay abed well past sunrise, only venturing out when the sounds of activity downstairs float upwards.

"Burglar?" asks Lucien, searching for the Louisville slugger Finn keeps, with the dust-bunnies, beneath the bed. She raises her brows, remembering how many times he's laughed at her for the concealed bat, then shakes her head.

"I'm not that lucky." They pull on pyjamas and head towards the din of an aggressive breakfast preparation.

In the kitchen, two men, both tall, handsome and blond; the elder veering more towards a kind of seared white, the other a faded gold. Well-dressed in matching chinos, sharply pressed shirts (one blue, the other green), and highly polished handmade shoes, Fae blood keeps them looking much younger than they are. On a bad day, they can pass for a couple in their forties. Indridi, peering over the top of impeccably designed spectacles, is perched on a high stool. His disapproving attention is split between the chunkiness of the furniture and the sight of Marc Fayette rummaging through Finn's shamefully sparse pantry. A large cardboard box smelling of fresh pastries sits on the counter, a testament to previous experience.

"Uncle Navan. Uncle Marc." Relief infuses Finn's voice with warmth. She's genuinely glad to see them, especially since it's not who she was expecting. Indridi enfolds her in a hug and she can feel, in his breast pocket, the hard square of a cold metal flask. Fayette's embrace is more perfunctory, not because of any lack of affection, but due to culinary despair.

"Coffee?" he asks, and she points him towards the freezer.

"It's the one thing she doesn't run out of," says Lucien, offering a hand that is large and ridged with scars, the price of his profession. Indridi looks him up and down, assessing the crumpled boxers and t-shirt, the mussed hair, the general height and breadth of the man with whom Finn is so obviously sleeping. He accepts after a suitable pause, approving.

Fayette, in contrast, looks at Finn and says, "You're in so much trouble."

"Hello to you too, sir." Lucien takes Marc's hand whether he wants him to or not, and Marc smiles in spite of himself.

"Oh, so much trouble. A *Laveau*."

"Just barely," mumbles Finn.

"Marc, we own three of his sculptures."

"Having the artwork in the house and the artist in your bed are two different things."

"I can *hear* you," says Lucien. Finn throws him an apologetic look, and moves to stand beside him, a gesture of solidarity.

"To what do we owe the pleasure of this incursion?" asks Finn asks, sliding an arm around Lucien's waist.

Indridi slips the flask from his breast pocket and takes a long draught. Marc rolls his eyes and returns his attention to assembling the moka pot. Unconsciously, Finn tightens her grip on Lucien's side and he gently prises her fingers loose. "Uncle Navan? Anytime you're ready."

"Well, we so seldom see you and were wondering how you were occupying your time . . . " he begins, then reconsiders when she glares. "Something's—up. But we don't want to start until everyone's here."

"Everyone *who*?" asks Finn, dreading the answer. As if on cue, there's the sound of the front door opening and the tap of chic, expensive heels. The click-clicking of purple beads. "Oh, God."

"You know what this means?" says Lucien.

"It means too many people have a key to my place!"

"Well, there's that. But it also means Fate has made the choice for us. There's no time like the present—especially when your relatives are bearing down on you *en masse*."

"That doesn't help," she hisses and tightens her grip on the love-handle he's developed since they've been together.

Grandmamma Tallulah holds her age well, but not as well as Indridi and Fayette—thinner blood. Her hair, which has been through as many possible iterations as any woman can have in a lifetime, is streaked red and white, just above her shoulders, a longer version of the bob Finn's seen her sport in the photos of her youth. She's lost a little height, but she's willowy and curvy in the right places and her dancer's body could still stop traffic. Wrapped in a green shantung silk dress, the colour setting off the large diamond tie pin she always wears as a brooch, with stylish black patent shoes and a matching clutch purse, Finn thinks she could pass for an excellent fifty. Gods know she's twice that if she's a day. Her large hazel eyes light up at the sight of Finn, but she gives Lucien a suspicious look. He doesn't flinch, which warms Finn's heart—she's seen lesser men melt from Tallulah's laser beam glance.

"Darlin' girl." Whatever else might change, Tallulah's inflections are still those of an older time. She envelops Finn in an embrace redolent of something expensive and French. "You don't write, you don't call."

"I saw you last weekend."

"Time passes so slowly. And you really should clean up out front. The sidewalk's atrocious. Marc, Navan." She manages to give an eloquent shrug and buss each man on the cheek, one gesture flowing smoothly into the next. Finn can't help but admire her grandmother's finesse. Lucien clears his throat. She resents him, briefly; at least he got to have the difficult conversation with his family out of her hearing. Any display of his moral cowardice, dissembling, or other failing of the backbone was hidden from her. But *she* has to perform in front of a very judgmental audience.

"Grandmamma, this is Lucien Laveau." She says the last name lightly, as if there is no meaning to it, no weight of Montague-Capulet years. Truth be told, if she could have coughed into her palm and mumbled when she spoke she would have. Tallulah narrows her eyes and offers a slim hand. Lucien, with his perfect feel for situations, kisses the back of it, as if he's a courtier. *Suck up*, thinks Finn. But her Grandmamma's mouth lifts at a corner and she holds onto Lucien a few moments longer than necessary. *The old flirt.*

"We had some high times with your Grandmamma Eugenia, my cousin and I." Finn notices that she doesn't say Maeve's name, that her lips flatten as if she's trying to stop it coming out. Finn's whole life it's been like this and she doesn't really understand—only that when Maeve married Trosclair Robillard, Tallulah decided she couldn't bear the stench of respectability. It didn't even seem to matter that Trosclair had been dead for the better part of thirty years; the cousins stubbornly refused to speak. Still, Finn dares to hope it might be okay.

"Well, looks like all the finest people in Charleston are here, though some of them are a little underdressed." Another caramel thick accent floats across the kitchen, which now smells strongly of coffee, pastries and perfume. "Navan, you are a sneak and a rogue. That goes double for you, Marc."

As quickly as they rose Finn's hopes take a nosedive, crash land and burst into metaphorical flames. It's not that she doesn't love her great-aunt, but the old ladies haven't been in the same room for over seventy years and they sure as hell haven't spoken to each other in just as long. Well, they haven't *spoken*, not *directly*, but each has become a master ventriloquist, sending messages, often acid-edged, through family members so that whole conversations have been exchanged with miles between them. Now, two sets of willow-green eyes flecked with yellow take each other in for the first time in decades.

Then Finn realises that the *belles* are the least of her problems. Behind Maeve, who is shaking her umbrella at arm's length to keep the drops well away from her suit—a symphony of black and white that matches her hair—stands Rowan.

Finn's little brother, who took in the family lore at Tallulah's knee after their parents died, who ate up all the legends and the resentments against the Laveaux. Rowan, self-proclaimed heir to an old, now groundless hatred, who tries to fill his own emptiness with things from the past, things that have no strong foundation in the present. Rowan who, in looking back, always stumbles. Rowan, who is staring at her like she's the worst person in the world.

Finn closes her eyes.

---

It has been so long since they've all been together like this, all gathered in one room, Mymnir almost wishes she didn't have to disturb them. Hours have passed, days—how many days? Impossible to tell without sunshine, without moonlight—*time* has progressed, as it has a habit of doing, without the raven caring to clock its movements. What's important is not the seconds ticking by, but the metronome beating of clay hearts, getting louder and faster and stronger as the gods quicken. *They look so peaceful*, she thinks. *It's unnatural.*

Their waxy faces placid, serene, flushed with gestation. Pink as babies, calm and happy. Not angry. Not full of mischief. No, not yet. *First, they need to remember.* An impatient caw tears from Mymnir—so long alone, she has forgotten words, or they have forgotten her. She coughs, essays a question, *How many days has it been?* Such tumbling sounds. Surely, enough. The lungs bellow evenly, the flesh is tender; it springs back almost immediately when prodded. They must be ready by now. She fumbles for the gilded receptacle pinned above her right breast. *They must.*

The brooch slips from its setting without a hitch. Mymnir runs a fingernail beneath its decorative lid, seeking and finding the concealed latch. *Too bad the old wolf isn't around to see this*, she thinks before pressing the little nubbin, hearing it click open. Lóki's kingdom box was an impressive trinket, certainly, and it served an important purpose. But its twin, the one Mymnir forged herself, is unforgettable.

Leaning over Baldr, she decants the slain god's memories back into his body, all the precious bits of the soul she'd taken before Ragnarok came—before she caused it or fled from it, she isn't sure which, not quite, not anymore. All the drops of what once made him *him*, stored all these centuries in a jewelled capsule that hung, sometimes, near her right shoulder; all the liquid history now slips like honey mead between Baldr's parted lips. She rubs his throat, forcing him to swallow, and keeps pouring until the essence changes from white-gold to crimson, then moves on. *Blood has always been Þórr's best shade*, she thinks, shuffling from replica to replica, repeating the rite for each of them as red turns to indigo, to ochre, to rust, to pewter, to ash. When the vessel is drained, she snaps it shut and reattaches it to her garment. Then she steps away, so excited she flutters from human to raven form and back, and prepares to greet her old companions. Her old masters.

*It will be different now*, she trusts, watching closed eyes flicker and tic as reminiscences settle behind their lids. *They will join me at last, they will see what I've become, and everything will be different. No longer a servant, but an equal.*

But after a few more hours—days?—of waiting, Mymnir begins to have doubts. Breath still soughs from their mouths, regular and even, in and out like the tide. Occasionally, fingers twitch.

Feet, once so stiffly pointed in their boots, relax. Armour clinks as slumbering limbs seek more comfortable positions. Feathers and wisps of hair ruffle in unfelt breezes . . . And yet, nothing. No change. The seven gods merely stir—they don't *wake*.

No, not even seven, Mymnir realises. Six. To say Baldr's reactions are sluggish would be too generous. Unlike the rest of them, his metamorphosis isn't productive; his aren't the fidgets and rustlings of one about to slough off sleep. He *is* moving, but in retrograde. What was smooth and whole moments—weeks?—before, is now crumbling. The elixir of his returned memories weighs him down instead of reviving him. His features sink in leaden increments, and come undone.

"Get up," she says, leaning over him, whisper turning to a shout. "Get up."

Baldr's sweet face blurs around the edges, and his head caves in like a cake pulled too soon from the oven. "No, no, no! Get up," she urges, but he does not hear, does not listen, does not obey. Mymnir straightens, face tight, expression cold and, abruptly, turns her back on him. *He's just as dead now, just as murdered, as he was after Lóki tricked blind Höðr into the deed.* But the others, the others . . . Death was no excuse for any of them. Baldr's homecoming may have been a vain hope, but the others!

*I've done everything*, she rails, *given everything. Beds, bodies, spirits. I've given it all back—and a new world besides—I've given everything* . . . But even as she thinks it, she knows this last isn't quite true. Not completely.

She runs a hand across her eyes, feels the jut of her cheekbones, the delicate plumed brow. Features of frost and ice, features of her own choosing, her own stealing. Hair and skin, pale as the murdered god's. Lips full as Frigg's, curves borrowed from Frey and Freyja. Lightning wit and temper, all Þórr. Cascade of silver hair limned, every so often, with a lustrous blue, like starlight on Njorðr's ocean.

Oh, how they'd screamed, Mymnir recalls, not for the first time, not for the last. How they'd wailed as she ripped through their skulls, small though she was, an ethereal bird sprung from Óðinn's mind, a sharp-beaked being of inspiration and air. And, oh, how she'd grown as she gobbled their memories, plumper, taller, more solid than ever as she added their dreams to her own. She'd been nothing before, she'd been *lesser.* A flimsy raven. A one-eyed man's reverie.

Not a woman.

Not Queen.

But then, but *then.* She'd flown, she'd speared, she'd taken what Óðinn should've offered in the first place. A life of her own. A form not attached to his. From each of them, she'd stolen. Adopted. Adapted. They'd made her what she is, these other gods, every one of them, together. By their selfishness they'd made her a thief. But by her own will she'd made herself something new, something unthought-of, something miraculous. Not borne of the All-Father; fathered by all. For over a thousand years, she'd been much more than a spectre hovering beside her master's ear. For so many lifetimes, she'd *lived.*

Alone.

*Little thief, little thief, it is time to repay your debts.*

Here in this world, far beyond Ásgarðr, Mymnir has been monarch and bird, reviled and revered. Confined by her own devices to these two shapes—woman and fowl. Incapable of transforming to her third, original, natural form. A glutted burglar, she became too substantial for shifting into something light and hollow, she became too full. Of herself. Of the seven. If they are to be reborn, if she is to set things right, she must give it all back. The woes, the beauty, the ambition, the loneliness. These are not her lot, not hers to carry.

The white raven flies around the cavern, gaining speed and momentum as she circles, as she dives. Sharp and narrow as a dart, she stabs, pierces, slices through skulls. Travelling so swiftly through foreheads and temples, she scarcely makes a hole. With each pass, screams erupt from long-silent mouths, ragged cries, wails of the newborns. With each pass, Mymnir relinquishes pieces of herself, of her godhood. Returns the things she stole. Six sets of heavy limbs rumble, six pairs of eyes open. The raven, a streak of silver, arrows through minds and hearts. Filling them up, emptying herself out, until she floats, ephemeral but whole. *If only Huginn was here.* She becomes lighter still as she realises every thought is a little part of her brother, just as she is in every remembrance. No matter how much she gives, no matter where his bones lie, neither of them will be lost.

She is Mymnir still, will always be.

Raven, woman, memory.

Around her, at last, the gods are awake and raging. Baldr remains dead; a precursor of greater sorrows. *As it was, so shall it ever be* . . . What began in the old world must be finished in the new. Ragnarok's long overdue conclusion.

Mymnir smiles as her gods, her masters and children, wield weapons and magic, and start climbing the root-trellised walls. They scramble to the domed ceiling, scraping with sword and spear and hammer. Quakes rattle the cavern, spreading deep and wide, disturbing tectonic plates. Showers of dirt, worms, and silt bury the biers, filling the undercroft to Mymnir's waist as she watches them disappear. As they burrow up, up, up.

---

"Wonderful, the family's all here," drawls Fayette and counts out the right number of coffee cups—no two look alike, but he manages to communicate scorn through nothing more than a flare of his nostrils. From the other room, Reg is rambling to himself about feathers and blood and clay, about life and memories and mothers. Finn makes a concerted attempt to block him out.

"*He's* not family," says Rowan, tone hard and sad, and Finn imagines him flinging her perceived betrayal around his shoulders like a cloak. She wants to roll her eyes, but keeps herself in check. He loves a dramatic gesture, does her baby brother. Quitting a law degree to go 'find himself' in Nepal. Using his inheritance, the whole shebang, to buy half-shares in a failing second-hand bookstore because the girlfriend *du jour* owned it. Getting saddled with the full mortgage—and the shop's upkeep—two months later, after the woman abandoned ship. Working there ever since like a sailor bailing out a sea-tossed rowboat. *A good investment*, Rowan claims, but Finn knows he keeps the place just in case Adele comes back. He'd have been an excellent knight, she thinks, sent off on quests for things that don't exist, pursing *ideals*. Chivalry would have suited him down to the ground. Relationships conducted from afar, with lovers placed on pedestals, forever yearned for, forever out of reach. No reality, never subjected to the harsh light of day or someone leaving the toilet seat up and the cap off the toothpaste. Rowan was a romantic, easily devastated. Rowan was *exhausting*.

"We are not here," interjects Indridi, his inflection telling all and sundry that he will brook no dissent, "to pick over old bones."

"But—"

"Rowan, your tenacity is admirable. *However.* Whatever problems you have with your sister's choices can be dealt with *after.* For now I need you to focus." He stares Rowan down as the young man's skin reddens, russet as his shoulder-length locks. Outside, there is great roll of thunder. "As it happens, Mr Laveau *does* belong here. His ties to this situation are as strong as yours."

Finn notes that no-one questions Navan's involvement—he's family in all but blood; Maeve and Tallulah's oldest friend, Fayette's husband and saviour. His place is nowhere but here.

"And quite frankly," adds Indridi sharply, "if that pair of old bags can keep quiet for five minutes—which they have and *bravo*—then perhaps you can try to do the same."

Finn accepts a cup of coffee and drags a bear claw from the pastry box. She looks around her kitchen at the strange assembly that's migrated to the long, scarred dining table: the belles, sitting close together at one end, heads almost touching, elbow-deep in pastry flakes, but still not talking; Fayette tidily dismembering a cruller while Indridi ignores the food for the contents of his small canteen; Lucien wholeheartedly attacking a clan of helpless beignets whose only defence is to release a snowfall of icing sugar; and Rowan, sitting stiffly, refusing both food and drink. Finn puts out a hand and touches his wrist. He pulls away.

The urge to shrug and to hurt come in equal measure. Lucien, beside her, moves his leg so their knees touch and she feels the warmth of him, the strength; impressed that he can comfort her without doing something to openly antagonise her brother.

"How to start?" says Indridi, almost to himself. Fayette puts a hand on his husband's shoulder, squeezes tight. Again, there is the growl of thunder overhead and both men raise their eyes skyward as if expecting something to come through the ceiling. Indridi begins, rapidly but surely.

He tells them the history of the Hrafn, of Mymnir who, tired of servitude, of being simply a palimpsest on which Óðinn wrote and rewrote the world, stole so much, caused such devastation, then fled. Of how she made her own folk, not immortal, no, but long-lived and strange. Of those who defied her and fell, of those who fled and survived, of wolves and weddings and wings, giants and drums and looms and demons. A story of blood and memory and feathers and family in which they are all involved, implicated, entwined. And, having, each one of them, grown up with such tales, with aunts and grand-dams, uncles and great-fathers, all with some skerrick of magic left in them, having seen the last flickers of these enchantments playing at their own fingertips or those of their kin, they know and believe that what he says is true.

"The Queen," Rowan intones, and Finn can tell he's love-struck.

"The Queen, indeed," says Indridi, and Finn sees from his expression that he knows Rowan has missed the point. But the Fae perseveres.

"She disappeared so long ago we refugees and exiles hoped she was gone for good. But things have been happening and we've been watching for a very long time," he says with a meaningful look at Fayette.

"Once a sticky beak, always a sticky beak." Tallulah laughs but there's no malice in it, just fondness.

Marc shrugs.

"It falls to us to see it through to the end," Indridi says.

"So what kinds of things? And what can *we* do about it?" says Lucien, voicing Finn's thoughts.

"People are disappearing. Items that had fallen to earth after the final siege of Ásgarðr were collected over the years—but their keepers have been taken or killed and the artefacts stolen. A sense of something growing, building, developing. A feeling of something being *made*. But we couldn't place it, couldn't pin it down. Until this morning.

"It's her. Mymnir. Only she can wreak such change. She did it once before. What can we do? Try to reason with her?"

"From what you've said rational thought isn't her strong point . . . " Lucien says.

"I'm sure she'll listen." This from Rowan.

"*Ragnarok*," says Maeve, the word almost bloody on her lips.

"You always were melodramatic," says Tallulah. "A little rain, a little thunder, a megalomaniac queen, and you assume it's the end of the world?"

Maeve gives a less than lady-like snort. "These pumps are Louboutins, darlin'. And apocalypse really takes the shine off patent leather."

Smiles ghost across the women's faces.

*So Armageddon is what it takes to get them talking*, thinks Finn. *That's a good start.*

Lucien is frowning. "So, we sally forth armed only with reason?"

Indridi pauses, then with the subtlest glance asks Marc to retrieve the rich brown leather weekender bag they'd left slumped inside the front entrance. From within its stylish plaid depths, Navan pulls a cloth-wrapped bundle, approximately two feet in length. The material is grey, oiled hide, with remnants of silver embroidery still visible. He gradually strips the covering away, revealing what appears to be a broken branch. No thicker than a broom handle, the wood is twisted and stained, knotted where twigs must once have sprouted. One end is splintered. Jagged barbs point where the spear's shaft would've extended, if it hadn't been snapped. The other end is polished, and sharpened to a deadly spike.

"This is very old, but I imagine it will do the job if required," he says quietly.

"No! You can't—that's barbaric! How can you even suggest such a thing?" Like all of his emotions, Rowan's horror is monumental, important, *performed* with great drama and feeling—and Indridi will have none of it.

"You think this is a *game*? You think it ungentlemanly to contemplate killing a woman? You have no idea, you *child*, no idea at all what Mymnir is like. She's hard and cold and capricious. You think living under her rule was any kind of a dream? You think we survived by playing nice with her? You, your family—*families*—no-one with your bloodlines, Fae or human, has lived this long through kindness. They lived because they ran and they fought to be free."

Rowan seems to be about to argue but thinks better of it. There's silence for a moment, disturbed only by the steady pounding of rain, the squawking of birds, their racket getting noisier as the downpour intensifies. Then Lucien spreads his hands as if grasping for meaning. "So, we're your crack squad of—what, god-killers? Is that what she is?"

Indridi grimaces as if to say *Good help is hard to find* and shakes his head.

"She's Mymnir, raven, woman, memory, all grown too big for her boots. She has power, much of it stolen, and she is dangerous, but she can still be *ended*." He says this last as if in deference to Rowan's chivalrous delicacy. He nods towards Tallulah. "And *that* thing might just come in handy."

Her eyes widen. "Ever the charmer, Navan."

"The stone, darlin'," says Maeve in a stage-whisper.

Tallulah's hand flutters to the gem, far smaller than it once was, but still impressive for all that.

As her grandmother reluctantly agrees—"I hope mankind appreciates this *sacrifice*," she grumbles—Finn gets up to rinse out her coffee cup, and put another pot on the boil. Towelling her hands dry, she stares out the window, watches as a starling drops down, glides a moment, flaps its wings to gain speed and slams head-first into the glass. It was so deliberate, so *suicidal,* that she is stunned. The loud *whack* makes the others turn.

"What was that?" asks Lucien and rises.

"I don't like the look of this," says Marc. Indridi joins them by the sink and they all follow Finn's gaze, riveted by the swelling armies of birds. Dozens of kamikaze fliers, then hundreds, thousands—owls, grackles, finches, nuthatches, warblers—lancing into apartment complexes and shop windows, bodies crashing through panels and alarmed doors. Spear-headed formations breaking off in many directions—the largest flank careening toward the antiques shop, toward such a thin barrier of glass . . . Reg's voice has risen several octaves, tearing in from the back room as he shrieks.

"What was gone has returned and walks once more! Annihilation comes on swift wings in the place of angels!"

"Time to go," says Indridi and draws his right hand upwards, a gesture both eloquent and efficient, as if he's unzipped the air. For a second, all Finn can see is a blinding white light. She blinks swirling afterimages away and focuses. Through the rent, it's winter. At least, everything seems frozen—cherry trees in full blossom, all sparkling and silver-leafed, line avenues of ice. Minimalist buildings in simple geometric shapes, airy confections of white concrete and glass, dot the landscape, illuminated by streetlamps of frost burning with blue flames. And everywhere, people. Some human, dark-skinned, but many—so many—with Indridi's colouring, his bearing, his feathering. Paying them no attention whatsoever. Between a towering sculpture and a shop much like Finn's, another door, another tear rends the scene, and through it stands an enormous oak tree. Mesmerised, she looks. Agog.

Indridi grabs her, brings her back to herself, right before the kitchen window smashes.

Daggers of glass and wood pepper the back of Finn's bare legs and arms as birds missile into the room. Everywhere, beaks and shards slash, driven by the hurricane winds outside, driven by madness. Shrieks and smashing, a cacophony of damage. Finn shields her face, lunges for the spear. She snatches it off the table while Indridi holds the Fae portal open.

"My dear family," he yells above the clamour, "step lively. Our time is up."

---

Mymnir, feathered, perches in the oak's uppermost branches. Corkscrew twigs thrash in the gale, flimsy green shoots bending against the onslaught of sleet and lightning and rain, beneath showers of robins and sparrows, gulls, crows. Some dead, some nearly so. Their little avian bodies twisted and broken, wings crumpled and bleeding as they tumble, as they snag on sticks, decorating boughs with feathers and gore. They fall around her, ice pellets and lightning and birds, but the white raven is not afraid. Her head twitches, twitches from side to side, twitches up and back. Not because she is nervous, but so she might see everything at once. The gods' ascension. Their rightful—righteous—havoc. She doesn't want to miss a second.

*This* is what they were born to do, all those years ago, today. Atmospheric turmoil. Elemental control. Þórr bulls across the heavens, planting sparks, sowing sky-fire. Forests of electricity lance their roots down from a soil of turbulent cloud. Njorðr geysers after them, turns giant and lets his feet splash. Emptying lakes and streams as though they were puddles, laughing to see their tidal crash. Torrents whirlpool over the ocean, stirring up great walls of water set to ravage the South Carolina coast.

*Yes*, Mymnir caws. *This.*

The landscape is reinvented, deconstructed, reconstructed. Freyja ploughs cities, suburbs, industrial wastes. Fields of wheat, rye and corn reclaiming broad avenues, parking lots and shopping malls, millions of spiked green heads spearing higher than church steeples. Hailstones the size of cars crush roofs, split bridges, crater highways. Frigg's tears unleashed, redoubled and trebled, pummelling the earth in the wake of Baldr's second death. Cattle of all breeds, two-legged and four, stampede as Freyr seeds riverbanks and causeways, houses and barns, nests and warrens and dens. Thousands of creatures desperately, frantically start rutting.

And Óðinn surveys it all, the lights and the darks, silence and noise. Stirring waters, rupturing hills, splitting the sun and impaling the moon with Gungnir. Catching all flying things; eagles and swallows, satellites and planes. Inspecting and destroying them. Searching for two that matched, a perfect fit for his shoulders. Two he once had, once lost.

*Oh, yes.* Mymnir is near-paralysed with ecstasy, to see them in action. To see this glorious display of power. Her eyes and head twitch, twitch up and down. She digs her claws into the bark, ruffles her wings for balance, doesn't blink.

Streaks of light across the firmament, glaring blue and white, are reflected, captured in a flash at the base of the oak tree. The Queen glances down the length of the gnarled bole, sees a vivid gash in its shadow. A shining hole sprung from nowhere, spouting a group of nothings. Humans, not Fae. Ants.

She turns back to the destruction above her.

Before her.

For her.

She sings.

---

"There she is! It's her!"

Rowan's voice is filled with such longing, Finn wants to slap him. Although he's shouting, she can hardly hear him over the fury of wind and rain. Chunks of ice and gobbets of filthy water plummet through gaps in the oak's sweeping foliage—but compared to the wrath of weather beyond, the shaded space beneath the massive canopy is an island of calm. The ground is churned, a froth of mud, hail and dead leaves, the footing unreliable. Holes the size of round dining tables breach the soil, tunnelling deep into the earth. Finn treads carefully, minimally, afraid she'll trip and fall down one of the dark shafts. White-knuckled, she clings to the knobbled length of the spear, holding it awkwardly in front of her, like a sword. *What the Hell am I supposed do with this? It's little more than a* stick . . . Through the branches overhead, she can see flashes of lightning. Flashes of huge bodies, too huge to float the way they are, dodging clouds, racing comets, hurling them. Flashes of arms and legs, shapeshifting at blink-speed; now skin, now steel, now translucent smog-limbs. Flashes of faces contorted with grief, with anger, with ecstasy. Flashes of the end.

In the sky, the gods play.

Finn wants to turn and run, but her muscles appear to be disconnected from her brain. She wants to dive back through the threshold Indridi opened, she wants to find calm and safety in the kitchen, but it's impossible, it's gone, the door sealed up, containing an insanity of birds. Blood trickles from nicks and gashes in her skin, but she can't move. There's nowhere to go.

Lucien braces her, helping to keep her upright and facing the magnitude of what they need to do. Standing where the portal has just winked out, Tallulah balances on one leg, steadied against her cousin's arm as she takes off her shoes. Once the footwear's safely wedged between the roots, she returns the favour for Maeve. The *belles* are dishevelled, slices of expensive material hacked from their outfits. Marc and Indridi approach the enormous bole, looking skyward. Only Rowan is alone, unscathed, seemingly unaffected by anything but awe, arm raised as though expecting the large white raven sitting atop the ancient tree to soar down and land on his wrist. The sound of the bird's cawing—*singing?*—reaches Finn, and she can tell, much to her astonishment, that the creature is *happy*.

"Why did you bring us here," she asks, shock draining any emotion from her tone. "Why all of us?"

"Because staying behind was *such* a good option," snipes Indridi, then clamps his mouth shut.

"Only the National Guard could contain this," says Marc, shaking his head at the impossible logistics. Rain spatters his chinos, ruins the crisp in his shirt. He points to the rampaging gods. "Or should I say *them*?"

"Just wait," Indridi says to Finn, repeating it as he turns to Fayette. He gestures at Mymnir. "The problem is *there*. We need to deal with her. And then—"

"How?" Lucien interrupts, squinting against the wind. "I don't think a peace conference will work from this distance."

"We have to get her down, for one. Make sure she doesn't fly away," says Finn, unsure how, exactly, they might do it. The bird is easily twenty metres up, and the spear is unwieldy, not particularly aerodynamic. She holds her hair back and eyes some of the low-hanging branches, the ones that skim the ground, then rejects the thought. Climbing in these conditions would be suicide.

Navan calls to Lucien. "How's your throwing arm?"

"It works," he says and shrugs. Finn thinks, *This is no time for modesty* and watches as Indridi looks speculatively at Rowan.

"No," she tells him. "He throws like a girl. So do I. Lucien's your man."

Indridi flashes a grin and turns to Tallulah. He taps the diamond on her shoulder. "Time for this to be put to better use."

"It was nice while it lasted," she says and grudgingly detaches the tie-pin and slaps it into the waiting palm.

Indridi turns the thing over in his hands. He works at the long metal stem until it snaps off and there is only the large, glistening ball. "This should hold a charge nicely."

Cupping the gem, he whispers something low and sweet to it, then blows on the stone until it glows, wreathed with a crystalline rainbow. He holds it out to Lucien with the warning, "It's a little warm, but I've told it what to do—it should fly. Just hit the damned bird."

Lucien nods.

"I do so hate to see good jewellery wasted," pouts Maeve and Tallulah seconds, scowling.

"Seriously," says Navan through gritted teeth. "*That's* your biggest concern right now?"

Lucien does his best to ignore them, to concentrate. His hair whips around, *just* short enough to avoid stinging his eyes. He moves back cautiously, a foot at a time, keeps going until he can get a clear shot through the branches. Everyone else watches his progress while they spread out, picking their way around holes and over grounded boughs, to take positions circling the trunk. Waiting to catch their prey. All but Rowan.

Buffeted by sleet and starting to shiver, Finn's brother gapes up at the tree. Several yards behind him, Lucien swings his arm, warming the muscles, loosening the joint. He does it for so long Finn wonders if he's showboating, but when he finally releases the stone it flies straight and true, hitting the target with an audible *thwack*.

"No," Rowan cries, quicker off the mark than any of them, running toward the shower of white feathers.

---

Mymnir falls.

Such a magnificent view, such awful splendour. The electric breath of her children illuminating the vault, the terrible beauty of their labour—And pain. Searing, jarring, numbing when there should be only satisfaction, only triumph on this day of days. Her body forgets itself, forgets—And green, brown, everywhere, everywhere, scourges lashing. Air whistling past her ears, thunder in her skull as it crashes, connects—And shrieks. Shouting and crying, her own, others', masculine, feminine—And the gods. Howling, oh the pain, as she tumbles and screeches, as she falls, a raven, a spirit, one form, another, another—And woman. Snow-feathers descending on her head, trembling from her eyebrows, her hair—And she hits, breathless. Writhing on the furrowed dirt.

Above her, a ragged group. *Ants*, she thinks, but no. No, they are up, she's down. She's the ant now, and they—Humans. *Ants*, no. Humans, and . . . And another. One of her own—oh, yes!—one of her seeds. *Still bright, still bright.* She grimaces, winces. This one smells . . . familiar . . . like . . .

"Eiðr," she croaks. "Eiðr. Get a nátt-lamp; it's too dark . . . "

"Hrafn." Oh, the scent of him, wonderful. Delicious. Not quite right, though, not quite old Eiðr . . . *Too warm*. "White—"

She opens her mouth and Not-Eiðr vanishes. *No, no*. She chortles, wheezes. *Pushed aside.*

Her vision swims, doubles, trebles, *so many ants*. One kneels beside her, reeking. She wrinkles her nose, knows the stench too well. Memory, heartbreak, loss. Dreams.

"My Queen," he says. "Mymnir."

It's his reverence that undoes her.

"Oh, Ari," she says. She can hear it in his tone—utter devotion, submission—but more than that, finally, finally more. *My Queen*, he said, but also, *Mymnir*. Just that, just enough, her title, her name, just her. "Ari," she says, and her face is wet, eyelashes sticking together, and he's blurred, but no matter. He can see her, he *sees* her, at last, just *her*.

"I'm sorry," she says, reaching up to touch his face. It is sweaty, cold. He nuzzles his cheek into her palm. With her fingertips, she examines his eyes. "I didn't mean it."

---

"Rowan," Finn cries, hoisting the spear. "Get out of the way!"

But he just keeps kneeling by the woman's side, oblivious. "Rowan!"

His stillness spurs her into action. She clambers over the bough between them, screaming at him to *get up*, to *move*, and sees Lucien doing the same from the other side. But the chance to gain her brother's attention is lost as the earth shudders, rocked beneath two sets of godly feet.

Þórr and Óðinn, attracted by the raven's song, have descended. At first tall as skyscrapers, they snap centuries-old branches and limbs as they land, blocking all light as they bend over and *peer*. The oak quakes as the gods shrink to the size of giants, one of them smashing huge pieces of wood with a hammer to allow a better view. Finn backs away, stumble-running. Within two steps, she skids on the edge of a hole, scrapes a groove up her shin, jars to a stop on her knees. The spear goes flying, jams broken-end down into the soil. With pain lancing through her right leg, she digs into the rain-swirled mud, pulls herself out, crawls after it. *Where's Lucien?* There—closing in on Rowan, but too slow! The fool is scooping Mymnir up, caring nothing for giants or car-sized hammers. And the raven—

She's now as unaware of Rowan as he is of them. Finn watches the bird-woman's expression, sees it evolve: rapt, beatific, delirious. Eyes trained on Óðinn, Mymnir shrugs Rowan off and opens her arms in welcome. The prodigal son—father—returns. For a few seconds she stands there, regal, maternal, until the thrill wavers. Her arms drop, inch by inch, as she realises the gods give her no such reception in return. The knowledge slowly dawns on her lovely face: there will be no happy reunion.

"What can we do?" shouts Finn, sensing that things have moved well beyond their control.

"What your families have always done, when it comes to immortals and gods," says Indridi, clasping her hand, reaching also for Lucien's. "Witness. Remember."

Rowan is still fixated on the Queen, but as her smile dims, he follows her line of sight. Takes in the gods, backlit by magic and lightning, smelling of rot. He plants his feet squarely, sets himself as a shieldman for his Lady. He raises his chin, a challenge, curls his hands into fists.

Þórr gives an ear-splitting burst of laughter and hurls Mjöllnir.

Finn will only recall these events later, and then only in flashes. She will see the gargantuan hammer hurtling at her brother, she will see in intricate detail the carvings on its head, will be fascinated by the way it absorbed light. But for the longest time she will refuse to remember the moment when the thing hit Rowan, lifted him off his feet and crushed him into the trunk of the oak with such force that the tree cracked and her brother became a pulpy mess of bone and blood.

And those terrible, drawn-out moments between realisation and agony, the moments when gods chuckle at what they'd done, when the white woman, flung from Rowan's embrace, screamed, then shifted, became a thing of feathers and fear, and began to rise, to fly, to flee once more. The weeping and wailing from Tallulah and Maeve as they threw themselves forward, sparks, such tiny sparks, flying from the tips of their manicured nails, catching at the gods' cloaks, snuffed almost instantly. And Finn saw all their chances of salvation, all their futures, would be lost, and she just didn't care, with Rowan gone, her sweet brother, the fool, she just didn't care.

And that horrible, deafening roar as one-eyed Óðinn saw what the raven intended, that she would again escape him. He hefted a spear—it has a name, too, she will learn it later, but though Lucien will patiently tell her that name over and over, it will always slip from her mind—and the All-Father hefted the deadly length and threw it, with all his might, at Mymnir.

And the tip caught her under the breast and was gone, passed through her slight, feathered body. White wings, paused in flight, became ivory arms, the talons were legs, supple, a woman's, and just as quick she was nothing but smoke and wisps, dissipating memory, a lifeless thing swallowed by time.

And how with her death, at that very same instant, the gods began to unravel. Óðinn *whoomped* to the ground, a puddle of soil and sinew, unmade by his own spear. Þórr followed with a rumbled sigh, and, one by one, the other four ceased their celestial display, broke apart, and fell through their own storms, lumps of clay raining from the sky.

Finn remembers her family, the old and the new, stood by silently, observing this unmaking, this unearthly chaos, witnessing it to the end. Mushroom clouds rising wherever a clump of god-clay fell, bursting silver and gold as it dug deep, deep underground. Smoke burning their eyes and still they watched, still they witnessed. And when the haze cleared, saw the primeval trunks sprouting, shooting a thousand feet into the sky, trees fully grown from each daub of clay, each corpse refashioned in spreading branches. Mymnir's last sowing.

And they watched, and they witnessed, and they remembered.

And they survived.

Ragnarok was an apocalypse for the gods alone.

# Afterword

*Music drifted like smoke from beneath the closed door. Slow rhythms carried a baritone's chocolate voice out the house's open windows, dripped it down the front porch and left it pooling beneath Maeve's high-heeled Mary Janes.*

This was the beginning of a story that became "Prohibition Blues", written originally for an anthology that didn't eventuate. Happily, this piece found a home in *Damnation and Dames* earlier this year. Even happier, "Prohibition Blues" also gave us the writer's equivalent of an ear-worm: a brain-worm. This first tale presented characters we loved and whose personalities and pasts we wanted to explore further. So, we had The Conversation. "Why don't we write another story?" we said blithely. And as things tend to do when we start a collaboration, ideas tumbled out in a flurry of emails and phone calls, escalating quickly. "No, we'll need to do two if we're going to tease out that thread, and that one. But then there's also *this* angle. Ooooh, and what about *this*? You know what," we wrote simultaneously, as we tend to do, "looks like we're writing a book. A mosaic novel or a collection of interlinked tales would be perfect . . . " But at the time we were both finishing Dread PhDs (yes, *precisely* like the Dread Pirate Roberts), holding down jobs (foot-on-snake kind of holding down, hoping one doesn't get bitten), writing our individual collections—y'know, stuff. So we agreed, *No. Not now.*

But, hey, who can take the word of a writer? Worse, two writers. We kept talking about this book, jotting notes about where everything started, making up histories for the characters, writing scraps from tomes that never were. Soon a series of story-tiles began to appear, forming a mosaic of a larger fable. We didn't want *Midnight and Moonshine* to have a traditional linear plot, but to comprise a series of puzzle pieces—each one adding to the greater picture, solving some mysteries but leaving others open. Tales that took you on a journey, then left you wondering where else the tessellated path would lead.

Thank you for joining us on our rambling pilgrimage! We hope you've enjoyed the wonders we dreamed up, and leave you with the old storytellers' maxim: "This is our story, we've told it, and in your hands we leave it".

ANGELA SLATTER AND LISA L. HANNETT<br>
NOVEMBER 2012

# Glossary

*À toi de voir*: Your call (French).
*Ætt-morðingi*: kin-killer (Old Norse)
*Ámur*: dark giant (Old Norse)
*Attends*: wait (French)
*Bláfótr*: blue-foot / black-foot (Old Norse) In Old Norse-Icelandic literature, "blue" and "black" were often used interchangably.
*Bokors*: sorcerers (Haitian Creole)
*Bylgjur*: engulfing waves (Old Norse)
*Caraque*: 17th century French ship for commerce and passengers (French)
*Chepi*: fairy (Algonquin)
*Coco macaque*: a magic stick that walks on its own (Haitian voodoo)
*Contes*: tales (French)
*Corvidae*: includes ravens, crows, nutcrackers, choughs, rooks (Latin)
*Draugr*: revenant (Old Norse)
*Dreki*: dragon (Old Norse)
*Ekla*: lack, fault
*Elskari*: lover (Old Norse)
*Et à juste titre*: And rightly so (French)
*Fjallkona*: queen of the mountains (Old Norse)
*Græmlings*: gremlins (Danish)
*Häxorna*: witches (Swedish)
*Hedera*: ivy (Latin)

*Hrafn:* raven (Old Norse)
*Hrímþursr:* frost giant (Old Norse)
*Húsringr:* noble house or holding (Old Norse)
*Hvíta:* white (Old Norse)
*Jé-rouge:* "red-eyes", werewolf spirits (Haitian)
*Jötunsbani:* giant's bane (Old Norse)
*Knorr:* type of ship (Old Norse)
*Kólbitr:* coal-biter (fairy tale character) (Old Norse)
*Lilla gullebit:* little gold piece (Swedish, endearment)
*Lykill:* key (Old Norse)
*Mais j'anticipe:* I'm getting ahead of myself! (French)
*Marbendill* (singular): merman (Old Norse)
*Marbendlar* (plural): people of the sea (Old Norse)
*Marraine:* godmother (Creole)
*Menthe:* peppermint (French)
*Menuets:* minuets (French)
*Mín bróðir:* my brother (Old Norse)
*Minou:* kitten/kitty (French) (colloquial, endearment)
*Nátt:* night (Old Norse)
*Niflheimr:* "mist home" realm of ice and snow.
*Pauvre étoile:* poor star/poor dear (French) (colloquial)
*Poupée:* doll (French)
*Prestr:* priest (Old Norse)
*Rastir:* (plural) unit of measure; (singular) rǫst, roughly a mile or a league (Old Norse)
*Ríki:* kingdom (Old Norse)
*Rousant:* rising (French; heraldic term)
*Santé:* health (French)
*Sáðsystr:* seed-sisters (Old Norse)
*Séfinn:* jarl/lord (Old Norse)
*Skitr:* shit (Old Norse)
*Skræling:* (Old Norse and Icelandic) In medieval Icelandic sagas (Íslendingasögur), this term is used for people native to the region known as Vinland (probably Newfoundland) whom Norse sailors encountered during their travels there in the 11th century. In *Midnight and Moonshine*, it is also used to describe humans with Fae blood.
*Skýja:* cloud (Old Norse)
*Skyr:* a sort of yogurt-cheese (Old Norse and Icelandic)

*Snáði*: boy/lad (Icelandic)
*Svartosattr*: black salt (Old Norse)
*Svín-fylking*: swine array (Old Norse) The term refers to the wedge-shaped phalanx of warriors, so named due to its being shaped like a swine's snout.
*Þórr*: Thor
*Vísla*: weasel/ferret/minkrat (Old Norse)
*Wanageeska*: white spirit (Sioux)
*Yuanlingshan*: formal Chinese coat for men; attire of both male and female officials and nobles in the Ming Dynasty.

# Also by Angela Slatter

AUREALIS AWARD FOR BEST COLLECTION 2010

"In this collection of 16 previously published and new stories, Slatter presents twisted, fractured, illuminating fairy tales and dark fantasies that beguile in their elegant simplicity. Many of the stories are reiterations of classic fairy tales from all over the world. Dark and sinister, these shorts place strong, empathetic female protagonists into harrowing, horrifying, or humble circumstances and see them triumph."

— PUBLISHERS WEEKLY

# Also by Lisa L. Hannett

### WORLD FANTASY AWARD FINALIST 2011
### AUREALIS AWARD FOR BEST COLLECTION 2011

"Hannett's first collection shows off her fondness for lush imagery, unsettling concepts, indirect prose, and multilayered plots. The 12 stories, all but one original to this volume, push boundaries and experiment with style, form, and meaning, rarely straightforward and often hovering between fantasy and horror."

— PUBLISHERS WEEKLY

## AVAILABLE FROM TICONDEROGA PUBLICATIONS

| | |
|---|---|
| 978-0-9586856-6-5 | Troy by Simon Brown (tpb) |
| 978-0-9586856-7-2 | The Workers' Paradise eds Farr & Evans (tpb) |
| 978-0-9586856-8-9 | Fantastic Wonder Stories ed Russell B. Farr (tpb) |
| 978-0-9803531-0-5 | Love in Vain by Lewis Shiner (tpb) |
| 978-0-9803531-2-9 | Belong ed Russell B. Farr (tpb) |
| 978-0-9803531-3-6 | Ghost Seas by Steven Utley (hc) |
| 978-0-9803531-4-3 | Ghost Seas by Steven Utley (tpb) |
| 978-0-9803531-6-7 | Magic Dirt: the best of Sean Williams (tpb) |
| 978-0-9803531-7-4 | The Lady of Situations by Stephen Dedman (hc) |
| 978-0-9803531-8-1 | The Lady of Situations by Stephen Dedman (tpb) |
| 978-0-9806288-2-1 | Basic Black by Terry Dowling (tpb) |
| 978-0-9806288-3-8 | Make Believe by Terry Dowling (tpb) |
| 978-0-9806288-4-5 | Scary Kisses ed Liz Grzyb (tpb) |
| 978-0-9806288-6-9 | Dead Sea Fruit by Kaaron Warren (tpb) |
| 978-0-9806288-8-3 | The Girl With No Hands by Angela Slatter (tpb) |
| 978-0-9807813-1-1 | Dead Red Heart ed Russell B. Farr (tpb) |
| 978-0-9807813-2-8 | More Scary Kisses ed Liz Grzyb (tpb) |
| 978-0-9807813-4-2 | Heliotrope by Justina Robson (tpb) |
| 978-0-9807813-7-3 | Matilda Told Such Dreadful Lies by Lucy Sussex (tpb) |
| 978-1-921857-01-0 | Bluegrass Symphony by Lisa L. Hannett (tpb) |
| 978-1-921857-05-8 | The Hall of Lost Footsteps by Sara Douglass (hc) |
| 978-1-921857-06-5 | The Hall of Lost Footsteps by Sara Douglass (tpb) |
| 978-1-921857-03-4 | Damnation and Dames ed Liz Grzyb & Amanda Pillar (tpb) |
| 978-1-921857-08-9 | Bread and Circuses by Felicity Dowker (tpb) |
| 978-1-921857-17-1 | The 400-Million-Year Itch by Steven Utley (tpb) |
| 978-1-921857-24-9 | Wild Chrome by Greg Mellor (tpb) |
| 978-1-921857-27-0 | Bloodstones ed Amanda Pillar (tpb) |
| 978-1-921857-30-0 | Midnight and Moonshine by Lisa L. Hannett & Angela Slatter (tpb) |
| 978-1-921857-10-2 | Mage Heart by Jane Routley (hc) |
| 978-1-921857-65-2 | Mage Heart by Jane Routley (tpb) |
| 978-1-921857-11-9 | Fire Angels by Jane Routley (hc) |
| 978-1-921857-66-9 | Fire Angels by Jane Routley (tpb) |
| 978-1-921857-12-6 | Aramaya by Jane Routley (hc) |
| 978-1-921857-67-6 | Aramaya by Jane Routley (tpb) |

## TICONDEROGA PUBLICATIONS LIMITED HARDCOVER EDITIONS

| | |
|---|---|
| 978-0-9586856-9-6 | Love in Vain by Lewis Shiner |
| 978-0-9803531-1-2 | Belong ed Russell B. Farr |
| 978-0-9803531-9-8 | Basic Black by Terry Dowling |
| 978-0-9806288-0-7 | Make Believe by Terry Dowling |
| 978-0-9806288-1-4 | The Infernal by Kim Wilkins |
| 978-0-9806288-5-2 | Dead Sea Fruit by Kaaron Warren |
| 978-0-9806288-7-6 | The Girl With No Hands by Angela Slatter |
| 978-0-9807813-0-4 | Dead Red Heart ed Russell B. Farr |
| 978-0-9807813-3-5 | Heliotrope by Justina Robson |
| 978-0-9807813-6-6 | Matilda Told Such Dreadful Lies by Lucy Sussex |
| 978-1-921857-00-3 | Bluegrass Symphony by Lisa L. Hannett |
| 978-1-921857-07-2 | Bread and Circuses by Felicity Dowker |
| 978-1-921857-16-4 | The 400-Million-Year Itch by Steven Utley |
| 978-1-921857-23-2 | Wild Chrome by Greg Mellor |
| 978-1-921857-27-0 | Midnight and Moonshine by Lisa L. Hannett & Angela Slatter |

## TICONDEROGA PUBLICATIONS EBOOKS

| | |
|---|---|
| 978-0-9803531-5-0 | Ghost Seas by Steven Utley |
| 978-1-921857-93-5 | The Girl With No Hands by Angela Slatter |
| 978-1-921857-99-7 | Dead Red Heart ed Russell B. Farr |
| 978-1-921857-94-2 | More Scary Kisses ed Liz Grzyb |
| 978-0-9807813-5-9 | Heliotrope by Justina Robson |
| 978-1-921857-98-0 | Year's Best Australian F&H eds Grzyb & Helene |
| 978-1-921857-97-3 | Bluegrass Symphony by Lisa L. Hannett |

## THE YEAR'S BEST AUSTRALIAN FANTASY & HORROR SERIES EDITED BY LIZ GRZYB & TALIE HELENE

| | |
|---|---|
| 978-0-9807813-8-0 | Year's Best Australian Fantasy & Horror 2010 (hc) |
| 978-0-9807813-9-7 | Year's Best Australian Fantasy & Horror 2010 (tpb) |
| 978-0-921057-13-3 | Year's Best Australian Fantasy & Horror 2011 (hc) |
| 978-0-921057-14-0 | Year's Best Australian Fantasy & Horror 2011 (tpb) |

WWW.TICONDEROGAPUBLICATIONS.COM

THANK YOU

The publisher would sincerely like to thank:

Elizabeth Grzyb, Angela Slatter, Lisa L. Hannett, Kathleen Jennings, Kim Wilkins, Margo Lanagan, Jeff Vandermeer, Theodora Goss, Cat Sparks, Jonathan Strahan, Peter McNamara, Ellen Datlow, Grant Stone, Jeremy G. Byrne, Sean Williams, Garth Nix, David Cake, Simon Oxwell, Grant Watson, Sue Manning, Steven Utley, Bill Congreve, Jack Dann, Janeen Webb, Jenny Blackford, Simon Brown, Stephen Dedman, Sara Douglass, Felicity Dowker, Terry Dowling, Jason Fischer, Pete Kempshall, Ian McHugh, Angela Rega, Lucy Sussex, Kaaron Warren, the Mt Lawley Mafia, the Nedlands Yakuza, Amanda Pillar, Shane Jiraiya Cummings, Angela Challis, Talie Helene, Donna Maree Hanson, Kate Williams, Kathryn Linge, Andrew Williams, Al Chan, Alisa and Tehani, Mel & Phil, Jennifer Sudbury, Paul Przytula, Kelly Parker, Hayley Lane, Georgina Walpole, everyone we've missed . . .

. . . and you.

In memory of Eve Johnson (1945–2011)

CPSIA information can be obtained at www.ICGtesting.com
Printed in the USA
LVOW061948240513

335457LV00001BA/159/P